ROCK
Bottom
SATAN'S DEVILS #7

MANDA MELLETT

Disclaimer

This is a work of fiction. Names, characters, businesses, places, events
and incidents are either the products of the author's imagination or
used in a fictitious manner. Any resemblance to actual persons, living
or dead, or actual events is purely coincidental.

Warning

This book is dark in places and contains content of a sexual, abusive and
violent nature. It is not suitable for persons under the age of 18.

ISBN: 978-1-912288-25-0

AUTHOR'S NOTE

Rock Bottom is the seventh in the Satan's Devils MC series, but can be read as a standalone.

If you're new to MC books you may find there are terms that you haven't heard before, so I've included a glossary to help along the way. I hope you get drawn into this mysterious and dark world in the same way I have done—there will be further books in the Satan's Devils series which I hope you'll want to follow.

If you've picked this book up because, like me, you read anything MC, I hope you'll enjoy it for what it is, a fictional insight into the underground culture of alpha men and their bikes.

GLOSSARY

Motorcycle Club – An official motorcycle club in the U.S. is one which is sanctioned by the American Motorcyclist Association (AMA). The AMA has a set of rules its members must abide by. It is said that ninety-nine percent of motorcyclists in America belong to the AMA

Outlaw Motorcycle Club (MC) – The remaining one percent of motorcycling clubs are historically considered outlaws as they do not wish to be constrained by the rules of the AMA and have their own bylaws. There is no one formula followed by such clubs, but some not only reject the rulings of the AMA, but also that of society, forming tightly knit groups who fiercely protect their chosen ways of life. Outlaw MCs have a reputation for having a criminal element and supporting themselves by less than legal activities, dealing in drugs, gun running or prostitution. The one-percenter clubs are usually run under a strict hierarchy.

Brother – Typically members of the MC refer to themselves as brothers and regard the closely knit MC as their family.

Cage – The name bikers give to cars as they prefer riding their bikes.

Chapter – Some MCs have only one club based in one location. Other MCs have a number of clubs who follow the same bylaws and wear the same patch. Each club is known as a chapter and will normally carry the name of the area where they are based on their patch.

Church – Traditionally the name of the meeting where club business is discussed, either with all members present or with just those holding officer status.

Colours – When a member is wearing (or flying) his colours he will be wearing his cut proudly displaying his patch showing which club he is affiliated with.

Cut – The name given to the jacket or vest which has patches denoting the club that member belongs to.

Enforcer – The member who enforces the rules of the club.

Hang-around – This can apply to men wishing to join the club and who hang-around hoping to be become prospects. It is also used to women who are attracted by bikers and who are happy to make themselves available for sex at biker parties.

Mother Chapter – The founding chapter when a club has more than one chapter.

Patch – The patch or patches on a cut will show the club that member belongs to and other information such as the particular chapter and any role that may be held in the club. There can be a number of other patches with various meanings, including a one-percenter patch. Prospects will not be allowed to wear the club patch until they have been patched-in, instead they will have patches which denote their probationary status.

Patched-in/Patching-in – The term used when a prospect completes his probationary status and becomes a full club member.

President (Prez) – The officer in charge of that particular club or chapter.

Prospect – Anyone wishing to join a club must serve time as a probationer. During this period they have to prove their loyalty to the club. A probationary period can last a year or more. At the end of this period, if they've proved themselves a prospect will be patched-in.

Old Lady – The term given to a woman who enters into a permanent relationship with a biker.

RICO – The Racketeer Influenced and Corrupt Organisations Act primarily deals with organised crime. Under this Act the officers of a club could be held responsible for activities they order members to do and a conviction carries a potential jail service of twenty years as well as a large fine and the seizure of assets.

Road Captain – The road captain is responsible for the safety of the club on a run. He will organise routes and normally ride at the end of the column.

Ronin – A biker who travels alone, sometimes wearing a patch denoting he's Ronin. Not affiliated to any club, but often bearing a token which will help ensure safe passage through territories of different clubs.

Secretary – MCs are run like businesses and this officer will perform the secretarial duties such as recording decisions at meetings.

Sergeant-at-Arms – The sergeant-at-arms is responsible for the safety of the club as a whole and for keeping order.

Sweet Butt – A woman who makes her sexual services available to any member at any time. She may well live on the club premises and be fully supported by the club.

Treasurer – The officer responsible for keeping an eye on the club's money.

Vice President (VP) – The vice president will support the president, stepping into his role in his absence. He may be responsible for making sure the club runs smoothly, overseeing prospects etc.

Brothers protecting their own

Contents

CHAPTER 1

Becca

3 months ago

Little tremors ripple through my body as I watch Hawk pacing the room, anger emanating off him like a palpable force, his hands clenched into fists at his side. Each time he reaches the window he pauses and shakes them out. By the time his long legs cover the six strides to the opposite side his fingers curl into his palms once again.

Is he going to hit me?

It has happened before, but as long as I'm good and do exactly what I'm told I usually avoid physical punishment. Having been married to Hawk for coming up to three years now, I generally know what to say and how to behave in most situations. But today is an exception. *Exactly how am I supposed to support my husband in these circumstances?*

Staying silent, not wanting to say anything that might provoke this enraged man, my eyes follow him warily as he prowls back and forth. Women at church adore him. Try as I might to see him through their eyes, it's impossible and leaves me feeling, like always, a failure when it's hard to bring myself to even like him.

He's a striking man. I suppose many would say handsome, his body tall and muscular—there's no denying he's kept himself in shape. But it's his hair that everyone notices first. Jet black with a pure white lock over his forehead. The result of an accident years ago, he'd once said. However it had happened, it gave rise to his nickname, his grandmother having said he resembled an osprey. Liking the handle, Hawk preferred it over his given name.

It suits him. Ospreys are hunters. It used to be thought they can mesmerise their prey, which then rolls belly up and surrenders. A good analogy for our relationship. I had no chance but to succumb when he determined it was me his sharp talons would sink into. Today, Hawk's as agitated as any caged wild bird, trapped like an animal. That the situation he's in is of his own making won't even occur to him. His focus will be solely on the part I played.

Hawk. My secretive husband. A man with so many sides to him. While he likes me to call him by his handle in private, in public he's Pastor Alexis Gardner. It's as if he has two distinct personalities.

I was thirteen when I was introduced to him. At thirty-six years old he, at first, seemed a breath of fresh air, the new pastor at the church my parents and I religiously attended every Sunday, as well as the Bible classes during the week. Shyly I'd shaken his hand, even then noticing the flare of interest in his eyes, but in my naivety at that time failed to recognise it for what it was.

It was only later that I came to realise my parents had been grooming me, preparing me for my future role when I became eighteen. That, together with teachings at Bible classes had laid the groundwork. God-fearing women submit to men. God-fearing women obey the man in the house who knows what is best for them, are quiet, and go about their daily tasks without complaint. God-fearing women never speak back or contradict.

A week before my birthday my mother had taken me to the doctor, and not the one I normally saw. The clinic surprised me.

services had become apparent. I had become his wife—or to be more accurate, his slave.

As my parents had schooled me to believe, I was just a woman, having no place or value in the world, existing only to serve a man.

My mother had shown no sympathy after he'd raped me. Her troubled eyes were because I'd come to her without first seeking permission from my husband, and she sent me back to him, telling me my duty was to obey. Her only words on the matter being to stress that Alexis Gardner was a man of God, and by serving him I was doing God's will. I'd barely had time to notice the new car already on the driveway, let alone, at that time, realised the significance. It wasn't later until it dawned on me prestige in the church may not have been all that they had received.

I dreaded the thought of having a child with Hawk, and with his healthy appetite for sex thought it would only be a matter of time before I fell pregnant. Until I learned the significance of that clinic visit the week before my birthday. The three-year implant my loving husband had demanded ensured that I wouldn't. Hawk didn't want children. My views on the matter not even asked.

No longer innocent, but still naïve and sheltered from the world, which in recent weeks has suddenly been turned upside down. I knew Hawk could be violent, but he hid it well from everyone else. Until he'd lost his temper with the wrong person.

I never knew who the man was, or his relationship to my husband. All Hawk would tell me is that disloyalty had to be punished. The easy-going pastor had personally half-killed him. Instead of being cowed, the man had gone to the police, got immunity from prosecution in exchange for information and pointed his finger and, well, the rest is history. It's not an exaggeration to say the man Hawk had beaten had been left close to death. For one thing, he'll never walk again. Unfortunately, they'd only managed to pin grievous bodily harm on Hawk, failing to prove anything else. The fact they'd looked had verified my suspicions that there was more to my husband than the day job he was known for. But I had nothing useful to offer when questioned.

As I walk out of the bathroom, dressed, Hawk watches me, then takes out his phone and glances at it. "I'll have to go soon," he says, his voice suddenly calm. "But what to do about you is the question."

His intense stare has me turning my head away. The way his brow creases suggests I'm a problem to be solved. "I can stay here. Or I'll go back to my parents. Whatever you want, Hawk. If you do…if you go away. When you come out I'll be waiting."

He barks a laugh. "Somehow I doubt that." He strides across the room and takes my chin in his hand, pinching the skin and making me wince. "Stay here as my obedient wife when I'm not here to tell you what to do? You'll run as soon as my back is turned. Don't think I don't know what you're planning."

He's right to be uncertain. The minute he's put away—and I hope it's for a really long time—I'll be off. To another state, hell, another country. Out of this trap which he and my parents sprung shut around me. Return to my mother and father who all but sold me to him? Never. He must have money somewhere in the house, something that can get my new life started. Enough for a bus ticket, surely?

"You'd never survive. You know nothing of life. Nothing other than pleasing me."

I swallow, my eyes watering with pain as his fingers dig in. "Hawk, you know I'll do whatever you want."

"Too right you will. You're my wife. Mine to do with as I like. And as you're mine, I'm going to make sure you will be waiting for me whenever I get out. I've got some friends who owe me a favour. You'll be staying with them until I'm a free man again."

Suppressing a shudder, doubting I'd enjoy the hospitality of any acquaintance of his, I go cold at the thought. While I'm not allowed to be close while he discusses business, apart from parishioners, sometimes evil-looking men come to the house, leering behind Hawk's back if they catch sight of me. If it's them he's suggesting, and I can't think of anyone else, the thought scares me. Hawk's so possessive. While I'm his, no one can touch me. I don't like to think what might happen if he's locked away.

"I can look after myself," I try to say firmly. Not totally sure whether I'm trying to convince him or myself. I don't remember who I am without him. Whether I was ever a person in my own right is an unanswerable question. First cocooned by my parents, then by him.

Ignoring me, he removes his hand from my face, takes out the phone and leaves the bedroom. I hear his voice mumbling from the next room but am unable to make out any words. Now that he's out of sight I allow myself to start shaking.

I've anticipated this moment since that night when the police came calling, and after I unwittingly dropped him in it. All the while hoping they'd send him away for a maximum sentence, thinking I'd be free once the door slammed behind him. Now I'm more than concerned. It appears he's making plans to control me from behind bars. I doubt he cares about my comfort in the meantime. He's changed. He's never pretended to love me, but now, me being the reason the police caught up with him, he's colder than ever. I suspect he hates me.

A clever man, he's not marked me. That I hadn't been able to back up his story had the police watching him closely. He's stayed squeaky clean to demonstrate his innocence, to prove that he isn't a violent man. His congregation had supported him throughout the investigation. I think they would continue doing so, even faced with indisputable evidence of his guilt. I've stood beside him each Sunday, played my part as his happy wife, all the time knowing my retribution is promised for some time in the future, when he walks free once again. Hawk can wait for his revenge. With the amount he's paying his lawyer, that might not be long coming.

The bedroom door opens. Hawk enters, now far more relaxed. "Well, that's all organised."

"Please, Hawk. Don't do this," I plead, even knowing it's useless. "I'm your wife. I'll stay here. Where else would I go?"

He crosses the room and fists his hands into my hair, pulling it painfully. "You know better than to question me. What I say goes. And this way, I know you'll have protection. And will be waiting for me when I come out."

I didn't even get to see him in court or hear his punishment declared with my own ears. I'd left the house before him. His *friends* arrived just after he'd finished putting his expensive suit on.

He was sentenced to three years in prison. *I* was sentenced to thirty-six months in hell.

CHAPTER 2

Rock

Present Day

It's Friday. The day Satan's Devils meet for church. Then, what else would we do? We party. It's the one day of the week we're all guaranteed to come together. A member doesn't miss church without a very good reason. Dying, or dead, would only just about do it.

Tonight, my brothers are assembling, ready for Prez to call us in, some having been here a while, others coming in, shaking off the autumn rain that's steadily falling. Having arrived back from town before it started, I, luckily, missed the shower and am already at the bar with a drink in my hand. Enjoying my beer, I'm standing in a companionable silence next to Beef, my oldest friend in the MC. On one hand I'm relaxed and at peace with the world. I fucking love being part of the Satan's Devils. It's more than a home, it's a family—and one far better than that related by blood. I'd give my life for any man here, as they would give theirs for mine. I can ride when I want, talk when I feel the urge, be silent if that's what I need. Fuck whenever I get the itch. Hell, if I want to fight there'll be a brother willing to go a few rounds with me in the gym. I live for the MC. Take it away, and there'd be nothing of me left.

As if he knows what I'm thinking, Beef raises his bottle and clinks it with mine. I take it as a toast to the life that we live. My friendship with the big, heavily-built man goes back well over a decade.

Yeah, being in an MC is like life's blood to me. Lately though, I've come to see how the Satan's Devils are changing. I've kept my thoughts to myself, but I'm actually beginning to question whether it's still the right club for me. I'm just musing over how much it's morphing into something I don't recognise when, as though to corroborate my thoughts, a child's scream of laughter pierces the air and Prez's young son, Eli, grabs my attention. I frown as my mood darkens.

Nowadays our hardened prez smiles. He's changed from the focused badass we respected and, I admit, viewed with more than a touch of fear. He's become a family man. If I'm not mistaken, judging by the looks and tender touches he's been exchanging with Sam, he'll soon be announcing that his old lady's expecting a second baby. There's something in the softening of his eyes as he catches sight of her that makes me suspect she's pregnant again. Presumably not wanting to be outdone by his VP. Wraith enlightened us last week that Sophie is pregnant with their second child.

The influx of old ladies and kids has changed the whole atmosphere of the club. Most of what we do nowadays is clean, our money decently earned. Our treasurer is tied up with honest tax returns rather than finding ways to put dirty money through the wash. Sometimes I wonder what type of fucking MC we're becoming. Where's the excitement, the danger, the high that comes with walking on the edge? Well my brothers might be going soft, but there's no way I'll be following them. Let's face it, I'm becoming bored.

I still wear the one-percenter patch on my cut, but the jury's out as to whether I truly deserve to. It's true we care little for civilian ways, but half the time I feel a fraud, longing for the days when Drummer's father, Bastard, was still around. Just knowing you'd survived another day was a buzz back then. Living life in the fast lane, having to watch what's in front as well as behind you… Well, yeah, fuck, I miss that.

"Have a good night, last night?" Beef enquires, interrupting my thoughts.

Momentarily I struggle to find the answer he's looking for, in the end settling for, "Win some, lose some. You know how it is."

He gives me a sharp look. "Be careful, Rock."

Nonchalantly I brush off his concern. "I know what I'm doing."

We don't get a chance to say more. Having given Eli one last swing around, Drummer, at last, puts his child down and circles his hand over his head. "Church!" Before kids had come on the scene he'd have suffixed that with fuckers, assholes, or douchebags. Yeah, we all have to watch our language now. In a fucking MC.

Beef puts his hand to my back and gives me a friendly shove. "Soon as this is over I'm grabbing a sweet butt." He places his hand on his crotch and thrusts his hips as though I need the emphasis to get the point.

I suppose we're lucky to still have their services, grateful that for now Jill, Allie, Pussy, Diva and Paige are still with us, available at all times to fuck. If the prez ever decides the sweet butts are leaving it won't be long before I'm following them out the door, and that's a given. Responding to Beef, I readily agree, "You and me both."

"Paige and Diva? Together?"

Now it's my turn to slap him on the back and give a genuine grin. "Why not, Brother? Got to have something to look forward to after church."

He laughs and strides off to our meeting room. I follow more slowly, less eager than him. We'll probably have to listen to stuff which quite honestly bores the fuck out of me. Dollar going through the finances, Slick and Bullet talking about their progress in building the new mall in town. I long for the days when we'd talk instead about killing our enemies. Or the risks involved in dealing with guns.

I'm not an officer, nor ever likely to be, so I take my seat halfway down the table. High-ranking posts are given for life, and as we no longer face danger on a daily basis, it's likely Wraith, the VP, Peg, the sergeant-at-arms, Blade, the enforcer, Dollar and Heart, who are the treasurer and secretary respectively, will be in their posts until they can no longer ride. While I'm not sure I'd welcome the responsibility that comes with being an officer, that in this chapter of the Satan's Devils I'm unlikely to get the chance is just another thing that irks me.

Drummer bangs the gavel. "Shut the fuck up."

My eyes snap to Prez. His irritation at those continuing their private discussions is clear, and more than a little surprising. Over the past few months he's been far more relaxed, normally allowing people to settle into the meeting.

Once quiet has fallen, others similarly startled by the sharpness of his voice, Drummer wipes his hand over his face. His mouth has thinned, his steel eyes homing in as one by one he looks around the table. Only the VP looks like he already knows what's the matter. Like the others, I sit forward, suddenly intrigued by the thought that today something's different.

"Unless anyone's got anything other than a progress report, or we're losin' money, we'll leave the normal business for tonight. We've got ourselves a situation, and that's what we need to talk about."

All eyes are on him. No one speaks.

"The VP and I had a meetin'." He pauses, takes a breath, then lets us know. "With Javier Herrera."

"Fuck. It must be gettin' on for a year now since we first tried to get a meetin' with him." Dollar peers over the top of his glasses. Then, realising he's not going to be reading from his prepared spreadsheet, takes them off, holding them in one hand. "Why now?"

Prez nods, showing the treasurer's asked a valid question. "Things are changin' in Tucson, and not for the good. I got a call from Herrera this mornin'. A summons you might say. The VP and I felt we couldn't turn down the invitation." He nods at Wraith. "We went there straight after."

"What the fuck does he want?"

It's the way the VP and Prez share a worried glance that has my heart beating faster. Drummer clears his throat. "You all know the link between the Herreras and Los Zetas." Yeah, we do. The Tucson crime family doesn't hide their connection to the cartel. I draw my attention back to the prez as he continues. "I'm not sure what part Los Zetas are playing in it, but Javier wants more guns going over the border. The Herreras can't handle the extra business, so Javier has decided that he'd use us as mules."

"What the fuck?" Peg's hand slams down on the table. "He thinks he can just use us?"

"Can it, Peg." Wraith's growl and admonishment is unusual. It's usually the other way around.

It hasn't had any effect on Peg, who ignores him. "I've promised my ol' lady this club is clean. Ain't gettin' back into that shit again."

"I hear you, Brother." Now it's Drummer's turn to snarl. "None of us want touch that type of business with a fuckin' barge pole. But we may not have the chance to avoid gettin' our hands dirty."

Blade spins his knife, stopping it when it points at the prez. "What the fuck do they think they've got over us?" he asks wearily.

I was wondering the same thing myself. My gaze, which had been caught by Blade's spinning knife, snaps back to the prez.

Drum's shaking his head. "There's a new MC settin' up in our fuckin' territory. Goes by the name of the Chaos Riders."

"Heard of the Chaos Riders, don't know any detail. MC based up in Phoenix. Keep to themselves. Not heard they were startin' up a new chapter, though," Viper contributes. "How the fuck did we not know this?"

Wraith nods toward the empty chair at the table. "Presumably because Mouse is off communin' with nature."

Yeah, he'd been gone a month, was due back soon. He's our computer guru and stays on top of all the information the club needs. But something to do with his Native American heritage has him occasionally going on vision quests or some such shit.

"We can take the fuckers on. Make sure they know they're not welcome."

Blade's comment makes me grin, and my hands twitch under the table. *Now that sounds more like it.*

But another look exchanged between the VP and Prez tells me it's not as easy as that, confirmed when Drummer speaks. "The Herreras are backin' whoever carries the guns for them. They've spoken to the Chaos Riders and are happy they're up to the job. Mean bunch of motherfuckers apparently."

"So why speak to us?" Road wonders aloud.

"Good point, and that's what we asked." Drum sends another worried look Wraith's way. "Don't think we got more than half the story, but readin' between the lines, seems the old pipeline the Herreras used has dried up and they need to find another. They're givin' us first choice. If we refuse they'll give the business to the Chaos Riders."

Slick lets out a sigh. "I'm with Peg. I've got an ol' lady. Don't want to explain to her that one day I might not be comin' home. I vote we let this new bunch of motherfuckers take the risk."

"I hear you." Bullet nods. "I remember those days. Saying goodbye to Carmen, not being able to promise I'll be seein' her again. Don't wanna get back into that."

Viper's in agreement too. "Dead or in the penitentiary. Don't fancy either option myself." He raises his chin. "I vote no, too. Let someone else take the risk." His thoughts are echoed around the table, while my eyes alight at the tantalising thought of danger. I glance at my brothers. Marvel's looking at me and gives me a slight nod as though he's reading what's going through my head. *At least it seems someone's on my side.*

"I wish it was that easy. Not so sure we have a choice." Drummer's deep voice stops all other conversation. He waits until he's got our full attention before delivering the punchline. "Javier's met with the Chaos Riders, who've made it clear they want to come in and be top dog. If they carry guns for the Herreras, part of their payment was they'd get help takin' us out. Seems they've got their eye on this compound."

The table erupts.

"Then we wipe them out. Before they get their fuckin' feet under the table in Tucson." Peg doesn't seem to think agreeing to kill them counts as us getting our hands dirty.

Drummer's looking weary as he draws his hands down over his face. "If we take out the Chaos Riders we'll still have the Herreras on our backs about gettin' back into the gun trade. Rock and a hard place pretty much sums it up."

"First order of business is to deal with this bunch of motherfuckers. Then we take on the Herreras," Blade says firmly.

Steely grey eyes fix on him. "I suggest we take a minute before puttin' anything to the vote. This is fuckin' serious, there's no doubt about it. Many of us now have ol' ladies and children, more to protect, and damn more to live for."

"If we don't fight, what we gonna do? Hand over the fuckin' compound and get out of Tucson?" Blood already racing, my features are arranged in a sneer, my hands fisted in anticipation of fighting. If that means taking on brothers who've lost the appetite to settle things the old way, by violence, then I'll happily do it for them. Don't want to be in an MC that rolls over and lets everyone stamp on it. I bang my fist on the table. "I say we make the decision now. To fight."

My fist thump was loud. Drum's even louder, and he uses two hands to do it. "Yeah. Or we could decide to protect the ol' ladies and children. Leave Tucson. That's one fuckin' option on the table."

"We're the mother fuckin' chapter." Marvel, whose views, as I already suspected, are similar to mine, interrupts him. His eyes are wide open as though he can't believe what he's hearing.

"Shut the fuck up and let me finish." Drum pushes back his chair, gets to his feet and leans forward over the table, resting on his hands. "We all need time to come up with options. Don't want to rush this and make the wrong decision. Think fuckin' carefully about what's important here. We don't have enough information about the fuckin' Chaos Riders for a start. All I know is they're situated somewhere south of Tucson. But how many of them are there? What's their loyalty to their club? What's their history? Is this threat real, or is Javier simply blowin' smoke up our asses?"

Everyone stares at Prez. Wraith clears his throat. "Laid a lot on you today, brothers. Prez is right. We all need to give some serious thought to it before bringin' our ideas back to the table."

Retaking his seat, Drummer nods at his VP then says tiredly, "Agree we need a minute to let this sink in." He rolls his head back and takes a breath. "We've seen some action over the years, but this tops it all."

Viper raises his hand. "Can I ask something before we split?" At Prez's nod he continues, "Might they go after our businesses?"

Drum points to the man who asked the question. "And that, right there, is the kind of thing I'm fuckin' talkin' about. If we don't carry guns for the Herreras, Javier suggested we'll face some kind of retaliation. So, yeah, Viper, they could. Or they could make a direct attack on the compound. Or go after the women. That's what I need you lot thinkin' about. All the areas where we're vulnerable. We've got a bit of time before the Chaos Riders get settled. Let's use it wisely. Once Mouse is back we'll be able to dig for more information."

"When is the fucker back?" Dollar, clearly unhappy, sits back, folding his arms.

Drum shrugs. "I'll get in contact with him. Get him here as quick as he can. Today's meetin' took us on the back foot." If anyone has been caught off guard it would appear to be the prez. This isn't how things would have gone down in the old days. Any threat to the club would have been eliminated, and fast. No doubt about it. Well, if he can't handle the heat, perhaps he better step down from his position at the head of the table.

As the conversation continues around me, I'm trying to hide my grin. Inside I'm reflecting; whatever decision we come to, there's no way we're going to avoid that excitement that I'd felt was missing in my life. I start to perk up. If Drummer isn't the man to take the decision to fight, perhaps it's time we vote in a new prez. Blade, perhaps. He's not got an old lady, and his only priority would be protecting the club.

One question breaks into my deliberations. "What does the dominant think?" I dip my head up and down, indicating I believe Joker's asked a good question.

At least checking with them is something Drummer seems to have done, as he informs us, "Had a word with the Wretched Soulz local chapter prez, just to see if they'd had warning of a new MC. They have. The Chaos Riders did it all polite. Got their permission to set up in Tucson. How we settle any difference that might arise between us, they're leavin' to us. Won't be gettin' any support in that direction. Unless it starts reflectin' on them. Then they'll decide who they wish to fuckin' side with."

I'm suspecting the Wretched Soulz, the dominant MC over most of the southwestern states, aren't so interested in us now we're so clean. Probably think we're a bunch of weekend warrior pussies. Maybe these Riders are more of a group they can get in bed with. They likely think we're weak. Either way, their lack of support is disappointing news. We've supported them often enough.

"So," Wraith starts to sum up, "we agree to carry guns for the Herreras, or we face a possible fight to the death with the Chaos Riders. Or Satan's Devils leave Tucson."

For me, it's good news. Unless they take the last option, I'm guaranteed some excitement to brighten my life. I can't believe anyone would agree packing our bags is the answer. This clubhouse and compound are too well situated to abandon to another club.

Peg's looking stunned, as are most of us around the table. The direction this Friday's church has taken being completely unexpected. "When do we need to decide?" the sergeant-at-arms asks.

Drum closes his eyes briefly, opens them again and says, "Javier has given us a month. The Chaos Riders are already in Tucson, but they'll still be settlin' in, and I suspect they won't want to make a move on us immediately. Like us, they're waitin' to hear if they've got the gun trade. Only difference, they might want it. "That's enough for now. Go drink, fuck. Do whatever you want to get your minds workin'. We'll reconvene in a day or two and discuss it more when it's all sunk in."

CHAPTER 3
Rock

I follow Beef and the others out of church, then hover around as they congregate in the clubroom. At first everyone's quiet, but it's not long before they stop acting bemused and murmured conversations start. Eager to see which direction my brothers are going to go in, I don't join in, just wander from group to group, picking up on the different vibes. Not unexpectedly, those with ol' ladies are focused on protecting the club, others talking about taking the new club out with a pre-emptive strike before the Riders make themselves at home in Tucson, and a couple are debating whether we should accept Javier's offer and start running guns. It could be a lucrative business. I'm just about to add my two pennies worth to the final discussion when all talking stops as the sweet butts come in and the old ladies emerge from the kitchen, kids trailing behind them. Club business doesn't get discussed in front of the women.

Beef jerks his head toward the bar. It doesn't take more than a second for me to decide a beer is a fucking good idea. I'm still shocked by the unusual discussion in church, and the bubbling feeling of excitement in my guts as though someone had been listening and had answered my prayers. Gun running or taking down another club... Whichever it ends up being doesn't much matter. Each carries sufficient danger to get the adrenaline running. Has Karma really picked up on the restlessness inside me that had me yearning for an end to the boredom?

As Beef asks Ally for two beers I'm reminded again of the changes that had come to this club. We're using the fucking sweet butts to tend bar rather than having them provide the services they're here for—with so many brothers hooking up with old ladies there's not so much call for their primary role. Except for us single and unattached men, of course. And we're fast becoming a minority. I wonder which brother will go down next. Seems like a fucking disease, and one that's catching. But not me. No way. I like my freedom way too much.

Taking a long swallow, Beef drains half his bottle then slams it down on the bar, pointing with his free hand to the women coming in the door. "Still up for it, Rock?"

I sure am. All the talk in the clubroom has my blood flowing, and going, predictably, straight down to my cock. I'll think on what Prez said later. Here and now there's something I want to exercise more than my brain. Lazily, I glance over the hangarounds, the hopeful women who've come up from Tucson to party, but there's none that particularly take my fancy. They all seem too young, giggling girls wanting to try their chance with a biker. Give me an experienced woman any day of the week. Out of the corner of my eye I see Road eyeing up Paige and Diva.

Nudging Beef, I point to Road. "We better hurry up or we'll lose our chance if we want those two."

Showing he can move fast for such a big man, Beef's up in their faces a footstep in front of Road. I laugh, then take myself over, ignoring our brother's scowl, and place my hand on Diva's arm.

"Suite, or?"

"Crash room," I reply to Beef. The rooms out the back are closer for one thing, and as to the other reason, I'd prefer my own bedroom not to smell of sex for the rest of the night. Keeps my sheets clean as well.

When Pussy hands me my beer I raise my bottle toward him in salute. As his eyes choose that moment to roll back in his head, I turn back with a grin. MC life. Fucking, fighting, and living life on the edge. Fucking brilliant.

The next couple of days pass like any other in the club. I work during the day, fuck and drink at night, and ride my bike as much as I can, enjoying the cooler autumn weather. I even manage to make it down to a casino in Tucson for a game of poker. It's only on Monday, when Drummer calls an emergency church, that anything seems out of the ordinary. Not that I wasn't half expecting it. Friday night's revelations obviously suggested we'd be meeting again soon.

As usual, I arrive early, giving myself time to grab a beer and to hopefully catch up with Beef. Today's sweet butt-come-bartender is Jill. Inwardly I groan. if I want that drink I'm unable to keep my distance.

"Rock!" Her eyes light up in delight as I approach. She puts her elbows on the bar and leans over. From here I get an eyeful of her bountiful breasts, the darker skin around her nipples clearly visible. "Hey. Wanna get together later?" Her hand comes out and touches my chest. "We're so good together."

Wrapping my hand around hers, I pull it away and place it back where it should be—on the bar, not touching me. "Nah, I'm alright." If I go with a sweet butt I'll make certain it won't be her.

"Pussy's taking over for me later, so I'll be free." When I shake my head she pouts, but isn't going to give up. "What about you take me for another ride on your bike sometime? It was so much fun when you took me before."

"No," I snarl. I don't like to be hard on the woman, but know I have to make myself clear. "Don't have bitches on my ride. You know the score, Jill."

A sly grin appears on her face. "But you made an exception for me."

I had. Once. And how I was regretting it. Jill had been stuck for a lift back from town. Drum had rung saying I was the nearest brother, and would I mind? He knows I'm not as fixated on not having any woman up behind me other than, for me, a fictional old lady, than some of the other brothers. As a result, I hadn't given it much thought at the time. It was only a short trip. The ride hadn't been the problem, that she'd now been on the back of my bike was. Stupid bitch boasted around the club, made out she and I were together. Sure, I'd fucked her in the past, but she'd never stayed in my bed. And she's not the first woman to have ridden up behind me. Meant nothing to me. But it had to her.

Reaching across the bar, I twist my hand into her hair, holding her face so she's forced to look into mine. "How can I make it clear to you? There's no you and me. Sure, we've fucked, but it wasn't anything special."

When I release her she's still got a gleam in her eye. *Stupid bitch.* Those words with Drummer might need to come sooner rather than later.

A slap on my back makes me turn to find Beef's joined me. Jill stomps off to get another beer, slamming it down so liquid spills and the bar top gets wet.

"Hey, clean that up!" Beef shakes his hand to dry it, his eyes narrowed on the sweet butt who does all she can to get out of bartending duty. He knows exactly what she's up to. "What d'ya reckon, Rock? Think I'll have a word with Drum to put her on the rota seven days a week. Bitch needs more practice."

I bark a laugh and watch in amusement as her eyes shoot daggers back, but Beef's got this. He seems to grow in front of her face, making her quickly back down and go get a cloth. His gaze never leaves her until the bar's been cleaned to his satisfaction.

"Fuckin' sweet butts."

"You've got that right," I tell him. At least when the prospects were tending bar they didn't talk back. "You know why we're here?"

"Not a fuckin' clue, Brother." Beef frowns. "The Herreras gave us a month. Still, I suppose we need to talk about it and decide what to do before then. Could be they've brought forward decision time."

I shrug. "Could be."

I see Wraith entering, watch him give a fond look at Sophie. Then, as he walks past the bar he catches my eye. His good-natured smile immediately slides off his face and I instantly go cold. *Fuck it. Does he know?* I turn away and make a big thing out of taking hold of the beer bottle, raising it to my lips and draining it. *Is this it?* A feeling of dread settles inside me as I suddenly realise I might, after all, know the reason for this emergency meeting. *Fuck, I hope I'm wrong.*

Nonchalantly, as though I haven't a care in the world, I saunter into church just as usual. There's nothing to show there's anything amiss. Wraith's now chuckling at something Blade has said to him, Prez is looking at some papers he holds in his hands. Dollar's polishing his glasses before perching them on his nose, and the others, like me, seem to be mystified at why we've been called in.

I relax and laugh at a joke Joker's finishing off, my attention caught in time to hear the punchline.

The sound of the gavel meeting wood makes me turn to Drummer. Once again he's staring down the table, his gaze settling on each of his men. His face, though, is not relaxed.

"You'll all be wonderin' why I've called you in." Prez's voice sounds strained, weary. "Fuck it," he suddenly snarls. "In all the

After a very pregnant pause, Drummer instructs, "Joker, escort Rock to the clubroom and get a prospect to stay with him. Rock, you gonna give me your word you'll not be a problem?"

I stand, knowing I've said all I can. They're not going to listen to my promise that I can win it all back. Fuck. All I needed was more time. Can't they understand that? Judged and found guilty, that's what's happened here. Now they'll pass sentence. I send a plea with my eyes to all my brothers around the table, knowing I'm leaving my fate in their hands.

"I won't be a problem," I give to the prez.

CHAPTER 4
Rock

ike I'm going to stay put like a stupid fuckin' asshole. I'll be out in bad standing for what I've done. They won't have a choice about kicking me to the curb. However long I've been a member, what they have decided was stealing from the club, and taking away their chance of buying another business is too great a crime for a slap on the wrist.

No one has to tell me what will happen. I've seen it before, though thankfully not often. First they'll slice my cut into pieces, then, and far worse, they'll burn my full Satan's Devils tattoo off my back. *If* I survive that, no club will ever take me in again. Not unless they want war with the Devils.

Nah. Only a pussy, or perhaps someone braver, would hang around waiting for that to happen.

Matt, our newest prospect, and who's only been here a couple of months, has been called away from his post by the gate. Instead he's given a different guard duty, and is now warily watching me. Joker issued strict instructions that he wasn't to let me leave. With Truck, our other prospect, on his firefighting shift, that means my route of escape is unguarded. All I have to do is…

I settle myself down at a seat by a table. "Any chance of a beer, man?"

Matt, not knowing why he's been asked to keep an eye on me, relaxes at my easy approach. "Sure." As the sweet butts haven't yet appeared, he leans over the bar to grab a bottle.

I move fast and have him in a choke hold before he knows it. I'm stronger than him, and he's yet to muscle up. He fights, but his face goes red. I let him go when he passes out, checking for a moment that he's still breathing. Killing a man, even a prospect, would mean the Devils would never stop chasing me down.

Without wasting a moment I take off my cut and disrespectfully throw it down, then I'm outside, astride my bike and walking it down the incline. When I'm far enough away I start my engine, pressing the remote to open the gate and get away cleanly. *I've escaped.*

I twist the throttle once I'm on the highway, increasing my speed without a clue where I'm going. After a while I pull up and realise I'm shaking.

I've been a Satan's Devil for sixteen years. I'd signed on in Bastard's time and escaped being rounded up with the rest of the brothers in the police raid that ended in a blood bath, as I'd been doing a stint in jail for possession. That a patched member had handed me, a lowly prospect, a bag of something which would be a misdemeanour for a man like me with a clean record, but a more serious repeat offence for him, I kept to myself. During those twelve months I kept my nose relatively clean, just bided my time until I was out, my silence earning me a full patch on release. The lesson learned was that I never want to go back to prison again.

I came out to find a much-changed club. One with Drummer, Bastard's son, at the helm. Until recently I hadn't looked back. Now it hits me. What the fuck do I do now? For the first time the enormity of my situation sinks in. It's not only mental but physical, my body feeling lighter now I've left behind the cut which hasn't been off my back for nearly fifteen years. Already I miss the creaking of the worn leather and the weight across my shoulders. More than that, I feel deeply the loss of the men I called brothers. I shouldn't be riding alone on the road. I should be sitting around the table with them. Drinking or fucking with Beef. Christ, what a fool I am. How the fuck did I get myself into this mess?

There'll be no more sitting around the table. The only thing they'll be discussing is how to catch up with me and make me take the punishment I deserve. Blade will be sharpening his knives, Wraith and Peg bunching their fists. They'll all want their turn with me, the turn I denied them by running rather than staying and facing the music. There will never be a way of putting this right. I've compounded my crime by escaping.

I put my hand in my pocket, pull out my phone and stare at it. Then, take the sim card out and break it. To be extra cautious, I throw it away. Mouse might not be there, but Drum may be able to get him to track it remotely. Next, I reach for my wallet and peer inside. I've got a total of five hundred dollars in cash on me. Feeling glad I don't trust plastic, as I didn't have time to detour to my suite to collect clothes or more money, at least it's something to be going on with. First thing to do is to get to some shady motel where I won't be asked for ID and can get my head down and start thinking where the fuck I go from here.

I wouldn't put it past Drummer to already have people out searching.

Restarting my engine, wanting to put as much space as possible between me and the compound, I start riding again, going through Tucson and continuing to the southern outskirts, where I turn off the main drag and head on into the area where I know I'll find somewhere to hole up for a while.

A motel sign flickering as it attempts to blink vacancies comes into sight. It's run down with weeds growing in the parking lot. I ride in, pass cash over the counter with no questions asked, take the key and enter my abode for the night. The cover on the bed is dirty. When I strip it off, the sheets underneath at least look clean. Without getting undressed, I lay on the bed on my back, my hands under my head. When moisture appears at the corners of my eyes I'm not surprised. *I've lost my family.* With no blood relatives living, they were like real brothers to me. Beef, of course. I'll miss him the most. *Fuck, the loss of our friendship hurts so much.* Then there's Viper, Slick, even Road and that strange pair, Joker and Lady. FUCK IT! All lost to me now. *How could I have been so fucking stupid? So fucking dumb.*

I really hadn't thought it through what would happen when they found out, or how it would feel. Now I know it's fucking killing me. I sniff, angrily wiping the tears away. I'm thirty-four years old, a fucking man. Now I'm blubbering like a fucking baby. *Don't look back. Look forward.*

But what the fuck does the future hold? What does it look like? Right now I have no fucking idea.

They were never going to listen to me. Wouldn't give me a chance to explain. After all the years I've done whatever my president—either Drummer or Bastard before him—had asked, without question. Look where it's got me. At least I've still got the tattoo on my back instead of charred skin. If I'd stayed, that was the least I'd have been left with. And a fuck load of other pain to go with it.

I'd have given my life for the club... But it was clear they weren't going to help me out. I could see that in their eyes. A brother in trouble just thrown to the wolves. I could have sorted it. I'd have suggested just a few more goes at the high rollers game and I'd have won the money back. But they hadn't listened, shown me no support or sympathy, weren't going to give me a chance.

Well, fuck'em. It's me for myself now. Rather than looking at what I've lost, the company of those self-righteous pricks, I should look out just for me. For my future.

I'll miss riding with my brothers.

I turn on my side as I think about the last time I was around that table. Not today, but at Friday's church. Particularly about what Prez—no, not my prez anymore—what Drummer had said about a new club starting up in our territory. It's somewhere south of Tucson, can't be far from where I am now.

A biker can't just walk in and ask to join a new club. It's not that easy. I've still got my Satan's Devils' tat for a start. No club would have me without first checking with Drummer. Then when they discovered the circumstances I'd left in, how I had run instead of waiting to take the punishment that would have been handed out, that would probably have them handing me over to the Devils.

Unless... *What if I could offer them something?* Pulling myself into a sitting position, I draw up my legs and place my arms over my knees. If they're looking to take out the Satan's Devils, I've got something to give them. Something that would be worth one fuck of a lot. *Information about the club.*

Could I do that? Betray my brothers? Only...they're not my brothers anymore, are they? They're men who hate me. Would probably kill me with no questions asked if they saw me...

I toss and turn all night, unable to sleep. Instead I try to sift through the thoughts in my head. Foremost, the danger I might be in by approaching the Chaos Riders. I know fuck all about them. They could shoot me on sight without giving me a chance to explain. Is there another option? Could I leave Arizona, try and get in with another club? No, that's impossible, no one would take in an out-bad member. If I want to ride with brothers, the Chaos Riders are the most likely club to approach.

My value to them might get me an in. Then all I'd have to do is prove myself.

If that's the route I'm taking, I know it will be a hard road ahead. It won't even be easy making contact with them. I can't just saunter into a new club. *Mean motherfuckers*, isn't that what Drum had said? They won't trust me on principle. To stay alive, I should steer well clear. But what other choice have I got? I'll die anyway. Riding alone would destroy me. Life's not worth living without brothers. What else can I do?

When morning comes I rise, get my travel kit out of my saddlebags—which means I can at least brush my teeth—then, sweeping back my hair, look into the mirror and splash cold water on my red-rimmed eyes. Sometime during my restless night the decision's been made. *I'm going to betray the Satan's Devils.*

Stopping briefly at the nearest mall, I pick up a couple of pairs of jeans, socks, boxers, and tees to tide me over. Eyeing my rapidly depleting funds with disgust, I get back on my bike and kick up the stand with new resolve. No point hanging around. Today's task, to find where the Chaos Riders are holed up. I eye the sun rising in the sky, knowing there's a good chance I won't see it rise tomorrow. A bullet to my head might be the best I can expect by way of welcome. Sure, I've got info I'm prepared to give freely, but there's a strong possibility they'll prefer to torture it out of me instead. This path I'm taking is risky.

Before I can find out what greeting I'm going to get, first I've got to find them.

Riding to the area where Drummer had indicated they were located, I pull up at a gas station, and there have my first bit of luck. The attendant divulges the direction bikes seem to come and go in, so I set off, heading further into the outskirts of town, and then out into the desert. I'm almost at the point of turning back when I spot a track off to the righthand side of the road, tyre marks in the sand suggesting it's used by bikes. Lots of them. As I proceed carefully down the unpaved road my heart is in my mouth, expecting every second the sound of a shot which might be the last thing I hear. My body is taut with tension.

In the distance an old two-storey farm house comes into sight. Surrounded by saguaro and with an ancient wooden veranda around it, it looks like something out of a Western. But the bikes parked up outside show it's used now for more modern purposes. Although the location seems idyllic, I can see why they've got their eyes on the Satan's Devil's compound. It's not a good defensive position, and they don't seem to have guards posted. Anyone can approach unhindered.

Warily, I ride closer, then hear the unmistakeable sound of a bullet entering a shotgun's breech. *Fuck! I am in the Wild West.*

I slow right down. A bullet landing about a foot in front of my bike makes me stop.

I wait on my bike, my head bent forward. My first job, finding the Riders' lair, seems to be complete. Doubt enters my mind. That warning shot could be my last chance to turn around. Though I thought I'd come to terms with the notion, suddenly comprehending heading on could mean this is the day that I'll die, I realise I want to live.

They'll be suspicious. They'll be right too. Perhaps they won't even ask questions, just shoot. And this time, to kill. I thought I had my whole life ahead of me. I may have thought wrong.

My internal discussion continues until I pluck up the guts to start moving forward again. As a man appears on the veranda, heavily armed, I reach the point of no return. One thing's for certain. *There's no turning back.*

A gun waves at me, and interpreting the action I cut the engine, kick down the stand and get off. I'm not surprised. I wouldn't let a strange rider anywhere close to our compound. *My old compound, that is.* The man says something over his shoulder through the doorway. As he turns I see one word on the back of his cut, *Prospect*.

It takes a good minute or so until the man standing on the veranda is joined by another of their members. I take a good look at the leather he's wearing as he waves at me to step closer. He doesn't appear to be an officer, but he is holding a gun pointed at me.

"Search him, Squirt," he instructs the prospect.

The prospect, who close up looks about sixteen, his face covered in pimples, approaches. He might appear young, but I admire his steely expression, how he gestures, then, when I open my arms, expertly pats me down. He finds everything, lifts my tee to check for a wire, even discovers the gun in my ankle holster. When my knife joins his collection I feel as naked as the day I was born.

As soon as he's finished he steps away with my weapons and goes to stand by the other man, awaiting further instruction.

"Who are you and what are you doing here?"

They know I'm unarmed, so I step forward and hold out my hand. "The name's Rock." There's no point giving him a fake one. I keep my voice confident.

He disregards my hand. "And?"

Shrugging, I tell him, "I want to become a member."

The man stares, then asks incredulously, "A member of what?"

I realise I've passed no signs. "Of the Chaos Riders." Again, I keep my voice even. "Heard you were around here." I point to the prospect. "Reckon I've come to the right place."

"You might have, you might not. Remains to be seen. Don't know an MC that you can walk up and just demand to join."

I shrug. "Appears that's what I'm doing."

"Just like that?" His eyes go wide, then he starts to laugh. "You might ride a Harley, *son*, but that don't make you Riders' material."

"I know that," I say firmly. "Ridden with a club sixteen years."

His eyes sharpen. "Which one?" he asks fast.

I don't hesitate. "Satan's Devils." No point hiding it. The tat on my back would give that away fast.

"Wait here," he says to me, and to the prospect, "Keep an eye on him, Squirt."

"Sure thing, Fester."

As he wanders off into the building I bite my tongue, wanting to know who decides the handles here, hoping to fuck they don't try and rename me. Then I wonder if I'll stay alive long enough to find out. I focus on being content that, for now, I'm still breathing.

The next person to appear after a few minutes at least gives me a nod of greeting as he approaches. "Krueger. I'm the VP," he announces, holding out his hand.

Taking it, I need no explanation of his name. He's Freddy Krueger to a T. All he needs is a striped sweater. I hide my grin.

"Hear you're looking to join us?" His voice is gravelly.

"Fuck yeah." Now I put some emotion into it. It's easy to hear the longing in my voice.

His eyes widen, then his brow creases when they narrow again. "Just the fuck like that? Brothers don't jump clubs easily. Gonna need an explanation if you've been a Devil for as long as Fester tells me."

I spit on the ground. "Fuckin' assholes. Brother gets into trouble, they cut him off." I only have to remember what they would have done to me for my face to burn.

He waves his hands, showing he wants more. "If you're a troublemaker, why the fuck would we want you? Better start talkin' else I might decide you're easier to deal with dead."

"Look, I didn't do much. Got into a bit of trouble gamblin'." I don't tell him I stole their funds. "Fuckin' straight assholes didn't give a damn."

His eyes crease with suspicion. "Okay. So here it is. Man doesn't turn up here and ask to join their club's enemies. Not unless they're stupid or lookin' for info. I'll give you one fuckin' chance. Step into the clubhouse, and if you can't convince us, well, you won't be steppin' back out. Not breathin' anyways. Or you can turn around and run back to your club sayin' you weren't successful."

I pull myself up straight. "Can't go back. They'll end me." I spit again. "Motherfuckers." Looking into his eyes, I make another attempt to persuade him. "Bunch of sanctimonious assholes. Walkin' so far the other side of the line they don't give a man a second chance once he's got himself into trouble."

A sneer appears on his face. "I heard rumours the Devils had gone against getting their hands dirty. Pricks probably don't even know how to fight anymore."

While suppressing down the thoughts of the likes of Peg and Blade, I nod. "You've got that right, Brother. We used to have boxing matches. Fucking ol' ladies put a stop to that."

He moves fast, his hands grabbing my tee while his leg shoots out, curls around mine, and before I can react has me on the ground. As I ruefully rub the back of my head where I banged it, he glares down. "Ain't got to the place where you can call me *Brother*. Not yet anyways. Perhaps not ever."

I could take him with one hand behind my back. But I don't. I lie there, at his feet. When he doesn't make another move I take it as unspoken permission that I can stand.

He takes another full minute to decide. "Okay, I gave you a chance. Be it on your own head. Best come inside and see if you can sweet talk Chaos." After half turning away he swings back and jams his finger into my chest. "On my part, I don't trust you."

I'm not surprised. I wouldn't trust a stranger appearing out of the blue either.

As I follow him inside, hearing the door clang ominously shut behind us, my mind's whirling. *Chaos. Chaos Riders. Wouldn't surprise me if I'm being taken to see the prez.* Might as well start at the top.

The clubhouse is small, but surprisingly clean, the typical bar along one side, a pool table off to another. Tables with mismatched chairs, and the unmistakable smells of stale beer and male sweat. Unlike the Devil's clubhouse, this is on more than one level, and Krueger leads me up some rickety wooden stairs which creak so badly I hope they will bear my weight as I ascend to the next floor. At the top, he points down the corridor. "Offices and the officers' bedrooms are up here. Members bunk in the bunk house behind this building. Prospects sleep where they can." The information he's sharing starts to make me think I might have a chance of being accepted here. Though, then again, it doesn't matter what he tells me...not if I'm going to end up dead.

He knocks on a door and pushes it open when a voice from inside calls out permission to enter. Stepping back to let me through, he closes it behind me then walks to take his place alongside another man standing behind the desk. The man sitting must be Chaos.

Seconds tick by while no one speaks. We're all examining each other. Krueger exchanges looks with the others, then points to the man seated at his side. "Chaos, our prez. Buff, our sergeant-at-arms."

"Rock." I introduce myself with a chin lift.

Chaos jerks his chin while the other two pull up chairs and seat themselves, and I'm left standing, feeling like a school boy summoned to face the headmaster. The prez stares at me for a moment, then instructs, "Turn around. Pull up your shirt."

I do so, exposing my full back patch tattoo. I give them a chance to study it, my skin crawling as though I can physically feel the touch of their eyes.

"Never want to see that again," Chaos informs me. I shrug my tee back into place and turn back around. "If you do get patched in, you get that covered with our colours. Until then, you keep it hidden. It's offensive. I see it again, I'll burn it off myself."

Making a mental note never to go shirtless, I nod.

Leaning back in his chair, Chaos folds his arms. "Right. So give me your story."

I tell him. All of it. No point hiding anything, except perhaps for the fact I stole. When I finish, Chaos glances at his companions and has a conversation consisting of raised eyebrows and chin lifts. It's a moment before he starts speaking again. "Don't make no difference you've been with another club. You haven't done anything to make us trust you. But you could be useful to us." He leans forward, his eyes fixed on mine. "You stay, it's on one condition. I want all the dirt on the Satan's Devils. You understand me? There ain't going to be no holding back. You're going to spill every detail down to how often Drummer takes a shit. You getting me here?"

I nod eagerly. "They're nothin' to me anymore. Didn't have my back when I needed it. All the years I called them brothers, and they were going to send me out bad for one fuckin' mistake. There's no loyalty left."

"Hmm." Chaos glances at Buff, who considers me for a moment, then gives a sharp nod. When it's his turn, Krueger does the same. "Okay. Here's the score. You start at the bottom as a prospect. Ain't gonna be wearing our patch until you've earned it. You hear me?"

Might not like it, but I expected it. A man's got to earn trust, and prospecting, showing you'll do all the shit, is the only way of doing it. "I know the score," I tell him, pulling my shoulders back. "Until every man here knows what I'm made of, I'm at their beck and call."

"Too damn right. You don't come to church. You don't get to know our business. Prospects don't go with the whores."

I raise my chin. Again, expected. And while I reckon my dick is going to get very familiar with my hand, I don't protest. "Agreed."

Another moment of silence, another exchange of expressions, then Chaos sits forward. "In any other circumstance we'd have taken you out back and killed you. But you've got something I need. Information. And I've got something you want, brotherhood. I'll do right by you, give you the same chance as any prospect. But one step, Rock. One fucking step out of line and you'll wish you'd let the Satan's Devils kill you. I won't take you out quick, though you'll be begging me to. You'll be praying for a fuckin' bullet. It will be a slow, agonising demise, I promise you. You'll plead for death long before you take your last breath. You hear me?"

"Loud and clear," I try it out, though after sixteen years it's hard to address a man wearing a different patch by that handle, "Prez."

"Not so fast." Now Chaos has a twisted grin on his face. "First you've got to pass our initiation."

CHAPTER 5

Becca

"Rebecca! Come inside now." I start at the angry voice coming from behind me, and the use of my full name. Grimacing apologetically to my new neighbour, I skip back to the front door.

"Mom! I was just talking to the girl who's moved in next door. She's twelve, only a few months younger than me. She goes to school and has loads of friends there. Can I go? It sounds fun." I know my words are tumbling out one after the other, but I can't seem to stop them. "She goes to church, but it's different from ours. Can we try that one?"

"Rebecca!" Mom snaps, ushering me inside. "We go to our church because we enjoy Pastor Gardner's sermons. Other churches warp the Bible. And you get a perfectly adequate education at home. We teach you everything you need to know."

"But, Mom, they use textbooks. You just use the Bible."

I don't read the warning signs. "That's not good enough for you anymore?"

I shake my head. "I'm not saying that, just that it would be nice to have a change."

"Stop talking back, Becca. How often do we have to tell you about contradicting your parents? Now go to your room, and I'll be speaking to your father when he gets home. There'll be no more talking to the girl next door. She's not good people for you to mix with."

I'd been excited to meet someone my own age, someone new. Someone with different ideas and outlook. I go to my room disappointed and remain there until my father comes home, knowing tonight's lesson will likely involve a strap meeting my backside.

But when Dad returns from work he's got another man with him. To my surprise, it's Pastor Gardner, the new pastor at our church. I don't take to his sermons, don't understand some of his teachings, but my parents like him and seem to hang onto his every word. Tonight, it appears, he's staying for dinner, as Mom scrambles to find an extra plate. At least that makes me view him favourably, the strap delayed, or hopefully, put off completely.

"Excellent pot roast, Mrs Salter."

Mom blushes. "Please, call me Anna."

The pastor nods as he helps himself to a second serving while I'm trying to eat what I've already got. He puts down the ladle and looks at me critically. "Dave's been telling me about your daughter." His eyes might be on me, his attention is not.

"Yes, this is Becca. Rebecca," Mom replies, her mouth thinning, presumably remembering our disagreement a few hours ago.

"You were right, Dave. She is exquisite." He nods to my father, then addresses me for the first time. "I've seen you in Sunday School, haven't I? And in the Bible and prayer meetings during the week?"

I glance at my father, who raises his chin. "Yes," I reply, meekly.

"We're bringing her up to be a good Christian girl," my father confirms.

"And she's what, thirteen now?"

I'm perplexed as to why he wants to know my age, but again, my father agrees.

That might have been the first, but certainly wasn't the last time Hawk came to dinner. Over the years he'd became a regular visitor to our home. Sometimes he'd be alone with me and would grill me on the scriptures. The parts he thought I ought to know. At first I was flattered, the other kids jealous at the attention he gave to me in our Bible classes. As the years passed, though, I noticed a different expression when he looked at me. It was only later I realised it resembled the way he'd looked at the meal my mother had prepared. With greed.

Now I'm caught in his trap.

By the light coming in through the small grill, I make another mark on the wall, taking a moment to tally them. Four-teen here, plus the seventy-five from when I was kept in Phoenix. Eighty-nine in total. That's almost three months I've been kept chained up.

For the first few weeks I was imprisoned on the biker compound in my home town. Two weeks ago I was moved here. The awful journey saw me blindfolded and transported in the back of a van with no idea where I was being taken. When we arrived the covering over my eyes had slipped and I got a quick glimpse of an old, run-down farmhouse, but no more than that before I was ignominiously carried in through the front door and down steps to a cellar. My location might have changed, my accommodation and treatment has not. Immediately after we arrived a cuff was again put around my ankle, the dreaded chain refastened around a sturdy support.

I'd have to be blind not to know who is holding me captive. Some of the men I see have *Chaos Riders MC* on their leather vests, others simply the word *Prospect*. That's all I know about the people who are keeping me for Hawk. My marks on the wall let me know how long I've been here and, unfortunately, how long I've got to go. Another thirty-three months, unless Hawk gets out early for good behaviour. I can't see how I can survive. My body has suffered, weak from lack of exercise and decent food.

Does he know the way his wife is being treated? Does he care? While I don't like to acknowledge it, part of me thinks that he does. Knowing I've no freedom to enjoy and that I'm incarcerated in the same way as him probably gives him some reparation for being locked up himself. Punishment for the part I unwittingly played in sending him down. Thinking back, he'd never treated me as anything other than a possession, and as such, me being held on ice for his enjoyment when he's released makes sense. Just like an old coat you'd throw into a closet and forget it's there until you need it.

I lie back on the filthy mattress, remembering that day, the last time I saw Hawk. Before he'd left to go to court his friends, members of the Chaos Riders, had arrived. Men who I never thought a well-respected pastor would have known, let alone have dealings with. These rough men had, with his blessing, taken me away and brought me to their compound. Since then I've been as much a prisoner as my husband. It's ironic. Hawk's also incarcerated, but I expect he's being treated much better than me. Don't they have TV's in prison? An exercise yard? He might be locked in a cell, but he wouldn't be kept chained twenty-four hours a day.

He'll have access to a bathroom, not a filthy bucket which is only emptied once in the morning. He won't have gone without a shower for almost three months.

I gave up screaming and shouting after the first few days. If it caught anyone's attention they just turned their music up louder. Realising it was futile, I'd stopped.

I'd told Hawk I'd wait for him. *I lied.* Somehow he'd known, and made sure I'd be around when he got out. It doesn't escape me that no one knows where I am. Am I only being kept alive so he can kill me with his own hands when he's released? My treatment suggests it.

I'm dead if I stay here. For three months I've tried to escape. I can't open the lock that keeps my ankle shackled, and the only man I see is the one who refuses to talk. I wait, biding my time, hoping for something to happen, though I'm unsure what I'm expecting. I've got thirty-three months to achieve my freedom. Lately though, my optimism of getting out has been fading, correlating with how quickly my body is growing weaker.

Initially I'd hoped my treatment would improve. I'd stopped protesting and complaining or pleading to be set free, hoping my good behaviour would be rewarded. When it wasn't I knew I'd lost any value. *Doesn't anyone miss me?* But there isn't anyone to care. My parents will trust Hawk to have made the necessary provision for me, and I have no friends who'd wonder about my whereabouts or miss me.

When I'd first met Hawk, the striking older man with the strangely attractive flash of white hair, I had no idea how much influence he was going to gain over my life. I was a young teenager, initially thrilled that I'd caught his eye, and preened when he gave me special attention, little jobs to do at Bible class which weren't given to anyone else. For five years I lived in ignorance of his intentions. My marriage was a complete surprise. Our coupling was just a bodily function, the moves mechanical. As his wife I had duties to perform, one of them obviously sex, which, for me, was painful. Uncomfortable at best.

After our wedding he allowed me to see the real man, the one neither my parents nor anyone in the church would suspect. He quoted scriptures which suited his purpose, justified all that he did with excerpts from the Bible. My subservience was demanded, my service of him justified. That he led a second secret life was obvious. I'd suspected another woman, but it wasn't until the police had contacted me that I realised I'd been on the wrong track. They'd wanted my help in building their case, and I would have given them every assistance, but I knew nothing. All I could say was Hawk was someone other than the pastor he showed to the outside world. If they had anything concrete they suspected him of, they never told me.

Hawk had been arrested for a misdemeanour. I've been caught like a rat in a trap. My only hope is that the police will keep investigating, won't be satisfied with the conviction they got. But even as I'm praying he'll never be released, I worry it won't just be his key that's thrown away. If he's not going to be freed, there'll no longer be a reason to keep me alive. Or protected.

Hawk is possessive. He liked to dress me modestly, but in a way that showed off my curves. Even at church he'd parade me around on his arm, showing other men what they couldn't have. It's that jealous trait that's stopped me from being molested. If something happens and Hawk doesn't get out, this biker gang will no longer have a reason to keep their hands off.

I've been through every emotion since I've been imprisoned. Fear of what might happen to me, disgust at the conditions I'm kept in, anger with my parents for placing me in this position, and sadness at the waste of my life. I'm twenty-one, I should have a future to look forward to. Instead, every minute ticking by is one less off my short life. Unless their treatment improves, it will be a miracle if I see my twenty-fourth birthday. Sometimes I think I won't even see my next.

I've lost weight, my hair has started falling out. My skin is greasy and atrocious. I've sores on my back, ass, and thighs where I lie or sit for too long. And the mattress stinks of sweat and often feels damp.

Forcing myself to my feet, I start doing stretches, compelling my tired, complaining body to exercise. Touching my toes, I almost lose my balance and fall over, the lack of good nutrition having its effects. I shake out my limbs and concentrate, pushing through my daily routine. When I finish, I collapse, trying to get my breath, relishing the brief rush of endorphins.

Footsteps descending the stairs have me looking up. They sound different. There's more than one person. A key turns in the lock—making me wonder, and not for the first time, why do they bother locking the door when I'm chained up?—and two men step in. The first very familiar, the man who usually brings me my food and empties my bucket. The second? Well, he's tall, quite broad. Muscular arms, one with tattoos emerging from the short sleeve of his tee. As my eyes travel up, even I grimace at the sight of his face. It's covered in bruises. There's a cut crudely stitched together running from his scalp to the corner of his right eye. The way he favours one leg suggests he's in pain. *He looks in a worse state than I am.*

He's wearing a leather vest, just like the man I know only too well, and when he turns around, like him, he too has a patch with the word *Prospect* on it.

What gives me hope is the brief flare in his eyes when they settle on me, but it's quickly extinguished.

As if he's not surprised to see a woman chained in a cellar, he simply turns to his companion and asks, "So what do we do here, Squirt?"

"*We* do nothing," Squirt sneers. "From now on this is your job." He passes the newcomer a small brown bag. "Put this in her reach. But watch for her claws."

Yes, I'd attacked him once out of pure frustration. To his credit he didn't retaliate, but had become wary about coming close.

He waves his hand, a silent instruction for me to move over. As he issues his non-verbal instruction I obey and make room for him to get to the bucket. I've never stopped him taking it away, the threat of him kicking it over and soaking the mattress with my faeces and urine enough to make me stay clear.

"Take the bucket upstairs and empty it."

The new man throws the bag at me. When Squirt passes him a bottle of water he rolls it within reach, then picks up the bucket.

"When it's empty, bring it back down. You do that once a day. You bring down more food and water in the evening. Oh, and if she tries to plead with you, to beg, just ignore her. Don't get into a conversation."

"Got it." He's got a deep voice, a velvety sound that's more pleasant than any others that I've heard. "Food twice a day, bucket emptied mid-morning." He pauses for a moment. "Clean clothes? Showers?"

"Nah, Rock. We don't bother with that."

No, they don't. After the time that I've been here, I don't smell myself anymore.

A quick glance my way, then the new man, apparently called Rock, disappears with Squirt. The door is locked and I'm left on my own once again.

It appears I've got a new jailor. But from what I've seen he'll be no better than the first. He barely looked at me, didn't seem to see anything unusual in the conditions I'm living in. I quickly regret my initial sympathy for the bruises on his face.

A few minutes later the door opens again, and my bucket is returned. Rock doesn't say a word. He doesn't even look at me. I was right. They're all made from the same mould. He'll be no help to me. If I'm going to get out of here I've got to wait for them to make a mistake. *At least drop a pin or something so I can try picking the lock.*

Time goes slowly in the cellar and the days are boring, so I hold out for the only thing that breaks the monotony and wait until my stomach growls before, at last, giving in I open the bag. A ham sandwich. It's dry and stale, but I force it down with sips of water. I had tried going on a hunger strike. But probably knowing if I was going to die Hawk would want to do it himself, they didn't let me get away with it. Once they realised what I intended, Squirt had come down with a scary looking man who'd held my mouth open while the prospect forcibly pushed food in. I had no option but to chew and swallow, or choke.

I wasn't brought up to be brave. My family had kept me secluded. I hadn't a clue how to cope or what I could do. Everything about this situation is beyond me. In the past I've had to make no decisions, only followed direction. Now I've no one else to depend on, it's hard to think for myself. I try to contemplate, *What would someone else do?* But don't come up with any answers.

The evening comes, and this time Rock enters alone. He doesn't even move far in from the door, just throws a bag to me and rolls a bottle of water across. *Is he too scared of me?* Hell, that's a joke. I do my best to look at him accusingly, lumping him in with the rest of these unfeeling men. But my expression has no effect on him. I don't know why I bothered, when within seconds he's gone. I'm left alone once again.

Three more marks on my wall. And still Rock hasn't spoken or replied when I address him by name. I don't waste my breath now. He's as bad as Squirt. Maybe it was because he's older I'd hoped for some sympathy, but no. Hawk must have got to him too.

The days go by, passing tortuously slowly. Then one day, the thing that I most dread happens, only for the second time since the Chaos Riders had taken me, my body obviously completely out of kilter. I wake with a familiar stickiness between my legs and cramping in my stomach. The first time I'd felt relief. Though I still had the implant, the idea of becoming pregnant with Hawk's baby filled me with horror. But my pleasure at the evidence I wasn't expecting soon disappeared when I'd plucked up the courage to ask Squirt for sanitary items. He'd laughed, and on this rare occasion, spoke to me, telling me he was a man and it wasn't his job to supply female shit. He'd told me to stuff toilet tissue up my pussy.

This time I don't even bother to ask.

Embarrassed, I try to fold the soiled paper so the blood doesn't show, certain I'd get the same dismissive answer from Rock were I to ask for something that obviously threatens his manhood. I curl into a ball, trying to ease the pain, knowing any exercise today will be beyond me.

It's times like this when I'm at my lowest and feel like I'm nothing more than an animal trapped in a cage.

Rock enters, presumably at the same time he does every day —I've no watch or clock to know for certain. A bag lands beside me, I don't bother turning. I hear the slight thud as a water bottle is put down, then the clank of the bucket's handle. Then…

"Oh fuck!" A moment passes, then rough calloused hands touch me.

"Get off me!" I flail with my arms, catching him on his face. Strong hands grasp my biceps, trapping me as he pushes me over onto my back.

Don't let him rape me.

Then I grasp it's not desire I see on his face, but concern. "Fuck, woman. Stop strugglin'. You're bleedin' and I need to find out where from. What the fuck have you done to yourself?"

I don't need his exploring hands finding the answer, so I hiss out. "I've got my fucking period, asshole." *I don't swear.* I didn't even know that I could. My shock at my profanity pales into insignificance at his unexpected reaction.

He lets me go immediately and sits back on his haunches. Looking me over from head to toe, and then around the area I have access to. It's not very large. His hand wipes over his cheek, ruefully rubbing the additional bruise I'd just given him. Then his eyes alight on my face, then move down to where my arms are now wrapped over my stomach. "Sore?"

Stunned, no one has cared enough to ask how I am since I was brought here, I automatically nod.

"Hey, Allie, one of the sweet butts in my last clubhouse, she suffered with cramps. Got fuckin' miserable with them. Sorry you're going through this." His eyes meet mine again. "What can I get you?"

He's asking what I want? Surprised, I take a chance. "I need tampons." But I've no hope he'll meet my request. To my astonishment, he raises and dips his head.

"Sure you do. I'll get them. Any preference?"

Dumbfounded, I tell him the brand I prefer. And then go for broke. "Some Advil?"

"You got it." His hand reaches out but stops in mid-air.

Was he trying to touch me? I must be suffering Stockholm syndrome, so lonely and lost, ready to welcome anyone's touch, but I find myself wishing he had.

He stands, and for some reason I feel bereft, particularly when he shrugs and looks apologetic. "I won't be able to come back down until tonight. But I'll bring you what you need then. I wish I could do more."

I don't want him to leave. "Why not? Why can't you come sooner?" He's the first person who's spoken to me like a human being.

He waivers, then turns toward the door, takes a step, then comes back. "What's your name?"

"I'm Becca." It's the first time anyone's asked me.

"Becca," he repeats as though trying it out, and something loosens inside me that someone's called me by name. "Look, they're watchin' me, okay? I have to be careful if I want to get my patch." His intense stare seems to burn into me. "Trust me, alright?"

This time when he steps away he leaves, shutting the door behind him. As I hear the key turning I gaze at the ceiling in disbelief. *Trust him? To do what? Save me?* But if they're watching him there's probably not much he can do. Or, perhaps not right now. That patch he's chasing sounds important to him.

There's one thing for certain. If it's him I have to pin any hope on, and let's face it, he's all that I've got, I won't be doing or saying anything that will give him away.

CHAPTER 6
Rock

Their initiation ceremony had been brutal. I could have taken their sergeant-at-arms or enforcer on easily had it been one on one. But with Buff and Wreck coming at me together, I did as well as I could, but it hadn't been long before I was down. They carried on until I was unconscious, coming round to find a wound on my head amateurishly stitched up, little skin on my head or body that wasn't bruised, my nose broken, two teeth knocked out, and my knee dislocated. I counted myself lucky not to be dead, but on trying to move, suddenly wished that I was.

Every movement hurts and causes me to groan, but when I force my eyes to open it's to find I'm lying in a queen-sized bed that's not long enough for me, in a small room with a TV on a dresser and a closet beside it. As I pull myself up, my feet feel something lying at the foot of the bed. Groaning as I pull it toward me, I find it's a leather vest with a prospect patch lying beside it, along with a handy needle and thread.

Allowing myself the first smile of the day, I awkwardly bend until I can reach it, then realise I won't be going far until I do something about my knee. I remember watching Doc when Tongue had once dislocated his. He'd got him to flex his hip, then straightened his leg and pushed his kneecap back into place. Hoping I'm making it better and not causing worse damage, it takes me a few attempts—not being the easiest thing to do to yourself—and I'm gritting my teeth to stop the scream escaping. But at last I feel a pop, and it's located right again.

Breathing heavily, I start sewing—as much to give myself something to do as to try and take my mind off my various pains and injuries. Also knowing, though, they wouldn't look on me favourably if I left the room without proudly displaying my new insignia. My job completed quickly, I realise I need a piss. Badly.

I'd been spoilt at the Satan's Devils compound, my suite there total luxury compared to this. It's immediately plain there's no convenient en-suite bathroom. Gingerly, I pull myself out of bed, slide on my new cut, and, with a heavy limp, go to find the facilities. At the end of the corridor I find what I want, a large enough bathroom with three showers, two sinks, and a stall. I go to the urinal, unsurprised to see my urine coming out tinged with red.

As I zip up, a sudden wave of all that I've lost washes over me, my lowly status setting me back sixteen years to when I last was a prospect. The pain I had to let them inflict has me finally grasping, *this is it*. The lowest I can get. I've reached rock bottom. All that I thought I'd accomplished taken from me, the love of my brothers lost.

I look in the mirror, then quickly away, not wanting to examine the damage to my face. *There's only one way to go now.* And that's upward. The Chaos Riders have accepted me into their ranks. Now it's only a matter of time until I get them to trust me and become a fully-fledged member of a new motor-cycle club. A new set of brothers. It's the best I can hope for.

I take a deep breath, well, as deep as I can until the sharp pain suggests I've got a couple of cracked ribs, draw myself up as straight as I can, and walk out of the barn that seems to still be in the stages of being converted into rooms for the Chaos

Riders. I enter the clubhouse with my head held high, proudly displaying my new cut.

Krueger, Buff, and Wreck are standing by the bar. They turn at the sound of my footsteps unevenly clanking across the floor, beckoning me toward them, nodding with approval as they notice I'm wearing my cut. I reach the bar and put my hand out to balance myself.

With a heavy slap to my shoulder which has me leaning my full weight forward, gasping with pain, Krueger laughs. "Welcome to the Chaos Riders, *Prospect.*" Then he waves to the man who'd been standing on the veranda when I first arrived, fuck it seems like a hundred years ago. "Squirt. Got you a helper. Show him the ropes, will you?"

"What's the matter with you?" Wreck, the enforcer, must notice me favouring my right leg.

"Dislocated knee," I manage to get out.

He smiles, as though proud of his handiwork. "Squirt. Find something to bind his knee, then put him to work."

Knee bound, I try to keep as much of my weight on it as I can bear, determined not to show weakness. The bar work is easy, learning what the different members like to drink slightly harder. I'm not yet trusted with keeping watch, presumably in case I let enemies slip by. But as the days pass and my leg and other injuries start to heal, I feel less pairs of eyes burning into my back. *I'm starting to earn their trust.*

Although the accommodation is far more basic, in some ways this clubhouse is better than the one at the Satan's Devils compound. For one thing, there's not an old lady or a kid to be seen. But in others... Well, as a prospect, the services of their women aren't available to me, and I've discovered I wouldn't be interested if they were. There's enough clues that the women aren't here by choice, nor being recompensed for their services. The men are rough with them, dragging them literally by their hair out to the bunkhouse, or fucking them in the open. It seems their only desire is to come themselves, uncaring whether the woman is satisfied or not, and in most cases, they're obviously not. Blowjobs are forced, men laughing as they make the women choke. During the day the women are hidden out of sight. At night they're brought in from the barn where they're kept, the front door locked to prevent any escape.

Manning the bar alongside Squirt, he nudges me and points to a woman being forcibly fucked by two men on the pool table, while another is shoving his dick down her throat. "Won't be long until I'm patched in and I'll be having me some of that. I can't fucking wait. You too, I expect?"

"Yeah, Squirt. Nothing I'd fuckin' like better." I feel dirty even saying the words. I like my women warm and willing. But I've noticed a couple of members don't partake. George is one of them, a man called King another. I was relieved to realise it's not obligatory.

I keep waiting, but Chaos himself doesn't start to quiz me until the first week's gone by. I'm pleased when I'm eventually summoned to his office. This time, I'm invited to sit.

"So, Rock. You're settling in well. Have to say I admire the way you cope with all the shit."

I've been trying hard enough. All their bikes are spotless.

"I had my doubts about you." He folds his arms over his chest, his keen eyes watching me.

"I've thrown in with your lot," I tell him, honestly. "Want to make my home here. Not going to fuck my chance up."

"I hear you. I thought you might have been a plant at first, but you've been giving us your all." He pauses, raises a hand and scratches his bald head. "Can't be easy with your first time prospecting well in your rearview. But the brothers tell me you do anything without complaint."

I smirk. "Wiping George's ass was going a bit far."

He chuckles. "Hear you did it though."

I had. I nearly puked. "I'm not a kid like Squirt. I know how this game goes. If I want my patch, and I do, I can't make any mistakes. I do whatever I'm asked."

Chaos nods. "Can tell you've got experience. And, I have to admit, I've taken a liking to you. Respect you. Hear some fuckin' sense coming out of your mouth, unlike some I could mention. We're still setting up here, got more members coming in in a couple of weeks."

I'm burning to ask how many, but I don't. As a prospect it's none of my business, and I'm not going to fall into any verbal trap.

He leans forward and places his elbows on the desk. "At the rate you're going, you might get patched in early."

I sit up straight, showing my interest. "I'm all for that."

Having dangled the carrot in front of me, I'm not surprised by what he says next. "Time to show your loyalty, Prospect. I want to know everything you can tell me about the Satan's Devils. Their compound, their armoury. How many men they've got. Where their weak points are. I don't want you to leave anything out."

I don't even flinch. All I have to do is remember how the Devils would have kicked me out. With the tat on my back itching, I don't hesitate. "I can give you all that." It's clear he's planning to take them all out, but again, I don't ask for confirmation. I'm just a prospect. If I need to know, he'll tell me.

It takes an hour, during which I tell him all I know about the Devils. It comes to one fuck of a lot. Well, I was there sixteen years. He'd grabbed a pen early on and has scribbled a couple of pages in a notebook. After the first five minutes he'd called Krueger, Buff, and Wrecker in to listen as well. All four men question me closely, a couple of times repeating queries already answered, but they don't trip me up.

"Okay." Chaos looks at the others. "I think that's all for now. Once we've looked at this we may well have other things to ask you."

I shrug and offer, "I'm an open book. Anything I can tell you I will."

There's a friendlier vibe coming off the four men now. They must know as well as I do, that by betraying the Devils I've signed my death warrant were it ever to come out. Wrecker raises his index finger, Chaos nods his permission for him to talk.

"Reckon Rock could take over some of Squirt's duties."

"The cellar?" Chaos asks.

"Uh huh."

"Don't see why not, Wrecker. I, for one, have started to trust him." The prez gives a crooked grin. "After all, we're all he has now."

Yeah. If the Satan's Devils get wind of what I've just done, they'll kill me on sight. Clean club or not, Chaos is right. Having opened my mouth and betrayed the Satan's Devils, from this point on, the Chaos Riders are all that I've got.

Well, I put myself in this position, came to the Riders with my eyes open, not worth worrying about the Devils now. Instead, I begin to wonder what they keep in the cellar, and what duties I'm going to take on. *Weapons? Drugs?*

I'm stunned the next morning when I find out what their secret is, certainly nothing I would have expected. A girl. Kept in conditions I'd immediately remove a dog from if I found it living like that. Kept chained, she's dirty and smells, wearing clothes which are tattered and obviously not recently washed. Her hair, which probably was once sleek and shiny, now falling out. The powerful odour alone had turned my stomach, but I couldn't let anyone see my disgust. I kept my mouth shut, didn't ask questions a prospect wouldn't get an answer to, and ignored her as best I could while I did my job.

Taking my cue from Squirt, I didn't talk to her. If I want my patch I need to follow every order. But the morning I'd learned she had her period was when I broke my silence. Leaving her, knowing now she was Becca, not some faceless female, was hard. I wanted to stay and comfort her, tell her I'd do anything to help her out of her plight. *But I couldn't.* The only thing I could do was get her the supplies she needed. She damn near broke my heart being so accepting of her captivity. *No one should be treated like she is.*

But I do things right. First, I asked Squirt.

"You fuckin' what?" he replies, laughing. "I'm not going to a drugstore for her. I've got a fuckin' cock."

I grit my teeth. *And that makes you a man, does it?*

For the first time since what I think of as my interrogation, I go to see Chaos. Knocking on his door, he gives me permission to enter.

"Prospect. Come in."

He doesn't invite me to sit, and I'm kept waiting while he looks over some paperwork. Eventually he glances up. "What d'you want?"

"The girl, in the basement."

He shakes his head. "Not saying nothing about her. You don't need to know. What's she said to you?" Narrowed eyes regard me carefully.

I'd expected that response. "Nothing," I deny. "But it's not what she's said, but what I saw."

I've got his interest, so I continue with just one word. "Blood."

He stands quickly. "She's cut herself?"

Keeping my voice even, I explain, "No, her period. And she hasn't got any…"

I suppose it would affect his manhood if I named what she needs, as he cuts me off. "Well, fucking get her some then. What you wasting my time for?"

"Squirt led me to believe she wasn't allowed any luxuries." I defend myself, while dropping the other prospect in it.

"Squirt's not got the brains he was fucking born with. Luxuries, fuck." His hand wipes over his head.

"Thanks, Prez." I shudder. "Didn't like thinkin' where that blood came from myself." Which is totally untrue. Women have periods. Full stop. Doesn't make me less of a man to know about them.

"With you there, Prospect. Women need to hide that shit." Chaos has paled, and he gestures I should leave. Presumably so he can recover from our conversation with his manhood intact.

I didn't break out in hives, and my cock didn't fall off as I searched through the aisles, finally finding what I was looking for. The girl behind the counter didn't belittle me as she rang my purchase up, and I successfully returned to the clubhouse without having grown boobs. Suspecting they'd frown on me giving her any comfort, I snuck a few Advil out of a bottle, placing them into my cut.

When evening came I took her supplies down to her. It felt like a punch in my gut to see the look of pleasure on her face, as if I was giving her an expensive present of jewellery rather than basic sanitary items.

Crouching down beside her, I clasp my hands between my legs. "Sweetheart, I'll go give you some privacy in a minute, but can you tell me who you are, and why you're being kept here?"

Her eyes meet mine, something in their depths leading me to believe she's summing up whether to tell me or not. Then the little shrug she gives suggests she realises she's got little to lose. But when light comes into her eyes, she asks hopefully, in a voice little more than a whisper, "Will you help me escape?"

Sadly, I shake my head. "Not right now, darlin'. But I'll see what I can do. Give me some details first. Let me know what I'm dealin' with here."

She looks down at her broken and dirty fingernails. "You're one of them, though, aren't you?"

"I am." Denying it would be suicide.

She's quiet for a moment, then, "I'm Becca Gardner. No one special. But my…husband is Hawk." As she names him she trembles.

"Husband?" I frown, while thinking, *She's married?* Do the Riders want something from him? Is she being held for ransom or some such shit? And who is her husband? "Hawk his first name or last?"

"The only name anyone calls him. It's a nickname, like yours." She puts her hand up to a straggly overgrown fringe and touches it. "He's got a shock of white hair, here. Apparently, Hawk was the name of a badger in an old child's story. His grandma named him. His proper name is Alexis Gardner. He is…was…a pastor in Phoenix."

A pastor? I don't know if that makes being kidnapped and held for ransom more or less likely. *What the fuck would the Riders want to hold over a pastor?* Knowing I've not got much time, I file the name away and move on to my next question, hoping to get some answers. "Do you know why you here?"

She nods. "Hawk got sent away to prison. A three-year sentence. He asked his 'friends'," she puts the word in quotes with her fingers, "to take care of me. Make sure I wait for him while he's gone."

And this is taking care of her?

"Three years? How long have you been here?"

She indicates the wall she's shackled to, and I see marks. Too many fucking marks. "Over three months."

This is the way they care for a friend's woman? It doesn't sound right. It breaks my heart to think she's been here that long, and if she's right, her release is nowhere in sight. "There's more to it, isn't there?"

She bites her lip as though to prevent more coming out. Trust, it seems, has to be earned on both sides. Knowing I've already spent more time in the cellar than I should, I put my hand out. When she doesn't flinch away I pat her arm, feeling how bony and skinny she is. Then I stand. "I better get back."

Staring at the floor as though it holds all the answers, she doesn't acknowledge me as I leave her, wondering what the fuck I can do to help. No one should be treated the way they're treating her. From what I've seen she's not going to last another three months, let alone the full term until this Hawk is released.

CHAPTER 7
Rock

I'm out of here, man." Taking the keys to my bike out of my cut, nonchalantly I bounce them in my hand.

"Have a good afternoon." Runner, the other prospect who I've taken a liking to, looks at me and grins. I'm not leaving them in the lurch—bikes are cleaned, clubhouse scrubbed down, both him and Squirt are around to deal with any of the members' demands. "Give her one from me."

Winking at him, in a move reminiscent of my old friend, Beef, I put my hand over my crotch and, bucking my hips lewdly, chuckle. "How about two, even three? And I'll make sure I enjoy them." I see him put up his middle finger as I turn away.

Fuck, it's good to get out into the fresh air and away from the clubhouse. Happy for once to have the afternoon to myself without being at anyone's beck and call, it's hard to keep the shit-eating grin off my face as I ride out through the gates. My expression quickly turns into a scowl as I look into my rearview mirror and see another bike following me. *Squirt.* It could be coincidence. Wanting to find out, I test him, taking one turn then another. He's sticking to me like fucking glue, not even trying to be discreet. *He is following me.*

I give up trying to shake him and go the direct route, turning into a residential area and pulling up at a low-budget house. He parks up behind me. Turning off my engine and pocketing the key, I swing my leg over the saddle and prowl back toward him.

"You're not fuckin' comin' in," I snap. "I don't fuckin' share."

He grins and absentmindedly squeezes one of his pimples. "Shame."

"Get fuckin' lost."

"Free country, ain't it? Think I'll sit here and enjoy the sun."

He can sit there all he wants. As long as he doesn't come any closer. "I'll be here all afternoon," I warn him. "Got some lost time to make up for."

He points to the door which has opened. Dressed in an almost see-through negligee, the woman I've come to see comes running out, screaming. "Rock!" She's beaming, excitedly showing how pleased she is to see me.

I can't do anything but swing her up into my arms, planting my mouth on hers as I put on a show. I can tell that she's giggling, my mouth isn't what she's had before—well, not north of her waist anyways. Holding her front tight to me as if I'm jealous of him seeing anything of mine, I flip him off over her shoulder, haul her up and carry her inside.

As soon as we're in the entrance I slam the door shut with my foot and immediately let go of her, wiping my mouth with the back of my hand.

"Oh, come on, it wasn't that bad, was it?"

"I don't kiss, Allie," I remind her.

"Shame. I enjoyed it." Her sly smile makes me chuckle.

"Go upstairs, Allie. Remember to put on a show." A very welcome and masculine voice instructs her.

Without needing to be told twice, she hurries away. I watch her go. "Who's up there with her?"

"Wraith."

"Wraith? But Sophie?" I frown. Wouldn't it have been better to have brought one of the single men?

A snort. "He's not gonna fuckin' cheat on Sophie. But he can still remember what to do. Your friend out there will see a lot of shadows movin'."

"Allie's solid?"

"Yeah. She's a good'un."

As Drummer steps into the light I can't hold back any longer. I hold out my hand, and when he reciprocates, wrap my fingers around his and tug him toward me. My hand goes around his back, his around mine, and we share a man hug for longer than normal. I haven't seen him to talk to since the day before my expulsion from the club. The day he'd offered to put excitement back in my life by giving me the chance to quite possibly lay my life on the line for my brothers. I'd accepted, of course. Hadn't hesitated.

"Fuckin' glad to see you, Brother. Fuck, thought you might be dead." The emotion in Drummer's voice nearly does me in.

I swallow and blink rapidly. Then answer calmly, "For a moment there, Prez, I thought I was. Nearly didn't survive their initiation." I take a step back, which enables Drum to see the new, still-red scar on my face, and the bump on my nose that wasn't there before. I open my mouth and point to the gaps where previously I had teeth. I haven't had time to visit a dentist.

"Fuck. Brother, I'm sorry." His voice catches. They might not have killed me, but I've been left with permanent scars.

Drum turns away, and I follow him into a back room where the curtains are drawn. He goes to the fridge and gets out two beers. "Now I'm sure you'd probably prefer to be upstairs gettin' your rocks off, but how about you update me instead?"

I grin. "I'll have to go back bandy-legged."

"Don't look at me, Brother. I'd do a lot of things for you, but fuckin' you ain't one of them."

We both laugh. *Fuck, I've missed him. Missed this camaraderie.* Leaning back, I take a swig of the welcome beer, feeling the most relaxed I've done in weeks. "So, Wraith knows. Anyone else?"

Prez shakes his head. "No one. Best warn you, Rock. You show your face anywhere near the compound or our businesses, and you're likely to end up dead. No one's got a good word to say about you." As my head bows, hating my brothers are thinking so little of me, Drum adds, "For now it's best to keep quiet. Someone gets questioned, they can't let anything drop if they don't know what's going on." He points his own bottle toward me. "Best way of keepin' you safe. Know how much you must hate it, Brother, but it won't be for long."

"Doesn't make it much easier." The thought of my brothers believing I'd actually steal from the club pains me.

Drummer nods, then chuckles as he changes the subject and indicates my cut. "Prospect, eh? Bet you're enjoyin' that."

I frown, growing serious. "That's something I need to change, and fast. Need to get myself around that table."

"You find anything out yet?"

"Nah. Oh, I've had the inquisition, told them everything we agreed. They think you're a bunch of pussies and won't put up much of a fight." I take another drink. "Prez, their bitches are forced. They don't respect women at all. Best look out for the old ladies and kids if we can't take them out first."

A pained expression passes over his face. "At least we're in the drivin' seat with you on the inside. Even if it's only to give us early warnin'."

"Nothing's going to happen for a couple of weeks. They've got more men comin' in. Don't yet know when or how many. And I'm not in a position to ask."

He shakes his head. "Prospects don't get told that shit. Not until they need to start making beds."

"That was my thought. Soon as I get involved in the preparations and know anything, I'll get word to you."

The corners of his mouth turn down. "It would have been better if they'd taken you on as a member, but at least you're on the inside. Any intel is better than nothing."

Annoyed I haven't more to divulge, I remember what I want to ask. "Prez, there's a girl there. She's chained in the fuckin' cellar. Has been for three months. She's in a fuck of a state."

"They use her?" His eyes become steely.

"Nah. That's the strange thing. No one touches her, or even speaks to her. Only take her food twice a day and empty the fuckin' bucket she has to use."

"Who is she? And why is she there?" He takes out his phone and holds it ready.

"Becca Gardner." I wait for him to tap her name into the notes app. "She has a husband named Alexis. Goes by the handle Hawk, because of a shock of white hair over his forehead apparently. He's gone away for a three-year stint. The Riders are holding her for him."

Drum's eyes go wide. "Three fuckin' years chained in a cellar?"

I shrug. "Seems that way." Her image comes into my head and makes me frown. "She's not gonna make it, Drum."

He rolls his head back on his shoulders. "I'm not fuckin' surprised. And Hawk? Hawk." As he repeats it, he looks thoughtful. "Not sure I've come across him."

"He may come from out of the area. Think they brought her with them from Phoenix."

"I'll get Mouse on it."

"Thanks. Mouse back home?"

"Yeah." Drummer taps his fingers on the now empty beer bottle. "Something happened while he was away, but he's not said what it is. Just seems quieter, deeper than normal."

Except when he's finding out our info, Mouse often seems that way. "Hope it's nothing to worry about." I change the subject. "I want to get Becca out of there, Drummer. Get her somewhere safe."

"You like her?" He grins.

"I couldn't say." My lips purse together briefly. Do I like her? Fuck if I know. Lookin' like she does at the moment doesn't exactly encourage a hard-on. "Feel fuckin' sorry for her." Yeah, I do. "I don't want to leave her there, Prez. I've had thoughts on how I can help her escape."

"She yours?"

What is it with Drummer and his questions.

"Fuck no, Prez…"

"Rock," he interrupts me. "You want to risk blowin' your cover for a girl you just met? Take it from me, you wouldn't do that lightly. You're going to ask me to take her in as well, aren't you?"

I stare at him. "Fuck. Drum, I don't know. Yeah, she needs somewhere to go, and I couldn't think of a better place for her. Pretty sure I can get away with helping her out without exposin' myself. As for the rest?" I pause, my hands go to my head. *Why do I want to help her?* "I just want to make sure she's safe," I finish, lamely.

His mouth thins. "Can she run?"

"She's too weak to walk or run far. But they don't check on her. There's only me going down twice a day. If I can get Chaos on board with my suggestion, I think I know how to get her away. Just need someone with a car waitin'…"

He doesn't hesitate. "We can do that."

"Prez, I'd like her on the compound until we know who this Hawk is and how long his reach is."

"I hear you, Rock." He examines my face for a moment. "There's a problem with that. As soon as the women get talkin' to her, and if she's in the state you say, they won't be able to stay away. She'll tell them it was you who arranged her rescue. Then we risk everything comin' out, which puts you in danger."

I press my own lips together. "I'll speak to her. Tell her straight. Her survival, and mine, depends on her keepin' quiet. I reckon she'll agree. I'll have to give her something so she trusts you. Doubt she'll trust anyone easily right now."

"Don't like includin' women in our wars. But equally don't like that we don't know what she's being punished for. You talk about her trustin' us, but how do you know you can trust her? She might be a snitch who put this Hawk away."

He's right that, I know nothing about her. But the memory of her expressive eyes that make you think you're looking into her soul comes back to me. "I don't know, Drummer. But I've got a feelin'. If you feel you need to put her on lockdown, so be it. But keepin' her in a suite on our compound will be luxury compared with where she is."

He takes in a deep breath, then lets it out slowly. "Rock, what you're doing for us? We'll never be able to repay you. If this is something you want, then there's no way I can refuse. Set it up, let me know where and when, and I'll sort my end out."

My hand reaches out and we bump fists. *I've missed this so fucking much. Just shooting the shit with my prez, my real prez.* The man I'd give my life for.

"I'll use the burner phone and text you the details as soon as I know them." He nods as I slip the phone he brought for me into my pocket.

Suddenly there's a new voice. "Hey. Allie's darn near worn me out and we were only pretendin'! Christ, you're going to have to go back lookin' like you're half dead."

"Wraith!" I stand, and we do the hand clench and man hug thing all over again. "Gettin' old? Can't keep up anymore?"

He pushes me away and smirks. "Went a few rounds with Sophie before coming here."

"So that's why you winced when you got on your ride?" Drummer asks, one side of his mouth turned up.

"What can I say? My woman wants satisfyin', she gets her needs met."

"Pregnancy hormones," laughs the prez. "Sam's already getting horny."

"Congrats, man!" I'd had my suspicions, now they're confirmed. Another kid in the clubhouse. Now I've had a chance to see a compound without them, I'm starting to think perhaps they're not as bad as I'd thought.

He brushes off my best wishes while Wraith fixes me with a stare. "Fuckin' good to see you, Brother. I know why Drummer kept it quiet, but it's been hell thinkin' you'd gone bad."

"Not been fun and games for me either," I agree.

"Can fuckin' see that. Someone's rearranged your face." Wraith, like Drummer before him, looks distraught.

"Two someones. Their enforcer and sergeant-at-arms. Initiation ceremony." I grin. "I passed, apparently. Found out when I regained consciousness."

A female voice calls out. "Is it safe for me to come down?"

"Yeah, Allie." I smile as she enters, and when she gets close enough, tug her so she falls onto my lap.

She winks at the VP. "He's an animal, that one. I'm exhausted."

Wraith growls as I take hold of her hair, wrap it around my wrist and pull her head so she's forced to look into my eyes. "We were never here, and this never happened, Allie."

Her sincere look convinces me, as well as the words she says. "I know, Rock. It would be dangerous for you, and for the club, if I said anything. My mouth's shut, my mind's already forgotten what happened this afternoon. Look, it's my home too. And I love you, Drum, Wraith, all the brothers. I won't do anything to jeopardise that." She breaks off and looks at Drummer, then at the VP. "I'm not stupid. If someone's comin' for the club, we need information to protect us. Rock needs to be kept out of it so he can get it for us. You can trust me."

"I know we can, sweetheart," the prez reassures her earnestly. "Already know that."

It was hell leaving Drummer and Wraith. Last time I hadn't had time to think about it, knowing the brothers were after my blood, I was being chased for real, and my mindset reflected that, making it easier to play the part of turning traitor. This time it's with man hugs and expressions of love. It fucking killed me. I'd have given anything to be able to go back with them. But I couldn't. Not when it's my job to get information to save our club.

I acted the part. Allie made the most of it, hanging on to me at the door, calling me back time and again for yet another kiss. In the end I pinch her and tell her not to overdo it, but she was enjoying herself, and deserved something for agreeing to keeping her mouth shut.

Squirt was still waiting, so I made a show of checking my zipper was done up, adjusting myself in my pants and grimacing as I sat astride the bike, leaning forward as though making myself comfortable. Before starting the engine, I call over my shoulder, "Going straight back to Long Horns. No need for you to try to catch up."

He scowls when I wave at him, but pulls away from the curb at the same time as I do. Allie and I had given Drummer and Wraith some time to get clear, just in case he lingered to check out the house. Allie had a gun on her, prepared if he tried to get inside.

I use the ride to get back into a prospect's mindset. Back at the Chaos Riders' compound nothing has changed. Not that I should have expected it to. Apart from getting Runner's middle finger again when I tell him I'd enjoyed two fucks on his behalf, it's straight back into the grind of being a prospect. Someone had cut themselves, and I cheerfully mopped up the blood.

My absence having raised no suspicion, I'm careful to behave just like everyone expects me too. That includes making sure I spend no longer in the cellar than necessary, which means I have no more conversation with Becca for just over a week. At first she'd look up expectantly when I went in, but I purposefully kept my mouth shut and didn't acknowledge her. I don't want her to know the compassion I feel so she wouldn't act differently if someone else was to come down with me. After a couple of days she goes back to ignoring me while I deliver her food and empty that fucking bucket.

A week after my visit with Drummer, the prospects are put to clearing out an unused barn and getting cots and bedding sorted. I ask the reasonable question and receive the answer to prepare for a dozen men, and to be ready in seven days.

Again I climb the stairs to see the prez, and again I'm called in and offered a seat.

"Glad you came up, Prospect. Need to know something."

I raise my chin toward Chaos.

"Armament. I'd like to go over it again. How are the Satan's Devils fixed?"

In case it's a test, I remember precisely what I'd told him before. "Not too good. They've been running down stocks. Sloppy as well. I've seen empty boxes of ammo where brothers take them out and just put the boxes back on the shelves." They do, but Peg knows to look for that. He wouldn't leave anything to chance. "All the men have their personal weapons, but they tend to be Glocks."

"AK15s?"

"A handful. But with all the kids around, they're kept locked up."

Chaos's brows rise. "Okay. Now what about explosives? I heard they were responsible when the Rock Demons' clubhouse in Phoenix blew up a couple of years back."

"Slick's the explosive's expert. I don't know what he has now. Since the wildfire in the summer they've been moving stuff off-site. Put the wind up them to have a fire come so close. They're paranoid about harming the children."

He narrows his eyes incredulously, and I worry I've stretched it too far, but am relieved when he scoffs. "Women and fucking kids dictating every move? Never heard the fucking like. Don't need pussy saying we should keep fucking guns anywhere but close at hand. Fucking assholes. Taking them out is going to be a piece of cake." He chuckles, obviously pleased with what I've told him. "Okay, so what did you want me for?"

He's in a good mood, perhaps this won't be too hard. "The girl in the cellar…"

"Not fucking bleeding again, is she?" He sneers. "If she is, keep that shit to yourself."

"Not in the same way." I summon up a worried expression. When I think of her condition it isn't hard.

That's caught his attention. "What do you mean by that?"

"She's lying on a filthy mattress, in dirty clothes. I saw her legs, she's got fuckin' bed sores." I'm not lying. I have. One day I'm going to wring Chaos' neck for letting her get into such a state.

"Not much I can do about that," he replies dismissively.

"Look, I don't know why she's here, but as we're feedin' her, I suspect you don't want the sores to become infected and have her dic on you."

That brings him up. "Die? She in danger of that?"

"Seen if before." I lie. "It's what happens with bedridden patients. They get MRSA or some such shit. Septicaemia if the sores fester."

It's his turn to look worried. "I can't have her fucking dying on us. What do you suggest?"

Got him. "Simple," I answer. "A shower, a change of clothes. That should sort her out."

He stares at me, huffs a laugh, then points his finger. "You suggested it, you fucking sort it. And, Prospect? Keep your fucking hands off her. You don't see her naked for a second, understood? Hawk would fucking kill me."

Being a good prospect, I don't ask who Hawk is. Instead, I suppress the grin that's trying hard to rearrange my features, battling to scowl instead. "Got it. I get her showered and don't touch her. No problem there, Prez."

CHAPTER 8

Becca

*I*t might be my eighteenth birthday, but like the other seventeen that have gone before, I don't expect anything to mark it. No cards, no good wishes, and certainly no presents.

When I wake I stretch, knowing today I've become a legal adult. It's words only. I'm not naïve, I know I haven't grown up. I've watched the girl next door from my window, who, while a few months younger, seems older than me. I've seen the young man who comes to collect her and take her out, and spied on her as she returns giggling and happy, wondered at her being kissed by him on the door step. I heard the party she had when she turned sixteen, watched all her friends, male and female, turn up. My parents prayed long and hard that night.

I know nothing but this house and the church, or the few outings and picnics attended with members of the congregation, or visits to the doctor or orthodontist. I couldn't catch a bus, never handled any money other than what I was given to put into the collection box. Eighteen years might have passed, but I know little more than I had at thirteen. I've never watched anything on TV but religious programs, or sometimes the news.

Enough self-examination. Time to get up. I eye the clothes my mother had laid out for me, my head tilting in puzzlement. Why a white dress? It's pretty, with a lacey insert making it demure up to the neck. My eyes crease. It seems far too delicate and fragile for my household chores. Never one to argue with her choices, just put on the clothes I'm expected to wear, so today's no exception.

Feeling awkward and strange, I descend and join my parents for breakfast. Dad's home today, as my birthday falls on a Saturday.

They seem excited, expectant, but I know better than to ask why. If I need to know, they'll tell me.

"So, Becca. This is a day that's been a long time coming." For once Dad is jovial. I didn't realise he could smile until now, or at least, not at me. All my life I've tried to be the good, obedient daughter he wanted, but somehow always came up short of his expectations.

"You've finished with your schooling now. You're an adult." Mom seems delighted.

As I sit wondering what is so significant about me reaching the age of maturity, the doorbell rings. I don't take much notice, knowing it will have nothing to do with me. Mum gets up quickly to answer it.

"Pastor Gardner. Come in."

"Call me Alexis, please, Anna. We're about to be family."

I turn at the pastor's strange statement in time to see Mom blushing. Like my father, she's beaming with pleasure. I start to rise, to make myself absent while the adults talk, but her next words have me pausing.

"Come in," she urges again. "Rebecca's ready and waiting." At my name my ears perk up. What am I ready and waiting for?

Imitating my father, I stand as the pastor enters the room. Has he come to wish me Happy Birthday? That would be strange. Neither of my parents have said it.

"Becca." Pastor Gardner stretches out his hand. "What a wonderful morning this is."

Still bemused, I feel his fingers wrap around mine, but he doesn't just shake it. No, he holds on. "Pastor," I greet him.

"Call me Alexis, or better, my nickname, Hawk."

My parents aren't allowed that formality, why me?

My father coughs and pointedly looks at his watch.

"Yes," Pastor…Hawk says. "Becca, today you're going to make me the happiest man in the world. You're going to become my wife."

It takes me a moment to process his words. Then I wrench my hand from his in horror. "No," I squeak, then try again more firmly. "You're mistaken, Pastor. I'm marrying no one. I'm sorry."

"Becca!" My father says sharply. "It's all been arranged. We're expected at church in an hour."

Arranged? I certainly had no part in the arrangements. "Dad, I'm sorry, I can't."

"Just do what you're told, Becca. Can't you see what an honour this is? You'll be the pastor's wife and will be well looked after."

My eyes flick to Mom, immediately sensing I'll get no support. I can't get my head around it. This must be a nightmare I've yet to wake up from. I try pinching myself, but it doesn't work. I look at Hawk. "You're too old for me to be marrying you," I tell him bluntly.

"Older men have the experience to cope with a young wife," the pastor explains reasonably, my father nodding his agreement.

"Pastor Gardner will be able to continue your education," Dad says. "Don't forget what you've learned to date." His eyes harden, his voice deepens. "Obey your parents and your husband."

I lean on the chair for support, looking down at my half-eaten breakfast, wishing I could wake up from this terrible dream. My eyes go to my mother, then my father. They both look as determined as I've ever seen them. "You can't mean this." My voice is little more than a whisper.

Again, Dad consults his watch. "Come on, Becca. Everyone will be getting to the church soon. We need to be there and ready.

Today will be the happiest of your life. Now take your fiancé's hand and let's get going."

My fiancé? I must have missed the bit where he asked me.

"I have a say…"

"No, you don't," Mom snaps. "You're going to church and saying your vows in front of God, and you will mean them. You will be a dutiful and faithful wife to your husband." She pauses. "If you don't, we'll disown you. We brought you up to obey. We know what's best for you. And that's marrying the pastor. What more could you hope for?"

I've been home schooled, which amounted to being taught little more than everything in the Bible. I'm not equipped for any job, except looking after a home. What could I do if they turned me out? I've no money, no prospects. No friends or relatives who could help.

Hawk's been quiet, letting my parents deal with me. Now he enters the conversation. "Come, Becca. You're eighteen today. Time to step into your new life. Time to set foot on the path that God's laid out for you."

His voice is gentle, almost mesmerising. He's a pastor, perhaps he does know God's plan. What choice have I got? None.

After three years, am I at last escaping his clutches?

There's a black SUV waiting just where Rock told me it would be. Suddenly cautious, I pause before approaching it. *Am I right to trust Rock? What do I know about him?* Nothing at all except he's been the only person to be kind to me, to treat me like a human being since Hawk went to prison. Actually, before that. I'd been Hawk's prisoner long before the Chaos Riders took me.

Is this another one of Hawk's plans? My escape had gone smoothly. Rock had helped me reach the tree growing outside the bathroom window, my own adrenaline aiding me, making me strive to reach out to grasp it and, with a strength I thought

I'd lost, managed to use the branch to let myself down carefully until I stood on the ground. *Freedom.*

Wearing the shoes and new clothes that Rock had managed to scrounge from one of the whores, I stepped off the veranda as fast as I could without making any noise. My skirt might be up around my ass, my top far too small, but I wasn't going to complain. Clean clothes for the first time in months, even if I had to forego the promised shower to buy extra time.

As I cling to the edge of the farmhouse following the instructions I was given, the sound of the water I'd left running in the bathroom above fades into the distance. There's a short run to make until I reach the edge of the treeline, but Rock had chosen a good time, all the members must be in the clubroom. I bend low, making myself as small as possible as I run, and am gasping for breath by the time I reach the safety of the trees.

I'm out. My muscles are already trembling, my limited exercise in the cellar not seeming to make up for the months of inactivity, but I force myself to press on, following Rock's instructions. Out the back, heading slightly to the right, across the open desert on my belly, getting to my feet when I'm far enough away…then running hell for leather until… Yes, just where he said, the SUV comes into sight, and at the same time doubts come into my mind. *Have I left one trap just to be caught in another?*

The driver must have been watching through his mirror. As the door opens a tall man steps out. He's dark, handsome. Not as heavily built as Rock. His face twists when he sees me, and I recall the brief glance I got in the mirror in the bathroom before Rock had helped me out. *I look awful.*

It's the compassion on his face that gets me moving, but I'm still anxious. Adrenaline still coursing through my veins, my heart continues beating fast. Though it would be sheer coincidence for there to have been another car waiting, I need to be certain this is what Rock had set up.

"A ride to safe haven for Becca," the stranger says.

Yes. Those were the words Rock had given to me so I'd know I could trust this man. If I was right to have faith in Rock.

I sway, partly with relief, partly with weakness, and partly in preparation to keep running, to take my chances and fend for myself. But I'm feeling faint, my escape already draining me. With no money, scanty clothes, and in a strange city, what chance would I have on my own?

"You're dead on your feet, woman. And we need to get out of here fast. I don't know how much time Rock will be able to buy us."

He's right. It won't be long before they discover me gone. They'll be out searching for me as soon as they know I'm missing. If I don't go with him, the chances are they'd soon find me. I start moving forward, the stranger holding out his arm as I stumble. I take it because I need the helping hand.

"Come on. We'll soon get you home and safe."

Still unnerved, I'm yet again being taken to a place I don't know where. I let him help me into the passenger seat, then fumble for the seatbelt. As soon as I'm situated he runs around to the driver's side and wastes no time starting the engine and driving off. My spirits begin to rise as I leave the Chaos Riders and that hated cellar far behind. *Anything has to be better than that.*

"What's your name?" I ask curiously when we've covered the first mile, then quickly wondered whether I should have spoken, relieved as he answers.

"Wraith."

Rock hadn't explained who he was sending me too. Couldn't even give me the name of the person collecting me. He'd said he hadn't been told when he hurriedly explained the arrangements. If he had to guess, he suspected it would be Drummer. *Mr Drummer I interpreted.* Now my companion has told me, I go cold when I realise it sounds like another biker name. "Where are you taking me?"

His face turns to meet mine, he grimaces, then says through gritted teeth, "Somewhere you'll be properly looked after, a place to heal and regroup. Somewhere you won't be treated like an animal. And with people who'll deal with your situation."

I replay his words in my head, recognising it sounds like Utopia, too good to be true.

Wraith speaks again. "You'll meet my ol' lady, and the other women. They'll be all over you. Rock told you to be cautious?"

I nod, then realise he can't have seen, so give him the words. "I'm not to talk of Rock, or the Chaos Riders. Just that you helped me escape, but not to give any details or where I've been or who I've been with."

"Keep it vague. Tell anyone who asks it's club business. We'll give the brothers enough information to keep them quiet. No one must know that Rock's undercover. We're trustin' you with this. If you mention him accidentally, you have to lump him in with the other Riders. Make people believe he's joined them." He throws another glance at me. "We've got brothers out searchin' for him. They want to bring him back to face a punishment they think he deserves. If the Riders hear we're no longer lookin' for him, they're likely to guess he's a plant. If that happens, he'll be dead."

He's put it so starkly. "I won't let anything slip. He got me out of there. I owe him so much."

"Lookin' at you, Becca, you owe him your life. You wouldn't have lasted many more months, let alone another couple of years."

We're through Tucson now, heading up the I10 toward Phoenix, when suddenly he indicates and turns off. It's a bumpy track, restored in places. Trees look like they've recently been burned by a fire, but new growth on the ground is starting to sprout. While I'm thinking a wildfire must have recently swept through here, we pull up in front of huge metal gates. A toot on the horn gets them opening, fear bubbling up as I feel trapped again when they close behind me.

I'd seen the signs he must be a biker—his name for a start, and the fact he'd mentioned his brothers. But the men milling around the auto shop wearing leather cuts no longer left any room for doubt. *I've been brought to a different biker compound.*

I whimper as I watch the leather-clad men. Wraith turns and catches my eye. "We're not the Chaos Riders," he says grimly. "We're the Satan's Devils, and we'd never treat a woman the way they've treated you."

"But I'm still a prisoner."

He pulls up in front of what looks more like a hotel than a biker club and switches the engine off. "You need a place to rest and recover. You need medical attention, good food to get your weight back on. We've got a gym which you can use to get your strength up. It's not safe for you to be out on your own, and you're in no state to look after yourself." He taps the steering wheel and sighs. "You're definitely not a prisoner. I'll turn around and drive you back to Tucson if that's what you want. But Rock's asked us to look after you, and because of what he's doing for us, we're not in a position to refuse." He pauses, turns toward me, and places his hand under my chin so I'm forced to look at him. "Rock must care for you. He's put himself in fuck knows what trouble helpin' you escape. You owe it to him to give us a chance. Whatever he's going through because he's helped you—and knowin' what I do of the Riders, he won't get away cleanly with whatever excuse he makes—you need to at least give him peace of mind that he knows where you are and that you're safe."

His long speech resonates with me. Rock had indeed stuck his neck out when he helped me escape, taking a big risk getting me away from there. The least I can do is comply with his wishes. It hadn't occurred to me he could get hurt on my behalf. I certainly do owe him a lot, and accepting what he'd arranged would be a good start with respect to repayment.

"A gym, huh?" I try a small smile. It feels unfamiliar. Though I've no energy for such things now, I used to use Hawk's equipment, one of my only pleasures enjoying the burn from keeping fit.

Wraith smiles, it transforms his face. But it's not at me. His eyes are fixed on a woman, who, as I turn, I see coming up to my door.

"Bloody hell! You look done in, babes. You want to come inside, have a cuppa or something?"

"That, there," Wraith informs me, "is my ol' lady, Sophie. She's got a heart of gold, but you might need a translator at times. She's from England."

"Sod off, Wraith," Sophie admonishes him but gives a wide grin. Then to me, "Come on, hun, I'll help you inside."

Taking her offered hand, I take my first step onto the ground of the Satan's Devils' compound. It's then I look around and *see* the place, and not my fears, for the first time. This is no converted warehouse in a rundown location, or a farmhouse out in the wilds. Instead, I could have come to a vacation resort. The views are stunning, looking down into a valley surrounded by two mountain ranges. Beyond the high robust fencing, desert borders the compound on all sides as far as I can see. Though it looks charred at present, I've no doubt soon all the vegetation will spring back. There's even the odd saguaro that's survived unscathed.

Shielding my eyes against the sun, I take a moment to breathe in the fresh air, noticing different aromas, which for the first time in months don't come from me. Though an under-lying odour reminds me I desperately need a shower, and being faced with the pretty and fresh-smelling woman, I feel ashamed.

"I need to clean up," I suggest, hesitantly.

"You need to see Doc," she contradicts, with a shake of her head. "Come inside, the others all want to meet you. But if it's too much I'll take you up to your suite."

Suite? While I'm anxious about meeting company and know I'm not at my best, as today's escape has already taken a toll on me mentally and physically, she's given me no choice. I let her take my hand and lead me in through the clubroom door.

Again, I'm surprised. I didn't see much of the Riders' club-house, but it certainly wasn't like this. There's the normal bar and pool tables, but the comfortable looking chairs around the tables match, and it seems freshly painted. There's pleasant smell in the air too, and I realise what's lacking. *Cigarette smoke.* The group of women who are seated on a couple of couches look up with their mouths dropping open as I walk in, and from the way they are dressed, and the young children playing at their feet, they look like wives—or what did Wraith call Sophie? Old ladies. Certainly nothing like whores.

With my free hand, I try to pull down the miniscule skirt, embarrassed again.

One gets up and approaches. "Hi, I'm Sam. I'm Drummer's old lady. He's the president."

I might not know much about motorcycle clubs, but if she's the president's wife, that probably makes her top dog. "Hi," I say weakly.

I don't have time to try to think of something to say, when another woman also stands and comes over. "I don't want to fuss, dear. And I'll get teased for this. But *I* know what matters most to a woman is her hair. You come to me after Doc's set you right. I *can* do something with it." As she touches it a strand comes out in her hands, and tears start to fall for the first time in weeks. I'd got used to my situation. Crying never changed anything. But the sight of this unknown, but compassionate woman holding my hair in her hands sets me right off. *She's right. A woman's hair is important.* "I'm Carmen, by the way," belatedly she introduces herself. "My old man's Bullet. I'm a hairdresser."

"Darlin', you ready for me to take a look at you?" A man not resembling anything like a doctor approaches, and I flinch, wondering who he is and what he intends to do.

Sam purses her lips and shoos him back. "Becca, Drummer's not shared much with me, and I won't ask for details you're not able to give. Just looking at you tells me you've been through a lot." Her eyes crease as she takes in my appearance again, then she indicates the man who's just spoken. "This is Doc. He was a medic in the Army and knows his stuff. If he thinks you need a hospital or a real doctor to visit, we'll arrange it. I suspect this all seems scary and you don't know who you can trust. If it's alright with you, I'll come in with you."

It's then I realise I'm still holding tight to Sophie's hand as I feel a squeeze on my fingers.

"Want me to come along as well?" she asks, her eyes softening.

"Please." My voice sounds weak, even to me. I look down at her. She's about two inches shorter than me. "But what I really want is a shower."

"Let me examine you first. Then I can advise how to look after your sores. And one of the old ladies will find you something better to wear," Doc says, his face grim.

Unnerved by the sudden change in my fortunes, I let Sophie lead me across the clubroom, down a passageway to the rear. She opens a door, and I enter a clean-looking room.

"Sit." Doc indicates the bed. Sam sits on one side of me, Sophie the other.

Wondering where he's about to start first, he surprises me by asking, "I understand you've been held prisoner. Tell me how long, where, and what food you were given to eat."

"Not enough, obviously," Sophie butts in. Sam hushes her.

I sigh and tell him everything I can. "I was held in a cellar. Chained up. A dirty mattress. No access to washing facilities. They fed me twice a day, either a sandwich or a burger. No fruit or vegetables, and just a bottle of water to drink." I swallow and admit, "I was there for over three months." The location of my prison had changed, but not the circumstances. I doubt they need the details.

"What?" Both women exclaim.

Doc silences them with a glare. "I can see the mark where your ankle was obviously cuffed, and other sores which have got infected. But what we're looking at here I can tell is a case of anaemia and other effects from a lack of vitamins D and C and probably a whole lot of other letters. In my view, unless you tell me different, I don't think you need a hospital unless your condition worsens."

He breaks off, looking at me closer, his jaw tensing. "Fuck, woman. I've seen cases like this before, but normally refugees living in immigration camps." He clenches his teeth together, then crouches down so he's at my eye level. "Anything else I should know about? Were you...abused?"

Rapidly I shake my head. "They didn't touch me like that." He seems relieved, and I sense that both Sam and Sophie relax. "What should I do?" I ask him.

"I'll give you iron tablets, and you're to eat lots of food rich in iron. Vegetables and fruit. And," he smiles at this one, "get plenty of rest and sit out in the sun." He points at the visible sores on my legs. "I'll give you an antibiotic cream to put on them after your shower. I think we've caught it in time, but if they don't clear up, get worse, or if there's anything I can't see that's worrying you, you'll need to see a doctor."

He kneels and opens a bag and pulls out the items he mentioned. Sam takes them from him. He says one last thing before he leaves. "Thank fuck you got out of there when you did." With a last tightening of his face, a muttered goodbye, and something else I didn't quite catch under his breath, which I take was an impolite comment about my condition, he leaves.

Tears come to my eyes, summoned by the sudden change in my fortunes and being overwhelmed by these strangers, who for some unknown reason are prepared to take care of me. Suddenly I'm crying all the tears I'd held back while I'd been chained in the cellar. Without saying a word, Sam pulls me into her, hugging me tight.

I cry for a very long time.

CHAPTER 9
Rock

I've given her twenty minutes to get clear. I daren't give her longer than that. I go down to the clubroom and approach Krueger.

"VP. I don't know what to do." I frown, hoping I look sufficiently uneasy.

He breaks off his conversation with Wreck and impatiently rolls his eyes. "What the fuck, Prospect?"

"It's the woman. The one in the cellar. Prez agreed she could shower, but she's been in there for some time. I can hear water runnin', and I've knocked on the door, but there's no answer."

"Well go in there, Prospect. Kick the door down if you have to. Don't know why the fuck Prez agreed she could wash."

Because she had fucking infected sores all over her. But I say nothing, just shrug as though agreeing, who knows what reason the Prez had, then hiss in a breath as I give my excuse. "I can't go in. I want that patch."

Krueger breathes in sharply. "What the fuck does checking on her have to do with you getting a fucking patch? If you bring this sort of problem to the VP, you ain't showing any fucking initiative."

I pull my shoulders back. "Prez gave me a direct order that I mustn't see her naked."

Surprisingly, Wreck comes to my defence, leaning over to speak into Krueger's ear. "Hawk."

Krueger sighs. "Fucking man and his fucking instructions." He looks at me and nods. "Okay. You did right, Rock. Come on. We'll come with you. If that water's still running, we'll check it out. Girl might have fainted or something."

"If she's drowned it would save us a problem," Wreck observes. "We need that fucking bitch stinking up the cellar like a hole in the head."

"Well it won't smell so badly now if she's been this long in the fucking shower." Krueger laughs loudly at his own joke as we make our way up the stairs.

Outside the bathroom, normally reserved for the officers, Runner's on guard. I'd grabbed him before going down. "Any movement?"

"Nah, that water must be stone cold by now."

Krueger pats him on the shoulder, then tries the door. It's locked from the inside, took some fiddling to lock it after I came out, but I'd managed it. He steps back. "Kick it down, Prospect."

It takes two sharp kicks and the door flies open.

"Fucking hell! Sneaky fucking bitch!" I'm ready for Krueger's punch to my stomach, forcing myself to relax my muscles, knowing he won't take kindly to breaking his fist. "This is all your fucking fault, Prospect!"

I knew it would be.

Wreck's pushed past and is looking out of the open window. "Where the fuck has she gone? There's no way she could have jumped and survived. Prospect, get down below. I can't see a body, but she might have dragged herself away. Dying animals do that, don't they?"

Runner takes off, true to his name, at a run. I move alongside Wreck. After studying the view for a moment I point out something he's not immediately noticed. "She might have made that tree."

He turns with an incredulous look. "She'd have to have leapt for that. I don't see how she could have done it."

"Neither do I. I checked, there was no route of escape."

Come on, come on... I don't want to be the one to find explanations. And I'm not. Krueger pushes me out of the way. "Desperate people do fucking desperate things. If she'd balanced on the window sill and jumped, she might have made it." *Thank you, God.*

"Chancy. More likely she'd have fallen."

"But possible."

Krueger looks at me. "Wanna give it a try?"

I look out of the window, eyeing the flimsy looking tree. "I wouldn't like to, no. If I made it, my weight would break it."

The VP's still staring at me intently. "I'll leave it to the prez. But if he wants you to give a demonstration, you'll be doing it." He grabs my collar. "And now, that's who we're going to face. Wreck, get the brothers out searching. In her state, even if she made the jump and survived she won't have gotten far."

"On it, VP."

Prez takes the news predictably badly. He stands, leans over the table, and spits at me, "You better hope she's found. You've got a fucking lot to answer for, *Prospect.*"

Weighing up my chances of getting out of here alive, in my head I go over my preparations hoping they will prove to be enough. I shift from one foot to the other, trying to appear embarrassed. "Look, I did what I could. I needed a dump, man. Obviously couldn't do it in front of her, so I got Runner to stand outside. Took me longer than expected—probably that chili last night—went back as soon as I could get off the fuckin' can. When I heard the shower still runnin' I got Krueger straight away."

"Why didn't you go right in? Wasted precious time."

Krueger huffs. "Because of Hawk's instructions that you passed along."

Chaos glares at the VP, then sighs. "Fucking man did this to himself with his fucking possessive instructions." The prez passes his hand over his face, then looks at me again. "You want me to believe you spent twenty minutes in the shitter?"

I shrug. "Had a lot to get out. Probably still smells." I rub my stomach. "Bad business."

Chaos has a weird grin on his face. "Check it out, Krueger."

Krueger startles. "You, what…?" Then realising Chaos means what he says, he huffs loudly and disappears.

"You better hope your story checks out."

Again I shrug, knowing it will. I'd emptied Becca's bucket down the can instead of the outside drain. On top of that I'd added in some dog faeces I'd found, making sure they didn't all flush down. And stank like hell. Wasn't pleasant, but I'd covered my back.

We wait in silence. It's not long until Krueger returns looking white, his disgusted face turning toward me. "Bad fucking stomach? You didn't even think to wash that shit away?"

"I was in a hurry to get back."

"Well you better…"

"VP!" Chaos roars. "Get one of the other prospects on it. I've not finished with Rock."

I'd rather be cleaning the heads than facing the prez, but I don't let my preference show on my face. Instead I do the expected, and smirk.

Krueger leaves, shutting the door. Chaos sits, leaning back in his chair, studying me very closely. "You better hope that she's found. And quickly."

I decide it's time to meet him head on. I step closer to the desk. "Look, Prez. I admit it was bad timin'. I could have alerted Krueger sooner. But how should I know what time it takes a bitch, who hasn't had a shower in fuck knows how long, to get clean? I don't know shit about women, I just fuck 'em."

His eyes seem to see right through me, but I refuse to back down. After a moment he sighs. "The only thing in your corner is that you've no reason to help her escape. She's nothing to you. Nothing to anyone in Tucson. And as far as Hawk said, she's got no access to money or friends. You want a patch, I see that hunger in your eyes. You've everything to lose and nothing to gain by letting her go."

I open my mouth, but he hasn't finished.

"But when we find her, and we will—she can't have gone far—she'll learn her treatment before was nothing. I can make her hurt without leaving a mark, and she'll tell us exactly how she escaped. Any mention of you…"

"There won't be. I didn't help her." My lips purse, partly in an effort to stop me crossing my fingers behind my back, hoping that Wraith got her away and she's not wandering around lost. She won't have a chance unless she's got to the Satan's Devils' compound.

"Any mention of you, and I'll make you wish you'd never fucking been born."

"If I'd helped her, I'd deserve it. But I didn't." I'll surely be going to hell for all the lies I've been telling today. But fuck if I care. I've already got a room reserved for me there.

Chaos pulls his chair back in while at the same time waving me to a seat on the other side of his desk. "I want a meeting with Drummer."

His sudden change of subject takes me off guard. I frown. "I don't think I should have a hand in arrangin' it. He wouldn't give me the time of day."

"Nah. I'll sort the deets out. But I want you there."

The why question must show on my face, as he answers without me asking. "We'll let Drummer know you've given us all the information you have. I want to back him into a corner knowing there's nowhere to hide." He laughs. "Can't wait to see his fucking face when he learns you've joined us."

Again, I suppress the question, but he answers anyway. "Fuck it, Rock. I want that compound. I'd rather have it without destroying it. And I don't want a rival one-percenter MC, even if it is a fucking pussy one, in Tucson. I'll get the dom on my side if I prove they're too weak to hold a charter."

"Satan's Devils have got other chapters."

A grin now covers his face. "Word is Red's pissed off with Drummer for all the pansy new regs. Hellfire and Snatcher want more freedom to go their own way. And Lost, well, he's having a hard enough time keepin' his own chapter together."

Good on you, Drum. You've got the word out fast.

"They won't get support from any direction. Yeah, there's no real bad blood. Drummer will lose the gavel, but they'll find a place. Don't care where, with their other chapters or setting up somewhere new. Don't give a fuck, as long as it's outside of Tucson."

I look down as though I'm thinking. "Drummer won't think you give much weight to what I've had to say. I'm only a prospect."

"Which is why," Chaos allows one corner of his mouth to rise up, "I'm proposing to bring you to the table. Get you patched in."

I grin widely, knowing I can show genuine pleasure, then grow serious, returning to the earlier subject. "And what if the girl isn't found?"

"Hawk's inside for another couple of years. When he gets out, where d'you think fingers will be pointing? You've got two years to figure that shit out."

If I have my way, this mysterious Hawk won't be a problem in two years. And I certainly won't be a member of the Chaos Riders then. It's not something I need to worry about.

"Fair enough, Prez. I get my patch, I'll help you run the Devils out of Tucson, and then that will be the time to face up to this Hawk."

"Fair enough," he confirms.

To my immense relief for both our sakes, Becca isn't found. Search parties are sent out, but there's no sighting, no clues. After a couple of days they turn to the hospitals, but no one resembling her description had gone to their emergency departments. While we're still instructed to be on the lookout for her, Chaos starts focusing on other issues instead. Tipping me off that this Wednesday, my position will be discussed in church.

I haven't said a word to Runner or Squirt. They've been here longer than me and won't take too fucking kindly to me getting a patch before them. I'd rather deal with any discontent after I've got a patch, as prospects are forbidden to hit a member. Yeah, I can be sneaky like that.

I polish the bar top *again*, wanting an excuse to be close by should I get called into church. I don't know how they do it here, but the Satan's Devils call a prospect into their meeting, make him think he's in trouble for some shit before dropping his new patch on him. Then there's a party to welcome him into the brotherhood.

In readiness for church coming out, Squirt is herding the women in through the door. Unlike the sweet butts back home, who'd be chattering and boasting which biker's cock they'd be riding that night, all of these look like they'd prefer it to be none. I grimace. As a prospect I've had to pretend to resent that the girls have been out of bounds. As a member, I'll be expected to fuck them. My excuse of having Allie to go to won't hold water. Not with this lot. I've heard Pistol's got a wife, and that doesn't stop him fucking around in the club.

Out of the corner of my eye, I try to pick one who seems the least reluctant. Could I take her to a room, do nothing and tell her to keep her mouth shut? No, I've accomplished so much I can't blow it now by trusting the wrong person. What I'm doing here is too important to my real family. I've got to pretend to be a good fit for this club, and that seems to include fucking in public. Hopefully once will be enough to keep up my act.

Maybe I'll…

"Prospect!"

Runner and I both jump up. King grins. "Not you. You." He points his finger straight at me so there can be no mistake.

"What d'you want?" I indicate the bar.

"You. In church."

Grinning widely, Runner gestures cutting his throat. As I follow King, I flip him off.

As though prepared for anything, I enter the room I've not been allowed in before. Unlike the Devils' rectangular one, this table is round, and Chaos sits one hundred and eighty degrees from the door. Krueger's on his left with Wreck next to him, and Buff sits on the prez's right. Fester, George, Ballsy, Buzz, Pistol, and Dong sit in a semi-circle around them, and there's one empty chair, which is now being taken by King.

Positioning myself just inside the door, I clasp my hands behind my back and stand with my feet shoulder-width apart, my shoulders back, ready to take anything they throw at me.

Chaos stares at me, his face unreadable. If I hadn't had his head's up, I'd probably be worried at this point. He leaves me to stew for a moment. When it's becoming difficult not to fidget or react to the scowls coming my way, he clears his throat.

"We decided it was time to get rid of that tat on your back."

If he's testing me, I'll go with it. "Sure, Prez. You want me to get it blacked out?"

"Well, do we boys?" He throws the question around the table.

Various responses come back, 'fuck yeah's and even a couple of 'prefer to burn it off's. I take it all stoically.

Then, suddenly, Chaos stands and throws a handful of patches onto the table. Three in fact. The insignias for the Chaos Riders. I walk forward and scoop them up, allowing a quick smile before growing serious again, and looking each of them in the eye, tell another lie. "I won't let you down, *brothers.*"

Fester's the first to reach me, slapping my back and pulling me close. "Knew you were a good fucker first time I saw you."

One by one they all do the same. Finally, it's the officers. By the time my back's been pummelled by eleven men I can feel a bruise forming. Chaos is the last, and after a hug he shakes my hand.

"Meant what I said. Find someone to get that ink covered with our patch. And soon. Offends me to know it's on you."

Hoping I can delay it until this mess is sorted and I'll be once again proud to display my real colours, I just agree. "I'll see to it, Brother."

"Patch party!" Yeah, some things are the same all over.

I take my knife out of my belt and slice off the prospect patch, throwing it into the bin in passing. So fucking glad to have member's privileges once again.

I don't waste time heading to the bar. Squirt has returned from wherever he was, and as I proudly wave my new patches in his direction his face goes red, pimples glowing like flaming beacons.

He comes around the bar and gets in my face. "Why you?" he splutters. "You've not been here five minutes." He points to himself. "I was the next one due to get patched in." His finger comes out and prods me.

Quick as a flash I grab it, bending it back near to the point of breaking it. "You don't fuckin' touch a member," I remind him. "Now go shine my bike."

As I release him he rubs his finger, hatred still glaring out from his eyes.

"What you still standin' here for? I want to be able to see my face in the chrome."

Still he pauses, but steps back, his gaze landing on each of the other members. They all stare back impassively. If he's prospected for as long as he says, he'll know the score.

Shaking off the remnants of my prospect's demeanour, I pull myself to my full height. "What you fuckin' waiting for?" Seeing as he's going to get no support, he turns and sullenly leaves the room, kicking away an innocent chair as he passes. Even from here I can see his body shaking with rage. I don't let him get away with it. "And Prospect?" I shout, making him falter. "I already know where every fuckin' scratch and dent is."

As though I've passed another test, someone slaps my back, and another brother puts a welcome beer into my hands. My eyes remain on the now empty doorway. Speaking to no one in particular, I ask the question I've wondered about but never asked. "How the fuck did he get his handle?"

It's Buzz who enlightens me. "Those pimples of his? He likes to squeeze them. He was standing in front of the mirror, gave one a good squeeze and it squirted out all over the glass."

Now I wish I hadn't asked. I really didn't need that fucking visual.

Thinking it might be a safer bet, I turn my attention to Runner, who answers for himself. "I was into track at school. Got the county record for sprint."

Yeah. That I can handle.

Turning, I notice Fester standing with an eyebrow raised. Having heard about Squirt, I don't want to question him.

"Well, aren't you going to ask?" He grins widely.

Dong wraps his arm around my shoulder, pointing at the other member. "He lets things fester," he informs me. "As you'll find out if you cross him. Weeks later he'll still remember that shit."

That's enough about handles. I don't want to know about Dong's. As the man in question turns me to face the worn couches where the women are sitting, he smirks. "You can use the bitches now, give your right hand some fucking rest at last. There must be one your tongue's been hanging out for. Which one is it?"

None. But I'm not going to get away with that. "You want to share?" I know that he does, I've unfortunately had to witness it often enough.

"Fuck yeah! Let's take Vice. She can handle two men." His arm still draped over me, he drags me over to the clearly reluctant women, looking away. Conspiratorially, he tells me, "Her cunt grips like a fucking a vice. You're gonna love it."

I don't. Taking a woman with someone other than Beef is something I've not done in a long while. It takes no time to get her naked—well, not with Dong impatiently ripping her clothes off—and onto the pool table then we get down to business. I soon find Dong has no sense of rhythm, just seems to race to getting himself off without a care if anyone else is coming with him.

But nature takes its course. My cock swells at the sight and smell of a cunt, and the sensations, though I hate to admit he was right, of Vice's muscles clamping down like her namesake, has the predictable reaction of squeezing the cum up from my balls and out the end of my, thankfully, condom-covered cock. I don't try and hold back, just get it over and done with, hoping to cause her as little discomfort as possible.

The sweet butts at home wouldn't have been pleased to go unsatisfied, but she just seems relieved when Dong moves away and I roll out from under her. But the poor girl gets no relief, Fester and Pistol quickly taking our places.

CHAPTER 10

Becca

My eyes open wide as Sam opens the door and ushers me into a large bedroom, a door off to the side leading to a bathroom. The bed is huge, but there's still plenty of space for a couple of arm chairs, a wall-mounted TV, a desk, and small table. It's obviously someone's room, there are personal possessions strewn around, but it's tidy and clean.

Crossing to the wardrobe, Sam opens the doors. "Hmm, there's a bit of space in here for anything you want to hang. If I were you, I'd shift some stuff around in the drawers to free one up when you feel like it. In fact, I expect Drummer will agree to dump all these clothes under the circumstances."

Somebody else's clothes. "Whose room is this, Sam?" There's a tremble in my voice I hadn't expected to share.

Her eyes snap to mine and she rushes to reassure me. "No one you have to worry about. He won't be coming back. It belonged to a brother called Rock. He wouldn't dare show his face here. I'd put you in an empty one, but Viper's crew are redecorating the others. Tell you what, I'll bring up some garbage sacks and I'll get it cleared for you."

No! I inwardly scream. *You can't dump Rock's belongings.* But I can't tell her that, or why. "It's fine, Sam. I'll just move stuff around. Don't bother to rush on my account."

"Hmm. Well, the sheets are clean. Got the prospect to do that while you were in with Doc."

I wish he hadn't bothered. To sleep with the scent of Rock on the bedclothes… What on earth am I thinking? I used to hate Hawk's masculine perfume left on the bed. Why is the thought of the smell of a strange man so enticing?

Rock's room. I admit, without understanding why, there's a kind of comfort in my new accommodation. *But what happens when he comes back?* That I can't ask her. I'm not supposed to let anyone even suspect I know who Rock is, let alone that he will be using these clothes again. I settle for an innocent comment. "Are you sure this Rock won't mind?"

Her face scrunches in displeasure. "He's not in a position to complain."

Oh, Rock. They have no idea what you're doing for this club. My heart bleeds for the man who they owe so much to, yet don't know it. Her reaction has re-emphasised, however much I'd like it to be different, keeping my mouth shut is imperative.

She crosses to the bed and examines me. "What do you want to do now, Becca? I can tell you're exhausted, but you must have had enough of being cooped up. Do you want to stay in this room, or would you prefer to come down to the clubhouse to eat? Either way's fine. It's no trouble to get something sent up." Her eyes narrow as she looks at my clothing, then indicates a chair. "The other girls sorted some clothes out for you. Might not be a great fit, but tomorrow I can go down to Tucson if you'd like, pick up some other stuff. You'll just have to tell me what you want."

I freeze. She's asked what I want to do. Asked what clothes I'd like. My brain goes into panic mode and shuts down.

"Becca? *Becca?* Are you alright? Come here and sit down." She must have moved fast without me noticing. Her arm comes around me and leads me to the bed. "Here, sit down before you fall down. Are you feeling worse? Do we need to get Doc back?"

I start shaking, overwhelmed by embarrassment and fear of the unknown. As she's regarding me so sympathetically, suddenly I want to explain. To tell her what's ordinary for her is miles away from normality for me. *I can't tell her everything, but…*

"I'm sorry. I'm no worse, Sam. I just lost myself there for a moment."

She steps back, putting her hands on her hips. "The way you've been treated, it's not surprising."

"It's not that, Sam. I, you…"

Sam's face tightens. "Have I said something to upset you, Becca? You've gone as white as a sheet."

I grit my teeth, sensing she won't be judgemental. Then when I find my voice the words all come rushing out. "It's just, you're asking me questions, giving me choices. I don't know what to do."

"Becca?" Her brow furrows. I can see I've confused her.

"I was brought up in a highly religious family," I start to explain, my voice choking as I realise even just a glimpse at how others live today has made me question all my beliefs. "My mother would tell me what to wear. I couldn't choose anything of my own. She prepared the food which I had to eat, whether I liked it or not. I was home schooled." I glance at her. "I've never had friends." I pause, then dive into the hard part before I lose my nerve. "On my eighteenth birthday I was married to the pastor of my church. He was much older. He took over from my mother, but if anything, was worse."

I break off and wave toward the pile of clothing on the chair. "You ask me to choose what to wear, I should be excited, but I'm not. I'm so scared of doing the wrong thing. I've never existed without somebody else controlling my life and my every move."

For a second Sam is still, her face showing twin expressions of horror and sympathy. The latter wins out. "Oh, honey." Coming to sit beside me, she draws me in for a hug. "I think there's a lot more you're not saying. I can't begin to imagine how you've been living. It sounds like you were a prisoner even before you were kept chained up. There's no one who's going to judge or control you here." She pauses, then, "How about I help you? First thing you need to know is that you can't do anything wrong. Wear whatever you like, no one will laugh at you. Hell, from the mishmash of stuff you've been given, you'd be hard put to find something that goes together. Wear what you feel comfortable in." She presses her lips together. "You sound like you were a slave…and that you've never known anything else. Like your body now has to heal, so does your head. I'll help you, hun. All of us will help you." Raising her hand, she turns my head to face her. "Baby steps, hey?"

"I'm sorry, Sam. I don't know which way is up anymore. I don't know what's right. All the teachings…"

She frowns. "I'm not here to question your religious beliefs. But just know I don't agree that women should be treated the way you obviously were. There's a different way to live, Becca. Only you can decide whether you want to take it."

"But here I'll need to make decisions for myself." I get to the root of my problem.

She chuckles. "You won't get very far if you just wait for someone to tell you what to do. Let's start small. Are you feeling well enough to come to the clubhouse? Be honest, now."

Honest I can do. "I've had a rough day. Escaping…" I shut my mouth fast, I can't give her any details. "Coming here. On top of the stuff Doc said was wrong with me." I pause, then say with more determination. "I'd rather stay here."

Her hands clap together as if I've done some kind of trick, and she smiles in encouragement. "I'll get some food sent up.

I'll also keep the other women away for now. They can satisfy their curiosity when you've had a good night's rest."

After I thank her she pats my shoulder then leaves. I'm alone. A state I've been used to for more than three months. It shouldn't worry me, but strangely, I miss her company. I stay seated on the bed, my head swimming at my change in circumstances. A few minutes pass before I pull myself together enough to examine my new surroundings. There's a photo on the bedside table. Reaching over, I pick it up, then trace my fingers over the face I'm familiar with. It's Rock, standing beside another man I've not met. Their arms are around one another, both grinning into the camera. Whoever the other man is, he now probably hates Rock.

I put the photo back where I'll be able to see it when I'm lying in bed, not understanding why. *Because it reminds me Rock was the first man to see me? To treat me as a human?* Remembering the cellar, I'm just thinking how much this suite is a far cry from where I was being kept when I notice something. Sliding doors which lead onto a balcony. Outside is a table and two chairs. My hand claps to my mouth as I start to giggle. From where I had been imprisoned to this fantastic suite? Even if I was locked in, it would be incredible.

My hands finger the sheets. *This is Rock's room.* Again, the thought brings me comfort, making me brave enough to look at the clothing the other women were kind enough to lend me. Then do something I wouldn't have imagined I'd dream of doing. I go to the wardrobe, select one of Rock's t-shirts, and quickly change. As I slide it over my head I know it's far too large and all but drowns me. But wrapping my arms around my middle, I imagine him wearing it, convincing myself I can breathe in his scent.

I hope he didn't get caught helping me escape.

Sometime later, still wearing the clothing of the man who saved me, I eat the food that a prospect brings up *and delivers with a smile and a greeting*, then, having touched my fingers once more to his photograph, sleep in Rock's bed, trying to analyse why wearing Rock's t-shirt calms me. *Thank you for saving me, Rock. Thank you for bringing me to this amazing place.* I hope and pray you've not suffered for it.

After two days on the Satan's Devils compound I'm still waiting for the other shoe to drop. I only left home on the day of my marriage, and since then have been provided for by Hawk. Here I'm still getting used to the fact I'm not constantly being told what to do, what to wear, what to eat, who I could speak to, and who I could not.

For the first time in my life I have nothing to do, no one to please, and time to simply relax and enjoy myself, and given the space to heal. I've accepted both my body and mind still have a long way to go, but there's small improvements. When Sam brought in armfuls of new clothing, I only asked once which I should wear. She'd raised her eyebrow, then smiled when I made the choice for myself.

It probably takes me far longer than anyone else, but I feel a sense of triumph when I match pants to a top. Then, having to leave my comfort zone of following instruction, I have to slow down my rapid breathing and force myself to stop worrying someone will criticise and send me back to change.

At mealtimes I hesitate, and Sam again comes to my rescue, telling me to choose what I want from the selection prepared, making suggestions as to which are most nutritious. When I'm asked my opinion it always takes me a moment to respond. As Sam had warned the other old ladies, they, too, are patient with me.

I'm embarrassed to find how hard it is to think for myself. Every decision I make I tell myself is a step forward. A move toward a new Becca. Earlier when asked if I want to go back to my suite and rest, or... I chose the option which means I'm currently sunbathing on an unseasonably warm autumn day, while Ella, Slick's old lady, Jayden, her younger sister, Sam, and Sophie and their kids play in the swimming pool.

The sight of them having fun and their joyful shrieks and shouts make me think my first impression that this was a vacation resort had been more on the money than I could have expected. I'd soon learned it actually had been a place where people came for their getaways before it burned out, enabling the bikers to buy it up cheap years ago. I pinch myself when I remember I'm actually staying in a suite, complete with a luxurious bathroom of my own.

Apart from the whores with their curious eyes, who I try to avoid, the women here are amazing. All so friendly, yet undemanding and accepting when Wraith shut down their questions with two words, club business. I've become friendly with Darcy, the sergeant-at-arms' old lady, whose job really opened my eyes as to what a woman could do—she's a firefighter. Today, despite being pregnant, she's on shift. I've learned Sophie and Sam are expecting as well. It makes me wonder if I'll ever have a child of my own. If I do, I've already vowed he or she would be brought up very differently from the way I had been.

I hear a sound and open my eyes, smiling as I see one of their younger members, Paladin, pulling out a lounger next to me and flopping himself down, drawing up his legs, shading his eyes with his hand as he waves at Jayden. The two youngsters never seem very far apart.

"Looking good." He points to my head.

I nod a thank you, but inside wince. Three months ago I'd been proud of my long, shining hair which had reached to my backside, but as it had thinned so much, Carmen had chopped most of it off. I'm still getting used to my shorn spikey look. *It will grow out.* But in the meantime, it's a constant reminder of all that I've been through. *Of all Hawk was responsible for putting me through.*

My sores are starting to heal, and I've already gained some weight. The women here seem to conjure up incredibly tasty dishes taken out of a worn handwritten recipe book. I don't know what secret ingredient they put in that lasagne yesterday, but it was the best I've ever tasted.

Paladin's not one for making small talk, or at least not to me. I lay back down, one man coming into my thoughts. *Rock.* It plays on my mind that he might have been hurt for helping me, and my constant worry is whether he got away with it or not. When I ran from the Riders' clubhouse I had no idea what I was heading into. It wasn't just my escape I need to thank him for, but enabling me to come here. When I'd known bikers were rescuing me, I suspected I'd just be exchanging one prison for another. I couldn't have been more wrong. If you now asked me, I'd say I'd have to be dragged kicking and screaming if they wanted me to leave.

Mmm. Rock. I picture his muscular body, his overtight tees, as though he had difficulty finding ones to fit him, stretching over his chest, leaving nothing to the imagination. His hand-some face despite his new scar, his strong arms covered in tattoos… If I met him again, if he was able to return to his brothers… What would my reaction be? I wriggle in my lounger to get more comfortable, realising thinking of Rock is causing a strange tingling sensation and a sense of longing to see him again. It has to be that Stockholm syndrome still hanging over me. Being attracted to the only jailer who'd been kind to me.

Attraction? I first lived with my parents, never allowed to date or even talk to boys alone. Then along came Hawk, and even if I had found him attractive I wouldn't have from the time he so cruelly took my virginity. What do I know of being attracted to a man? *Nothing.* The only benefit that came with Hawk being sent down was I didn't have to submit to him anymore. I believed I never wanted a man to touch me intimately again.

So why this longing? This overwhelming compulsion to see Rock? Even I know it's more than just to thank him for enabling my escape which led me to this amazing place. This compound, where for the first time in my life I'm allowed to be me. Sometimes I worry I'm still wearing the shirts he left here to bed. *Is that right?* What pull does this man have over me?

"Scat." A deep voice has me opening my eyes once again.

Seeing Drummer, the president, taking Paladin's seat, I sit up and pull my wrap around me, suddenly shy in the presence of the man who must have okayed my rescue. If it wasn't for him, and his club, I wouldn't be feeling safe or finally becoming healthy again.

He looks me over, his eyes tracing my body head to toe. If any of the Chaos Riders had subjected me to such scrutiny it would have made my skin crawl, but Drummer's steel-grey eyes have softened, and I see only concern in them.

"How are you doing?"

"I'm doing good, Drummer." Wrapping my arms around my knees, I stare at the women and children in the pool. "Thank you for getting me out of there and allowing me to stay."

He looks around him. When he sees no one in earshot, confides, "Rock took the risk. We ain't done nothing."

He has. More than he'll ever know. He's shown me a lifestyle I didn't know existed. People living a way I'd never experienced. Men who don't constantly bark orders. Affection clearly demonstrated between bikers and their old ladies. Apart from Drummer, there's another man I owe all this too. I lower my voice and whisper, "Rock, is he okay?"

He continues to gaze at those in the water, and I feel him going tense. "Heard nothing from Rock. But Chaos is setting up a meetin'. If I'm right, Rock will be there."

"Why?" Then I want to choke back the question, I probably shouldn't ask.

"Because it's what I'd do," he says enigmatically, then, sensing I don't understand, clarifies, "If I had one of his men who'd turned traitor, I'd get all the information I could out of them. Then flaunt that in front of him."

"Will Rock have told him your secrets?" I wonder aloud, keeping my voice low. Then realise I'm pushing my luck, flinch. *I shouldn't speak without being given permission.*

Drummer just chuckles. "What do you think?"

I bite my lip, then smile. His question giving me the go ahead to give my opinion. "I think he'll have told Chaos exactly what you wanted him to say."

He gives a full laugh now, leans over and pats my arm. "You'll do," he says as he stands, still chuckling, then looks down at me again. "You'll fuckin' do."

"Hang on." I pull myself to my feet, my eyes wide. "What do you mean, I'll do?"

He raises his chin and examines me again before leaning in and enlightening me. "You'll make Rock a great ol' lady."

Then he turns and goes, leaving me with my mouth hanging open. *Rock's old lady?* I've been here long enough to know that's akin to being someone's wife. *But I'm still married to Hawk.* Adultery is a sin. I tense, wondering whether I could use that for protection. If Rock wanted sex… The thought makes me freeze, and I start to wonder whether I really do want to see the man again. Men take, women must give.

My eyes alight on Sophie, who's just got out of the pool. Wraith, the VP and her old man, has appeared to greet her. She quickly approaches him, wrapping her arms around his waist, leaning into him. *She doesn't act afraid.* When his hands go to her ass and he pulls her against him, she giggles.

I bite my lip. *She's not submitting.* None of the women seem to here, despite the fact the men call them their property. *Could all my teaching have been wrong?* Was it just Hawk and not all men? If Wraith took from Sophie what Hawk took from me, she wouldn't be behaving as she is. *She'd be timid and trying to avoid his touch.* I shouldn't be watching a private moment, but I can't drag my eyes away. When they exchange a very un-PG kiss I'm still staring, until they check with Sam that she'll watch their daughter, and Sophie happily follows Wraith. It's obvious what they'll do next, and she's certainly not scared or reluctant.

The afternoon starts to cool, I reach for my wrap and put it around me. Leaving the others sorting out their various children, I take myself back to my suite. Drummer's comments, my observations and my thoughts, have unsettled me. Trying to be honest with myself, the question isn't only what Rock might expect from me, but what *I'd* like from him. To have him hold me like Wraith held Sophie? To be happy in a man's arms, not scared? *Only bad women enjoy sex. You're a good girl, Becca. Submit to your husband and fulfil his needs.* As my mother's voice comes back to haunt me, I remember again that I'm a married woman. Which would be the greater sin? Adultery, or actually *wanting* to sleep with Rock?

All the sun, food, and good company are doing me good, and over the next few days I make great strides into my recovery. Although the men here are all dressed the same as the Chaos Riders, in jeans and black leather, there are subtle differences. For a start, they're polite—at least when the old ladies are around. Although I've taken my cue and make myself scarce when the sweet butts appear to offer their services late in the evening, when I do see them around the club none of them look forced and all seem happy to be here.

Two days after my strange chat with Drummer, now having made a determined effort to push his parting comment out of my mind, I go down to the clubhouse hoping to find the old ladies there. Instead I walk in to an almost empty room, with the biker I recognise as the one called Beef sitting by the bar, and Truck, one of the prospects, tidying up. I'd found out Beef's name as he's the one next to Rock in that photograph I still stare at each night when I go to bed.

I make an about turn, ready to go back out.

"Hey, Becca. No need to run off."

I pause, uncertain.

"Here, come sit with me for a while. Have a drink." He raises his chin, then tilts his head to the empty stool beside him. "I could do with the company."

Unsure whether I should talk to an unknown man with no old ladies around, I nevertheless obey the command and, albeit hesitantly, walk over.

"'ere, Jill. Get Becca a drink. What you want, Becs?"

Taken aback by the shortening of my name, as well as the choice he's left to me, I turn to the woman behind the bar and stammer my request for a soda. The look she gives me makes me think the sooner I'm out of here the better. If I hadn't already recognised her as a sweet butt, her skimpy clothing would give it away. She couldn't be accused of providing this particular service with a smile. When I politely ask for the bottle to be opened, it takes Beef's growl before she complies, then walks off with a huff.

I turn to thank Beef, who gives a quick smile, but his heart isn't in it. I immediately sense there's a reason he's sitting on his own.

"You okay?" I ask, recognising the signs of being down.

"Uh huh," he replies, then glances at me. "How you doing, yourself? You're lookin' better. Got some colour in your cheeks."

"I'm getting there," I confirm. "I'm just grateful that you're all letting me stay here."

His eyes narrow. "Don't know your story. Not going to ask. But just one look at you when you arrived showed you've been through something no woman ever should fuckin' have to. Ain't going to turn you away, even if Prez isn't lettin' on why you're here." Then he winks at me. "Tell you what, when you're feelin' better, come and see me. Wouldn't turn a pretty woman like you away."

I may be naïve, but I'm not stupid. *He's talking about sex.* I feel like a bucket of cold water's been thrown over me. "I, er, I…" My voice trembles, my stomach drops. *Is that what they expect?* "Er, no, er. Do I have to?" I peek at him quickly from under my eyebrows. He's good looking even though he's heavily built, but I'm not in the market for a man. Any man. And particularly not one who'd want me in his bed for a night. *And I'm still married.* Would that work if I tell him?

Beef's looking at me with his eyes wide open, his jaw dropping. "Ain't no one gonna push you to do something you don't want, Becs. Not here." As he sees my hand trembling when I pick up my soda, he shakes his head. "I wasn't serious. It was just a stupid attempt at being friendly." He rubs at an invisible spot on his head. "Awh fuck. I'm fuckin' this up, ain't I? See, if you were interested, well, I would be to. But if you're not, well, that's okay as well."

It's almost sweet the way he's stumbling over his words, trying to work out how to tell me he finds me attractive while leaving any decision to me. I take a deep breath and try to say the right thing. "Sorry, Beef. I'm not here for that. I'm, er…"

"You got someone waiting for you?"

Have I heck. Hawk. It's easier just to nod. Then I add, "It's complicated."

"Know about complicated, darlin'. Fuck yeah, I know all about that."

"Yo, Beef?"

Beef swings round. "You want me, Prez?"

I haven't turned, so can't see what gesture has Beef hastily swallowing the last of his beer then leaving me sitting alone at the bar. It seems that's a signal for the sweet butt to return.

"You keep your hands off him. And any of the men," she snaps.

"What? Okay, er…?"

"I'm Jill."

"Jill, I'm no threat to you. Or any of the sweet butts. I don't want any of the men." Or not the ones that are here, anyway.

Leaning over the bar, getting right up in my face, she spits out, "What you want and what they want are two different things. Only two types of women here. Old ladies or sweet butts. We've already got far too many of both. Not losing another of our men to the likes of you. And you ain't joining the sweet butts. Not if I have anything to do with it."

She's got no problem, either way. "I don't fall into either of those categories," I start, trying to put her mind at ease. I might not have taken to her, but I don't mind reassuring her again. "I'm not looking for a man."

But she's not going to let it drop. "I'll have my eye on you," she warns me.

Her attitude is getting to me. Hawk might have walked all over me, but now faced with her animosity I find a new confidence. "What I do or don't do is none of your business."

"You tell her, Becca." Sam, who I hadn't heard entering and, from the look on her face neither had Jill, cups her hand around my shoulder. "Jill, Drummer won't be happy you've taken it on yourself to lay down the law. Best keep your thoughts to yourself in the future. Else you might find yourself out of a job."

The steel in her voice must show Jill she's not joking. It's the first time I've seen her anything other than easy going. Then realise, as the president's old lady, she has to be able to pull out the grit when she needs to.

The sweet butt and old lady stare at each other, and it's like time stands still as they have their stand-off. But though Jill's mouth works as if she's got something else to say, the words don't escape her lips, and it's her who backs down and storms off, leaving the bar untended, the door slamming behind her on the way out.

"She's a bitch," Sam says conversationally as she walks around the bar to get herself a soda. "Don't let her get to you, Becca."

Nodding thoughtfully, I query, "She said there are only two types of women in the club."

Sam laughs. "I bet she did. And she's mainly right, but there are exceptions. Old ladies, sweet butts, and," she pauses to smile at me, "those under our protection. And that's why you're here, Becca, isn't it?"

As I nod, she climbs up onto the stool next to mine. "Have you had women under your protection before?"

"Certainly have. Though before my time, that's how Sophie arrived. She won't mind me telling you she was in a wheelchair then. Peg got her up and walking, and Wraith, well…"

"She's Wraith's old lady." I smile remembering how there can be no doubt about that.

"That she is," Sam agrees.

"She switched categories," I observe.

Sam's smile turns into a grin. "Nothing to stop you doing the same."

My mouth drops open in horror. "I'm not old lady material." *And there's the small matter that I'm married. Albeit to a man I hate.*

Now she chuckles and nudges my arm. "Hey, never say never. When you've got your health back I can see you'll be one stunning lady. You could probably have your choice. Now, which would you go for?"

I can tell she's joking, and it makes me giggle.

Sam taps her fingers against the bottle she's holding. "Hmm. What about Marvel? Now those tattoos… If I wasn't with Drum I might like to find out just how much of his body is covered."

She makes me think of another tattooed man. I shake my head to dismiss the errant thought, which she takes as the dismissal of the man she mentioned.

"Not Marvel then. What about Beef? He's been walking around like a bear with a sore head for the last few weeks, since Rock…" As she breaks off I wonder if she means since Rock had left them, and have to bite my tongue so I don't let on that I know. *Beef's missing his friend. They look so happy together in that picture.*

"Beef's okay," I play along, but try to deflect her. "But there's no spark." *Not that I'd know what a spark is. Unless it's that feeling I have for Rock.* My thoughts go back to him, hoping he's alright and not in trouble for having helped me.

"Shooter?"

"Too young."

"Hmm, there's Mouse. I don't think you've met him yet. He's a stunner." She raises her eyebrow. "Clever man, too. He's our information and security expert. Though since he's been back he's been keeping to himself."

"Oh?" I ask, not because her description interests me at all, but because an information expert might be able to help me discover more about Hawk and what I can do to get out of his clutches for ever. Until then I'll be trapped and always looking over my shoulder. *Hey, look at me. I'm actually thinking of a future.*

She gives me an intense look as I go quiet, then starts going through the men again. "What about Blade?"

My eyes open in horror. "I've got an aversion to knives."

"You're hard to please," she says, chuckling once more. "Peg's taken, but…Dollar. He's not too young."

No, he's older. But quite dashing, those spectacles he wears when he needs to see something close up give him a distinguished look. I give myself a mental slap on the wrist for even considering it.

"Sam, I am not going to be anyone's old lady," I say firmly, trying to shut the conversation down.

For an answer I get a knowing look.

CHAPTER 11
Rock

The meeting is arranged at a point halfway between the two clubs. It's to be held in the hired backroom of a bar, one frequented by neither of our members. I'd assured Chaos that, to the best of my knowledge, the Satan's Devils had never used the location or had any connection to the person who ran it. In my personal opinion, it was too seedy even for bikers to meet.

I'd told him the truth. One sniff that something wasn't right, and not only would I be a dead man, but Drummer would find himself walking into an ambush. Wreck and Buff had checked it out and reported back after they'd made the arrangements, so when I drive up, bringing up the tail with Runner behind Chaos, his VP and Enforcer, I'm not surprised to see what a dive it looks. While I don't envy the prospect for his job of staying out with the bikes, I can see why Wreck insisted he tag along.

We arrive early, Chaos wanting to get here first, but Drummer, Wraith, Blade, and Beef pull in only seconds after us. I'm amused to see they're equally protective of their bikes, Truck having come along with them.

I steel myself for the reception I'm about to receive. As I turn around I see Beef's eyes open, his jaw nearly dropping to the floor. Blade's first to move, flying forward, snarling, his fists swinging. Wreck faces off in front of him.

"Blade!" Drummer stops him.

"Prez, it's…"

"I can see who it fuckin' is, Blade. I got eyes." Drummer spits on the ground, then addresses Chaos. "I don't deal with fuckin' traitors."

Chaos shrugs, unaffected. "He ain't no traitor. Leastwise not to me. You want this meeting to go ahead? Well, he's standing alongside me."

"You know what he did?" Blade's about as angry as I've ever seen him. "You should hand him over to us."

"Nah, he's too useful." Chaos stands his ground. I let out a breath, only just letting go of the idea he could have brought me just to hand me over, to show a good turn to the other prez. While they wouldn't have killed me outright, Blade, Beef, and Wraith would have had to give me a beat down that would have to look good. Blade and Beef wouldn't have pulled any punches. As far as I know, and from the genuine way they're reacting, they still believe I've betrayed the club.

Beef, obviously brought with them as his size would impress, is just shaking his head. Disappointment oozes out of him. *I miss the fucker.* Everything I am makes me want to reassure him, or at least give some signal to let him know the truth, but all I can do is put a sneer on my face and play my part. *I'm doing this for my club, and for Beef.*

"Right, everyone. Weapons stay outside." Chaos is trying to take charge from the start. Drummer sizes up the area, then nods and waves to his men. The Riders and Devils take their guns out of their holsters and put them in their saddle bags, then follow Chaos into the tumbledown building. I bring up the rear as the rest trail in, keeping well clear of Blade and out of range of what I know will be his hidden knives.

Chaos sits, with Krueger to one side, Wreck to the other. I take up position behind him. Drummer, Wraith, and Blade have a similar arrangement, with Beef standing at Drummer's back.

Drummer kicks off. "You've called this meetin', Chaos. I ain't got all the time in the world. Suggest you start talkin'."

Chaos relaxes and leans back. "Don't mind if I do, Drummer. You see, we've got ourselves a situation."

I see Drummer's eyebrow go up, but that's his only response.

"Got more brothers coming in. We need larger accommodations. We want your compound."

I thought he might talk around it for a bit, but instead he's gone straight for the jugular. Drummer's mouth drops open. Then he leans forward, giving an incredulous laugh. "You fuckin' what?"

"Your compound. We want it. Can't say it clearer than that."

Blade, his hands twisting as though feeling empty without one of his customary knives, laughs. "We can accommodate you alright. In our fuckin' graveyard."

Chaos laughs, a chilling sound. "Now I know for a fact that right there's nothing more than bluster. Your ex-member, here," he pauses to wave his hand back at me, "has been very helpful. I know exactly what your position is, your state of readiness, or not, as the case may be, and your arsenal. Or lack of."

Four faces are looking at me in disgust. Beef, moving quickly for the size that he is, is round the table and putting his fist in my face before I can react. As I go down, Wreck, not small himself, retaliates for me.

"Drummer," Chaos snaps. "Control your man. Or this meeting is over. I don't need any more from you, this is just a formality. I have all the information I require to take the Devils down."

Drummer waits until Beef's in position again behind his chair, his steel eyes glaring at Chaos. "Maybe you have, maybe you haven't. But us Devils aren't giving up our compound."

"You've got no choice, *Brother*," Chaos sneers. "You and the rest of your men are the ones who're going to get put in the ground if you don't do what I say. Your women, well, we can always use more sweet butts."

"Our women," Wraith gets into the conversation, saying through gritted teeth, "are old ladies, not sweet butts." His body trembles as though he's finding it hard to hold himself back.

"Don't give a damn what you call them. If it's got a cunt we can make it work." Wreck and Krueger laugh with him, and I force a smile onto my still hurting face, trying to ignore Beef's look of utter disgust.

"Kids too," Wraith continues, looking like he's having difficulty spitting out the words.

"There's always a market for brats."

I cough to hide my grimace, and can't look at Drummer or Wraith, knowing what will be going through their minds. The thought of Eli and Olivia ending up in the hands of men such as these is just horrific to imagine.

"You're making a lot of threats, Chaos. How do I know you can back them up?"

Now showing his hand, Chaos grins. "As I said, got a lot of men coming in. Men who mean you'll be outnumbered. And my men ain't soft. They're well trained and ready to kill. Unlike the pussies you've got in your clubhouse."

Drummer still looks unperturbed. "You're talkin' about the Satan's Devils. And I lead the mother chapter. I can bring in more men than you."

Chaos laughs. "Ain't anyone gonna lift a finger to help you. You've pissed off the other charters, they won't mind you being taken out." He shrugs. "They might give you shelter, but they're not going to lay down their lives for you."

Now my real prez puts on an act, letting the first show of concern appear on his face. He exchanges a glance with Wraith, then addresses Chaos again. I can only guess Beef and Blade have been told to shut up and go along with whatever is said.

"What are you proposin', Chaos? You can't believe we're going to up and leave our compound."

"That's exactly what I am proposin'." It's Chaos's turn to lean forward. "Herrera wants someone to run his guns. He's only gonna give it to one club, and that's the one he thinks is the strongest. You ain't got a chance in hell of taking me down, Drummer. Hell, I doubt you want to run guns again, having got out of the business. I'm gonna give you a chance. You, your women, your fucking kids, you pack up and get out by the weekend and I'll let you walk out of Tucson."

I take the chance to lean over and whisper into his ear. He grins, then adds, "You can leave the sweet butts. Rock here wants to reacquaint himself with them. And we don't have any aversion to fresh fucking meat."

"Fucking meat." Wreck chuckles. "That's a good handle."

Drummer's hand is toying with his beard, his face expressionless. Blade and Beef aren't so pokerfaced, twin looks of hatred alternating between being thrown at me, Chaos, and his companions. Chaos, on the other hand, is already tasting success, as relaxed as Drummer is tense.

It's a pregnant pause, the ball in Drummer's court. His eyes go to Chaos. "I need to take this to the table."

"Of course you do," the man in front of me agrees. "Wouldn't have expected different. Today's Monday. I'm being generous with the time I'm giving you. But Saturday I'll be coming to your compound. If any of you are still there, you'll be dead. As long as you're gone, there won't be any trouble. If you stay out of Tucson, we'll leave you alone."

Drummer's face remains impassive, no inkling to give away his answer. Suddenly he points straight at me. "I want the traitor back."

"I need someone to show me around your compound. He stays with me."

Now I'm the one who has to force his face to be blank. For a second I thought I had a chance of escape. I make myself bend down and whisper to Chaos again, who laughs loudly. "Yeah, Drummer. Make sure you leave your best whiskey."

My impudence has Drummer moving, standing and kicking back his chair. "This meetin' is over, Chaos. You've just declared war on the Satan's Devils. And we won't be takin' that lightly."

Chaos also stands. "I don't make empty threats," he snarls in response. "Best remember that, Drummer."

Drummer walks out, followed by Wraith and Beef, with Blade trailing behind. As he passes it's only my quick reflexes, and that I was expecting it, which save me from a potentially fatal stab to the stomach. As it is, he uses a knife he had hidden to slice through my flesh as he passes.

As Wreck and Krueger leap up, Chaos waves them down. "Let him go. Should have expected they'd try something like that. Who is he, Rock?"

"Enforcer," I gasp.

"Yeah, might have guessed. Well, he's yours on Saturday if they don't run away like the scared motherfuckers they are."

"Thanks, Prez," I manage to get out, trying to hold my gut together.

"You okay to ride?"

"Yeah, will need some stitches though."

Back at the clubhouse, being stabbed all over again, this time with needle and thread, I question my intelligence in signing up for this job. I've been hurt worse over the past few weeks than I have in the last few years with the Devils. *Because you're protecting your club. Drummer entrusted that task to you.*

But even the pride of knowing I hold the trust of my prez doesn't bring me any relief. The pain of my wound being sewn up pales in comparison to the mental anguish I feel knowing how much Blade and Beef hate me. I'd known what to anti-cipate, of course, but seeing the men I still call my brothers demonstrate the depth of their hostility toward me is far worse than the gash in my gut. If I hadn't known of Blade's quick reflexes I would currently be bleeding out, dying a painful death. In their minds, I'd deserve it.

After suffering through the ministrations, I grab a bottle of Jack and take myself off to my bed.

Self-medicated, I sleep through the night and don't rouse until early afternoon when I'm woken by a commotion and a woman's voice screaming. At first I pull a pillow over my head. But the screaming gets louder, and although it's muffled, there's something about the tone that jerks me fully awake. *I know that voice.*

It can't be. Why the fuck would she be here? *Would Drummer have sent her?* No, no way. She's a troublemaker. If he needed to get a message to me he'd use a burner phone. Or he'd send Allie—Squirt's seen her before and thinks she's my fuck buddy.

With a feeling of dread, I pull myself up, wincing at the pain in my stomach which seems to have stiffened while I'd been sleeping. Ignoring it, knowing I've got to get down to the club-room fast, I quickly pull on my jeans and boots, forgetting my t-shirt in the rush, going down the stairs bare-chested.

Fuck. It is her. *What has she said?* Fester's behind her with his arms holding her pinned tightly, Ballsy's ripped her top, exposing her tits as she's frantically trying to get loose and screaming my name. I saunter toward the trio as casually as I can, seeing the rest of the brothers looking on partly in confu-sion and partly in amusement.

"Let her go, Fester. She's not one of your whores."

He's clearly reluctant. "If it looks like one, walks like one, talks like one, then it probably is. What's up, Brother? Thought you were into sharin'."

Lazily I reply, "I want to know why she's here. Then maybe you can have her."

"I think that's something we all want to know, *Brother*." Chaos has come up behind me and slapped his hand down hard on my bare back, leaving it there as though sending a message. *Fuck, I should have got dressed.* He slaps me again. "Thought I told you to keep this covered up? Maybe we'll remove it ourselves."

Inwardly I cringe, knowing he'll have no problem carrying out his threat. Chaos might be a lot of things, but he's not stupid. As his fingernails dig into my skin, he speaks again. "Now, who is this slut, and why has she been screaming the place down for you?"

That's exactly what I want to know. "She's a woman I've fucked," I say dismissively.

"Then you'll have no problem with your brothers fuckin' her, will you?"

"Fuck no. But I want her first…"

"You can't give me to them," Jill screeches, letting loose tears which start streaming down her face. "Why Allie, Rock? Why did you want her and not me? What's so special about her?"

I go cold. "Come with me, Jill. You wanna fuck? I'll fuck you." My tone's menacing, but I still can't shut her up.

"What's her cunt got that mine hasn't?" she yells. Her voice so shrill I fear it will break the glass in the windows.

"Jill," I say sharply as I try and warn her again. "Keep your mouth shut, bitch."

"Beef said you were here. Allie wasn't fucking surprised. She knew all along. Said she'd fucked you. *It shouldn't have been her.*" Her voice rises. "I'm the head of the fuckin' sweet butts, not her. And with that new bitch comin' in too. She got something to do with you, Rock?"

"Whose sweet butts?" Chaos asks casually. "The Satan's Devils?" I'd have been taken in if I hadn't seen him in action before.

Jill shrugs as if signing my death warrant is no big deal. "Of course."

Now it's my arms that are grabbed and forced behind my back. Pistol and Dong have moved fast. Chaos must have signalled them.

Jill's eyes have opened wide at their swift actions, her face working as if she's trying to understand what's going on. The stupid cunt that she is, she still hasn't quite realised yet what, or who, she's dealing with. She might be slow, but there's already acceptance inside me. All I can hope for now is that I've already done enough to save my true club. I can't do more if I'm dead.

Chaos walks around me, blocking her from my view, but I hear him clearly as he asks, "This new woman on your compound, sweetheart? Anything seem odd about that?" His voice is far too laid back for the words that he's asking. And by lulling her into a false sense of security, she throws me to the wolves.

"Sure is. Fucking bitch. Scraggy cow. Can't even make a decision for herself."

"And would that bitch be called Becca?"

"Sure is."

She must think she's buying her way in with information. If I could get my hand on a knife I'd gut her myself. *All our plans gone to shit.* Because of a fucking sweet butt.

When Chaos opens his mouth again his voice and tone change. "Take both of them to the fucking cellar!" he roars out.

CHAPTER 12

Becca

It's so beautiful here just outside of Tucson, I think to myself as I open the door to the balcony and step out. While the desert beyond the compound is still blackened from the fire which I'd learned was only a few months back, even that retains a rugged beauty. Beyond the destruction my eyes can see right across to the Tucson Mountains. After the months spent in the cellar, I still can't get enough of the fresh air which I now breathe deep into my lungs. There's nothing that's anywhere near claustrophobic about this place, and it's here, for the first time in my life, I feel free.

Here no one barks instructions at me. No one controls every moment of my day or forces me to submit to their sexual demands. I no longer need to tiptoe around, frightened of doing the wrong thing or making a mistake. No parents to admonish me, no husband to criticise or dole out punishment. No one to tell me how I should think or what I should do.

Sometimes I think I'll wake up to find it was just a glorious dream. But no, I'm still here. Standing alone on the balcony I smile, though there's no one to see, realising my facial muscles now form the expression of pleasure without feeling stiff and unused. Is this what happiness feels like? It sure seems that way to me.

It's not all plain sailing. I haven't shrugged off all my conditioning of the past. Sam's a clever woman and has understood the support that I need. A little nudge here when I stand too long in the queue for food, undecided which items to take. A compliment there when I put on a combination of clothes that I've chosen for myself, uncertain if they're the right thing to wear. Her gentle encouragement has had me slowly gaining confidence to step out of my shell. She doesn't know how much it helps when she goes out of her way to ask my opinion, then gives me time to formulate the answer.

Sophie, Ella, Darcy, Marcia, Carmen and Sandy have followed her lead, all giving me the assistance I need to become my own person. I've come a long way, but there's still a distance to travel.

Indulging myself, I breathe in more of the glorious fresh air. The time when all I could smell was myself seems in the distant past now. I'm getting stronger every day. I still need to put more weight back on, but I don't feel anywhere near as weak as I did when I arrived. Later on this morning I'm going to meet with Peg, and he's going to help me get started in the gym. He offered, when he'd heard me talking to Sam about how much I used to love keeping fit but wasn't sure where I should start now. My muscles have atrophied, being unused for so long, but Peg said he's seen that before and will act as my personal trainer to help me build up my strength again. I can't wait. Another sign that I landed on my feet when I ended up here.

The sun is shining straight toward me, so while waiting until I go to meet the sergeant-at-arms in the gym, I pull up a chair and relax back, letting my skin absorb that precious vitamin D. Reaching over to the table, I pick up the sunscreen and, bending forward, start to cover my legs. It's then I hear voices below.

"Allie. *Allie*. Wait up." I shudder as I recognise the voice of the unpleasant sweet butt.

"Jill. You can ask all you want, I'm not going to tell you anything you don't need to know."

"I think you're forgetting yourself. I'm in charge here. I need to know where you are and what you're doing." It's not hard to distinguish Jill's shrill, angry voice.

"Well you don't need to know what I'm not allowed to tell you. It's club business. Now butt the fuck out."

I hear what sounds like a hand hitting flesh, then, "What the fuck did you do that for?"

"You don't talk to me like that!" Jill screams. "I can get you kicked out of here. You don't get to keep secrets from me. I'm more part of this club than you are."

"Ouch, Jill. Fucking let me go!" I risk peering over the balcony to see Jill's got her hand wrapped in Allie's long hair and is pulling it. Hard. "Jill, Jill, for fuck's sake." Ashamed of myself, I hide again, my hands fluttering as I don't know what to do to help.

"I can make your life hell, bitch. Now tell me what's going on. Drummer told me you could."

I'm still watching, they're so intent on themselves they don't look up and see me. I don't like anyone getting hurt, and it makes me feel guilty to admit I wouldn't want to take Jill on, even if I was feeling stronger. I've never been in a cat fight before, so would clearly be at a disadvantage.

Relieved, I see Jill loosen her hand at last. "I'm the head sweet butt, bitch. Don't you forget it. Now tell me about you going out with Drummer and Wraith."

"I *can't*," Allie insists.

Jill bunches her fists. "Well, you better get ready for a whole load of pain. And not just from me—from Drummer, when I tell him how you refused to follow his direct order. *Tell me!*" Her last words are a scream, and I wonder why she's not attracting more attention. Anxiously, I look up and down the roadway outside but there's no one around.

Allie's clearly indecisive, Jill now shakes her hard. "I know it's got something to do with that bitch, Becca."

Now my ears are burning. I try to inch closer to hear better. *What business do they have talking about me?*

"Look, Jill. I don't know anything about Becca. She just turned up, that's all I know."

"Well, tell me about where you went with them."

"Jill, let's take this to Drummer. He can tell me if he wants you to know."

Jill softens her tone. "Allie, apart from me, you've been here the longest, and you know only too well what Drummer's like if he thinks his word's being questioned. I wouldn't want to be in your position if you don't follow his order."

Allie shakes her head and looks around carefully. I duck down as it looks like she's going to glance up. "It's Rock." She speaks quietly. I have to strain to hear.

"Rock? What's that traitor got to do with it? I've heard the brothers talking about him. He stole from the club."

Allie sounds thoughtful. "I don't think he did. He's doing something for them. Drummer and Wraith took me to meet him."

"Did you fuck him?"

"Of course I did."

There's another slap. "How fucking dare you! You know he's mine!"

"For fuck's sake, stop hitting me. What do you mean he's yours? He's not even fucking here. And when he was, I didn't see him with you…"

"It was just a matter of time. I've already been on the back of his bike, and you know what that means. Why did they take you and not me? You put yourself out?"

"They asked me, Jill. As you yourself said, I couldn't refuse a direct instruction from the prez and VP, could I?"

"Where did you go?"

Allie lets out a sigh so loud even I hear it. It sounds like she's given in. "Just to a house. They kept me out of the way while they were discussing business."

"You didn't think to eavesdrop?"

Whether she did or not, Allie's not saying. She's sniffling as though she's in pain. "Jill, I can't tell you more, as I don't know it. And Rock had a prospect's patch on…"

"A prospect patch? For what club?"

"One called Chaos Riders. Oh, but there was another biker waiting outside for Rock. While I was waving goodbye from the door, I heard Rock say they were going back to the Long Horns."

"Anything else?" Jill asks tersely.

"No, that's everything. Will you tell Drummer…"

"I'll tell him you brought me up to date. Now go back to the house and clean yourself up. You look a fucking mess with your nose bleeding."

I give it a minute, thoughts racing through my head. No one knows better than me how Rock being with the Riders was meant to be secret. Now the person I like the least on the compound has got information she shouldn't have. *What's Jill going to do with what she now knows?* I've no idea. But the fact she's just been told where he is and who he's with sounds like it's dangerous. *I have to speak to Drummer.* I'm almost one hundred percent certain Jill wasn't meant to bully the information out of the other sweet butt.

I pause. Has my distaste for her influenced my reaction to their heated and, on her part, violent conversation? I don't really want to intrude on the president if there's no real reason. Perhaps I should ask Sam's advice? *But then I'd have to tell her...* I'm ashamed to say I take longer than normal to choose what to wear, my indecision exacerbated by my fear of saying something out of turn.

Eventually, wound up and worried in more ways than one, not least my concern for Rock's safety, I make my way down to the clubhouse. In the clubroom I see Marvel sitting with Joker and Lady. They're in the middle of a late breakfast.

I stop in front of them, already shaking as I prepare to make my request.

Marvel looks up. "Becca. Need anything?"

It's the opening I want. "Er, I'd like to see Drummer. Please, can you tell me where he is?"

With narrowing eyes, Marvel probes, "Why?"

"Um, I've something to tell him." *Why can't I be more forceful?* But faced with a challenging man, my trembling worsens.

Marvel leaps on my uncertainty. "Prez is a busy man. You shouldn't interrupt him unless you've got a good reason. Perhaps we can help instead." Marvel's eyes rake over me, and then he cocks his head to one side. "Want to keep me company for a while?" He pats his lap in invitation.

"Oh," I squeak, wondering whether I should do what he's asked, then make myself remember what Beef had said. *No woman is forced here.* From somewhere I dig up some confidence and inject a little more strength into my voice. "I need to see Drummer."

"What's this?" A voice barks. "You givin' Becca a hard time, Marvel?"

"Nah, Peg. Just messin' with her. But she wants to see Prez. I've been tellin' her she shouldn't bother him."

"Does she now?" The sergeant-at-arms looks at me. "Drum's tied up with something at the moment. Tell you what, we'll start a bit early. Let's go to the gym and I can start gettin' together a plan that will help you build your muscles back up. Come on, Becca."

I look up at the giant and find myself taking a step in the direction of the gym when the vision of Rock helping me escape flashes through my head. For maybe the first time in my life I prepare to disobey a direct instruction. I owe it to Rock to make a stand, and will just have to deal with any consequences. Imperceptibly, I straighten my back. "I'm sorry, Peg, this is too important. I need to see him, and I think he'll want to hear what I've got to say without losing any time."

"Prez is dealin' with something. Now's not good for him," Peg insists.

Rock's face in my head enables me to summon up determination. Even the sergeant-at-arms can't make me back down. But I can't summon up much more than a squeak as I ask, "Please, Peg. Where's Drummer's office?"

"Look…" Peg draws his hand over his face. "Perhaps I can help. Tell me what it's about and I'll decide whether to interrupt him."

Gritting my teeth, I tell him, "I can't do that. This is between the prez and me. Or maybe, Wraith?"

"Wraith's in with him." He waggles his fingers in a come-hither gesture. "Come on, woman. Talk to me. Prez doesn't want to be bothered by bitch problems right now."

Taking me by surprise, my frustration at being thwarted and my concern for Rock causes a hitherto unknown blinding rage to rise within me. Without thinking it might be unwise, I take a step forward and prod him in his firm chest with my finger, my voice rising. "It's not up to you to determine whether he wants to be *bothered by 'bitch problems'* or not. It's up to him. And I'm telling you, he'll want to hear what I'm saying." Immediately my words are out of my mouth, my hand goes to my lips and I flinch, expecting the blow that will surely follow. So intent on Peg, I don't notice everyone looking behind me.

I hadn't realised how loud my voice had got until I hear a growled, "What the fuck is going on?"

Swinging around I see Drummer. My relief so great, I feel I could burst into tears. "Drummer," I cry out. "I need to speak to you," then add incautiously in my anxiousness to make him listen, "I think Rock might be in danger."

The room erupts behind me. Peg's got me clinched with my back to his chest, roaring into my ears, "What the fuck do you know about Rock?"

Drummer's staring at me, then his eyes go to the sergeant-at-arms, and says wearily, "Let her go, Peg."

"Prez, she might know something about what Rock's up to." Peg's hold is tight and he's not letting me loose. "We need to question her."

Obviously not a fan of being challenged, Drummer's snarls out, "Let. Her. Go. Peg. I know exactly where Rock is and what he's doing." He doesn't even let those words sink in before pointing to the other three sitting behind me. "Get everyone in church now." Then he indicates to me. "Come on, Becca. You're coming in too. Might as well get this all over with at once."

Peg still doesn't trust me. As I hear men quickly talking on their phones, the word Rock repeated incredulously time and time again, the sergeant-at-arms leads me with a firm grip on my arm into their sacred room, the one even I know women aren't usually invited to enter. He sits me at the bottom of the table and stands behind me with his arms crossed over his chest, as though he's cutting off any route of escape. I feel intimidated as the rest of the members walk in, tossing me dirty looks as they pass. *Rock, remember Rock,* I repeat to myself as I hope I'm not going to dissolve into a puddled mess of nerves on the floor.

When all the seats are filled except five, Drummer and Wraith come in. Wraith pauses as he passes, putting his hand on my shoulder then squeezes it, then Drummer orders Peg to sit down.

"What do you know about Rock, Prez? You found him?" Peg asks. His eyes tight with tension, he seems reluctant to leave his position behind me. "We going after him? I want to fucking kill him with my bare hands."

"And what's she got to do with it?" Blade's spinning a knife. I don't feel any happier when it stops, pointing straight at me.

Shooter edges his chair a few inches from mine, as though wanting to distance himself.

The prez bangs his gavel. "Shut the fuck up. Now." His voice is so loud it makes me tremble. "Where are Road and Bullet?"

"On their way back from Tucson," Marvel explains.

"They'll just have to catch up when they get here. Becca. You said this was urgent?"

I nod. Hoping I'm right and it is. I'd expected to speak to him on his own, not to be dragged in front of all his men. My hands shake uncontrollably. I put them in my lap and clasp them together to try to stop them.

His stare, which had been steely, softens. "Becca. I know this must be hard for you. You have my word no one will hurt you here. Just take a deep breath and tell us what's going on. You've news about Rock? We want to hear it."

I swallow a couple of times. "I think, well, there's a chance he could be in trouble."

The room erupts with laughter, but there's no humour in it. The men either say he already is, or that they couldn't give a fuck if he's in danger.

Banging the gavel and roaring for them to be quiet, Drummer shoots me a compassionate look, then wipes his hand over his beard. "Everyone shut up and listen very carefully."

When there's silence, he starts, "Okay. Becca might have pre-empted this meeting, but I was going to let you in on what's going on shortly anyway."

At last taking his seat at the right-hand side of his prez, Peg growls, "And what the fuck is going on, Prez?"

Drummer stares around the table, then gives it to them straight. "Rock's no traitor. He never stole from us."

"*Fuckin' what?*" The queries start, the banging of the gavel getting their attention again.

"You're all aware of the problems we've got with the Chaos Riders."

"Yeah, Rock the fucking traitor is with them." Beef's so angry his face is red.

But Blade's quicker. "You set Rock up?"

More incredulous shouts.

The gavel bangs again. "Listen and learn, will you? I wanted a man on the inside who was above suspicion. Brave fuckin' man that he is, Rock jumped at the chance to help us, his brothers. Yeah, I set him up with his full agreement. Worked like a charm. Chaos brought him in as a prospect, then made him a full member so he could grill him about us."

Beef slams his fist on the table. "Fuckin' knew it. Knew Rock would never steal from the club. Knew he wouldn't have gamblin' debts. He's got far too good a head on his shoulders to get out of his depth. Christ, what a fool I've been." He lowers his head into his hands.

"Park it for now, Beef. We were all in the dark." Ella's husband tries to calm him.

"I've been a fuckin' tool," Beef mumbles into his clasped fists.

Marvel's been mulling Drummer's last words. His eyes open wide, then narrow and fix on the prez. "Why the fuck would you want him to know our set up?"

Peg frowns. "Because he fed him a bunch of lies, didn't he?"

A quick flash of satisfaction crosses Drummer's face as he raises his chin at the sergeant-at-arms. "Yeah, Chaos thinks our other chapters won't support us and that we're weak, almost out of ammo, and have no appetite for a fight."

"So that's what all the crap was about the other chapters." Blade looks like a man who's just seen the light.

"Why the fuck didn't you tell us?" A man I hadn't seen before speaks. His long dark hair and other hints of a Native American heritage make me realise this is the elusive Mouse I've only so far heard about.

Drum looks weary as he spells it out. "Chaos had to believe Rock's story. It would only work if his old club, us, were out to kill him. Rock's life depends on his backstory holdin' up and nothing happenin' to make Chaos suspicious."

Peg's eyes land on me, his attitude still not very trusting. "Becca said Rock might be in danger. How would she know that? You in contact with the Riders?"

The question's directed to me, but Drummer speaks before I can. "That's what I want to know."

Being subjected to the full force of Drummer's stare makes me squirm, but signals it's time for me to speak. Almost hyperventilating, I squeak out, "I've got a bad feeling, Drummer. I hope I'm wrong. But you know Rock got me out of the Chaos Riders club…"

"They're the fuckin' bastards that kept you chained up?" Blade interrupts, looking at me in amazement.

"Go on." Drummer glares at the enforcer.

I swallow rapidly, trying to moisten my mouth. "Allie. I think Allie did something to help. I don't know what, she said she fucked Rock."

Wraith snorts. "Lyin' bitch."

For some unknown reason I'm glad to hear that.

Impatiently Drummer points at me. "Why the fuck would Allie speak to you and tell you something like that?"

I breathe in deeply, knowing it's important to get my story straight. I steady myself, and when I start my voice is a little firmer. "She didn't. Jill stopped Allie on her way to the club-house. They didn't know I was on my balcony listening." I continue to tell them everything I heard. When I finish there's a stunned silence.

Drummer is the first to break it. "Marvel, get Truck to find where the fuck Jill is. I want her in the storeroom now."

"She's overdone it this time." Viper looks tired as he watches Marvel leave the room. He looks toward me. "And Allie's hurt?"

I nod. "Jill slapped her around, pulled her hair. But it's Rock…"

"Fucking bitch. If she does anything to put Rock in danger, she's gonna feel pain." Beef looks incensed, his words echoed by his brothers. When they first came into church they still thought Rock had betrayed them. Hastily they've had to rearrange their assumptions, and like Beef, now would do anything they can to protect their brother.

When the murmuring starts getting louder Drummer bangs the gavel. I've lost count how many times he's had to call this meeting to order. Before he can speak there's a knock on the door.

It's Truck, the prospect, who enters. "Jill's not on the compound, Prez. She's taken her car and gone out. An hour ago or so now."

"She wouldn't know where the Riders have set up," Wraith suggests.

"Er," I raise my hand to get their attention. "Allie overheard Rock and the other prospect saying they were heading back to Long Horns. She told Jill."

For a second you could hear a pin drop.

Drum looks at Mouse. "Can she find it with that?"

Mouse is tapping on his laptop. "There's a Long Horns out in the desert south of Tucson. An old ranch. If that's where they are, then, yes. Clearly marked on the map."

"We escalate our attack," Wraith starts. As Drummer nods at him the rest of the expressions around the table look quizzical.

Seeing the looks thrown his way, Drummer sighs. "You all know we discussed gettin' the other chapters here. Hittin' the Chaos Riders before they came at us. Rock was feedin' us info."

Slick shakes his head. "Can't do it now. Can't blow shit up if a brother's inside. And certainly not one who could have given his life for this club. Dude took one fuck of a chance. Chaos could have just killed him. Might already have by now if Jill's found her way there."

Drummer scowls. "The plan was Rock would have gotten himself out. He might not be able to now." There's nods around the table. "What I want to know is why the fuck would Jill go after Rock?" As Drummer wonders aloud, I agree with him asking. It was what I had wanted to know myself.

Beef stretches out his long legs under the table, leans back in his chair and sighs. "Bitch had her eye on him. Kept the fuck on about the time Rock let her up behind him. He thought nothing of it and kept his distance once he noticed her clingin'. I suspected it would come to a head, but when Rock left, well, thought she'd latch on to someone else."

"And did she?"

"Nah, prez. No chance anyone would want her permanent, except if you're stuck for choice. We all tend to go for the others." Marvel shakes his head. "Bitch's body is alright, but unless you've got your cock in her mouth her spiteful tongue is off putting."

That sentiment, which I would rather not have heard, is echoed around the table. I suspect they've forgotten I'm there. I don't bring attention to myself, firstly because I'm used to taking the back seat, and secondly, well, I'm as worried about Rock as they are.

Drummer draws his hand over his beard. "You think she's got it so bad for Rock she'll try and jump clubs?"

"Wouldn't have seen it comin', Prez, but given the circumstances, I think that's a yes." Beef looks completely confused and off balanced by the disclosures this morning.

Drummer's hands still. "Right. If Jill doesn't make an appearance soon, we act on the assumption she's gone to find Rock. If she has, she'll drop him straight in the shit. Whether she means to or not. Bitch is stupid enough to fuck up."

"Which means Rock may not be able to get out as planned. Can you contact him, Prez, warn him?" Wraith obviously knows more about what's going on than the rest.

Drummer shakes his head. "Nah. He rings me. Too dangerous to have his burner turned on. Fuck, what a mess." He bangs his fist down on the table. "Fuck it! We need to know what the fuck that bitch is sayin'. He won't be able to walk out if he's being held prisoner."

"Or if he's already got a bullet in his head." Peg's frowning. Beef's eyes shoot to the sergeant-at-arms, pain shining out from them.

The expressions on everyone's faces show with so much to take in, from learning Rock hadn't betrayed them, to knowing how much he's done for the club, the joy at their brother coming back to the fold to the thought that he might even now be dead. I might not know what he's done in the past for them, but I do know what he did for me. *He saved me.* Now it's time I stepped up, my turn to do something for him. Shakily, I get to my feet and lean on the table for support, my movement getting their attention.

"Yeah, you can go, Becca. And thanks."

"No, Drummer," I say firmly, having gathered up my courage while I'd been deciding to speak. "You need someone to go inside. You use me."

"What?" His eyes sharpen.

"You need information. You need to know whether he's still trusted, or hurt, or…" my voice breaks, but I continue. "I'll go in and find a way to tell you."

"Can't fucking ask you to do that, Becca. You've not even healed yet from the way they treated you."

"You didn't ask, Drummer. I'm offering. I owe Rock my life. I'd have died long before Hawk got out. Or gone crazy. But one thing's for certain, they won't kill *me*." My voice catches again. "But they might kill Rock. You could try to exchange me for Rock, or if that doesn't work, I don't know… Get me a phone or something. I can at least know if they've found out he's still working for you, and if so, where they're holding him, or whether he's…" I can't even say it.

"Prez," Dollar speaks for the first time. "We can't make a move until we know if Jill has gone there, and if she has, how she's played it."

"Or if Jill's even found their compound. She's not the brightest tool in the box." Wraith jerks his chin toward me. "But if we need too, we can use Becca, and without exposin' Rock. We could suggest tradin' her for our traitor." He pauses to make sure everyone's with him. "If Rock is safe, then we'll just be getting him out earlier than planned."

"It could work." Peg's nodding. "They'll just think we're desperate and trying anything."

"And when we go on the offensive and blow up their club-house, what happens to Becca?" Drummer's fists hit the table.

The blood has slowly been draining from my face as I realise getting in is one thing. Getting out, quite another. *Why am I sacrificing myself for a man I barely know?* But he's the man who's done more for me than any other. Than anyone in my whole life. He took a risk helping me escape and trusting me to keep his secret, as well as arranging somewhere to stay where I'd feel safe. *I owe him.* More than that, I'm driven by an emotion I don't understand.

I look Drummer straight in the eyes. "I'm scared, Drummer." I let my eyes roam around the table. "But I'm prepared to do this. I couldn't live with myself if we didn't try. You might be able to come up with something else, but I can't see what."

The president's gaze meets mine and holds it, the steel fading as his eyes soften. "Becca, can you leave us now, please? We'll discuss your idea and what other options are on the table, then let you know our decision."

I don't want to leave them, but am unable to disobey the president. As Drummer nods toward Shooter, who stands and holds out his hand to indicate the door, it's clear I'm already dismissed. Reluctantly I turn, but say one last thing before leaving. "Just tell me what you want me to do and I'll do it. I'd go back by myself if I thought it would save Rock." At that moment, I mean it.

CHAPTER 13

Becca

Mom." When she opens the front door my tears start to fall. I step inside, my arms reaching for her, wanting comfort like a child.

Instead she pushes past me, looking out into the street. "What on earth are you doing here, Becca? Are you on your own? How did you get here?"

"I walked." The three miles between what's now my home and my parents' house. But why is she worrying about that, and has taken no notice that I'm clearly upset?

Her face scrunches. "Does Alexis know you're here?"

Why should that matter? I shake my head, and before I've even completed the action she's reaching for the phone. Moving fast, I cover her hand with my own. "Mom, I've come to talk to you. I can't go back to him…"

She turns sharply. "What do you mean?"

Now's my chance. "He's so cruel. He hurts me. His…" How can I put this? "His desires are unnatural."

Her brow creases as she begins to understand what I'm saying, and her lips thin. "You said your vows in church. To honour and obey your husband. We brought you up to do exactly that." Her voice starts to rise. "You cannot leave Alexis, if that's what you're suggesting. You've barely been married a month. Think how it would look, Becca. You married him in God's house, in front of God." Then wincing slightly as though it's an unwelcome subject,

145

she adds, "It's a woman's place to submit to her husband. That's what we taught you." Her eyes meet mine and must see the tears there. The longer she stares, the longer I realise there's no way to get her on my side. I start to accept her words. Whether I had any choice in the matter or not, she's right. I had married Hawk, and now I was tied to him. For life. At last, having seen my capitulation, her face softens and she leads me over to the couch. "It's not always easy for a woman, but it's our lot in life. It's your duty, Becca. As Alexis' wife."

Stunned at her lack of support, I say nothing further when she goes to the phone to call my husband and tell him where I am. I start shaking, knowing he'll punish me for this. Wondering when I had my chance, why didn't I just keep running? Because you can't look after yourself. No money, no job, no one else to run to. Except my parents, and all Mom is doing is sending me back.

"He's coming," she announces, unnecessarily, putting down the phone. "Now, Becca, let's pray together. We'll pray for God to give you the strength to be a good wife."

I might have failed at being a good wife, but perhaps now I can be a good friend. But I'm scared.

I never drank before I left home, and Hawk didn't let me touch alcohol either. While I doubt whether drinking would do my poor abused body much good, I remember Hawk using it as a crutch when he was stressed out. If it was a cure for him, maybe a shot of tequila would help my frayed nerves.

Truck's back behind the bar. If I was him I'd be itching to know why I, a mere female, had been in the meeting in church, and why they're so desperate to locate Jill. But he doesn't ask, not even a raised eyebrow to encourage me to spill. He must really be chasing that patch.

His eyebrows lift as he pours the drink I request, and stay raised as I lift it to my lips and take a large sip, then cough and splutter. People drink this for fun? I wrap my fingers around the glass, not completely sure the tequila will help, but something has me raising the drink time and time again, now taking it more slowly.

Some kind of fucked up Stockholm syndrome this is. They better invent another word for the kidnappee returning to save a kidnapper. Tucson syndrome, perhaps?

I down that first shot, then ask for another, the burn in my throat and the warmth in my stomach at least works to take the edge off my anxiety. Dutch courage for certain, but I don't ask for a third, however tempting it is. I want to retain some semblance of a clear head for what I've offered to do.

I would have thought nothing could have tempted me back to that place, to risk being imprisoned in that cellar again. But I hadn't realised how important Rock had become to me until I understood he might be in danger. *I want him to be safe.* I don't want him hurt. The memory of how he'd appeared when I'd first seen him comes back to me. I remember thinking he looked worse than me. He'd taken a beating then, that's for sure. I'd do anything for that not to happen again. *This time, thinking he's a planted mole, they might not stop.*

I take my half-finished drink over to the couch and continue to take small sips until it's empty. Then I lose sense of time as I sit rolling my empty glass around in my hands. Lost in thoughts of things I'd prefer not to have to think about. Especially about Hawk telling me it was ordained that I should give myself to him.

Is it God's plan that I go back to the people who are saving me for Hawk, my *husband*? Has this only been a brief interlude to show me I could lead another kind of life? To wave temptation in front of me, then to snatch it all back?

It's not until I feel the couch dipping beside me that I start and look up, seeing the men have come out, and that it's Beef who's sat down beside me.

He gives a timid smile and takes my hand. Then looking at his massive paw resting on my, in comparison, tiny one, he starts to speak. "Rock and I are tight. We go way back. Came out of the blue when Prez said he'd stolen from the club. Wouldn't have believed it but for the way he'd run, and not doing much to explain himself. That made me believe he was guilty for sure." He squeezes my fingers and chuckles. "Fuckin' Prez is one crafty asshole. He probably even had that arranged and set up. If Rock had stayed he'd have had his club tat burned off."

I'm not sure where he's going with this.

"Becs, Prez took a risk, but he balanced it up. And Rock's a brave fuckin' man to have agreed. Knowin' him, he'd have volunteered for this shit. He lived, *lives*, for this club and everyone in it."

I nod. I'm sure he does. He must, to have done what he did.

"Prez isn't stupid, Becs. He always has plans A, B, and fuckin' C. If you go into the Chaos Riders compound, he'll sort it so you get safely back out." Another squeeze. When he next speaks, his voice sounds choked. "Want both you and Rock out of it."

"Becca?" Drummer's voice booms.

I stand, pulling my hand out of Beef's grasp. Our eyes meet for a moment, and then I nod. What he wants is exactly what I want too.

Drummer's standing with his office door open. He waves me inside and to a seat in front of his desk and in the middle of Wraith and Peg. Blade's standing with his back against the wall.

After taking his own place, Drummer sets me in his sights. "Don't like using a bitch to do what should be a man's work."

Bristling a little at the term he used, I ignore it and shrug. "You didn't. I offered."

Blade speaks from behind me. "You changed your mind, we can think of something else."

"I presume Jill hasn't returned?" I ask, then when told she hasn't, offer sadly, "If she went to their compound..." I don't need to finish the thought that they might not allow her back out. She'll soon find that Riders are completely different to Devils.

Drummer looks grim. "If she's not back tonight, I'll take it she did. None of the other sweet butts know where she was going. And it is unusual for her to take off. Allie's sobbing her heart out, she knows she did wrong."

"Jill didn't give her much choice." I jump to the friendlier woman's defence. "Jill wasn't going to let up until she told her. She got violent, as I said before." I look down at my hands, admitting quietly, "I'm just sorry I didn't try to do anything to prevent it."

"Now stop right there," Drummer interrupts. "Girl, you're still weak as a new born foal, and I doubt you've been in a fight in your life. Jill's got street smarts, she'd have taken you down with one hand tied behind her back. No one's blamin' you for what happened. You weren't to know what she was going to do with the information. I wouldn't have expected it myself."

"Thank you, Drummer." Some of the guilt eases off me. I look at each of the men in turn. "What happens now? Are we going straight away?" I doubt Drummer will delay when a man of his is in danger.

"No. We go tomorrow." As my eyes open in surprise at the short reprieve, Drummer continues. "Not tellin' you anything else. Though your eyes and ears will tell you a lot. Hopefully you won't be there long, but what you don't know, you can't tell Chaos."

"You expect him to question me." I hadn't thought about that.

"She's not going in," Blade insists, his jaw clenched. "It's not right." I turn and look at him straight on as he continues, directing his comments to me. "They might torture you for information. Have you thought about that?"

"Blade! We've discussed this. She won't need to hang out for long. We'll be going in right behind her."

I hadn't thought about torture. It had been mental torture last time. Now it seems they're suggesting it might get physical. *But it's for Rock.* I take a deep breath and pull my shoulders back, wondering whether it's the tequila that's made me braver. "What should and shouldn't I tell them?"

Drummer looks at Wraith, then Peg. They both shrug. "Thing is, Becca, old ladies don't know anything at all." I nod. I'm not even an old lady. "But you'll hear other bikers arriving tonight. If Chaos gets close enough to question you, the only thing you don't tell Chaos is anything to do with our numbers. Can you manage to do that?"

I open my mouth, then shut it again, seriously considering the question. Then answer it with one of my own. "If keeping quiet is the difference in *me* and Rock being alive or dead, what do you think, Drummer?"

Slowly his face is transformed by a smile. "I think, as I may have said before, that you'll do."

It's that enigmatic statement again, the one I don't understand. But I don't question him further. What I don't know can't hurt me.

Returning to the clubroom, I decide to stay for a while rather than returning to the solitude of my suite. I want to enjoy the company for what time I've got left. Alone I'd only give myself a chance to brood on what the following day will bring. I can't see it having a happy ending.

The buzz of conversation is all about Rock. At first incredulous that he's not been a traitor, then when they've discussed that enough, starting up with all sort of anecdotes about him as they talk of him with fondness. I listen eagerly, trying to soak up information about the man who, in truth, I barely know, even though I've offered up my freedom, and possibly my life to save him.

Apart from his sexual antics, which I try to close my ears to, I hear nothing that does anything except leaving me wanting to know him better. My initial reactions that he's a good man are only confirmed by all they're revealing.

During the evening, and into the night, the air is filled with the thunder of engines as more and more bikers pile in. Matt and Truck are kept busy finding places where men can place their sleeping bags. The crash rooms are full to overflowing, the mats in the gym brought into play, and the sweet butts are trying to man the bar as well as keeping the men occupied. When their particular services are required, they disappear with various newcomers into the back rooms in deference to the old ladies who, it being relatively early, are still around. Not for the first time I wonder how the sweet butts can do it, voluntarily allowing their bodies to be used for sex. But I suppose it's no different to me allowing the man who'd put a ring on my finger to use me.

Eventually, when it becomes clear my space on the couch is in high demand, I rise with the intention of taking myself off to my suite, even while dreading being alone, knowing tonight it will be hard to get any rest. It's only when I start walking toward the door that I realise while I've been lost in my reverie, just how many new men had arrived. As I start to make my way through the throng, I discover it's heaving with strangers that I'll have to walk through to get out. No faces I recognise are in the immediate vicinity.

With a growing sense of unease, politely I ask bikers to move out of my way. A few do, then suddenly my progress is halted by a jolt. Swinging around, my hand goes up to try and loosen the grip of the man who's got hold of my t-shirt.

"Yeah," he leers as he looks first at my face, then down my body. "Not the best specimen, but you'll do. Ain't enough women to fuck tonight." As he speaks his free hand pulls my tee away from my breasts, exposing them.

With a sense of horror my hands shoot down to try to make myself decent again, as another man nudges the first.

"You're right about the lack of pussy. Mind if I share?"

Oh no. At that moment I remember Jill saying there are only two types of women in the club. The reason for the old ladies all having worn their leather vests with their property patches evident tonight immediately becomes clear. Needing to correct their assumption, I try to explain. "I'm not a sweet butt." It comes out shakily.

The first stares lazily at my face, then his eyes roam back down at my still exposed breasts. I've yet to be successful in fighting to regain control of my shirt. "You ain't wearing anyone's patch, darlin'. That says you are. And a sweet butt's job is keep the men happy. Drummer ain't gonna be pleased if you don't give that pussy up."

The other man's hands try to still me from behind, and he's shoving his hard cock into my ass. I start to get frightened, my puny efforts to get away aren't working. *Women should do as they're told. Women submit to men. We don't force women here, Becca.* My mother's voice fights with Beef's in my head, all the while these two men are pawing at me. Frantically looking around, I see there's no one I recognise within sight.

As the first man rips my tee in two, the action startles a loud terrified scream out of my mouth.

"Hey, ain't havin' none of that. You're club property. A whore for us to use, whichever chapter we're in."

A voice from behind speaks into my ear. "Stop struggling. We know how to make you feel good, sweetheart. Ain't that right, Petty?"

"Sure thing, Roller. Now stop resisting before you get hurt. You know what you're here for." As he talks, Petty lowers his head and puts his mouth around my nipple. It does nothing for me except to start me panicking, my head full of Hawk taking me whenever he wanted. *Beef promised I wouldn't be forced.*

My heart's beating so fast it feels like it's going to leap out of my chest, my breathing speeding up as if I've done a full workout. I'm finding it hard to get air into my lungs, and as I start screaming and screaming, my vision starts to go black.

"What the fuck's going on here? Petty, Roller. Leave her a-fuckin'-lone. She ain't no sweet butt! Here, darlin'." As the two men assaulting me take a step back, new arms come around me, stopping me falling to the floor.

"She's not wearing a property patch, Beef."

"She's our fuckin' guest. She's under our protection." While his arms are comforting, Beef's body shakes with rage.

Petty's not going to give up. "How the fuck were we to know? And we weren't going to hurt her. Just give her a good time. Hand her over Beef. There's not enough pussy to go around tonight."

Beef steps back, taking me with him. "You watch your mouth, Petty. She ain't for you. She's Rock's."

Roller's hand lands on my shoulder. "That fuckin' traitor? If she's his and he left her behind, that makes her fair game."

"Rock's no fuckin' traitor," Beef roars, his loud voice making me jump. Angrily he swats Roller's fingers off my shoulder. "As you'll find out yourselves when Drum updates you."

I want to protest there's no way I belong to Rock, but if it's going to save me, it won't hurt to let them believe the lie.

"I'm taking her out of here. Now get out of my fuckin' way." Then, more softly, to me he adds, "Come on, sweetheart." He turns me around so I can face him, and that's when he sees my breasts exposed. His jaw tightens as he looks up and growls.

"Don't think you've heard the last of this, *brothers*. This ain't the way we treat women in this club."

He lifts me as if I weigh nothing at all, cradling me to his body so my naked breasts are no longer on display, and completes what was only a short distance to the open door. He carries me through the numerous bikers who have spilled out of the clubhouse into the night and, at last, we're out of the medley and walking up to the suites. Ignoring Rock's room where I'm staying, he takes me into the adjacent one I've never entered before. I realise it's his.

Again I start thrashing. "Beef! No!"

"Hey, I'm not gonna hurt you." Putting me down while he opens the door, he pushes me inside then gently lifts me and places me on his bed.

I start wailing, thinking I've jumped out of the pot and into the fire.

"Hey, hey. It's alright, darlin'. I ain't gonna hurt you." Sitting on the mattress he turns me to face him. "I'm gonna keep you safe, you hear me? You stay here. I just got some business to take care of. I won't be long. Don't go wanderin' around."

The voices of numerous raucous bikers can be heard outside. I recognise none of them. Whimpers still coming from some-where inside me start getting louder, and while a second ago I wanted him to leave me, my mind does an about turn and now I grasp his cut, not wanting to be alone. He understands without needing me to express it. "I'll be back in a minute, I promise. I'll lock the door. No one will come in while I'm gone."

He pries my hands away from his leather, and then he's gone. I curl into a ball, unable to stop shaking. Memories rushing back, threatening to overwhelm me. *Hawk*. Always Hawk. Taking what I didn't want to give freely. As fresh tears fall, I start to rock back and forth.

CHAPTER 14
Rock

Jill's been chained to the same shackle as Becca had been, but I doubt she'd appreciate the irony. Her eyes are wide as they flick around, gradually taking in her surroundings. She pulls on the chain and cuff around her leg, quickly realising she's no chance of escape. Her gaze lands on me, strung up to the ceiling, my toes only just touching the ground, the position causing the stab wound Blade had given me to start oozing blood again.

Already I can feel the burn to my shoulders. As she looks me over, her scared expression shows she's only now acknowledging we're both trapped and at the mercy of the Chaos Riders. *And it's all her fucking fault.*

"I'm sorry," she whispers.

Glaring, wondering how she thinks a simple apology is going to cut it, there's venom in my voice as I spit the words out, "What the fuck did you think you were doing?"

She looks sheepish, then turns her red-rimmed eyes toward me. "I've missed you, Rock. Never thought you could have been traitor. You know I wanted you...want you. When I heard you'd joined a new club I wanted to come and be with you. I thought you might have missed me too. I knew if I could just talk to you..."

I roll my head back, trying to ease the pain in my shoulders. "Well it seems you've got my undivided attention now. And we'll both have to accept neither of us will be getting out of here alive." Her eyes open as large as saucers at my words. Finally, as the enormity of what she's done seems to dawn on her, she at least has the grace to turn away.

Beef had been right when he'd pointed out Jill wanted me months ago. I'd have done better to have taken it more seriously myself. I'd fucked her many times, hell, in the same way I fucked all the sweet butts. She's been in the club long enough, and I assumed she knew the score, just like the others. As had my other brothers, I just watched on with amusement as Jill started to give herself airs and graces, lording it over the rest of the girls as though she was head bitch. They looked up to her just because she'd been with the Satan's Devils the longest. When Paige and Diva had joined, she'd shown them the ropes. It was easier for us men to just go along with it.

I had listened more when Beef said he'd seen signs she was getting attached to me in particular. It had started after she'd misunderstood the significance or, in my mind, lack of it, of riding on my bike. Unlike some of my brothers, I think the pillion seat is there for a reason. After Beef's warning I'd distanced myself, making use of the likes of Diva and Paige instead. It wasn't a great loss. Jill's slack pussy had lost any attraction years ago, but the things she could do with her mouth… Still, Allie was no slouch in that area either.

We all know a sweet butt hopes to be up riding behind one special brother, that eventually she'd be made an old lady. However, I've never known that to happen in my club—maybe in others. Whether it does or not, as far as I'm concerned, the thought of having a woman who's freely offered up her pussy to all my brothers is a complete turn off. If I ever settle down, it will be with one special woman who none of the other club members have known. *Someone like Becca.*

Why did that thought come into my head? Is it because this situation reminds me of the times I saw Becca chained and neglected? It's only sympathy I feel for her, nothing more than that. All I hope is that she's being well looked after by my club, and that Drummer will keep her far away from the Chaos Riders. *They know where she is now.* I don't doubt, having heard what they had, that they'll go all out to get her back. Shit, what a fuck up. It's all due to the woman who's next to me, chained up.

Jill's quietly sobbing, the sound grating on my nerves. At least she's sitting comfortably on the mattress that I never heard Becca complain about. *I'm* the one strung up with my arms being pulled out of their sockets. I bite my tongue as my patience begins to run out. No point wasting my energy on anger.

"How is Becca?" I'll die happy knowing that she's safe and recovering. It had been a risk getting her out of here, and one I'd been willing to take. Luckily my part in it had been put down to stupidity. If they'd had suspicions that I had helped her escape, I would already be dead. I've got away with a lot here, hopefully fed enough back to Drummer. Now my time is fast running out. It's worth it if what I've done means Becca is able to live the life she deserves, and that I've done sufficient to save my club.

Jill's accusing eyes meet mine. "Is she all you care about?"

That makes me snap. "Fuck, woman, I barely know her. No one deserves to be treated like she was. I want to know she's recovering." The thought that I'm soon to take my last breath has me wondering what it is about Becca that draws me in.

"Oh, she's doing that alright." Her tone is snide as she adds, "I hope you weren't thinkin' of makin' her your ol' lady."

Whether I was or wasn't is no business of hers. Anyway, I'm far from taking a bitch for myself. I never wanted an old lady. But for some reason I'd go as far as considering it with Becca. Not that I really know her, and now I've lost my chance to see who she really is when not cowed by captivity. There's no doubt she intrigued me. I'd have given anything to see what she looked like, physically fit and free. My cock twitches. Fuck, who am I trying to kid? She'd had me from the moment I first saw her. I didn't do anything selfless. I wanted to know she was safe with Drummer so I could explore what I'd felt for her when I got back. Yeah, being honest, I could see her as mine. Her wearing my patch. Her riding behind me… Now that I could picture. Her breasts squashed up against me…

"She's getting attention from all of the brothers." Jill's voice breaks into my thoughts.

That makes sense. They'd all protect her. They're good men like that. We don't treat our women like the Chaos Riders. I smile, knowing she'll be looked after even if I won't be there to do it myself. After what's she's been through, she deserves to be treated with kindness. Drummer owes me for giving my life for the club. He won't throw her out to the wolves. I just wish it had been me watching out for her. Being the man in her bed.

Jill hasn't finished. "She seems particularly close to Beef, practically moved into his suite. Oh, when she's not with Marvel of course, or Dollar."

My chains rattle as I pull on them, incensed that she's insinuating Becca is bed hopping. *But how do I know whether she's telling the truth or not?* Becca's a stranger, a closed book. What bothers me is I've lost the chance to open it. From what she says, it sounds like my brothers already know what the pages hold.

I need to know, so punish myself as I growl, "Are you tellin' me she's behaving like a fuckin' whore?"

Again her eyes open, this time in surprise. "You're saying you didn't know? Oh, Rock. I'm sorry."

"You lyin', Jill?" I ask straight out, still not quite believing her.

She gives a little shake of her head, motioning around her. "Why would I lie now? What have I got to gain? Rock," she gets to her feet, the ten-foot chain bringing her closer, but, thank fuck, not close enough to touch me, "she doesn't give a damn for you. Not like I do. *I* love you, Rock."

What the ever loving…? "Jill, I never hinted, never gave you anything that would make you think you were anything special to me. Whatever you're imagining is all in your fuckin' head."

"Yes, you did," she contradicts. As my jaw drops, she continues. "You let me ride on your bike. You didn't use me like the rest of the brothers, so I knew I was special to you."

Now it's my head shaking at the twist she puts on things.

"Rock, if we get out of here, can I ride on the back of your bike again?" She sounds breathless with hope.

"Ain't never havin' a bitch riding up behind me." It might not have meant anything in the past, but now I was aware of Jill's erroneous interpretation, if I ever get out of here, it's a vow I'll keep. Then again, I imagine Becca, her arms around me, holding tight to my waist. Previously that thought had had my cock swelling, although no longer. If Jill's telling the truth, Becca's not waited. Not given me a chance to come home and explore the attraction that had at least been on my side, if not on hers. Too impatient to wait, giving what I belatedly realise I'd come to think of as mine to whoever wanted her.

"But, Rock," Jill wails. Then when I don't reply she tries a different way. "If you promise me another ride on your bike, I'll tell Chaos whatever you want me to."

"You threatenin' me, bitch?" She flinches at my harsh tone. "The only way you're getting out of here is if we can convince Chaos to set me free." *And if by some stroke of luck that happens, I'll kill her myself.* Or if I don't get the chance, some-body else will be doing it for me. She's put a brother in danger, and Drummer won't stand for that. "You think you hold all the cards, Jill. But you don't. The most likely outcome is that you'll die along with me."

"Chaos might need a new sweet butt."

"They don't have sweet butts, you stupid bitch. They have woman they use, abuse, and keep as their sex slaves." I try to make her open her eyes. "You can't flutter your eyelids and get men under your thumb here. Don't try appealing to Chaos's better nature, he hasn't got one."

But I can see by the gleam in her eyes she's going to try. *Will she drop me in it to save her life?* I'm afraid that she might.

Before I'm anywhere near ready, I hear footsteps coming down the stairs to the basement. Taking a deep breath in preparation for what's coming, I stare at the door as it opens, seeing, not unexpectedly, Chaos and Wreck. The president and his enforcer. A few steps behind are Krueger and Buff. The whole top team, their faces set, showing their only intention is to cause me pain and suffering, and, eventually a death, as Chaos had once told me, I'll probably long for.

Ignoring the woman and the flirty smile she's planted on her face, Chaos steps up to me. A moment of considered silence, then, "I trusted you, Rock. Made you a member. Called you *Brother.* Gave you a home when you said you had nowhere else to go." His tone changes from sadness to disgust. "But that was all a fucking lie, wasn't it? You're a fucking Trojan horse."

I put every ounce of entreaty that I can into my voice. "It wasn't a lie, Chaos. Jill can confirm, I was thrown out of the Satan's Devils club."

He spares a glance for her, then turns back. "I wouldn't trust a fucking bitch any day of the week. They lie as easily as breathing."

Jill must have dropped her plan to seduce Chaos. Unexpectedly she lends me her support. "He's right. He stole from the club. He was thrown out…"

Buff's blow to her face has her falling onto the mattress, her eyes wild when I catch them, blood flowing from her mouth.

"Rock," she calls out as if I can save her. But I've got more important things to do. Like trying to save myself and my real club. The Satan's Devils. Not a bitch who, for the fucked-up reason of thinking she had a chance with me, had betrayed us.

I focus my eyes on Chaos. "You're makin' a mistake if you kill me."

"Give me one good reason why I shouldn't." He walks across the room and kicks out a chair, bringing it in front of me and sitting on it back to front. His chin rests on his folded arms leaning on the back.

"Because I'm not a plant. I can continue giving you intel which will help you take out the Satan's Devils and take their compound. And you need all the men you can get. I'm one more piece of muscle you'll have at your disposal."

His comeback is quick. "Not much good if that extra muscle stabs me in the back."

I try again to persuade him. "When we met Drummer and Wraith, did they look like men who wanted me back? For fuck's sake, Blade stabbed me. It was only by luck he didn't kill me."

Chaos stands and kicks away the chair. "I don't like you, Rock. Only voted you in 'cause you had useful info. Doesn't surprise me none if the Devils didn't take to you either. Yeah, the enforcer attacked you, but that could be personal shit. You take his woman or something?"

"No."

"And talking of fucking women," he moves closer, "how come Becca ended up on the Devils' compound? Tell me that, eh? If you didn't have a hand in her escape, how come she found them?"

"I've no fuckin' idea." My voice gets louder. "I don't know or give a damn about the woman." If Jill hadn't told me she's already fucking my brothers, maybe I wouldn't have been so forceful in my denial of her. But she had, and I was. And, from the expression on his face, I've confused him.

Chaos smooths his hands over his bald head and wonders half to himself, "How the fuck did she end up with them?"

I remain quiet. It wasn't a direct question, and I'm not opening my mouth just to run it for no reason. That's sure to get me in more trouble than I want.

His companions have remained still and silent up to this point. Now Chaos turns and waves them forward, my skin crawling in expectation of what they're proposing to do. Especially when Wreck unrolls some canvass, exposing an enviable collection of knives. The careful attention he's paying to them leads me to believe he keeps them well-sharpened.

After watching him prepare, Chaos switches his attention back to me, asking lazily, "What was the one thing I asked you to do for me, Rock?"

Fuck. Through gritted teeth, I give him the answer. "Get my back-patch blacked out."

He nods. "And I warned you if you didn't, I'd get it removed for you."

They're going to flay my skin. Get the tat removed that way. I could scream, I could beg. But I do neither.

"If you're truly a Devil no longer, I'll be doing you a favour."

"I'm not a Devil." I take my one last chance to get through to him.

He steps close, his eyes having to slightly turn up to meet mine. "That tat says you are while you're still wearing their patch. Do it, Wreck."

Krueger and Buff step forward, each crouching then taking one of my legs, pulling me down so my shoulders start screaming. With my body stretched taut I can't move. Wreck disappears behind me.

At first I feel no pain, then a mild stinging, then agony as the skin of my back starts to be peeled off, leaving the pain receptors underneath to start screaming. Each breath he breathes out I feel hit my subcutaneous tissue like a burn, followed by warm blood trickling down my back. It's a full back patch he's removing, from the middle of my shoulder blades down to the curve of my ass.

My mouth opens in a silent scream, but I don't make a sound, unsummoned tears streaming from my eyes as the pain grows with each strip of skin he takes off. My body's natural reaction is to fight him, but Krueger and Buff are strong, and while I automatically try to jerk and twist away from the torture, I can't evade that knife and the slow, methodical way he's removing the surface of my back.

It's only minutes before I start trembling as both physical and mental shock set in. Wreck pulls an arm around my body to keep me steady, and still that blade mercilessly separates skin from flesh. I make no sound as his attentions grow lower. I feel the top and middle of my back exposed now. Each area he clears multiplying the pain a thousand-fold.

My half-closed eyes see Chaos walking around me, his voice is almost gentle when he says, "Almost finished now. Good job, Wreck. Just that one last bit. The patch is completely gone now. Hey, Rock, good fucking news. You won't be offending me any longer."

"Done, Prez."

As though from a distance, I hear slapping on leather, presumably Chaos congratulating Wreck on a job well done.

Chaos walks back around to my front, putting his hand under my chin to raise my head. "Don't want you getting an infection now, do we?"

As I stare blindly at him, from the side of my eye I see Buff opening a pack and passing a bottle to the enforcer.

Then I'm no longer able to keep dumb. I scream in agony as the strong smell of brandy fills the room when the liquid splashes all over my back. I pass out.

When I come to I've got cold water running down my face, my back is sore and stinging, leaving me in a level of anguish I've never known before. Looking down I see blood pooling at my feet. A high-pitched cry has me turning my head to see Krueger and Buff raping Jill, one in her cunt and one in her ass. She's a seasoned club whore, but from the way they're taking her, they're overly rough, and even she can't take what they're dishing out.

Chaos is standing, looking first at me then at her, then back again. His jeans are open, and he's got his dick out and is stroking it. He sees me watching and grins evilly. "The smell of fresh blood gets me every fuckin' time. Add in a scared cunt… fucking incredible. Don't know which makes me harder."

Jill might have already signed her death warrant, but I don't like the thought of her being used like this. Especially when Wreck steps forward, readying his cock too.

"Stop." My voice is weak. "She doesn't deserve this."

"No? Well, what do you suggest I do with this, then?" Chaos looks down at himself, and his dick which looks like it's throbbing. "You know what? I'm almost there." He winks at Wreck, who grins back. Then they both walk behind me.

Their grunts let me know they've come, and while my bared flesh doesn't feel the warmth of the semen running down my back, the stinging from the salt certainly registers. *They've come all over my raw flesh.*

CHAPTER 15

Becca

Lost in the reruns of the two unknown bikers preventing my exit from the clubhouse repeating on a loop in my head, I don't know how many minutes have passed before Beef returns, but when he does I feel the bed sink. I whimper again and try to move away.

"Hey, I'm not gonna hurt you, Becs." Gentle hands pull mine away from my face. Opening my eyes, I see his concerned ones looking into mine. "Hey, girl, it's over now. No one's going to force you to do anything you don't want to."

His knuckles are bloody, grazed. As my eyes hone in on them I notice someone standing behind him. Beef hasn't returned alone.

"Go wash up, Beef. While Becca and I have a chat."

The mattress rises again, then another weight settles down, and a finger comes under my chin. "So fuckin' sorry, Becca. Should have made sure someone was looking out for you."

For some strange reason I don't want him taking the blame. "It's not your fault, Drummer. I shouldn't have stayed so long. Got lost in my thoughts, didn't see the room was filling with strangers."

He gives a dismissive shake of his head, his voice tinged with anger. "You've felt safe here, Becca. There was no reason you shouldn't." He moves his hand away from my face and clasps it with his other between his legs. Nodding toward my torn tee, which my hands are desperately trying to hold together, his lips go thin as he presses them together before asking, "They hurt you?"

I swallow. "Beef got there before they could."

"Don't agree with any man layin' hands on an unwillin' woman. I'll be havin' words with Red. He's their prez."

"They thought she was a sweet butt, Drum." Beef appears in the door to his bathroom, drying his hands on a towel. "Thought she'd be willin'. Thought they were entitled."

"Should have taken her word for it that she wasn't. From what you said, Beef, they didn't give her a chance to explain."

"Won't be questionin' it so much now," Beef mumbles, and the way he flexes his now blood free hands spells out the reason why he's so sure.

"You're still shakin', sweetheart." A hand smooths over my forehead. "Ease your breathin', darlin', you can relax now."

I shake my head. I feel cold, though my palms are sweaty. "No need to panic, Becca. You're safe now. I'll make your place here clear to everyone so you won't be put in the same position tomorrow."

"Wh-wh-what if they c-c-come to my r-room?" My teeth sound like they're chattering.

"Thought you might worry about that. You won't be going to your room, you're stayin' here with Beef."

My eyes flick to the man still standing in the doorway, his elbow bent and his hand resting on the side.

"No, I…"

Immediately understanding my concerns, Drummer reassures me. "Beef isn't gonna touch you. He's just here to make you feel safe. And tomorrow he'll stick to your side like glue. He's your own personal protector. He wants to help. He owes it to Rock."

I watch Drummer, his eyes now softened, and he's looking worried at my overblown reaction. Sure, I was threatened, but nothing actually happened. I have to give him something to explain my terror. "Hawk, my husband, used to force me, Drummer. All the time. I thought that was in the past now. What they did, it brought it all back." I half turn away, my voice fading. "I was supposed to submit."

His expression sharpens, and he exchanges looks with Beef before looking back at me. "Fuck. I'm sorry to hear that, sweetheart. And that raises more questions than it does answers. But those are for later. Why don't you try and get some sleep now? It's late, and you'll need all your strength for tomorrow."

That's what I should have been lying here worrying about rather than something that hadn't happened. His words make me remember what I'd promised to do. Any bravery I'd managed to summon up has disappeared with the reminder of just how cruel men can be. It was one thing to make the grand gesture and say I'll be the inducement to get Rock out of the Chaos Riders' clubhouse. But Petty and Roller have reminded me what I've got to lose. I never want to be used again, and this time I fear the Riders won't keep their distance like they did before. They'll want to punish me for escaping, and what better way to reduce a woman to nothing? I try to stop them, but the words come out.

"I don't t-t-think I can do it, D-d-drummer. I-I-I'm s-s-sorry."

Drummer's lips thin, then he looks at Beef. Beef nods, and Drummer stands to leave. "I can't, and won't force you," he says. "Fuck knows what hell you'll be walkin' into there. But it's the only way I can see to get Rock released. Jill hasn't returned, so we can only make one assumption. If she found the Riders, whether she did willingly or not, Jill will have given the game away. They'll know you're here, Becca."

"I n-need to get away."

"I'll talk to her, Drummer." Beef looks tired and tense.

Drummer stares at him, then back at me. "I'll speak to you in the morning, Becca. You can tell me your decision then." He starts toward the door, then turns back. "Whatever you decide, Becca, no one will think the worst of you. Especially after our lack of protection tonight." Then, finally, he's gone.

Beef's big, tall, burly. He might have saved me... *He scares me.* "I-I-I-d prefer to go back to my room, Beef."

Leaving his post by the door, he comes over. "If you do, you won't feel safe, not with all the drunken fuckers walkin' around. You need rest, Becca. Need to regain your strength so you can think straight. You'll be better off here stayin' with me."

Shaking my head, I refute that. "I d-d-don't want..."

"Fuck it," he snarls as he comes over and lies down on the bed, his arms pulling me toward him, his front to my back. "Just relax, don't fight me. Rock's my best fuckin' friend, and if you're his woman, ain't gonna be me or anyone else makin' you do anything you're not comfortable with."

"I'm n-n-not Rock's," I protest.

Beef doesn't argue. "Even if you're not Rock's, he cared about you enough to get you out of that place. Nothing will happen to you while I'm around."

He sounds so sincere. Although I'm surrounded by him, can smell his perspiration tinged with beer, for the first time since Petty and Roller trapped me I feel protected. Beef's hand gently strokes my arm, and, against all odds, gradually I start to relax. The tremors shaking my body slow, and when I speak next my stutter has all but gone. But I know I won't be able to sleep.

"Tell me about Rock, please?"

He sighs, and while I can't see it, I think he's smiling into my hair, his voice vibrating against my shorn head as he tells me. "First met Rock when he was a prospect and Bastard was still the prez. He was a wild'un back in those days, but from the start he gave his all to the club. When he was a prospect he took the rap for a patched member and spent a year in the joint. He was still inside when the cops invaded the club. Like a few of us old timers, he was one of the only ones not arrested or dead. He'd grown up when he was released. When he came out Drum had become the prez. Of course, doing what he had, Rock was patched in immediately. Threw himself behind getting out of all the shit Bastard had us into. Never gave cause for any of us not to trust him. That's why it was so hard to believe he'd turned traitor."

"That's him as a member, what about him as a man?" My eyes feel heavy and close at Beef's almost hypnotic voice.

"I think that's for him to let you know, not me," Beef murmurs. "But he'd never hurt a woman, never dream of it. Whatever you think, he never led Jill on. Sure, he'd fucked her, but not recently. Anything else was all in her head. He backed right off when he saw she was thinking that all her sweet butt dreams would come true. But a sweet butt never ends up riding up behind a brother."

If he says anything else, I didn't hear it. His voice, having gone so soft for such a big man, lulls me into a restless sleep, brimming with bad dreams. Visions alternating between being back in the cellar and being forced by Petty and Roller wake me with screams. Beef's soft touch on my arm and a gentle rocking motion each time I rouse soon has me back to sleep. His calming presence makes me thankful I didn't insist on going back to my own room.

Morning comes far too soon. Beef, true to his word and not leaving me for a moment, escorts me to the suite next door and waits outside while I dress in jeans and a light sweater, a nod to the slight chill in the autumn air. Then he takes me down to the clubhouse. It's full, but again he's there, right at my back.

Drummer's been waiting for my arrival. Bolstered by Beef's presence, remembering Rock as I'd known him, and his friend's confirmation that he was a good man, I nod to the president. A little hesitantly, but definitely positively. Taking it as a signal, Drummer jumps up onto the bar and whistles loudly with two fingers in his mouth to get everyone's attention. Then he gestures at me. Once again, Beef doesn't leave me as he helps clear a path up to the bar.

"Okay. Now this here's Becca. Take a good look at her. She ain't wearin' a property patch, as she's Rock's, and as he's not here, he hasn't been able to get her one yet."

"Is Rock a traitor, or…"

"Rock's a fuckin' hero," Drummer snarls. "He went under-cover. I kept that quiet, even from my own brothers, in order to protect him. And today we're going to get him out." He pauses and tugs at his salt and pepper beard. "Thing is, we've reason to believe they no longer trust him. We wanted to go in yesterday before they could hurt him too much, but needed more brothers at our back."

Shouts of 'We're with you! Let's go get Rock!' go around the room, along with a stamping of feet. I shrink back into Beef. They're like a bunch of angry animals, baying for blood.

"We did our part, Drum. Hopefully made them believe we weren't gonna support you," a deep voice shouts out.

"Thanks, Red. As did you, Hellfire, Snatcher, and Lost."

"Sure did!"

"Fuck yes."

"They're not expecting us to have back up. You'll go before us, and we'll give you time to get set up. Becca…" He breaks off and looks down at me. I close my eyes briefly, summoning up the tenuous courage that I'd lost last night, and then open them and again nod. "Becca, here," he continues, "she's coming with us. They were holding her prisoner, treating her badly, but we

170

know they'll want her back. We plan to offer her in exchange for Rock."

"If you're wrong and his cover's not been blown… You asking for him lets them know he's still one of yours, Drum."

Drummer gives an evil looking twisted grin. "It might, Hellfire, though not if I ask to exchange her for *my* traitor."

"We know you're rescuing a brother. But what will Chaos believe is so important for us to make the exchange?"

"Chaos will buy that we're looking for two things. Information and retribution. Same reasons he took Rock in."

Hellfire's not giving up. "Stupid bunch of motherfuckers. As you say, Rock's brave. Any other club would have killed him or kicked him back to you. He took one fuck of a chance walking in there."

"Exactly. And Chaos's stupidity, over-confidence of any of that shit, is why I think we have a good chance of making this work."

The tall man with the striking red hair speaks again. "What if they won't make the exchange? What if the bitch isn't as important as you think to them? Or you could be overpowered, she could be taken or simply…"

Killed. That's what he means. Beef's hand rubs up and down my back.

Drummer looks down at me and winks. "They need her alive. We threaten to kill her if they don't let Rock go."

The man pushes through the crowd and stands in front of Drummer, which puts him beside me. He's even taller up close, with freckles on his face which no way detract from his features. A colouring that normally doesn't appeal to me, but he wears it well. His hand comes out to rest on my shoulder making me jump.

"Look at her, Drummer. You must see the state she's in." Glancing down at me, he mouths, 'sorry', then lifts his face toward the Satan's Devils Tucson chapter prez. "You're leading her straight into the hands of those motherfuckers. I don't like that part of your plan."

Neither do I.

"Red. When have I ever let you down?" Drummer roars, then waits until quiet settles again. "As soon as she approaches the door, you'll be waiting. They want her so much, their focus will be on the front of the club, you'll be hidden in the treeline behind, and on my signal attack from the back, that will push any left inside out to where we're waiting. We'll have snipers set up to take out as many as they can when they flood out the door, then we'll come join you and mop up. After that Slick will set explosives to bring that fuckin' place to the ground."

Red stares at him for a moment, then says in a voice equally as loud as Drummer's, "That will work. I brought my best snipers, as you asked."

Drummer nods as though he had no doubts anyone would support him. "Time's of the essence. Workin' on the worst that could have happened, need to seize the best chance to rescue Rock while he's still breathin'. That's why the attack, originally timed for Saturday, has been brought forward to today."

Wraith snorts. "It'll work whenever we do it, Prez. With all our brothers behind us."

Another man comes forward, Red greeting him as Hellfire, who I've heard speaking but had been unable to get sight of. He's nodding his head. "Whatever chapter we're from, whichever part of the country, we're all Devils, and Rock's one of ours. We don't leave a brother to be tortured and killed."

His words are a signal for everyone to start shouting something which sounds like a battle cry. 'Ride Satan's Devils.' 'Satan's Devils Ride.' It's deafening when it repeats around the room, almost never ending as it's carried by echoes.

While Beef nudges me in the direction of the kitchen I know I'm dismissed. Beef stays glued to my side as I grab a coffee while avoiding taking anything to eat. As I drink I hear shouts and orders from the clubroom. The men are obviously sorting themselves out as cries go up for the snipers to identify themselves. While that's going on I raise my eyes over my coffee cup, then tug Beef's hand. Petty and Roller are standing in the doorway.

Both look very worse for wear. Petty's nose looks broken, and Roller's got a swollen jaw. Both have black eyes and walk stiffly. They nod at Beef, then at me.

"I'm sorry," Petty starts.

"Me too," Roller butts in.

Petty gives him a quick look, then his eyes come back to me. "We didn't know who you were. Would never have touched you if we did. You're a brave fuckin' lady, didn't need us to pressure you."

I still don't trust them, but feel braver with Beef with me. It only takes a second to connect their injuries with his sore knuckles last night. I don't know what will happen today, whether Drummer's plan will work or I'll find myself a prisoner again. In the scheme of things, what didn't happen last night pales into insignificance.

After a few awkward seconds pass I sigh and give them absolution. "I wasn't wearing a cut."

"Didn't matter if you were or not," Beef snarls, making both men flinch. "It's not you, Becs, who needs to apologise."

Petty and Roller look contrite. Petty shakes his head. "Lesson learned, Becca."

"Not yet," Beef says inscrutably. "But it probably will be once Red's dealt with you."

With identical chin lifts, one causing a wince, they turn and re-join the others in the clubroom.

"Not your fault, Becca." Beef gently raises my head to face him. "Not your fault. Nothing you did wrong."

Then I can think no more of the odious pair as the roaring of bikes reaches us. Drummer's plan's now in action, and I understand there's no turning back as the Devils mount up and ride out to take up position. My stomach boils with acid each passing minute, thinking there are a million things that could go wrong today. I trust and hope Drummer knows what he's doing.

Beef sees me wringing my hands together and covers them with his own. "We've got this," he starts. "We'll get both you and Rock home. You'll never have to worry about the fuckin' Riders again." He squeezes my fingers. "After that, we'll sort out your problems with this Hawk. You'll be free to do whatever you want."

I've got over two years to deal with Hawk. It's the next two hours I'm more worried about. I'm unable to forget how much danger I'm heading into when at last Drummer fetches me and takes me out to an SUV. Beef leaves me to ride his bike with the rest of his brothers.

Drummer's voice mumbles reassuringly. "Chaos will accept the exchange, I've no doubt of that. I'll let you go to him." Drummer advises, "Try not to go inside. The snipers should take out most of their men who come out front to see what's happening. Any others that stay in the clubhouse will find themselves fighting a rear action against Red's boys. As soon as it's safe I'll give you the signal to run to me." He turns his eyes from the road for a second. "We won't leave you with them, I promise you that."

"I thought you were going to give me a phone..."

"Change of plans, Becca. We've got the manpower behind us. Not exposing you to those bastards again. If Rock... If Rock's not able to come out, we'll go to him instead. But hopefully Chaos will bring him to us."

I bite my lip. That plan sounds better to me. "Drummer, if it goes wrong… If there's a chance he'll take me for real, please shoot me instead, will you?" I can't go back to that cellar. I just can't.

His jaw is set firmly as he replies, "It won't come to that."

I just wish I was as confident as him. "But will you promise?" The desperation in my voice must reach him.

He's silent for a moment, then, "I promise," he answers grimly.

When you're going somewhere you're looking forward to the journey seems slow. When you're approaching the last place on earth you want to be, it's over far too fast. Long before I've made peace with myself or am anywhere near ready, we're approaching the outskirts of Tucson, and then out into open desert. All too soon we start travelling along the track and the farmhouse, and outbuildings come into sight.

Drummer pulls up and goes to join his men, who have left their bikes. We're still some way out, but within sight of the place the Riders use as their clubhouse. Almost before he reaches his brothers his phone rings. Straining to hear from the inside of the SUV, I can only just make out his side of the conversation.

"Not a social call, no. You've got something I want, and I've got something in exchange."

Beef opens the door, helps me out, and stands me where I can be seen. I grow cold when he puts a gun to my head and the reality of the situation catches up with me.

"Give us Rock and I'll send Becca in unharmed. If you don't. We'll shoot her," Drummer tells the man on the end of the phone. There's a pause, then his voice changes as he snarls, "Because we want to deal with the traitor ourselves, of fuckin' course. Why do you think we want him?"

Drummer swears. "He better be able to walk out. And yes, we'll come closer. Any funny games and she's dead, I'm warnin' you, Chaos. I know you need her alive."

He ends the call and signals us. Drummer, Blade, and Peg start walking forward. Beef puts a hand around my arm, and without changing the position of his weapon at my head drags me after them. I don't have to pretend my reluctance.

It seems like a mile, but is no more than a few hundred yards, and soon we're about fifty feet from the veranda where a dozen or so Riders are waiting.

Chaos stands in no man's land, halfway between us and the door to the clubhouse, a smaller group of his men surrounding him. As Drummer predicted, others are coming out the front, swarming like bees to honey to see what's going on.

"We don't let her go until Rock comes out," Drummer calls.

Beef bends his head. "Look like you're scared."

He doesn't have to tell me to act. I'm terrified. Now faced with Chaos, I want to go back to the Satan's Devils' compound. Or anywhere. Just not here. I whimper softly.

There's a pause when nothing happens, a space of time that seems to draw out to the point where I want to scream. Then the clubhouse door opens, two men walk out carrying Rock. They throw him to the ground. He catches himself and rolls over, preventing himself landing on his back. I gasp. From his shoulder blades to his waist, his skin looks like raw hamburger meat.

Chaos steps back and kicks him on the ass. "Crawl back to your *brothers*," he sneers. "Sounds like they want to finish the job I've started." As Rock starts to move slowly forward, clearly in terrible pain, Chaos changes his attention to me. "Bring the girl to me."

I start struggling, no pretence needed, my body automatically protesting even being near to the man who'd treated me so cruelly. But it has no effect, Beef pulls me relentlessly forward. Chaos is eager, taking more steps as though anxious to come face to face. His men dog his footsteps.

As we come alongside Rock, Beef suddenly falls, dragging me down with him and rolls over to cover me as shots start ringing out.

CHAPTER 16

Rock

They tried to pump me for more information. I repeated only what I'd previously said, trying to convince them I was on their side, that they were fools if they thought I was planted to gain intelligence about their club. Lying to give myself time. Time for a rescue. The problem is, Drummer might not know I'm in trouble. We hadn't arranged regular times for me to check in, the threat of exposing me too dangerous. I don't know how the fuck Jill knew about the Chaos Riders, or where to find them, or what the Satan's Devils know about why she's missing. She could have given them a valid excuse for all I know. Even if Drummer is aware of my situation, I'm not certain I'll last long enough for him to come for me.

My back is agony. At times in the night I'd have welcomed someone to kill me, a merciful bullet instead of this constant burning and throbbing pain which feels like a thousand hot knives poking into me. Finally, when daylight broke, it wasn't me they came for, but Jill.

They strung her up next to me and started to interrogate her. As sweet butts are kept out of the loop, she couldn't give anything away. No, there were no extra men at the compound, and she hadn't seen any signs they'd been preparing for more. When she was asked what made her walk into the Chaos Riders' club, she said she'd overheard where I was and wanted to switch clubs to be with me. The only info she kept to herself was that at least some of the Devils knew I wasn't a traitor. Though by then she wasn't capable of saying much at all, but she kept that material evidence to herself, which was the only thing that might have saved her. That was the reason I'd turned my head and forced myself to watch when Chaos at last got bored and shot her through the forehead. She'd known what was coming, and met his gaze head on, even as he pulled the trigger.

Chaos had left her dead body hanging next to mine. Then he left only with his suspicions, still undecided whether I was a traitor to him or the Devils.

Left alone, I'm alternating between going hot and cold, and also very dehydrated. My shoulders no longer have any feeling at all, and when I can separate out the different pains, my legs feel tingly and ache with the effort of balancing on my toes. But my comfort, or lack of, is probably the last thing on Chaos' mind. When I'm conscious enough to think, I use the time dreaming up different ways to kill him. She might have fucked up coming here with her misguided intentions, but in the end Jill did what she could. *Kept quiet.* All I can do for her now is revenge her.

I've no idea of the time when I next hear footsteps on the stairs. I go rigid, wondering what hell they'll put me through this time. But to my surprise, they start untying my arms.

Fester stands and laughs when my legs don't support me and I crash to the ground, my knees taking the brunt of my weight. He kicks me. "Just think, what we've done to you will be nothing to what you've got to come."

I clear my throat. "What?" I croak.

"Chaos doesn't trust you, whether you're with us or not. And the Satan's Devils want you back to kill you. He's going to exchange you for Becca."

Drummer wouldn't give Becca back. He guessed my interest in her... Well, the interest I previously had before I knew what she was. But Drum doesn't know that. They have to be wrong, he's not here to exchange her. But if I open my mouth I'd drop myself in it. On the other hand, Drummer might have heard she was fucking all the men… He might know more about her than I do, and that she deserves to go back to Chaos. Fuck it. Jill had been right. That's the only reason Drummer would make an exchange. I won't have to go back to the club with her in it. Better this way. Never can trust bitches…

"Get up." Fester kicks me again.

I try. I really do. Apart from wanting to avoid Fester's steel toe capped boots meeting my flesh for a third time, the thought that the Satan's Devils might be here gives me determination, but I've been strung up too long, am too weak, and my back, fuck, my back…

Annoyed, Fester waves to King and George. Uncaring of my injuries, one takes hold of my shoulders, the other my feet, and with grunts and oomphs of effort, carry me up the stairs, through the clubroom, and into the daylight I'd given up all hope of ever seeing again. Before I have a chance to see who's there I'm thrown down, only at the final moment being able to twist to stop myself landing with the raw flesh of my back on the coarse and filthy gravel. *Drummer's here. Thank fuck.* Half of me thinks I'm still tied up and hallucinating.

When Chaos kicks me in the ass I start to crawl forward, but Drummer's a long way away, and I know for a fact Chaos will shoot me before I reach him. There's Becca, her face twisted up. *At the state of me? In fear of going back to the cellar?* She's not moving voluntarily, Beef's forcing her across the compound toward Chaos.

Chaos will have the last laugh. He'll shoot me as soon as he can take her. He won't take the chance that I'll turn on his club, especially after the way they've treated me. Every second I anticipate that bullet slamming into my skull. As I come alongside Beef I try to speak, to plead with him to leave her and get himself safe. My mouth opens as he suddenly pushes her to the ground, then drops, his body half on me, half on her.

Then the shooting starts, and I wait for the shot which will hit me in the part of me that's exposed. It's agonising lying helpless knowing with all the bullets flying around one has to hit its mark. Or it will hit my best friend. Or the woman. *She fucked my brothers. She didn't know what she meant to me.* Still, she doesn't deserve to die.

As sniper rifles continue to fire and men drop around me, I know it will be a miracle if we get out of this alive. Rapid fire is now coming in all directions. Chaos Riders will take a defensible position in the clubhouse. There's far too many for Drummer's Devils to take on, and they'll be picked off one by one.

From my position I see Riders are now flooding out of the clubhouse, but instead of joining the fight in front, they turn and shoot back inside. As soon as they're out they become targets for the men who've advanced closer. *Drummer's got help. He must have summoned the other chapters.*

With my limited view I have to rely on my hearing, which alerts me that the shots from the assault rifles are gradually slowing. Now there's single shots, execution style. Men begging and pleading, their cries cut off as another bullet must find it's mark. *It's a fucking massacre.* I start hoping that the right people are the ones winning.

Beef jerks, and his weight feels heavier. *Fuck no. Don't say he's been shot.*

"Beef?"

"Stay down, I'm alright."

It seems to go on forever, but at last there's silence, echoes of bullets that have been fired bouncing off the walls of the farmhouse and outbuildings. My ears buzz in the silence, and I'm as pleased as fuck when Beef pulls himself up. Once he's off me I agonizingly slowly pull myself up to a crouch, my eyes settling on the blood pouring out of Beef's side.

"You're bleeding."

"I'll be fine. Just a scratch." But already the colour is leeching out of his face.

Becca stands, her hand covering her mouth, and I'm not surprised when she turns away and vomits as she takes in the scene. It's been a blood bath. My eyes narrow as they find Chaos, his dead eyes staring up at the sky, a look of disbelief on his dead face. *I wanted to kill him myself.*

Fester's body is lying still, as are Wreck's and Krueger's. Squirt and Runner are piled on top of each other, with King and George nearby. One by one I count up the Riders I know and see quite a few of them I don't. *Chaos' support must have turned up while I was being tortured in the basement.*

"Time to go home, Brother." Drummer's voice is the most welcome sound I've ever heard, his words causing a lump in my throat. "Fuck, Brother. What have they done to you?" He's holding something in his hands, and he chokes up when he shows me what he has. "Brought this for you, but I think I'll need to keep it safe a little longer." It's my cut. My Satan's Devils cut. I've never been so pleased to see any object before in my life. Nor similarly as pissed off to know I can't yet wear it. Drummer's staring at the reason I can't put it on. "Rock, you need to see Doc. You too, Beef."

"I'm okay," Beef insists again, but as he tries to walk he stumbles.

"They both need to go to hospital," Becca insists. Her voice is weak and she's visibly shaking.

"No." Drummer is equally adamant.

Turning my head, I see bodies being lifted by, yeah, I smile as I recognise Red and Crash, his VP. There's Demon, the VP from Colorado, and I'll be fucked, Dart and Lost. And if I'm not mistaken, I can make out some of the Utah boys. No wonder Drummer had the upper hand. Even with their reinforcements the Chaos Riders had been outnumbered and didn't stand a chance.

Wraith steadies Beef, helping him stand. I watch him being led away, leaning heavily on the VP. Something warns me, despite his protests to the contrary, he's seriously injured. He's got to be okay. I can't have found my best friend to lose him again just as fast.

Becca is standing, looking like she doesn't know which way to turn or what to say to me. "Go with him," I growl. She means nothing to me now. Not after I heard what, or rather who, she's been doing. Not waiting for me and instead becoming a whore. It's not what I'd expected from her.

She still looks scared, and now, confused. But Drummer reinforces my instruction, his voice gentling as he tells her. "Go with Wraith, we'll get Rock back."

With one last look and her mouth working as though she doesn't know what to say, she at last nods at Drum and runs after the VP and Beef. She's clearly much stronger than when I'd last seen her.

"Can you stand?"

"I need help, Prez," I say through gritted teeth. Now the excitement has died down my back is protesting all over again.

He calls Shooter over, and together they each take an arm and have me on my feet. I stagger, but they get me moving in the right direction and soon have me lying face down on the rear seat of a second SUV as explosions ring out behind me.

I'm half out of it on the journey, my mind playing tricks on me. I feel hot, though I'm sure the air-conditioner's working, then go cold and wish they'd turn the heat up. I drift off, then come too with a start fully believing Becca's sticking knives into me. Then, when I doze again I see her lying on a bed with my brothers, being passed around between them, smiling as one by one they fuck her.

I'm almost completely out of it when I'm carried into the clubhouse and taken to a crash room out the back. Then I pass out completely.

When I come around I'm still lying on my stomach, and now there's an IV in my hand, and I hear Doc's voice mumbling.

"Welcome back." Prez gets down on his haunches so he can look me in the eye. "Thank fuck we got you out when we did. You're not going to die from your injuries, but infection had set in. Doc's set you up with intravenous anti-biotics and dressed your back. Fuck man," he toys with his beard, "why the fuck did they have to go and do that?"

"Chaos told me to get the ink blacked out."

"They removed the top layer of skin, which will be fuckin' painful." Doc walks around, but all I can see is his denim-clad legs. "The important thing is to change the dressin' daily and let new skin grow without formin' scabs. You should be able to get a new tattoo eventually, which will cover any scarring we can't prevent. I'm also giving you intravenous morphine, as you must be in a fuck-load of pain."

But it's not me I should be worrying about. Instead it's my best friend, and the man who quite possibly saved my life. "How's Beef?" My head feels woozy, but I've enough sense about me to ask after him.

"Took a bullet that nicked his stomach. I managed to get it out."

"Will he be alright?"

There's a pause and neither of them answer me. I go to sit up, but Drummer easily pushes me back down.

"He'll be fine. Man's strong enough to fight anything off," Doc says. "You worry about you for now."

But Doc can't keep the edge of worry out of his voice. I squeeze my eyes tightly closed to stop the threatening tears escaping as our long history together flashes through my mind. "Drum, tell him I love him, you hear me?" He might have fucked Becca, but he wasn't to know she'd meant something to me.

"I'll tell him."

Fuck, what Doc put in that IV must be strong. I barely feel the pain in my back, and now I've closed them, my lids are so heavy I can't reopen my eyes. Drummer and Doc are talking, but I can't distinguish any words.

The next time I come around it's to see a chair pulled up by the bed and Becca in it, asleep. For a moment I allow my eyes to feast on the sight. She's looking healthier already, there's colour in her face which wasn't there before. She's still too skinny though, and needs more meat on her bones. Her hair's been cut short to the scalp, enabling me to see the beautiful features of her face. Her ears are delicate, her nose straight and narrow, and she's got a luscious mouth I'd just love to put my cock inside.

But I'd just be one amongst many. I turn my head away. Taking a deep breath, I pull myself up, wincing when my back twists. The sound of me moving wakes her.

She sits forward, her face showing concern. "Rock, Doc said you had to take it easy. You ought to stay lying down."

Her voice makes me look at her again, the woman who I'd fantasised about and who I'd got to safety, dreaming about the time I could get to know her properly, to explore this strange attraction I felt for her. Before Jill had opened her mouth I'd toyed with the idea of getting her away from that fucker Hawk and taking that huge step of making her my old lady. Only to find she couldn't wait and had had all my brothers before me.

She's been with Beef, that's what Jill had told me. She never had any intention of waiting. I don't blame Beef, he'd had no idea. No, I blame her.

"Get out of here, Becca."

Her face scrunches. "Rock?"

"I don't want to see you."

She shakes her head. "Rock? What are you saying?"

"I'm saying I'm already sick of the sight of you." The pain in trying to find a comfortable position makes me angrier than I might have been. *She didn't know what I felt for her.* You can't betray someone you've never had. "I don't want to see your fuckin' face." *There I go, far too brusque once again.*

Fuck me. She's wiping moisture away from her eyes, crocodile tears I expect. *She'll soon be after her next conquest.* Then she stands, her back straighter than I'd seen it before. "I don't know what the hell's got into you, Rock," she starts stiffly. "I just wanted to see you're alright. You saved me, and I'm sorry if helping me escape was the reason for this." She waves her hand at my back. "That's all I wanted to say. I'll go now."

She wastes no time leaving, doesn't even slam the door behind her. I'm left feeling like an asshole. I wanted to hurt her because she'd hurt me. Not my physical injury, but the pain in my head. *Why couldn't she have waited? Why did she have to jump into the bed of the first brother to ask her?*

Only a couple of minutes later, the door opens again. It's the prez. He's looking at me strangely. "Just seen Becca crying in the corridor. You say something to upset her?"

I don't want to admit to being weak, and explain how her betrayal had hurt me. "We just cleared the air, she thanked me for saving her." I'd said a lot more, but I don't tell him what.

He affords me one of his steely gazes. "Fuckin' brave woman, is Becca. She volunteered to be used in exchange to get you out of the Riders' clubhouse. Girl didn't need to do that."

Fuck. I'd got it wrong. Drummer hadn't come up with the idea of using her, she'd done that herself. *For me.* She'd no need to thank me for arranging her escape. She repaid me yesterday. Offering herself to be used so I could be rescued, and with all those bullets flying, it could be her lying dead or dying.

Seems I need to thank her. But to do that I'll need to try to forgive her. For something she didn't even know that she'd done. She didn't know how close I'd come to claiming her.

CHAPTER 17

Becca

Shocked by Rock's cruel words and dismissal, I stand leaning against the wall outside his room, needing the physical support as I try to put together what the hell just happened. Perhaps in my head I'd built his concern for me up into something it wasn't. Maybe my dreams of our joyful reunion had all been in my head. At the very least, I'd expected him to ask how I am, how I was adapting to life on the compound. For him to be polite. Not rude and obnoxious.

Tears stream down my face. Angrily I wipe them away, uncertain why I'm crying. I didn't know Rock except as my jailer, and then my saviour. Had I built him up as a fictional character in my mind? A woman would have to be blind not to find him attractive, and my eyes are working just fine. Is that all he is? A pretty shell with nothing inside? Why do I feel so disappointed?

Lost in my thoughts, I'm only aware of footsteps approaching at the last minute. I look up to see Drummer has paused in front of me, his head tilted slightly, eyes creased. Then he shrugs and moves on, heading into the room I just left. I'm glad he didn't ask me to explain why I'm crying in the corridor.

I feel lost, unsure of my place now. *People referred to me as being Rock's woman.* So much so, perhaps I'd come to believe it myself. How wrong they've been, how far from his true intentions. He's made it clear he wants nothing to do with me.

He's in pain. But how does that explain his rudeness? Christ, his back looked so terrible yesterday it had been hard to see. Could that account for him being unrecognisable from the man who had been so sympathetic when I'd been kept in the cellar, and who had put his life on the line to help me escape?

What has changed? What's made him so adamant he wants nothing to do with me? It can't be anything I've done, I've had no contact with him, and while I've been at the clubhouse, I've been too weak to do much other than laze around and concentrate on allowing my body to heal. *I'd been looking forward to seeing him again.* Hoping for a chance to get to know him.

A sudden commotion at the end of the corridor catches my attention. It's coming from Beef's room, loud voices, exclamations and hurried feet rushing around. Now, Beef, he's really been kind to me. And yesterday he quite possibly saved my life, sheltering both me and Rock with his big body, and taking a bullet that otherwise might have had either mine or Rock's name on it.

As Drummer exits Rock's room abruptly and races down the corridor, I follow, anxious to know what's going on with the man who, unlike Rock, has treated me well. I pause as Drummer stops outside the open door, noticing how drawn he looks as he peers in.

When he asks, "What's happened? What's up with Beef?" I listen avidly.

Someone, I don't know who, answers from within. "He's bad, Prez. Went downhill suddenly. He's got to go to the hospital. Doc's got a bus on its way."

Scared for Beef, I move closer, now able to see that Drummer's normally forceful steel eyes have lost their intensity and appear hooded as he continues to look inside the room.

Knowing they hadn't wanted anything about the shooting to become public, I immediately comprehend how serious it is. It must be their last resort to give in and take him somewhere the authorities could be alerted. When the medics arrive I stand back, giving them space to work. Hearing the worry in their voices as I listen to their conversations. Watching until Beef is stretchered out and taken away. Automatically I start to follow, Drummer holds me back.

"I want to go with him. Please." I'd pinned so much on seeing Rock again. Now, Beef, the man who'd stayed glued to my side to protect me, who held and comforted me only the night before last, feels my only friend. I can't stand to be parted from him. The support he'd given me makes it seem I'm watching my lifeline be taken away.

Squeezing my arm, Drummer shakes his head. "Not yet, sweetheart. They need to settle him. Wraith's going with him."

Though neither man knew it, I'd been dividing my time between an unconscious Beef and equally out of it Rock. Now I'm at a loss to know what to do. *I wish someone would tell me.* Thinking for myself isn't as easy as others make it look.

"As soon as I know more I'll tell you. Beef took a liking to you, didn't he?"

Maybe Beef, too, wouldn't want to see me. He was kind to me for one reason. *Because he mistakenly thought I was his friend's woman. That, Rock's made quite clear I'm definitely not.*

"If you want to visit him I'll get someone to take you once we know the score. He's strong, Becca. Beef will pull through." Patting my shoulder, Drummer walks the short way up the corridor, disappearing back into the room where I'd find no welcome. Rock's.

Tears fall again. I feel like I've lost the only two men I've ever become close to today. One doesn't want me, the other might be dying, or already dead for all I know. The empty feeling inside reminds me I'm alone.

I've been stupid, thinking there was a connection between me and Rock. I couldn't wait for Rock to come back to his true home, to get to know him under the right circumstances, to have a chance to analyse what this strange emotion I feel for him might mean. Did I just hang onto a dream as he'd been the first man to offer me kindness? I must have read into things… something that wasn't there. Rock would have done the same for anyone, it's who he is. He didn't get me out of that cellar because he particularly liked me. From his reaction just now, he seems to hate me.

Trying to dry my tears, convincing myself Drummer will tell me any news about Beef as soon as he had some to share, I make my feet walk into the clubroom, and see Darcy. She's taller than me, with red hair, a definite pregnancy showing. She's standing up to Peg. I hover in the entrance, unashamedly watching curiously as she pokes him hard in the chest. "You promised me, Peg. You fucking promised me."

"We didn't have a choice, sweetheart." Peg looks tired. "There'll be no blowback on us. I promise you that, Flash."

"I'm not stupid." Darcy swings around, indicating Sam, Sophie, and Ella, who are avidly observing the conversation. A reason why I feel I have permission to eavesdrop. "And neither are they," she continues. "Something went down, Peg. You can't hide two injured men. I don't know what happened to Rock, but Beef was shot. Shot! You told me you were out of that business."

"I told you we earned our money clean, and we do." Peg's eyes have gone cold. I get the impression he doesn't like the challenge, or not publicly. "But when there's a threat to the club we sort it out our own way. That's all you'll get from me, darlin'. Anything else is club business." He nods at the women sitting around the table. "As you all know full well."

"Plausible bloody deniability." Sophie doesn't seem much happier than Darcy, but she sounds more resigned.

"Too fuckin' right," agrees Peg.

I hesitate about entering the room. Tears once again prick at the back of my eyes, wondering how they're going to treat me now I have no place here. Drummer allowed me to stay as a favour to Rock. Perhaps he'll want me to go now.

I feel foolish and lost. Part of me doesn't want to mingle with the old ladies as I realise I'd had foolish hopes of joining their number. Of being important to someone.

I hate this situation. Hate myself. I don't belong here, but where else could I go? And how can I leave? I don't even own the clothes on my back. Turning, I bang my fist against the wall in frustration.

An office door opens behind me, and a man I haven't been introduced to before, but who I'd seen in that meeting emerges.

"Becca?"

I swing around, memories of my unpleasant interaction with Petty and Roller slamming into me. *Who am I now that I haven't got Beef's protection, nor, it seems, will ever again be referred to as Rock's woman.* All my insecurities slam back into me as, warily, I nod.

The tall man with long straight hair and Native American facial features holds out his hand. "Mouse. I'm the go-to computer guy around here. We've not been properly introduced."

This is the man Drummer had told me would dig to find details about Hawk. Some of the tension seeps away as I return his handshake.

"If you've got a minute, Prez has asked me to do some investigating on your behalf. Find out what you're up against."

My concerns about Rock, my fear of returning to that cellar, had put my husband right out of my mind. Rock made it clear he doesn't want me around. Even if he comes to tolerate my presence and I'm not thrown out, I'll find it hard to stay with the

Satan's Devils. I need to start thinking about a new future now. The sooner I'm armed with information the sooner I can be away. I need to know how far Hawk's reach is before I can make any plans. *Plans.* Has God a new plan for me?

Wiping away my tears, I reply, "I've nothing else to do." *Except worry about Beef or mope about Rock.* I'd rather not be alone.

"Hey, I know you're worried about Beef. But, darlin', he'll be fine. I'm certain." Mouse's eyes soften as he watches my action. "Come in and let's discuss your situation. Take your mind off everything that's happening. Unless you'd rather be with Rock?"

As I quickly shake my head but offer no explanation—he'll find out where I stand with Rock soon enough—Mouse steps aside, holding open the door. Walking inside I'm immediately greeted by a strong aroma of marijuana, and smoke rises from a joint still burning in the ashtray. The desk top is covered in monitors, with more behind on the wall, and there are several keyboards dotted around as well as an open laptop.

Mouse waves me to a seat in front of the desk, then takes his chair behind it. He looks at me searchingly. "You sure you're okay not being with Rock?"

What's he asking? "Have you spoken to Rock?"

"Nah. Not since he's regained consciousness. But did you want to wait to go through this? You've probably got things to talk about with him."

"No." I put him right. "We've said all there is to say." As he looks at me strangely I continue, "Rock will come good in time. I'm more worried about Beef. But you're right. There's nothing I can do to help either of them, so let's get this over with." The sooner we do, the sooner I can be somewhere else. I look down at my hands as I remember how ill-equipped I am to deal with life on my own.

Mouse coughs, and I realise I'd been lost in my thoughts. Coming back to myself I see his eyes narrowing, then he shrugs. "Okay, so, tell me about Hawk."

The door opening interrupts us. Mouse takes a drag on his joint as Drummer steps in. "Ah. Peg said you two had got together. Okay if I'm in on this, sweetheart?"

I can't see why not, but I'm surprised the president of the MC wants to know about my problems. My expression must give away my thoughts as Drummer continues. "I don't know why the fuck Chaos was holdin' you. Nor, though I'm glad they did, why that bunch of rapin' motherfuckers kept their hands off you. I want to know exactly who your husband is. If we're going to get blowback for shelterin' you, I need to know in advance."

I suppose it makes sense he wants to protect the club. Despite Rock's abrupt dismissal of me, I've had nothing but kindness from the Devils. I'll do what I can to help them, though it might not be as much as they expect. Frowning slightly, I tell him. "Drummer, I'll give you whatever I can, though I doubt that I've got much that will answer your questions. But I need to give you some background first."

Drummer settles back into a chair, stretching out his legs, folding his arms and raising his chin to me. "Go on."

"I come from a religious family. Hawk became our pastor when I was thirteen. I only ever saw him as a pastor, didn't know anything else about him." I pause and bite my lip, admitting the next bit isn't going to be easy. As Mouse fidgets I try to get a grip on myself. "It was only later I learned that he'd planned everything from that moment. Agreed to it all with my parents. The first I knew of it was my eighteenth birthday, when suddenly it was my wedding day as well."

"Motherfucker!" Mouse suddenly looks animated. "Did you even like him?"

I shake my head. "I'd never thought of him in that way. Sure, I was flattered when an older man paid a teenager attention—he used to single me out in Bible classes—but I never thought of him as a potential husband. He was almost the same age as my father."

"How old is he now?" Mouse asks, pulling a tablet in front of him.

"Forty-two."

"And you're…what?"

"Twenty-one. We've been married just over three years."

Drummer and Mouse exchange glances. They look like they're doing the math for themselves. It's Drummer who speaks first. "You said he forced you. You weren't attracted to him?"

"Never have been. Never will be." My teeth shut together, they can fill in the blanks. "If I'd had a choice Hawk would have been the last man I'd have married, and that was even before I started to know who he really was. He's a controlling, possessive man." I smile self-deprecatingly as both men are giving me strange looks.

"So why did you agree to marry him?"

"I was home schooled, brought up by strict parents. I wasn't allowed boyfriends, or to go out with my friends. It had always been that way, but looking back, when Hawk set his sights on me my parents became worse. Before Hawk, I'd never…"

As my voice drops away, Drummer prompts, "Never what, sweetheart?" His voice is as gentle as he can make it.

"Never gone to a movie, eaten in a restaurant, or been kissed." I look down at my hands rather than into their pitying eyes. Naïve isn't a strong enough word for what I was. "Hawk wanted everything done his way. He'd lay out my clothes in the morning, give me set times to do things, tell me what to do every minute of the day."

"Sam mentioned you were kept like a slave." Drummer rolls back his head and stares at the ceiling for a moment. "You never had a chance, did you, darlin'? It goes back further than this fucker who married you."

I flush red, embarrassed to remember when I'd waited for Sam to tell me what to wear.

"Rock know this?" Mouse interjects. When I indicate 'no' he continues, "He ought to be here to hear Becca's story."

Drum shoots him a quick look and a shake of his head, leaving me to wonder exactly what Rock's told him. Mouse's eyes become slits, but neither man mentions Rock again.

Presumably trying to get the conversation back on track, Drummer asks directly, "Hawk's a pastor. So why did he end up in prison?"

I send him a grateful look as he removes the focus from my non-existent relationship with Rock. "Because, though his congregation never saw it, he's got a violent temper. This time he got caught. He put a man in a wheelchair, got sent down for grievous bodily harm."

"He ever violent toward you?"

The look I send Drummer answers his question. Now it's going to get awkward. I close my eyes while I gather my strength. "They caught him because I didn't give him an alibi."

The president of the Satan's Devils isn't stupid. He gives me a considering look. "Did you drop him in it on purpose?"

I shake my head. "That's why I gave you my sorry back-ground. I'd never been allowed to think for myself. Hawk would always tell me what to say—that's if he wanted me to say anything at all when people turned up. This time, he hadn't been expecting the man he hurt to report him. It's down to me why he got sent down. He was arrogant and didn't think he'd get caught. But..." I breathe deeply. "I wanted to get away from him. I didn't know how I'd survive, but I couldn't stand him. Hated him."

"And?" Drum prompts.

"The police turning up couldn't be good. Even I knew that. But I didn't ask them why they wanted to know. Just answered the questions truthfully when they asked."

Mouse puts down his tablet and leans back in his chair, raising an eyebrow toward Drummer. His long black hair seems to float around his head as he shakes it. *Here it comes.* They probably don't take kindly to people who tell everything to the police. Does that make me a snitch?

"Hawk blames you for sending him down."

"Yes," I admit. "You want me to leave now?"

Drummer's eyes suddenly open. "Why the fuck would you think that?"

Shrugging, I reply, "Because I was responsible for sending a man to prison. I might be used to following instructions, but I'm not stupid. The fact the police wanted to know where Hawk was that night probably meant they suspected he was up to no good. I could have said he'd been home with me. I didn't."

He laughs. "You did what you had to, sweetheart. You only told the truth. After the way you've been treated no one could have blamed you even if you had done it intentionally. What does make more sense now, is knowing that's why Hawk didn't care much about how the Riders treated you. And it gives us more to think about when he gets out."

Mouse looks thoughtful. "I'll look into when he's eligible for parole."

His comment makes me start and inhale a sharp breath. "I hadn't thought about that. He could get out early for good behaviour. He'll be coming after me…"

Suddenly Drummer leans forward, taking my hands in his. "Don't worry your head, Becca. One way or another we'll sort this mess for you."

"I'll need to leave Arizona before Hawk gets out..."

"Woah, slow down. For now, Becca, you're safe here on the compound."

But Rock clearly doesn't want me here. How can I stay? Drummer will back his brother over an unknown woman any day. *Perhaps Rock hasn't told him how he feels yet?*

"Tell me more about Hawk? What's his full name, darlin'?" Mouse asks, startling me.

"Alexis Gardner." His real name feels alien on my tongue. It's become hard to think of him as anything other than Hawk.

Mouse taps again, then turns the screen around to face me. "This him?"

I don't need more than a glimpse before I nod. "Yes. That white stripe in his hair makes him quite distinctive."

As Drummer examines the photograph his face tightens. He turns it back around to Mouse. "Apart from Hawk being violent, have you any idea why he hurt the man he did? Has he done anything like that before? Is there more to Hawk than just being a pastor?"

"I'm sorry, Drummer. He never talked to me about anything. If there is anything more to him, he never let on what it could be." I bite my lip before concluding, "But on the other hand, I wouldn't be surprised if there is. He's not a nice man."

Drummer studies me for a moment then raises his chin toward Mouse. "We'll let Mouse do some diggin', get you free of him, Becca. I promise you that. Took a brave fuckin' woman to offer herself up yesterday. We got a brother back who might not have been breathin' if we hadn't got to him when we had. Owe you one, Becca." One of his intense looks comes my way. "I'm not worried about you talkin' to the police. You proved you can keep your mouth shut when you need to by not speakin' about Rock when you arrived on the compound. Now I've got to ask you to trust us."

"I don't want to see Hawk again," I tell them. "I know he's my husband…"

"Man like that," Mouse points his finger at the tablet in front of him, "doesn't deserve a woman like you, Becca. You'll be better off without him. I'll look into how you can get a divorce."

Divorce? My eyes snap to the man behind his computer. It's what I want, isn't it? Of course it is. A small smile comes to my face, then disappears as I remember his possessive streak. *Hawk's not going to let me go.* "I don't think I'll ever be free of him."

"You will be," Drummer promises just as his phone pings. Taking it out, his eyes skim a text as he says, "Thank fuck." He's almost wearing a smile as he looks up, addressing both me and Mouse. "Beef's come through surgery. The doctors think his prognosis is good." He glances at me. "We'll have to cut this short. I'm going to the hospital to visit him."

"Can I come too, Drummer?" I don't want to stay and watch the old ladies play happy families. Knowing Rock hates me, that would hurt. Beef feels like the only friend I have here. Unless, I remind myself, he was only being friendly because of my tenuous connection to Rock.

Mouse offers, "I'll carry on digging, see what I can find out."

Giving Mouse a chin lift, Drummer stands. "Come on then. If Beef comes around he'll probably prefer seeing your pretty face to my ugly one."

I'm not certain I'm anywhere near pretty…or not yet. But I'm happy to get off the compound and interested, as we drive down into Tucson, when Drummer explains that normally an injured member would have all of his brothers around him. But they're going to limit his visitors so as not to draw too much attention to him being in the hospital with a bullet wound. The story is that his gun went off by accident when he was cleaning it.

"What about the Chaos Riders' clubhouse? Won't the bullets be traced back to your club?"

Drummer laughs. "Unlikely. We know our job. There were a series of explosions in their badly stored ammunition. All the bodies were inside, badly burned. Likelihood is the cops won't investigate too deeply as they'll just be glad that the scum has been taken out. It's an isolated location, some way out of Tucson. They may not even have discovered it yet."

"What about Jill? What happened to her, Drummer?"

Drummer's face twists as he answers in a cold voice. "Club business." Just like that, he shuts me up.

I don't dare question him further on the matter. I wonder about asking whether he wants me to leave the compound now it's clear I mean nothing to Rock, but something warns me I don't want to pre-empt that conversation. *What if he said yes? What on earth would I do?*

We've arrived. Drummer turns into the hospital and finds a parking space. Before we get out he drums his fingers on the steering wheel and throws me a thoughtful look. Then he gets out of the car without letting me know what he was thinking, comes around to my side and opens my door without speaking.

Once inside the hospital it takes us a while to get the right directions to, and then find, Beef's room. He's unconscious when we arrive and has still not come round by the time Drummer needs to leave.

This time there's no decision for me to worry about making. The last thing I want to do is return to the compound to be confronted by Rock. "You go on, Drummer," I offer. "I'll stay with him. Make sure he doesn't wake up alone."

Drummer nods and looks relieved. "Appreciate that, Becca. Don't like the thought of no one being with him."

CHAPTER 18
Rock

D oc's been in and changed my dressings, clearly pleased that any signs of infection are receding. He's using an old trick, Vaseline to cover the skin and stop it becoming dry with bandaging over the top to keep the air out and prevent scabs forming. While it still hurts like a bitch, I want to keep moving. I'm not a man who likes lying around in bed. Unless there's a woman keeping me company that is, and I'm not up to that yet.

Last night Diva and Paige came in, both giggling, both offering to suck my dick, but I excused my lack of arousal on the morphine even while knowing that had nothing to do with it. The only woman my dick seems interested in is one who prefers the cocks of other men. I'm mad with myself. Why hadn't I seen how shallow she was? How could I have been so taken in by her beautiful deep blue eyes? Madness. I must have mistaken my sympathy for a deeper emotion on account of the conditions she had been kept in.

Apparently Beef woke up this morning. Despite my pain, nothing's going to stop me going to visit him, needing to see with my own eyes the evidence that he's going to make a full recovery. It was him, my oldest friend in the club, I missed most when back at the Riders' clubhouse I'd thought of my brothers.

Although nothing's going to keep me from his side, it's harder work than I expected to slide my t-shirt over my raw, bandaged back. Pulling up my jeans is even trickier, muscles rippling and tugging at the ruined skin. However slowly I tried to take it, I'm breathing heavily by the time I've finished.

"Hey, Matt!" I call to the prospect I've spied as hunched like an old man I enter the clubroom. "Need a ride."

"Sure thing, Rock. Where we going?"

"The hospital to see Beef."

"Cool." Looking eager, the kid runs to find the keys to the spare SUV, returning quickly with Marvel by his side.

I can't help glaring at the man. It's easier to forgive Beef seeing as we've shared women in the past, but Marvel? I'm unable to hide my disgust that he's been with the woman I can no longer consider mine.

Marvel's quick to notice. "Was gonna come with you, Brother. But from the look on your face you look more like you want to kill me. Though I've no fuckin' idea why." He looks mystified as he shakes his head.

Pinching the bridge of my nose, I breathe deeply. "Sorry, man. It's not your fault, shouldn't blame you. You weren't to know."

"All of us thought the same, Brother." Marvel's face drops. "Prez did his shit too well. He wanted us to believe you'd turned on us so we'd act the right way if we ran into you."

Rapidly I shake my head to reassure him. There was a reason for what Prez did, it kept me alive. "Not talking about that."

"Then what?" The brother who likes comics looks perplexed, his brow creasing as he seems to think through all possible ways he could have upset me.

Taking pity on him, I shrug, then wince and regret moving my shoulders. "You fucked Becca." I sigh. "You weren't to know I wanted her."

"*Becca?*" Now it's Marvel who's rapidly moving his head side to side. "I've never been near the bitch. You think I fucked her?" His eyes open wide.

Maybe Jill was wrong to put him on the list.

"Sorry, Brother. My intel was obviously wrong."

"Sure fuckin' was. Now we got that cleared up, you trust me to drive, or are you still gonna shoot me?" As Matt chucks him the keys I see he's smiling. Marvel doesn't bear grudges.

Carefully I raise my arm and slap him on the back and hope he's wise enough not to reciprocate. When I see that he is, I accept the ride. "Sure thing. I'll be glad of the company."

When we turn onto the 110 and the journey becomes smoother and easier for me, Marvel looks over. "What was it like in there, Brother?"

"With the Riders?"

"Yeah."

I gaze out of the window as I remember. "Fuckin' awful, man. Women forced to take the members dicks. It wasn't pleasant."

"Red got the women out, didn't he?"

"That's what I heard. Took them to Vegas. Was going to get them settled somewhere they could recover."

Marvel's face has gone grim. "The youngest was only fifteen."

I nod. Another thing Drum had confirmed. "Just glad they're all in the ground." I only hope Beef is truly recovering and won't be joining them.

"It's good to have you back, Rock. Fuckin' hard thinkin' you'd stolen from the club. With you and Mouse gone, the club felt different."

"Have you noticed anything different about Mouse since he's been back?" I don't know if I'm imagining things. He'd only popped his head round the door briefly, but he seemed distant.

"He's quieter, as though he's not really with us."

Dipping my head to show that's exactly how I read it, I look ahead once again, wondering what's going on with my brother.

Normally he returns from his vision quests refreshed. Maybe no spirits appeared to him this time.

It's not long before Marvel is indicating, and I can't wait to get out of this seat. Being in the car has meant leaning on my sore back. Sliding out is painful, but Marvel's patient and walks with me slowly as we follow the directions Drum had given us to get to Beef's room. I walk down the hall alongside my brother, glad he's slowing his pace for me. When we're at last outside, anxious to see my old friend, I'm the one opening the door...

That's when I find them. My best friend and the woman I'd considered making mine. Beef's laying on one side, Becca's behind him, her arm draped over his shoulder. Both fast asleep.

"They make a good couple, don't they?" Marvel murmurs from behind me, not knowing how close I am to throttling Beef. *He's my best friend and he wasn't to know.* The mantra repeats over and over again in my head as I try to calm myself down. *He didn't know.* Not that it helps much.

Although he'd spoken quietly, Marvel's voice wakes Becca. She opens her eyes. On seeing us a smile lights up her face. When she notices only Marvel's reciprocating, the unfriendly scowl on mine makes her happy expression slip away as quickly as it came.

It shouldn't have surprised me to find them snuggled up together, but it does, and feels like a punch to my jaw. My face grows darker. Becca slides off the bed, her action disturbing Beef, who starts thrashing. Immediately she turns back to soothe him, he settles right away. *The fucker misses her.* But then he probably doesn't know he's sharing her with everyone else. *Except for Marvel, who's assured me he hasn't tapped that. Man's probably got too much sense.*

"We'd like to sit with him. Alone." My words are clipped, and I hope I'm sounding polite. She made me no promises, it was all in my head.

Marvel looks from Becca to me. "Hold on a minute, Becca. Tell us how he is first."

She looks at Beef, reassures herself he's quieted again, then at us and indicates the doorway. Once outside she leans against the wall as she tells us. "They removed his spleen, that was a success. He's got an infection, and when he came around was hallucinating. When he sleeps he keeps thrashing around. I'm worried he might pull the stitches out. It calms him if I lie next to him."

Of course it does. Lucky motherfucker.

"Is he going to be okay?" Marvel asks.

"It's sepsis they're worried about. The medical staff are keeping a close eye on him."

"When will we know if he's going to make a full recovery?"

"I'm not sure, Marvel. When the infection settles I should think. But the signs are good."

At that moment we hear groans through the door, and Beef's arms and legs are being thrown about again. Becca's straight back inside, up on that bed, holding him, and fuck me if he doesn't go back to sleep immediately. My first thought had been to send her away, now how the fuck can I separate them? Knowing however much it hurts to see her with him, if it brings my brother peace and helps him heal I couldn't be such an asshole as to deny him that. *He's my best friend. She's nothing to me.*

Marvel offers to get coffee, I accept. I'm left alone with the brother I love and the girl who'd taken up residence in my brain. While she hadn't known it, until Jill spilled the beans she'd kept me going in the deepest darkness of the Chaos Riders' club.

We sit in silence. After the update on Beef's condition I can't ask anything else. I've no wish to start a conversation during which I might say things I'd regret. I've no right to criticise her. I never told her of my intentions. Can I cope if Beef and Becca end up together? There's certainly something between the two of them. As I lean forward to keep pressure off my back, I decide when he's able to understand I'll enlighten him that she's fucked other members. It will be up to him what he does then. But unlike me, at least he'll be armed with all the facts before he makes any decision.

She's closed her eyes, but she's still awake. Her hand is gently stroking Beef's shoulder. As I watch her soothing him I can't believe I read her so wrong. I'd never have taken her for being promiscuous, but slut she certainly is. Even though she still looks poorly herself. Perhaps if she'd done less fucking and saved her energy for healing she'd look better.

Placing my elbows on my knees, I put my head into my hands. She owes me nothing. We're quits. I rescued her, she rescued me back.

Marvel returns, our coffees are drunk. An hour or so later Marvel reminds me that we should get back to the club, as it's church tonight. Becca tells me she's going to stay, unwilling to leave Beef alone. I have to admire her fortitude, and realise while it might slowly kill me inside each time I look at her, I'm not risking my friend's recovery just because I object to his choice of woman. But for his sake I will be having a conversation with her. If she wants to have something with Beef, she'll have to give up everyone else.

Back at the clubhouse I've only time to pop a pain pill before Drummer calls us in. There's an awkward moment when Hyde rushes out to find me a chair, as mine had been removed. It's harsh to think all the men sitting around me had believed me to be a thief and a traitor. They had to, I accept that. Though it's still painful.

While they've welcomed me individually, this is the first time we've met as a group since my return. Drummer addresses it head on. He bangs the gavel. "Brothers, tonight we officially welcome Rock home."

There's a general banging of hands on the table and stamping of feet, as well as numerous vocalisations of welcome.

Drummer nods at me before sparing a glance for everyone. "Before we go on to other business I want to go over it again. Make sure we're all on the same page as to what Rock has done for us. As you're too well aware, another outlaw MC tried to set themselves up in Tucson. I needed a man on the inside, couldn't ask for volunteers, as the only way to convince the Chaos Riders that that man wasn't a plant was for everyone to believe he was no longer a Satan's Devil. I needed his name to become dirt all over Tucson.

"I approached Rock, and he agreed immediately. Didn't hesitate for a minute. Even knowing that had he come across one of the men he used to call brother, that brother would probably have killed him. That is, if the Chaos Riders hadn't doubted what Rock told them and shot him on sight. I took the gamble he was worth more alive to them. A gamble which luckily paid off. But that doesn't change the fact that in accepting this mission Rock put his life on the line for his club."

Drummer pauses. The table's gone silent as the implications of what he's said sink in. He gives them a moment, then continues, "Wraith and I met with Rock to obtain information. Then once again Rock went back to the Riders, again potentially sticking his head in a noose. *For this club.*" Raising his head, he looks around the table, meeting the eyes of every man here. "I don't think I need to tell you, Rock is a fuckin' hero."

Murmurs of agreement float around, none of dissent, while I sit wishing I could disappear under the table. *Any brother would have done what I did had they been the one asked.* But that doesn't stop heartfelt thanks coming from every chair. Viper comes around with his hand up and I flinch away fast. He goes back to his seat with an apologetic look. *Thank fuck*. It doesn't stop my back burning at just the threat.

Prez waits for everyone to settle. "We were successful in taking out the Chaos Riders because of the intel we had from Rock. Without him there we wouldn't have been able to plan it so well. While the loss of any Devil from whatever chapter is hard, it could have been a far higher number."

"We were lucky, Prez," Viper butts in.

"No, Viper, we weren't. It wasn't luck. Our success was down to Rock."

Peg's looking at his clasped hands on the table. "Got us a problem though, Prez. While we had to get Rock out, Christ, he'd already got hurt bad enough," he breaks off to look at me with a grimace, "we had to go in fast, and I worry we didn't cover our backs."

"Agree with you there, Brother. But we couldn't wait any longer to go get Rock. Not once fuckin' Jill got a bee in her bonnet and went after him."

Mouse looks up from his laptop. "While the Riders' club-house was far enough out of town that the shots didn't attract attention. Blowing up that farmhouse certainly caught the police's notice."

Prez looks tired as he nods at Mouse. "Our hope is that they won't be investigating too hard. They won't waste much resources on trying to discover who took out an outlaw MC."

Slick raises his hand. "They were storing hard drugs there. Probably part of a pipeline and had just taken delivery. The cops will be more focused on that. Hell, we did their work for them and saved the money they'd have spent on them doing prison time. I made sure to leave enough evidence before blowing that shit up."

Raising his head again from his laptop, Mouse nods. "Shoot out among themselves is one of the reasons they're putting forward."

My brow creases. "Anything that might connect Beef's injury with the Riders?"

"Nah. Medics bought the story his gun went off while he was cleaning it. Luckily Doc got the bullet out and disposed of it. Only the timing might have made the cops suspicious, but the hospital staff didn't see any reason to record it other than as an accident."

Thank fuck for that.

But I'm still worried there may be a weak link. "What about the women. Can they be trusted to keep quiet?" I know Red got them out of state, but it's still a worry.

Blade grins. "They will if they know what's good for them."

A glare from the prez stops the enforcer continuing. "They were bemused, just grateful to be free as they'd given up all hope of rescue. Red's keeping an eye on them, but he doesn't think they'll cause problems." He looks to his right. "Peg, I know why you're worried. And there's nothing more I want than to run a clean club. But when we're threatened we are going to retaliate. It does bother me that it was easy for Chaos to believe we were weak and wouldn't have put up much of a fight. Or that I'd lost control of the other chapters."

Peg frowns, but raises his chin. "Have to agree as sergeant-at-arms, that's a bad position for us to be in. We earn our money clean, but we're always going to do what's necessary to protect the club."

"While we're talkin' about protectin' the club, I want to talk about the sweet butts." Prez glances at me. "Jill should never have been able to put us in the position she had. All our plans almost went south because of one club whore. Rock, did you know she had feelin's for you?"

"Yeah, Prez, I did. That's why I stopped fuckin' her. Never thought she'd take it as far as she did though."

Drummer wipes his hand down his face and tugs at his greying beard. "Any other sweet butts getting ideas above their station?"

There's a general shaking of heads.

"Jill's been causin' problems going way back. Challengin' the old ladies," Wraith observes.

"So she should have been out on her ass long ago," Drum says sharply. His eyes narrow as he looks from one man to another. "I don't want to get into this position again. If a sweet butt is latchin' onto a brother, or getting above herself, I want to know about it. I'll shut that shit down fast."

"Sweet butts learn too much," Marvel says. "Can't cut one loose if they leave with bad feelin's. You suggestin' we take them out?"

Drummer bangs his fist on the table. "I'm suggestin' I put the fear of God into them and set them straight."

"Jill's dead," I observe. "Prez, in the end she died protectin' me. Sweet butts have a loyalty to the club, and when it counted she showed it."

"She almost got you killed, Rock."

Yeah, she did. But in the end she didn't. "Just sayin, Prez, when it mattered she did have my back."

It was perhaps not the right analogy, as my back starts to sting and throb, and the winces and grimaces suggest my brothers all know what I'm thinking.

Though none of them can know where my thoughts go after that. To the one woman who certainly didn't stand up, or wait, for me.

"Talking about the sweet butts," Viper begins. "I had a chat with Allie. She's distraught that she was taken in by Jill. Knew at the time she shouldn't be spillin' what she knew, but Jill, well, we all know what a bitch she was."

"And?" Prez queries.

"Jill called herself head whore. I'm suggestin' we make that an official title and give it to Allie. Then she can keep the other bitches in line."

Prez's eyes widen, and he looks around the table. "Get them to police themselves, so to speak."

Viper lifts his chin. "That's what I was thinkin'."

"She get a pay rise?" Blade is grinning. "Extra cock?"

The chuckles that follow together with other lewd suggestions make me fucking glad to be back with my club.

CHAPTER 19

Becca

What are you still doing here, Becca? I'm out of the woods now. Doctors say I'm well on the mend."

"Wouldn't you be lonely without me?" I smile at him, pleased to see he's looking tons better. The greyness has gone from his face, his temperature has come right down. He seems to have fought the infection off, and they're keeping him in another day or so just as a precaution.

He presses the button to move the bed higher and reaches out his hand to take mine. "You know I've enjoyed you keeping me company, but you've got to start living your own life, girl, and hell, we both know that won't be with me. You've got another man to get back to."

"Rock doesn't want me." I turn my head away, not wanting him to see the hurt in my eyes. It's not the first time we've had this discussion.

Beef sighs. "You won't know what he's thinkin' if you're spendin' all your time here with me. You've got to stop hidin' away and need to give him a chance. Go after something *you* want for once, Becca."

My lips press together before I reply, "What do I know about him, Beef? Only that he's made it pretty clear he wants nothing to do with me." I'm still trying to convince myself what I feel for the man who'd been so rude was only an attraction brought on by circumstances. I suspect Beef knows I've been unsuccessful.

Shaking his head, Beef won't give up. "I've no fuckin' idea what's up with the both of you. Prez seemed convinced you were Rock's girl, and you, whatever you say, are attracted to him. You might not admit the words, but your actions speak volumes. That you were prepared to do what it took to save his life. He's hurtin' now, maybe not thinkin' straight. If you keep runnin' from him you'll never have a chance to show him you're interested."

Every time Rock's turned up to see Beef I've made an excuse to make myself scarce. Hanging out in the cafeteria until he departs. "Can we drop it? Rock helped me out, I returned the favour. It's settled and done." Frowning, I add, "I'm just sorry you got hurt in the process."

"Nah, don't worry about that." He fixes his gaze on me, then rolls his eyes. "I give up. If you insist on hidin' here, then keep an invalid entertained. Tell me about yourself, Becca. And how you got mixed up with that fucker Hawk in the first place."

Leaning back in the chair, I stretch my hands up over my head, flexing my shoulders while I pull my thoughts together. My brow knits together as I think back.

"My parents wanted a big family, but they ended up with just me. I had to become everything they wanted."

"You didn't have a good childhood?"

"I wasn't abused or mistreated. I was given everything material that I needed, but let's just say they were old-fashioned in many ways. Both only children themselves, I had no aunts, uncles, or cousins. The only people I knew were folks belonging to the church that they attended."

"Hawk's church?"

"Not until I was thirteen. That's when he became the pastor. My parents didn't like the old pastor, thought he was too lenient. Were even thinking of changing to another church until Hawk came along. I suppose you could say they were looking to choose the God who fell in line with their views. But that's all I ever knew. Home and church."

I stare across the room, my eyes seeing nothing that's in front of me as memories go through my head. "Hawk suited them down to the ground. They wanted to hear about fire and brimstone being brought down on the heads of sinners, not about how easy it was to repent. That's what they got with Hawk. I was thirteen when I first met him. He waited until I was legal before he made his move."

"Fuck. Didn't your parents see anything wrong with that?"

"My parents, Beef, you have to understand, had accepted it was God's will that they weren't going to have any more children. They wanted to do what was best for me. If I acted like a normal teenager, they thought I was unruly. If I rebelled, wanted to go out, they wouldn't permit it. I wasn't even allowed to go to the mall on my own. Hawk provided them with the ideal answer. A God-fearing man who'd take me off their hands. My marriage would be a continuation of their religious upbringing."

"Jesus."

I'm still staring at nothing. "I certainly had no leeway with Hawk. As well as his unwilling sexual partner, I was his unpaid assistant. He taught me about the job he wanted me to do, and exactly how he wanted me to do it. At first I had naïve hopes from my marriage. I was free from the restrictions my parents placed on me at least, even if the physical demands Hawk made on me were unwelcome. I was determined to do the best that I could. In the beginning I saw nothing wrong in the minute instructions as to how he wanted his paperwork sorted. Any letters had to be laid out in a particular way. I just thought he was fastidious.

"His need for control flowed out into his, and my, personal life. Not only was I given times I should be working, but he gave me a routine including when I was to get up or go to bed. He even insisted on choosing the clothes that I should wear. Except pants. Pants were forbidden in his house.

"I was to be available to him at all times, I quickly found. If one of the parishioners invited me to a lady's afternoon, for example, he'd come up with a reason why I shouldn't go." I risk a look at Beef, his eyes have opened wide.

"One day, Beef, soon after our marriage, I didn't do my work quite right. When Hawk reached for a letter the pile fell onto the floor." My face reddens as I recall that horrible night. "He's big, strong, and could easily overpower me. And he did. He pushed me down over the desk, pulled up my skirt, pulled down my panties, and spanked my bare ass. Hard. I literally couldn't sit afterwards. Then he, he…"

Beef's expression shows he'd completed the sentence for himself. "Why didn't you get out of there, then?" Beef rasps.

"I did." My voice starts to break. "My mother didn't see anything wrong in the way I was being treated. You see, a pastor always knows best."

"You went back."

"Hawk turned up to collect me. My father, who'd just returned from work, horrified to find me there, shook his hand, apologising for my behaviour. He told me to try harder at my marriage and not be a disappointment to them."

"Fuck."

"I was torn, Beef. Deep down I knew what he'd done to me was wrong. On the other hand, I couldn't fail at my marriage. My parents were proud I was married to the pastor, it was something they could boast about around town. That they censored me, and not him, made me wonder if it was me at fault. So, yes, I went back. But what else could I do?"

"Don't tell me. The spankings got worse."

215

I nod. "And the sex got more brutal. If I complained he'd tell me it was what God wanted. That as a good God-fearing woman I shouldn't expect to enjoy it."

"For fuck's sake." Beef looks disgusted. "You were completely trapped. Friendless. And I presume your parents continued to take his side?" As his face darkens I can tell he's becoming angry on my behalf. I glance at his reddened face in worry. He's supposed to be resting, not getting riled up.

"He couldn't do anything wrong in Mom and Dad's eyes. Nor in his parishioners'. Let's change the subject, Beef. Let's talk about something different."

His head moves from side to side. "Finish it, Becca. Tell me how he came to be put away."

I sigh, but his eyes don't waver from mine. Deciding to be brief, I tell him what I'd told Drummer.

"He must hate you," Beef observes. "That's why he let the Chaos Riders treat you so badly."

I tilt my head to the side. "If I was to guess, the instructions he left would have been not to touch me, to keep me until he got out. That's when he'd deal with me himself."

Stretching forward, Beef takes hold of my hand. "Satan's Devils are gonna sort this for you. Make it so you never have to worry about him again."

"Can't do anything for another couple of years," I observe.

One side of Beef's mouth turns up as if he knows something I don't. "I'm gonna have a word with Drummer."

Despite the determination in Beef's voice I know there won't be anything they can do. Hawk's safe in prison. All I can do is disappear right out of the state. Only problem with that, I've got no money and nowhere to go. That's what makes the situation with Rock so upsetting, and why Beef is right, I am hiding out here as I no longer feel welcome on the compound. Rock's home with his brothers, and his continued disinterest in me makes me feel like an interloper.

"You in touch with your parents?" Beef asks, out of the blue.

"No. Hawk will have concocted some story for them and his congregation, and, Beef, they love their pastor so much they've made excuses for him. They'll expect me to be waiting for him when he comes out. They trust him to take good care of me. In their eyes, and they're probably right, I couldn't take care of myself. If they find out where I am they'll see it as their duty to get word to him."

"Keep away from them, Becca. Fuck, I don't know how people like him do it. But it wouldn't be the first time a man of God has got away with sinning. It makes him human, I suppose. But the person you've described to me sounds more like a monster." He pulls a face. "You reckon you were the only one he was fuckin'?"

I've thought about it, admitting the truth only once I was out of his clutches. "I doubt it. The times he used to come home smelling of perfume made me suspicious. But when I asked he said he'd been consoling a lonely widow or wife whose husband had deserted her."

"I bet he had." Beef scoffs.

Our conversation is interrupted by a knock on the door and someone entering. I bend down and pick up my bag when I see that it's Rock, and he's scowling at me.

"Hey, Rock, Brother. Good to see you." Beef holds out his fist, Rock bumps it with his. "When you go back to the compound, take Becca with you, will you? She needs a good night's rest, and she's not getting that here. I'm well enough I no longer need someone with me all the time."

I glare at Beef. I like him, like our conversations. And to be truthful, here I feel safe when not surrounded by all the members of his club. "I don't mind staying with you. I thought you liked the company, Beef."

"I love your company, Becca. But you need to look after yourself too. I'll be out of here and back at the compound soon enough. Until then, Rock will look out for you."

The man given that responsibility looks horrified, his eyes flicking to me, then to Beef. It's not long before he voices his objection, and when he does it's through gritted teeth. "I'm on the bike, Brother. I don't take bitches on the back."

Beef raises an eyebrow. "Not even Becca?" he asks incredulously.

"Especially not her," Rock spits out.

The blood drains from my face at his blatant declaration. There's nothing else for me to do but leave them, and with as much dignity as I can muster. Leaning over, I place a chaste kiss to Beef's forehead and tell him, "I'll see you soon."

"Hey, Becca," Rock calls out, stopping me just as I reach the door. "I'll call a prospect to give you a lift back. Stay in the cafeteria and he'll meet you there."

CHAPTER 20

Rock

T hat was cruel, Brother." Beef's narrowed eyes are giving me a full-on stare packed with censure, the lines on his forehead showing his lack of understanding. He should know better than anyone else.

"Put a bitch up behind you and they start to get ideas," I explain, feeling I shouldn't need to. I've got the answer to one question at least. Beef is just fucking her, he's not serious. Otherwise he wouldn't want to see her on the back of another man's bike.

Beef shakes his head. "I get it you're hurtin', Rock. Shit, the state of your back, I'm surprised to see you ridin' at all. But fuck, even so, it's not like you to be so direct and hurtful."

"If she's got ideas about me it's best she forgets them fast." I don't want a woman who can bed hop so easily.

Beef rolls his eyes. "Rock, man. There's something fucked up about all this. The way she talked about you... Seems she misunderstood the situation. I thought you and her would be good together. She *likes* you."

My jaw feels tense as I reply. "Heard she likes a lot of people. You givin' me your seconds now, Beef?"

His face goes red, his mouth opens and shuts, and it's a few seconds before he gets out, "What the fuck?"

I sit down on the seat still warm from Becca's ass. "Just drop it, okay? I came to see how you were doing. I don't want to talk about *her*."

Beef pulls himself up. I can tell the effort it causes him. "Not lettin' you get away with that, *Brother*. You can fuckin' explain yourself."

For some reason I point at him and the door. "It's plain to see. You had something with her, and it's still going on."

"I had something with her?" If Beef was fit and well, his tone would have me questioning my sanity in staying close by.

"She stayed in your room. You slept together."

This time Beef manages to pull himself away from the supportive pillows. I feel guilty as he grimaces, but my features are set, and I'm not backing down. With a surprising amount of strength in his voice he growls, "Yes, she slept in my bed. Because two fuckers from Vegas thought she was club property. Scared the fuck out of her when they wouldn't accept her word she wasn't. What did you expect me to do? Leave her alone to worry? I watched over her, that's all." He leans forward, his forefinger pointing at me. "I. Did. Not. Fuck. Her."

My best friend doesn't lie. A look at the intensity in his eyes has me immediately believing him. "Well, if you didn't, plenty of others did. Guess she wanted the chance to enjoy her freedom…"

"How long have we known each other, Rock?" Beef snaps out, his eyes blazing.

Surprised at the question and the force he put into asking it, I automatically answer. "Twelve, fourteen years?"

"Sixteen fuckin' years," he corrects me, almost shouting. "And in all that time, Rock, I never took you for a stupid man."

I jerk back. "What the fuck are you talkin' about?"

Looking at me as though I've lost my mind, he continues. "That girl was in a terrible state when she arrived on the compound, weak as a fuckin' kitten. Fuck, she still ain't right. That's why I wanted you to take her back to the compound. Girl can still barely stand on her feet. If you do nothing else for me, you make sure she starts takin' care of herself. No, let me finish." He holds up his hand while giving a good impression of Drummer's death stare. "She wasn't in a state to fuck any brother, even if she wanted to. And the way she reacted to Petty and Roller showed she'd no fuckin' inclination neither."

But I was given the information. "Jill said…"

"Jill? *Jill?* You're takin' the word of a whore who did her best to get you killed over mine and Becca's? You ever stop to think she might have had her own agenda? Fuck, Rock. I thought you'd know better than that."

My eyes narrow. I hadn't stopped to think Jill might have been lying. My experience with women hasn't been great, my own mother cheated on my father, the argument about that probably causing the accident that killed them. Beef's got a point, Jill perhaps wasn't the best source of information. But then again… "She was in bed with you, Beef. I saw it myself."

Beef's eyes roll to the ceiling then back down again. "She was only giving me the same comfort as I gave to her. Nothing sexual involved. I don't have the hots for her, and she's none for me."

I stand. Having to rapidly reverse everything I thought about Becca makes my head spin. "I liked her, Beef. Even through how she was being treated, they didn't break her."

"She's strong, she's had to be." He nods at the door as though she was still standing there. "What she's been through… She had no chance with Hawk, he targeted her, made her dependant on him. Isolated her. She became nothing more than his fuckin' sex slave by the sound of it."

I go to speak, he stops me again. "She barely knows how to look after herself, Rock. But she's fuckin' trying. Shit, she's only just got used to choosin' her own clothes and what food to eat. Hawk controlled her, told her what to do, think, and believe. She's so fuckin' used to followin' instructions, she was terrified when Petty and Roller were pressurin' her. She hadn't a clue how to respond. That's why she's been hidin' here with me. She's frightened to return to the compound. I'm not there. You've made it clear what you think of her. She feels alone and unprotected. Fuckin' around is the last thing on her mind."

What? It seems I don't know anything about the woman I helped escape. The woman who's taken root in my brain. The woman I dismissed as a whore. *Becca.* "Fuck." I run my hands through my hair. "I've fucked up, haven't I?"

Beef nods toward the door. "If you go now you might still be able to catch her."

I might. But the things that I've said, the way I've acted toward her… Would she even want to ride back behind me? I've already called the prospect, he'll be on his way to pick her up. I'll finish my visit with Beef, then go back to the compound. Drawing my hands down my face I realise exactly how badly I've handled this. *Will I ever be able to repair the damage?*

"What can I say to her, Beef? From what you say, she was with a man who treated her as his property. I took one look at her and assumed she'd put out for anyone who wanted her."

Beef closes his eyes, and in that second before he opens them again I can see he looks tired. But when he speaks he gives me food for thought. "I don't know what she was thinkin' when Petty and Roller boxed her in. I tell you this, Brother. Hawk raped her throughout her marriage. She's not likely to jump into anyone's bed."

Raped her?

My mouth drops open as Beef continues. "She was taught that a good girl submits and gets no enjoyment."

What the fuck? Blame crashes down on me. What I accused her of is so far from the fucking truth it's unbelievable.

"He beat her too. Punished her by spankin's which were not erotic."

I have to sit down. Every word Beef is telling me emphasises how badly I fucked up.

Beef gives me a moment to start to re-evaluate everything I've been thinking about her, before asking, "We've been friends a long time, Brother. So let me ask you. You haven't bothered about a girl fuckin' your brothers before. Shit, we've shared enough together. Why did you react so badly, Rock, to the idea she'd been sleepin' with me?"

His question pulls me up and gets me to start thinking— honestly for once. Resting my chin on my hands, I decide to share my thought process with him. "I don't know what it is about her. Don't even know her, so it seems crazy to say some- thing in her calls to something in me." I don't wait for his response, just quickly check he's not laughing. "I dreamt of coming back to the compound, of explorin' our connection. Half afraid the hell I was livin' in was making me build it up into something it wasn't. So when Jill gave me her version of the truth, I leapt at it. It gave me the excuse I needed. I didn't need to analyse these weird fuckin' feelin's anymore."

"Tell her," Beef advises. "Just tell her straight. Tell her you've got feelin's for her and were afraid she wasn't as perfect as you believed. She needs someone like you, Rock. Even if it's just as a friend. Someone on her side. And someone to end Hawk for good."

"Mouse is investigatin' him," I say absently, still thinking of Becca and how I've wronged her.

"He got anywhere?"

"Not that I've heard. But he wouldn't necessarily tell me." I pick at one of my fingernails as I admit, "I've made it clear I want fuck all to do with her."

He sighs. "Best you correct that then. Be in her corner, Rock, won't you? I like the girl, I like her a lot." His face turns to me, and he growls, "Like a fuckin' sister." I hold my hands up to show he doesn't have to make his point again. "Promise me you'll look after her. Even if there's nothing between you. She needs someone in her corner. Now scat. Isn't there somewhere you ought to be?"

He means I need to go to Becca. Try and make this right. Show her she's got someone to lean on. "Yeah. If I can get her to listen to me. To forgive me. I promise you, Beef. Even if she wants nothin' to do with me after the shit way I've been treatin' her, I'll have her back."

Beef had long since collapsed back down on the pillows. With my agreement to go to Becca, any energy he had seems to have left him. One more thing I need to feel guilty about, I've overtired him. He can hardly keep his eyes open, so as I had when I entered the room, I bump my fist against his.

"Shiny side up," he mumbles, already half asleep.

"Dirty side down," I respond.

I check the cafeteria before leaving, but Becca's not inside. Starting my job of looking out for her, knowing that she's nervous of the very thing I've been accusing her of—being too close to my brothers—I call the prospect and get his confirmation that she is indeed almost back home. Going to my bike, I sit astride it, then pause before starting the engine, knowing I've no idea how this conversation is going to go. But there's only one acceptable ending as far as I'm concerned, Becca beneath me in my bed. *But fuck.* From what Beef had said, Becca will have a very different interpretation of what I want from her. I'm aiming too high. Friends. We'll be friends. Give it time. See where the road takes us.

Now anxious to see her, I push the speed limits, reaching the compound in record time. Backing into my spot outside the clubhouse, I then have another moment of *what the fuck am I going to say?* before I kick down the stand and leave my bike.

First thing, I need to find her and not allow myself to be distracted. Tempting as it is to take the coward's way out and put things off, I bypass Slick with just a wave, and in answer to his enquiry tell him Beef's doing good. Inside the clubroom my eyes search for her, but she's nowhere around. *Is she, as Beef seemed to suggest, scared and hidin' in her room?* I don't like the thought of her licking the wounds that I caused in private. There's a strange feeling in my gut which I can't put a name to at the thought having sent her away, she's alone and hurting. *She likes me.* I all but told her to fuck off.

Women's voices come from the kitchen, so I walk that way. I stand in the doorway unnoticed as my eyes find the woman I'm searching for, with a pile of peeled and a few remaining unpeeled potatoes in front of her. At first there's relief that she's not brooding on her own, then my analytical brain takes over and I think about the sight in front of me. Far from being the flirtatious girl looking for fun which my mind had conjured up in my too easy acceptance of Jill's lies, I'm seeing a woman strong enough to shrug off my insults.

As I watch and observe, she finishes her task. "Sophie, that's all done. What shall I do next?"

A simple enough question, but one which after my talk with Beef, I interpret in a different way. *She's never been allowed to make decisions for herself.* I regret to say my cock twitches at the thought of some instructions I could ask her to follow. Ignoring his input, I lean against the door jamb and try to come up with a plan to help her. First, though, I'll have to get this difficult conversation out of the way.

"I'm not sure what we should do next, Becca? What do you suggest?" Sophie smiles at her and I feel like I've been kicked. *The women know.* And they're tryin' to help her. They're doing what should have been my job. Giving her support and encouragement.

Before Becca can do more than smile at Sophie gratefully, I enter the room. As though she senses me, she looks up. Our eyes meet. Instantly she looks away.

I find my voice. "Becca, can I have a word?"

She glances up again, her brow furrowing. "Is Beef okay?"

"He's fine," I confirm. "I need to talk to you."

"You go, Becca. We've got this." Giving her no choice, Sophie scoops up the peeled potatoes and shoos her toward me.

Flustered, as though she doesn't want to cause a scene, she comes over. "I don't think we've got anything to say to each other," she hisses as she passes me. "Please leave me alone, I think you've said more than enough already."

I'm not letting her go without having my say. She's halfway across the clubroom by the time I catch up. Putting my arm around her, I steer her toward the crash rooms. This time of day they'll probably be empty. When she tries to pull back I tighten my hold on her, halt and look down into her worried, scared face. "Give me five minutes, Becca. Please. That's all I ask. Five minutes to *talk*."

I think it was the please that did it, along with my emphasis, as she doesn't protest again. When I see a door open I push her inside. It's a room the brothers use for fucking. There's a bed and very little else in it. But it will give us the privacy I want.

She doesn't sit down, her eyes focusing on something on the floor. Being what this room is, I'm hoping it isn't a used condom.

I take a step closer, she raises her hands as if to stop me, gives a quick glance at my face, then speaks hurriedly, as though the faster she talks the speedier will be her retreat. "I didn't have a chance to thank you properly for enabling my escape."

"I didn't thank you either." As I bring myself nearer, she steps back and comes up against the bed. "You took one hell of a risk to get me out." The thought that she could have been killed trying to save me gives me a chill. I can't believe what an ass I've been, talking to her the way I have.

She shrugs as if it wasn't anything. But it was. She must have been petrified, having to put her trust in Drummer, a man she'd only just met, to ensure she'd get out alive.

"I'm an asshole." I don't try to sweeten it. "There's no way I can ever apologise enough. I shouldn't have said any of the things I did to you." I've caught her attention, so I continue without giving her a chance to speak. "You had me from the moment I saw you, Becca. The very first fuckin' moment. Other women would have been cryin' and screamin' kept chained in that cellar. But you? No, you showed your strength from the very first time I came down."

She shakes her head dismissively. "The last thing I am is strong, Rock. I'm anything but. I did my crying and screaming a long time before I met you. It didn't do any good, so I stopped."

To my mind that doesn't mean she's not brave, just that, unlike me, she's not stupid.

I raise my hand to touch her face, she flinches away. I decide to lay it all on the line. "Becca, it broke my heart to see you kept that way. I knew I had to get you out, get you somewhere you could be protected."

"And you did," she puts in quickly. "Thank you for that."

"Darlin', listen to me, please? Yeah, I wanted you to be safe. But what kept me going in that fuck-up of a place was the thought of you being here when I got out. Fuck knows why, but

I couldn't stop thinkin' about you." She looks so doubtful, so unbelieving, I know I haven't got a chance unless I get this all out. "I know we don't know much about each other, but once the thought got into my head I couldn't get rid of it. I've never wanted that special woman on the back of my bike, but I went to sleep dreamin' of you there."

Her eyes snap to mine. "Well you certainly didn't jump at the chance earlier."

Momentarily I close my eyes. I deserve that. The memory of my rudeness causing me actual pain. Stepping past her, I sit on the bed and pat a spot on the mattress beside me. "Sit, please?"

She scrutinises me for a moment as though suspecting a trap, then shrugs and sits down. There's a good foot between us.

I swallow before speaking. "I've never wanted a bitch to call mine. Last thing on my mind. Saw my brother's findin' old ladies and laughed at them. That was before I met you."

She puts one knee up on the bed and turns to face me, her eyes hardened. "Whether you want me or don't want me, or if you'll ever be able to make up your mind, I've got news for you. You don't just decide you want a woman, *a bitch* in your language. Hawk decided he wanted me, and I had no say in it."

I've noticed one thing. She's not as meek with me as she is with everyone else. Maybe there is a chance for us.

I put my finger to her lips, which makes them snap shut. "I know, I'm puttin' this badly. Of course I didn't know if the feelin' was mutual. I had hopes it might be, but then you might just have felt gratitude toward me because I helped you escape."

She stays silent when I want her to speak. Want her to confirm I'm not making a fool of myself by laying my feelings on the line. Shaking my head slightly, I look away. "Look, Becca. I was screwed up in my head, alright? I might have been overthinkin', assumin' my feelings for you were reciprocated. You were out of sight, but not out of mind. I wasn't sure what to do with the overwhelmin' desire to see you again." I break off, replaying events in my head, determined to hold nothing back from her. "Then Jill arrived. Chaos was suspicious. He sent us both to the cellar to soften us up. While we were there all I could think of was you, so relieved when she said you'd made it back to the compound. I was strung up, already hurtin'. But if I closed my eyes, I could see you."

I feel warm skin against mine. *Fuck me, she's holding my hand.* I enjoy the sensation while I can, knowing she's more likely going to be hitting me in a minute.

My voice is even. Unemotional. "Jill wouldn't shut up. When I asked about you, she told me you'd started fuckin' my brothers. Beef, my best friend, being one of them."

She gasps. "Rock... You believed her? No one better than you knew I was in no state to do that, even if I had the inclination."

If I hadn't been swamped with feelings of jealousy I might have played a different hand. "Look, it wasn't good timin'. I got so mad. But even if you were, I had no reason to be jealous. You hadn't promised me anything. Any relationship we had was all in my head."

She stands up, her hand covering her mouth.

I get to my feet. "Becca, when I saw you in bed with Beef, it all seemed true. I'm sorry I didn't stop to ask you, or Beef."

"I haven't fucked anyone. Why would I want to?" The words come out forcefully, even staccato. "Beef protected me when I thought I was going to be raped. When he was ill I just comforted him the same way he'd comforted me."

"I know." I raise my voice. "I fuckin' know. And I'm so sorry. So damn sorry."

She's not going to forgive me.

CHAPTER 21
Becca

I've listened to Rock. Heard what he has to say and have done some reading between the lines myself. He's apologised, but what he hasn't quite admitted is the obvious motivation that lay behind his cruel rejection.

The pain in his eyes shines through as though he fears my response to his heartfelt plea will be negative. I step forward, my hand trembling as I raise it, and place my palm gently against his cheek.

I breathe in deep and take a leap. "You were jealous." My voice shakes as much as my fingers touching his skin.

His hand covers mine, not letting me move it away, and he leans into my touch. "Yes. I was jealous," he confirms, his own tone uncertain.

"Hawk used to get jealous," I start, softly. "He'd punish me if another man even looked at me. Would say I encouraged them."

Instantly his fingers curl around mine and tighten. "I wanted…want you, Becca." His stare becomes intense. "I had thoughts of you being my woman. I didn't want to share you with anyone else. If you ever agreed to be with me, yeah, I'd need you to be mine, and only mine. I wouldn't want anyone else to touch you." He sounds too much like Hawk. I start shaking my head, but Rock hasn't finished. "Look at you?" He huffs a short laugh. "Yeah, they can look. If you were mine I'd be so fuckin' proud that I'd got what another man's not. And if they can't keep their eyes off you, that's on them, not you. I'm not Hawk, sweetheart. I'd never hurt you. Say you'll be mine, Becca."

He's moving too fast. He wants me to be his. Hawk regarded me as his possession, there was no pleasure in that. I don't know who I am, starting to feel my way to learning my own needs and wants. I've seen the property patches the old ladies wear proudly, and have wondered why such strong, independent women allow themselves to be owned by their men. To me it's a prison without bars.

He's waiting for an answer. I can't ever give a man custody over me again. "Rock," my voice breaks as I try to speak. "There's no words to tell you how much I yearn for you in ways I don't understand. But I can never be someone's property. If that's where this is going, I'd rather part as friends now."

He reaches for my other hand and brings them both together between us, his large, strong hands cupping mine. Staring down for a moment, he then raises his eyes and gazes at me intensely. "I can't tell where this will be going, Becca. I never thought I would ever be thinkin' of makin' someone my ol' lady." He shakes his head before going on. "But you've got me twisted up inside. Jealous? Fuck yeah I was. It was that which made me so spiteful to you. Takin' an ol' lady? Well, fuck me. All I know is with you the idea excites me instead of scarin' the shit out of me." As his fingers gently caress mine he adds, "I can't promise where this is going. But I don't think it impossible that one day I'll be asking you to wear my patch."

I pull my hands away. "I wouldn't be able to do that, Rock." It breaks something inside to know I'm throwing away the chance of being with him. But I can't allow myself to be tied in any way with a man with the same views on women as Hawk.

It's his turn to touch my face, stroking me gently, then touching my shortly shorn hair, his eyes sharpening as he runs his fingers over it, then relaxing again. "Becca, there are things you need to understand. Property is something to be treasured, protected. To give your life for. If I ask you to wear my patch, I'm not owning you. It's the opposite, you're owning me. I'd be giving myself over to you, committing to you. It isn't a way that I'd use to control you. I'd nurture and support you in everything you wanted to do."

The way he puts it sounds different. Hawk had always taken, never given. If I'd tried to touch him the way I'd touched Rock, he'd have ripped my hand away as I hadn't asked for permission, or it hadn't been something he'd instructed me to do. I'd sneaked glances at Rock before, but never have had the opportunity to take the time to examine him properly. He's tall, probably a whole foot taller than me. His short hair and well-trimmed beard suits him, enabling me to scan his features, his brown eyes which now have creases around them, his nose slightly crooked, his mouth sensual and inviting.

"I'm not being fair on you, am I?" He raises his hand, hovering it close to my face. Then, as I'd touched him, he touches me. "You've just got free of Hawk, and now I'm puttin' pressure on you. What is it they say, if you love someone set them free? Not sayin' I love you," he adds quickly. "Too early for that. I wanna fuck you, sure. Love? Ain't loved a bitch before so don't even know if I'd recognise it. But I do know I'm pushing you too fast. You should be enjoyin' your freedom, not puttin' up with my wants and needs."

There are a few things wrong with what he's said. I enlighten him. "I'm scared. I don't know how to function alone, Rock. Never had to. Never was allowed to. And secondly, I'm not free of Hawk. I'm still married to him." I look down at my feet.

Rock sighs. "You're not wearing his ring on your finger."

Almost surprised, forgotten I'd taken it off, I look at my hand. "I hated it being there. It was a reminder of him."

"A symbol. Like all the other trappings of marriage. It's only your signature on a piece of paper binding you to him."

"It's not," I contradict. "I said my vows before God."

"Vows?" he sneers. "You wrote vows? Said them and meant them?"

My teeth worry my lip as I consider his words. "The vows were handed to me. I just read them. But I said them, Rock. In church."

"You think your God would hold you to them? To something you were forced to do? With the result you ended up being abused and hurt? And fuck it, with a man who let the Chaos Riders treat you as they did? You think your God would condone that? Fuck, woman, I'm glad I'm not a believer if that's what you think."

"Sometimes *I* don't believe in Him," I whisper.

"Not questioning your faith, Becca. Just that the teaching you had was twisted." He stares at me for a moment. "You need a divorce, Becca. But that's not going to happen fast, let's be realistic. The first step is to believe in your head that you no longer belong to him. You've no thoughts of reconciliation or going back. In the eyes of the law it may be committing adultery, but no one with an ounce of compassion would blame you for taking something for yourself for once in your life."

Wrapping my arms around myself, I think on his words. Not for the first time I know I've used my marital status as armour. Rock needs a better explanation. "Leaving my marriage to one side, I don't want to lead you on, Rock. But I'm not like Sophie or Sam, or any of the other girls." I feel tears prick in my eyes. "I can't be in a relationship with you or anyone. I never want a man to touch me like that again. I don't enjoy…"

"Babe." He silences me with just one word. Shushed, I shut up, which gives him the chance to examine me. After a moment stretches out he nods knowingly, then gives me an instruction. "Kiss me."

Kiss him?

"Becca, babe." His hand softly brushes my cheek, a barely there caress. "You trusted me, right? When I helped you escape? You reached for that tree and took hold, knowin' I wasn't going to let you drop."

I had.

"Trust me now."

"Why?"

He shrugs. "Just go with it, okay? If you don't like it, we can stop. You're in control."

This man must have kissed hundreds of women before, while I've only kissed one man. That was only a peck on the cheek when he demanded I showed my allegiance to him. I retreat to safe ground. "I can't while I'm married to Hawk." But haven't I already betrayed my husband by even thinking about another man? Rock's given me something to consider. Do I owe loyalty to a man I hate? Who's hurt me and left me to suffer?

Another gentle touch of his fingers to my cheek proves he can read my mind when he asks, "Do you want to stay married to him, Becca?"

"Of course I don't," I scoff.

"Then we'll go and see Mouse. If it's a divorce you need to feel free, then we'll find out how to do it." Staring into my eyes, he says softly, "But even before that, you're not married, you're separated. You never wanted to be tied to him in the first place. You're committin' no crime by being with another man."

My teeth worry my lip, then I whisper the truth. "Hawk being locked up was the best thing that ever happened to me. Even though I was kept prisoner by the Chaos Riders. It meant I didn't have to suffer his attentions any more. Now I'm free, I don't want to be subjected to that again. Even by you. We can only be friends."

I don't know what reaction I expected from Rock. For him to get angry? Disappointed? What I didn't expect was for him to simply repeat his earlier instruction as if I'd said nothing at all.

"Kiss me, Becca."

Despite my protestations and that my mind remains adamant, my body starts leaning toward his. Quickly I pull back and ask one question. "Why? What would that prove."

"Oh, Becca. Sweetheart. You were never attracted to Hawk. There was no chemistry between the two of you. With us things might be different. You owe it to yourself to give it a try. I'm not asking you for more, just a kiss. An experiment if you like."

He's tempting me. As I stare at his lips butterflies make my stomach flutter as though he's awoken something long dormant. I have an overwhelming desire to see if he tastes as good as he looks. I move closer, then leaning forward again, gently give him an innocent kiss, just a peck, a brief meeting of our lips. As I draw back I see the corners of his mouth curve up. Emboldened, I do it again, this time not moving away.

Neither does he. Bravely reaching my hands up to his head, I pull him nearer so his mouth presses against mine and opens. Accepting the invitation, my tongue sweeps inside to explore, his own coming to meet mine, the soft tissue enticing as they slide sensually together. He tastes faintly of coffee, and there's a tinge of salt in the background. The smell of him surrounds me, the leather of his cut, the detergent in his clothes, the soap that he uses and his deodorant, breathing in each individually then combining them to give me the scent of a man.

He's stopped being passive. His hands slip around my back, gently supporting me and urging me yet even closer as his mouth starts to dominate mine.

Hawk never kissed me. That makes this my first kiss by a man. It's causing sensations that Hawk never aroused.

As feelings overtake me I lose myself, wanting more of him, needing him closer. I slide my hands down first to his shoulders, then around to his back. He hisses and breaks our connection.

My eyes fly open, my hand covers my mouth. "I'm so sorry."

He takes in a few deep breaths, then the creases around his eyes gradually disappear and he smiles. "It'll be tender for a while." Putting me at arms-length, his fingers stroke my bare arms as if he doesn't want to stop touching me. He looks ruefully down at his crotch. As my eyes follow the direction he's looking, I see a bulge pressing against the denim. Glancing up again he says ruefully, "I can't control myself around you."

Blushing, I look away. No one's ever told me I'm desirable before. For Hawk I was his convenient wife.

"Hey, what's up?" His hand gently moves my face back.

"I've never kissed a man before," I admit.

The muscles of Rock's face tighten. "What the fuck? Hawk fucked you, didn't he?" He shakes his head as though he might have misunderstood.

"Fuck's the right word. There was never any emotion or tenderness involved. God gave me to him to cope with his natural urges."

"God had fuck all to do with it."

I look away. Rock's right, and I think I'd always known that. But Hawk was a force to be reckoned with. I'd had nowhere to run, no means of escape. Everything I'd ever been taught told me Hawk was right.

Suddenly Rock has let me go. He spins around, his hands sweeping through his hair as he stands, resting his forehead against the wall, his back toward me, tension showing by the set of his shoulders. I get to my feet confused. Is he angry on my behalf, or is something else eating at him?

My hand reaches out, then I draw it back, remembering in time not to touch his back. "Rock?" I ask softly. "This is all new to me. Did I do something wrong?"

His face still turned away, he shakes his head. "You, Becca? Nah. Nothing at all. But I'm this close..." he holds up his thumb and forefinger a fraction of an inch apart, "to taking what you're not ready to give. Fuck, if just a kiss turns me rock hard in a flash, touching you, *tasting you* will drive me insane."

What should I do? The fluttering in my stomach has increased to a throbbing ache. "Rock?" My quiet entreaty has him turning around. When he looks down into my face I make myself meet his eyes. "I don't understand what you do to me, Rock. I don't know why I want to get closer to you. To hold you. To let you..."

His expression isn't cocky, it's almost pained. In a surprisingly sweet gesture for a biker, he takes hold of my hand and raises it to his lips. "We'll take this slow, Becca. I don't want to push you. But when you're ready, I promise you. You will be in my bed."

With wonder I realise the thought doesn't frighten me. Instead I'm considering what that would be like.

CHAPTER 22

Rock

I don't trust myself right now. Becca's got my cock so fucking hard it's pressing painfully against my zipper. I'm going to need to get myself somewhere private soon to take the matter in hand before my fucking balls explode. I'm not even sure what it is about her that affects me so much.

I affect her too. She doesn't understand what her body's telling her. Has she really never been turned on before? While I want to throw her down on the bed and thrust my cock into her, make her understand how good I can make her feel, I know it's too fast. What I can do is keep her at a simmer until she comes to me, begging for me to take her, to show her what making love should be about.

Making love? What the fuck am I thinking? I'm a biker, I don't make love. Wouldn't know where to start. Except, with Becca I'll have to give it a damn good try. Suddenly I feel the weight of responsibility on me. Another bad experience would send her running from men for the rest of her life. *No pressure there then.* It's got to be right. And the time isn't now.

Hawk never kissed her? He treated his wife the same way we treat our whores. No, worse than that. The way the Riders treated theirs. I'd lay good money down he never worried about her getting off. *Christ!* For a moment I wonder how he's doing in jail, hoping he's become some big man's bitch and is now finding out what it's like being on the receiving end. Wouldn't that be good?

But now I need to concentrate on Becca. If I stand here much longer with a rock-hard cock I'll be the one pressuring her. "Come on."

Her face turns up at me. She's still biting her lip. Her face is flushed, that pulse in her neck beating fast. *She wants me.* But she's scared.

"Let's go see Mouse."

The sudden relaxation of her facial muscles makes me realise I was right to put my own desires on the back burner. I've got to lead up to it gently, give her time to get used to the idea that she and I are now an item. I hold out my hand. She takes it.

Mouse is in his cave, but he's not the man I remember from before I swapped clubs, subtle changes perhaps not everyone else would notice except for his brothers. You still have to nego-tiate the fog of smoke as you step into his office—the club smoking ban hasn't extended to in here—and as usual there's a joint burning in the ashtray. The bank of monitors is as it always has been, and in fact, I think he's recently added to the number. His keyboard and laptop are open alongside him. On first impressions everything is the same.

But his eyes seem hooded, his expression wary as, still holding her hand, I pull Becca inside.

Mouse raises his chin toward me, but his eyes fix on Becca. "Just the person I wanted to see."

She glances up to me as if seeking permission, but I wave her to one of the chairs in front of Mouse's desk, taking the adjacent one for myself. "I want to be prepared, Mouse. While now may not be the right time to initiate things, Becca wants to know how to get a divorce."

He simply nods as though distracted. "I can look the process up. But now you're here, there's something I want to ask." He spins his laptop around so that Becca can see it, leans forward, and points a pen toward a plan on the screen.

She studies it for a moment, her face scrunching deliciously as she tries to convert the lines on the plan with an image in her head. After a moment, she nods. "Our church."

"It is," Mouse confirms. He clicks a couple of times, then points again. "What's this area used for?"

Becca brings herself closer, her brow furrowed in confusion. "That's wrong. What are these plans?"

"They're the originals submitted when the church was built about twelve years ago," Mouse tells us.

With a shake of her head Becca informs us, "Then they had to have changed it before starting work. There's never been a basement under the church. I'd have known about it. There's certainly no door, and no steps leading down. Inside or out."

Mouse and I exchange glances. That's a big area, and if Becca's wrong and it does exist, a fucking good place to hide something.

"Hawk was a pastor, Becca. Was there anything unusual about him? Anything that made you suspicious?"

Her lips press together as she thinks. I realise I'm starting to catalogue all the adorable expressions she makes. *I can't wait to see what she looks like when she comes.* Shit, there goes my cock again. Luckily Mouse is behind his desk and won't notice, else he'd give me some shit.

"He could have been, done, anything." Becca's sweet voice brings me back to the here and now. "It wasn't unusual for him to be out a lot, all times of the day and night. His excuse was that he was seeing parishioners for this or that, but he could have been anywhere."

Mouse is staring at me, and my eyes fix on his. I nod. Just because a man works for the church doesn't mean he's necessarily a good man. A good man doesn't buy a young wife, he doesn't fuck her any time that he wants, he doesn't beat a man half to death. Pastor Hawk has something else going on, I'd stake my life on that. What he is, or was until they caught up with him, is a man without a stain on his reputation.

I place my hand on Becca's arm. When she turns to look at me I ask, "Can you get us into the church?"

Again her brow creases, and she puts her hand to her forehead. Then, like the sun coming out, she smiles. "Unless someone's moved it, there's a spare key hidden for emergency use. I can show you where it is. We'll have to be careful nobody sees us."

"Go in after dark?" I direct my suggestion to Mouse.

"Sounds like a plan. Prez will probably want in on this."

"Reckon you're right. Why don't I go and update him while you talk to Becca about getting that divorce? Sooner she's free of Hawk the better. Oh, and Becca?" As I stand she looks up, her head tilted to one side. "You're not going anywhere near that church. You'll have to explain where the key is left." If anyone saw her with us, word could get back to Hawk who she's with. Who knows what other friends he might have and might prefer looking after her.

Mindful of Beef's warning, surreptitiously I check before leaving her alone with my brother. Becca isn't giving off any vibes that she's worried about staying with Mouse. I raise my chin toward him, silently requesting he looks after her. He gives me a nod of understanding back. With a clear conscience, I leave them alone and go next door to see Drum. Wraith's in with him, which kills two birds with one stone.

"Rock. How's your back?"

"As long as I don't lean hard on it, not too bad, Prez. Doc's still changing the dressings every day."

"Costing us a fuckin' fortune havin' him make home visits," Drum grumbles, but his eyes crease showing he truthfully doesn't give a damn. I reckon he believes he owes me, but he's wrong. This club has given me the best sixteen years of my life.

Wraith extends his fist and I bump it with mine. "I know I've said it before, but it's fuckin' good to have you back, Brother."

It feels damn good. There's not one day when I don't think of how different the Satan's Devils are to the now extinct Chaos Riders. But I'm here for a purpose. Quickly I bring Prez and VP up to date on what Mouse has discovered.

Prez gives me a sharp look once I've finished. "You pulled your head out your ass about Becca at last?"

Shifting awkwardly, and it's not down to the pain in my back, I give it to him straight. "I've been an asshole."

"Ain't that the truth, Brother. And good. I like that little girl. She's got guts. Proved that when she volunteered to sacrifice herself to get you out."

I hold out my hands, palms open. "What can I say, Prez? I believed some rubbish that came out of Jill's mouth. Shouldn't have done, but it is what it is. Got things turned around right in my head now. Gonna do what I can to make it up to Becca."

Now he nods and raises his chin toward Wraith, then his steely grey eyes find mine. "You remember Stub?"

The name's familiar. Scrunching my eyes closed, I think back, dredging up a memory from the depths of my mind. "He rode with the Wretched Soulz, didn't he? Must have been ten, twelve years ago?" As Drum smiles as though he's a teacher pleased with his favourite pupil, I continue to comb through what I know. "He murdered his ol' lady when he caught her cheating on him. Was pretty brutal about it if I'm recallin' it right. Got sent down for life, didn't he?"

"He did that." Drummer confirms my memory is correct. "Found out he's in the same pen as Hawk."

Knowing there has to be a reason for this history lesson, I wait for what's to come.

"Got a visit arranged to see him. You want to come along?"

"What you thinking, Prez? Think Stub could get to Hawk?"

Drum's eyes narrow. "I'm thinking he might be able to get us some information so we know what we're dealing with." Prez sits back in his chair, his hands steepled under his chin. "Things don't sit right with me. We've got a pastor with a violent streak who's capable of nearly killing a man. A pastor who has links with an outlaw MC to the extent they were happy keeping Becca locked down while he was inside. Now, I might not have much time for religion, but that doesn't sound like your normal man of the church to me."

Nor to me. "And that possible basement under the church which no one knows about?"

"No one?" Drum's eyebrow rises. "The good church goers possibly not. If it does exist, I'm fuckin' curious about what might be hidden there. And exactly who knows about it."

"I'd like to know too." Wraith's been quiet until now. "Might be nothing, Becca could be right, the plans were changed for some reason. But if she's wrong and we can find the entrance, might be very interestin'." He pauses, tapping his finger against his lips. "Rock, I know you don't want Becca anywhere near that place, but she's spent darn near half her life there. Might be useful to have her along."

"Wraith, I don't think..."

"VP's got a point, Rock. Bring her with us. Nothing's gonna happen to her with us there."

I don't like it. Don't like it at all. Girl's been through too much as it is. Don't want to distress her again, or fuck it, take her into a situation where someone might see her and recognise her. But her knowledge could be useful. On the other hand, I don't want to expose her to any risk. "I'm sorry, Prez, I don't like the idea."

Prez and the VP share a knowing look, which I don't understand, then Drummer says firmly, "Know you care for her, Rock. But you can't deny it will be easier if she comes along. She'll know the layout for one thing. We go tonight. You, obviously, Wraith, and myself."

"Might need more, Prez. Don't know what we're walkin' into." Wraith waves his hand toward me. "If it was Sophie I'd want to know we had enough men to keep her safe. Whatever we find there."

Prez nods. "Good point, VP. I'll see if Joker and Lady are up for it. Maybe Marvel too. Slick could be useful as well. We'll go in the trucks. Want to go in quiet."

I frown. "Any suspicions of what we might find, Prez?"

"Not a fuckin' clue, Brother. Just got the feel in my gut that something's not right."

I'm completely with him there.

While my gut tells me it's wrong to take Becca, I can understand why Drummer wants her along. Now I've just got to tell her.

She might have been kept sheltered from the world, but Becca's got an innate bravery. To my surprise, she hadn't made any protest when I contradicted myself and told her she was coming with us to Hawk's prior church after all. If she had appeared concerned I'd have gone back to the prez again. But it seems Becca can't do enough to help the club which has given her sanctuary, however she personally feels about it.

After dinner we leave. Becca is quiet on the drive up to Phoenix. When I put my arm around her she tenses, but then leans into me after a few moments, relaxing. It's then I realise she's had one hell of a day. The vile accusations I'd thrown at her, then our argument when I hoped she'd forgiven me. That kiss. And now this.

"Becca. Does the new pastor live near the church?" Drum calls from the front passenger seat.

"No, there's no houses near. It's quite isolated."

I catch Wraith's eyes in the rearview mirror. That only give's our suspicions more substance.

"And he's not the new pastor, only the temporary one until Hawk comes out."

"Fuckin' what?" I exclaim.

Becca shifts under my arm, then says, "He's been forgiven and promised his job back by the elders. They put it down to a temporary aberration. I don't know what he told them, but he even went up in the estimation of some of the men. He'll be returning as the pastor."

"Christ." It's probably an inappropriate term to use, but these upstanding citizens go down in my opinion. Just because they liked the way that he interpreted the Bible they'd forgive him anything.

Becca's speaking again. "I think this is a wild goose chase. If there really was a basement, everyone would know about it. I've all but lived in that church. From when I was a teenager, and even more while I was married to Hawk. Every Sunday, most days during the week too. There are no hidden doorways, nothing to find, I assure you."

"It's still worth checking out," Wraith calls over his shoulder before putting his eyes back on the road.

Not much more is said, and Becca is quiet as we drive up the 110 then arrive at the suburbs of Phoenix. Wraith's programmed the GPS so has no need for directions. Becca's hand goes to her face, and in the light from the streetlamps I see her chewing on her nails. Curling my fingers around her, I pull her hand down and squeeze it.

"You'll be fine," I murmur into her ear. "I'm not leaving your side for a second. Trust me, Becca."

"It brings back bad memories," she whispers back.

It's just a church. A modern building. But as I watch it loom in front of us I find I'm seeing it through Becca's eyes. If it wasn't for the beliefs of the people who worship here, she wouldn't have been tied to a man like Hawk with their blessing. Or be so cowed she doesn't know how to think for herself. Every Sunday she'd be here, listening to the man she hated spouting his sermon, knowing even her parents didn't support her. Fuck, the men with old ladies call their women property, but we worship at their feet. These churchgoers think a man holds dominion over his wife. Property in its basest sense. The patriarchal view that a man makes all the decisions, his wife existing only to serve him. Under my arm, Becca seems to shrink.

"Do you still believe in God?" I wonder aloud.

She glances at me, then at the building ahead and shudders. "God, I think, yes. The church, no."

I squeeze her tight, only letting her go when the truck rolls to a stop a hundred yards away from the structure we've come to explore, wondering whether it will really give up any secrets tonight.

Or whether we're on a fool's errand.

CHAPTER 23

Becca

I hate coming back. I hadn't realised how much it was going to affect me. While the church will be empty at this time of night, my mind conjures up all the sanctimonious people who would attend every Sunday. Who really knew what they got up to behind closed doors Monday to Saturday, only to receive absolution once a week? Since I married Hawk and got a taste of what could go on out of sight of his parishioners, the building had ceased to hold any comfort for me.

Rock holds my hand as I get out of the back seat, keeping it tight in his as the other truck parks behind us.

"You were right, Becca. It's quite isolated here." Drummer's staring around. I know he's seeing the large, and at this time of night, empty parking lot surrounded by parkland.

I start trembling, but as Rock squeezes my hand I try to make myself think. "There are motion sensors that trigger lights to come on."

"Can we approach without setting them off?"

"Yes, if we go around the back," I explain to Drum. "There's no cash kept on site, no reason to think the church would be robbed. They're there for convenience, not security."

"Explain the alarm system to me," Slick requests.

"It's on the doors and windows. We'll walk around the side once I've got the key. I can disarm it…"

247

"They might have changed the code, Becca," Wraith says patiently. "What Slick's asking is who it's connected to."

"The pastor's house. But it's never gone off all the time I've been here. Hawk didn't want the police to attend before he did."

It's dark, but I can hear shuffling of feet as though my words had triggered a reaction. As I rerun what I'd just said through my mind it dawns on me I'd never thought that was suspicious before.

"What you thinking, Slick?"

"Disable the electric. You know where the fuse box is, sweetheart?"

Although Slick's married to Ella, I'm still wary of the baldheaded man, not having had much to do with him. But Rock's arm that's drawn me into his body gives me confidence. "Yes. I can show you."

I lead them in the direction that I know won't trigger the lights, and at the back of the church come to a junction box. I point to it. "That's where the electric comes into the building. The fuse box is on the other side of the door."

Slick gets out a flashlight and fiddles around for a moment. Soon he stands up. "I've shorted it. Will fix it again before we leave."

"Where's the key, Becca?"

Answering Drummer with an action I go to a vent on the wall and use my fingernails to pry off the cover. There inside is a full set of keys. Still thinking they're wasting their time, I select the one to the back door, put it into the lock and open it. The alarm stays silent.

"Right," says Drummer. "Let's fan out. We're searching for anything that might indicate there's a basement."

As the men fade off into the darkness with only their flashlights to guide them, I again lean into Rock. "There's nothing to find. I know this place like the back of my hand."

Rock gets out his own flashlight. "Come on, Becca. Let's go looking. Before you weren't looking for an entrance. Now you are, you might see something different."

Alongside him I walk around, answering all his questions. He points at a doorway. "Kitchen," I tell him, and then go inside with him. He opens cupboards, even looks under the sink, but as I'd said, there's nothing. I start hoping they'll soon give up. This place brings back nothing but bad memories. Hawk shouting at me when the sandwiches I'd cut weren't absolutely even.

I'm standing, staring at the counter, trembling as my mind dredges up the expectation of past punishments, when there's a muffled shout from the main church room. Rock quickly grabs my hand and leads me back out. The flashlights play on the altar which, to my surprise, isn't in its usual place. As I watch, Lady and Joker push it over further, seemingly with ease.

"Well, lookie here. What have we fuckin' got?"

I find myself waiting for the bolt of lightning that will strike down the man who's dared swear in church, but none comes. *Maybe God's forsaken this building.* A thought confirmed when Drummer triumphantly lifts the handle which opens a trap door. The hand which isn't being held tightly by Rock goes to my mouth. *How did I not know that was here?*

Rock and I are the last to descend the wooden stairs into a cavernous space that seems to mimic the size of the church above. In between the numerous support pillars are boxes upon boxes. The area is chock full of stuff. Wide-eyed, I watch as Slick and Wraith start opening them.

Guns. More guns than I have ever seen in my life, or even imagined I would. Evil looking assault rifles, handguns. *Oh my, are those grenades?*

"Hawk didn't even own a handgun," I find myself saying incredulously. "He can't have known these were here."

"Oh, sweetheart. I think Hawk was very much in the know." Rock moves me forward and starts examining the contents himself. "Lot of AK15s here. Bump stocks too."

Drummer's eyeing everything carefully. "Reckon we've found out why Herrera needs a new mule. His pipeline dried up when Hawk was committed."

"The timing fits." Wraith seems to agree, while I haven't a clue what they're talking about.

Slick's looking around. "Something doesn't add up. Why would the stock still be here? Surely Hawk had people working for him? Why wouldn't they carry on the business?"

"I don't like this, Prez." Rock's voice rumbles against my head. "This isn't necessarily old stock. Hawk's men might still be working for him. You might be wrong about the Herreras."

"Um," I don't like to interrupt, but I've got a feeling they'll want to hear this information. "I think you might have killed them all." Hawk may have made me into someone who acted like a puppet, but he hadn't been able to stop me thinking. As all eyes turn to me, I continue. "The Riders came from Phoenix. Most of the chapter moved to Tucson, the rest stayed here. If Hawk knew them well enough for them to keep me prisoner, maybe they were who he was using."

Rock picks up when I break off. "She's on the right track, Drummer. The extra men he brought in to take us down were from Phoenix. We wiped them all out. It also explains why the Herreras were so keen to give an unknown MC their trade. They were either already dealing with them, or knew they were in the business."

"Slick, catalogue exactly what's here, will you?" Having given his instruction, Drummer looks sharply at me. "You forget you've seen this, you hear me?"

I quickly nod. I can do that. I don't want anything to do with it. Just seeing all the guns around me is making me nervous.

"I've got a rough estimate, Prez. But in case Becca's wrong about the Riders, don't want to hang around much longer."

"Just what I was thinking, Slick. This is one fuck of a haul, and if there's anyone left breathing who knows about it, they'll be keeping an eye on it."

"Expecting trouble, Prez?"

Prez pulls at his beard. "Always expect trouble, Joker. Always. Now let's get the fuck out of here."

Again Rock and I are the last to go up the stairs. As soon as we're out the altar is pushed back into place, Lady getting on his knees and checking with the aid of the flashlights that there's no tracks left to leave a sign it's ever been moved, brushing away any marks that were made. Then we hastily exit the building. I lock the door and put the keys back behind the vent while Slick does something to the electric again.

Immediately when he does, the lights go on in the church. *Someone must have come in the front door.*

"Make a run for it?" Rock's voice sounds tight.

Drummer points to the light flooding out of the window and illuminating the ground. "They'll see us if they look out."

A voice comes from inside. "Can't see anyone's here."

"The alarm definitely went off?"

"I heard it."

"Fuckin' alarm must have battery backup." Slick bangs his hand against his head as though he should have thought about it.

I recognise one of the speakers. It's the new pastor. Hawk introduced me when he had to step away from the role after being arrested. Quickly I think. "Drummer, get your men round the other side. I'll handle this." I pull away even though Rock has me held tightly.

"No..."

"Rock," I hiss. "Go. Now. I'll be alright."

Drummer drags him away as the men fade into the dark shadows of the walls. As the back door opens and light floods out, I'm standing there in full view.

"*Becca?*"

I meet his eyes for a second, then look down at my feet. "I'm sorry, Pastor Alton. I didn't mean to disturb you. I thought the alarm was the same code…"

"Never mind that. Why are you here, Becca?" Pastor Alton's voice sounds full of concern, while the other man stands impassively. His eyes though, they roam. In a way that makes my skin creep.

"I…" I pause, giving myself a moment to think. "I was just missing Hawk so much. I wanted the comfort of his church."

The two men exchange looks. Looks I don't like.

"Come inside, Becca. We'll…pray together."

"It's alright, thank you. I already prayed by myself. I'll just be on my way…"

But before I can turn, the second man's hand takes hold of my shoulder. "Please, the pastor is right. You must be missing your husband and need to talk to someone. Come in and let us give you comfort."

"No. I'm fine." I shrug off his touch and get prepared to run. "I've finished now. I'm so sorry for disturbing you." Then I add what they must know. "Hawk wouldn't like me to be talking to men alone. Not even you, Pastor."

"Hawk wouldn't like you running around in the middle of the night on your own. Especially when you're supposed to be dead," the unknown man observes.

My eyes go wide, and I don't move fast enough.

Suddenly I've got a stranger's arms on me. He twists my arms behind my back and starts pushing me into the church. I dig in my heels, but he's too strong.

He doesn't even wait until I'm completely inside before he snarls a question I didn't expect. "Who was it that died in that fuckin' cellar if it wasn't you, *Becca*? Who's been helping you? And if you're so concerned about Hawk, why did you let him think you were dead?"

"Not so fast." The sound of a safety being taken off right by his head makes the man stop.

"And you, *Pastor*." A second gun comes into view.

As the man's arms drop away I throw myself at Rock, tears running down my face as I silently sob.

"Take her back to the truck," Drummer says. "We'll deal with everything here."

I let Rock lead me away, waiting for the sound of gunshots which I expect I'll soon be hearing, expecting them to deal with the two men the same way they dealt with the Chaos Riders. I grimace. *They can't kill a pastor, surely?* But I've no say in whether they do or don't.

Something's playing on my mind. Once I'm in the truck I let go of Rock's hand and turn to face him. "Why does Hawk think I'm dead, Rock? Tell me. Why would he think I died in the cellar?"

Rock purses his lips and looks away. Then turns back. "Chaos' men killed Jill, Becca. There was a woman's body in the cellar, but it wasn't yours."

He'd told me it was club business when I'd asked about Jill. I'd just let it drop, being too concerned at the time with myself, Beef, and Rock. I cover my mouth. I didn't like the woman, but I don't like hearing she died in the place I'd been kept in. It had been bad enough seeing the men killed, even though I knew they deserved it. Rock tries to pull me to him, but there's too much going on in my mind. I slide to the opposite side of the seat.

"Either the pastor or the other man must be in contact with him. Otherwise they wouldn't have known Hawk thought I was dead." As the realisations dawn on me, I go cold. "Rock, this means the pastor might have known who was keeping me for Hawk. He probably knew how they were treating me as well. How could he condone that? How many others are involved in this?"

"Becca, don't torture yourself. We'll have no answers until Drummer comes back."

He's right. But I can't avoid the thought that the pastor could have known. If he did, he's as dirty as Hawk. Is the whole damn church involved? Who was the other man? I can't remember seeing him before. Or have I? Wasn't he someone who visited the house one of the times I was sent out of sight. He might well have been, now I think of it.

"Come here, Becca. I'll never let anything happen to you."

This time when he reaches out I go to him.

The front doors of the truck open. As soon as Drummer starts getting in, I ask, "What happened? Did you kill them?" I don't know if I'm hoping they've been left dead or alive. Dead men can't talk.

Drummer turns and looks at me over his seat. "They're alive. The pastor didn't seem to know anything, but the other man, well, I don't trust him. I'd put money on it he's in contact with Hawk. Which means Hawk will get to know that you're under our protection."

I gasp. "What will he do?"

"That's for us to worry about, not you, Becca. But," he raises his chin to the man sitting next to me, "Rock won't let anything happen to you, sweetheart. You can bet your life on that."

Whether anything else was discussed remains secret, and nothing more is said as we drive the two hours back to the compound. Worried about Hawk and my future, I ask, but get shut down each time. After a while I start fuming. It's like being with Hawk all over again. Women aren't trusted with business. I deserve to know how much and what risk I'm in.

By the time we drive in through the gate which one of the prospects slides open for us, my fear has made me beyond furious, certain they should let me in on more of what's going on. I get out of the SUV and tear up to the suite I'm still using. Rock lets me go, staying behind presumably for Drummer to update him on the stuff they wouldn't discuss in front of me.

Opening the door to my suite, I throw myself on the bed, my hands punching the pillows in frustration. *Is Pastor Alton involved with the guns? Who was the other man? What threat is he to me?*

I've still not got myself under control when the door to the suite opens. I sit up fast, my jaw dropping when I see it's Rock.

"What are you doing here?" I spit out.

He snorts. "This is my suite, Becca. Have you forgotten that?"

Shit. I had. He'd been staying in the crash room since he got back. I start to get to my feet. "Well I'm certainly not staying in it with you." I start to grab the clothes I'd been given. "I'll go to Beef's."

Rock advances, and as quickly as I'm gathering tees and jeans together, throws them back down again.

"Will you let me get my stuff?"

"No."

"No?" I'm too angry to notice the gleam in his eyes. "You're as bad as Drummer. Not wanting to tell me the things that I need to know."

I try to snatch my panties back out of his hands, he doesn't let go. "Why do you need to know, Becca? Don't you trust us? After Drummer took you in and hid you. After we gave you board and lodgin' askin' for nothing in return. Drummer could have turned you away, instead he helped keep you hidden and safe."

"They did it for you," I scream at him. "Everything's done for the men here. Women aren't told anything…"

We're still stupidly fighting for possession of my underwear as Rock replies. "For their protection. Nothing else. What you don't know you can't tell anyone."

"You don't trust me."

"You don't trust *me*," he retaliates. It's then he notices what he's holding, and a sly grin comes over his face. "Nice underwear."

I release my hold quickly. "You can have it!" I scream, dropping everything and running for the door.

He's quicker, there first and slamming it shut as I reach to open it. I swing around, my back up against the wood. He's standing close, one arm up, his hand holding the door shut over my head. There's only inches between us. My breath is coming fast, his is too. The air feels electric. Striking as fast as a snake, Rock closes the gap and his mouth slams down on mine, his tongue insisting entry.

I respond, opening for him. Instead of remembering we were arguing, my brain processes his taste, which I already recognise. The kiss is brutal. I give as good as I take, each of us fighting for dominance. Somewhere in the back of my mind I register I'm not submitting, not allowing him the lead. Both of us equally engaged.

His cock presses into me, a very hard, very aroused cock, and I feel strange sensations. Not the dread I would feel when I knew Hawk was in the mood, but anticipation and an embryonic hope that Rock *won't* stop. Right now I'd let him do anything. I *need* him, need some kind of outlet for all the pent-up emotions I've gone through today.

As rapidly as he started the kiss he pulls away. The roles have changed. Forgetting I was trying to escape as much as I've forgotten my reason for escaping, now I'm the one stalking him, not wanting to lose the contact. Listening only to my body and not to my mind. For the first time ever wanting to encourage a man to touch me, believing down to my soul Rock would never hurt me.

"Rock…"

He turns to look at me. My flushed face and still rapid breathing must give my needs, my desires away, as he almost wails, "I can't do this. I fuckin' want to, but I can't." He drags his hands through his hair, his gaze meeting mine. "I want you, can't deny that. But you're not ready, Becca. I know that. Let's back off, take this slowly. I need to know you're ready for the type of loving I want to give. I can't give you what you need." He brings his hand toward my face. It hovers there briefly, then without touching me, goes back to his side. "I'm a biker, Becca. I don't know how to make love. I fuck. I'm so goddamn worried you'll think I'm treating you the same way he did."

While I can't elucidate the reasons why I'm able to reassure him, my reciprocal arousal being high on the list, I take the step that separates us and rest my face against his chest. "You could never be like him, Rock."

"How do you know, Becca? I can't even imagine what you went through with him. Being raped for three years. I don't want to know the things he did, I'm already ready to smash up the room, the bloc, hell, the compound. Fuck, I'm having a hard enough time just imaginin' it. But if I don't know, I can't avoid doing the same kind of shit. I don't want to hurt you. You're only just startin' to heal."

He's helping with that. So much. My body still tingling from being so close to him, I'm more afraid of him backing off than I am of him touching me. "How about if I tell you the things you do that he didn't?"

He tilts my head so he can see into my eyes. "Babe, I don't do well under instruction." He smirks, then frowns again. "I could get carried away… Fuck, Becca, that's a certainty. You have no fuckin' idea how hard it is to control myself around you."

I process, but don't respond to his comment. "You kissed me. Hawk never did that."

"He was an idiot."

Again I ignore his valid input. "And," my voice becomes shy, "you're making me feel things I never have before."

"I am?" His face starts to lose some of its tension. His soft chuckle shows he's more interested as he puts me on the spot. "What kind of things?"

I go red. There's only one explanation for this unmitigated throbbing in my core, but I don't know how to explain it. "Like, like… Like I want you."

A finger touches my chin and turns it up. "And how do you know that, Becca?" The lightening of his tone tells me he's teasing.

I turn away without answering, unable to describe the unfamiliar feelings he's brought to the fore. Incapable of using words to define the fluttering in my stomach and the burning itch between my legs that needs relief. Instead, I clutch at his cut. "Please, Rock. Please show me what it should be like between a man and a woman."

"I don't want to hurt you."

"Don't you want me?"

He's silent for a moment, then he breathes in. A massive sigh leaves his body as though he's lost the battle with himself. "I want you, Becca." His mouth descends and covers mine once again, this time a gentler but still passionate kiss. Our tongues glide together, our tastes combine, our lips caress. When he pulls away his eyes hold mine as his hands move and his palms cover my fully clothed chest. I know he's asking permission as well as making a statement.

I can only say, "Yes."

"Here. Now." There's urgency in his voice. His ability to form sentences failing, yet he still gives me another chance to back out.

I'm nervous, of course I am, but knowing I'm as affected as he is, again I give a simple agreement. "Yes." *I want this. God help me, but I do.* As the words *I'm still married* come into my head, I chase them away just as fast. *If this is going to make me a sinner, I'll just have to pray for forgiveness at some point.* God knows, I'm no stranger to retribution.

As though he'd been waiting for my consent, his hands waste no time ripping my tee over my head, then my bra is expertly unfastened, letting my breasts drop free. He sucks in air, allowing only his eyes to feast for a moment before bending his head and sucking a nipple into his mouth while simultaneously his fingers toy and pinch the other. The dual attack has my legs weakening.

"Fuckin' perfect," he mumbles while his teeth close on my nipple. But instead of hurting, it sends a zing straight down to that overheated area between my legs.

As he moves from one side to the other, feasting as though he can't get enough, my limbs go weak. Sensing my capitulation, he sweeps me up into his strong arms, placing me reverently on the bed, then comes over me, holding both my hands in one of his above my head. Next he returns to my breasts. His exuberance makes me giggle.

"Fuck, Becca. You're even better than I expected, I dared to hope. Your tits are fuckin' perfect."

Half embarrassed, half delighted, my response is another snicker as his voice vibrates against my skin. I've never felt this connection between my nipples and my core, nor believed I could get such pleasure from a man's attentions. I arch my back as the almost constant tingling zips its way down my body, knowing I've never felt so alive before.

When Rock finally lifts his head, I whine at the loss of sensation and raise mine to see what he's going to do next.

"Keep your hands there," he instructs. I do, realising the reason he doesn't want me to touch him is that I'd hurt him if my arms encircled his back.

My eyes follow his head, hair untidy as he moves down my stomach, pulling himself up with his abdominal muscles so he has room to take down my zipper. He moves to the side and pulls down my shorts and my panties. I'm completely open to him. I wait for the feeling of dread that I got when Hawk saw me naked, but it doesn't come. Then the realisation hits. *This isn't my husband. I'm with another man.* Embarrassed and mortified, I try to close my legs.

He looks up. "There's no room for anyone else here, Becca. Put him out of your head. You've left him, remember."

He holds my legs apart, his eyes instructing me that he's in charge, the intense heated gaze giving me assurance. Then any shame flees as he lowers his head, zooming in on my clit. *Oh my God.* The feelings. If I'd felt overwhelmed before, I don't know how to cope now. My hands flutter, uselessly grabbing at nothing, until I grab hold of the top of the pillow. My body comes alive, making me aware I had needs and desires I've never imagined before. As his tongue licks and teases I reach up for more, then sink back down as my tender clit throbs with something that's becoming excruciating, almost akin to pain, but it's not that, it's something else. Something tangible yet which remains out of my grasp. The way Rock plays me, like an instrument he's very familiar with, he incites reactions that prove he knows female equipment better than I do myself. Picking single notes then making chords as he makes my clit pulse, my muscles tense in my legs, my stomach tightens, then everything comes together and builds up.

I need something, I'm reaching for it. As if he knows, Rock's finger breeches me, and then he adds another, curling them around, touching something inside I didn't even know was there. My body automatically starts to rise, and he pushes me back down, keeping me there with a hand to my sternum.

I'm straining for that elusive release. Exactly what form it will take I haven't a clue, but this tension he's built up must lead somewhere. Even if I don't understand it, he's taking me on an incredible journey, and before it kills me I need it to end. His tongue circles, his teeth graze gently, then his lips apply suction. Now he's pressing down, his breath oscillating over my most sensitive part as he speaks an unfamiliar instruction. "Come, Becca. Let me see you lose control."

I don't understand what he's asking, but my brain doesn't need to be involved, as without fully comprehending what's happening my body starts to convulse and my lungs stop working. A cry leaves my mouth as I see stars. Then I'm shuddering uncontrollably as the pent-up pressure is released, and the rigidity that's held me in its thrall loosens and recedes.

When I gasp and start breathing again I open my eyes to see Rock grinning, leaning over me and planting his lips against mine. This time he tastes different, and I realise the flavour is my own. Although I've just had an incredible experience, in no time at all the kiss incites my body all over again.

Pulling away, Rock reaches into the drawer of the bedside table, fiddles with something and selects what he needs. "Thank fuck I still had some," he murmurs, and I realise that while I was out of it he's removed his jeans and is now smoothing a condom over his impressive cock. My eyes widen when I see it. He's far bigger than Hawk.

"Lubrication," I stammer out.

His eyes narrow and his head tilts to one side, then he chuckles. "Won't need that."

He will. Hawk always did, unless he chose not to use it when he wanted me to hurt. "You're too big."

"Hey, don't worry. You're soaking."

Now it's my turn not to understand what he means. Slowly comprehension dawns as he wipes his hand from my clit to my slit, then holds up his fingers, which are glistening. "Won't need lubrication, darlin'. You've got enough of your own. But if it hurts, tell me and I'll stop. Okay?" He touches his dry hand to my face. "I'll never do anything to hurt you."

Hawk never stopped. But Rock isn't Hawk. The two men couldn't be more different. I jerk my chin, giving my cautious agreement for him to continue, tensing as I feel his cock at my entrance.

"Relax, babe."

He gives me a moment while I try hard to obey him, my brain trying to find the right pathways to connect so I can do what he's asked. When at last I get some semblance of control and release the tension, he starts to push inside. I squeeze my eyes shut, expectantly waiting for the tear and the burn…and the friction. But there's no pain, only pressure. As my body responds and accepts him, a sense of joy washes over me as, at last, I feel able to enjoy our joining. I begin to relish the feeling, and, wanting more, welcome him inside.

With small, controlled thrusts he advances, sliding in and out, gaining ground slowly. Far from being unpleasant, it's amazing, and now my eyes open, watching his face, lined with concentration. As his breathing speeds up his brow creases more. He's focusing on his effort to hold himself back, to go slowly, giving me time to adjust.

As last he gives a grunt of satisfaction. "You feel fuckin' amazin'. The way your muscles are tight around my cock. Fuckin' incredible, darlin'."

He starts to move, I lie passive. He stops. My eyes are still watching him as he looks down at my face. I bite my lip, not understanding his unspoken question. But I need him to push in again, no time for teasing now. I want more of this mind-blowing sensation, so I whimper my frustration and experiment-ally start pushing myself down on him.

"That's right, doll. Fuck me back."

His encouragement makes me want to give something to him. I try squeezing my internal muscles.

"Fuck. That right there, babe. Fuck!" He takes over again, but this time I try to move with him, raising my hips to meet his thrusts. "Fuck, darlin'. That's it, oh fuck, doll. Are you close?"

What is he asking? But my body knows and tells my mind to shut up as the feeling of everything tightening starts all over again. He changes his angle, starts hitting that spot he'd found with his fingers, and it becomes impossible to stop the wave of sensation that starts flooding over me, and the high-pitched wail that comes from my mouth.

"Becca. Becca. Fuck!" His simultaneous cry mingles with mine, our bodies pulsating as he stills inside. A few seconds pass, then, "Darlin, Becca." He leans down and kisses me gently. "Fuck! You must be the best I've ever fuckin' had." Using one hand to keep the condom in place, he moves away from me and ties the end of the latex and throws it down by the bed.

As the euphoria fades from my body my brain kicks in and starts working again. My skin, previously flushed with arousal, is now tinged red with embarrassment. "Rock, I'm sorry. I've never…"

His fingers cover my lips to stop anything else coming out. "Becca, I love that I'm your first in so many ways. The first to make love to you. The first to make you come. The first to prop-erly arouse you. The first to teach you how to respond to a man.

Fuck, woman. You're mine, you know that?" Lying carefully on his side, he pulls me close.

"I'm going to hell."

It's only when he starts laughing I realise I've said that aloud. "What the fuck makes you say that?"

I purse my lips, then say primly, "Because a woman shouldn't enjoy sex."

"Then it's good I'm a Devil, isn't it? And I'll keep showing you pieces of heaven on your journey to hell, 'cause, fuck it, woman, I'm not gonna fuck you unless you're satisfied too."

As I smile and lean into him Rock starts to laugh. "What?" I can't see anything amusing, and his mirth is spoiling the mood. "What did I…"

"Hey, hush, darlin'." He pulls me closer, kissing the top of my head. "Of all the times I thought about making love to you, I didn't think the first time would be make-up sex."

I frown, and then recall how angry I'd been when he'd entered the suite. For the life of me I can't remember what we'd been arguing about. Or why it seemed so important.

CHAPTER 24
Rock

I walk into Drummer's office the next morning, already regretting having to leave Becca still asleep in my bed—where she'll be tonight and every night after if I get my way. I can't wait to help her explore her newfound sexuality. There's so much I can teach her.

I'm unable to understand a man like Hawk. Even the club girls know they won't go unsatisfied. We'd not keep them here long if the men just used them to get off. The hangarounds up from Tucson who attend our weekend parties only come because they know they're in for a good time with a biker. I grin to myself. *Becca's got no idea what her body is capable of.* I'm going to make her addicted to me, and the pleasure my dick, tongue, and hands can give her.

Drummer waves me to a seat, then finishes off typing something on his laptop. Finally he looks up. "Everything okay with Becca?"

"Yeah, Prez. She's good." That's an understatement.

He smirks. "Kind of got that impression when I walked past your suite last night."

Making a mental note not to tell Becca Drummer had heard us, I ask what I hadn't yet found out. "What happened, Prez? With the pastor and that man who was with him."

Drum gives a twisted grin, smiling with just one side of his mouth. "Now that's interesting." His brow furrows as his face forms a frown. "On our part, we didn't say anything about finding the guns. Just reinforced Becca's story that she wanted to visit the church."

"A blind man could see through that shit."

"Flimsy at best," Drummer agrees. "But if they don't know the guns are there, it's possible they'll believe it."

"You think they don't?"

His hands toy with his beard. "If they did, and they thought we might have found them, I think I'd have had a different conversation. I've got a feelin' the pastor is out of the loop, but the man with him was hiding something. He also has some sway over the pastor. They'd have been in their rights to have threatened us with the police, but they didn't. They were, however, very curious about our presence. And interested when I told them Becca was now under our protection."

"They bought it?"

Drummer shrugs. "I'm not sure they believed us, but they found us outside the church, only Becca admitted to going inside. There wasn't even any breaking and entering, as she used the spare key."

"You're saying no one, other than Hawk and now us, knows the stash is there? Or even that the basement is under the church? This isn't some new thing that's just started," I observe.

"I'm not sure about the other man. He carefully avoided giving us his name, by the way. He might know, but until he checks in with Hawk he won't know where we stand."

"You think he's meeting with Hawk?"

"I'd put money on it. He knew there was a body of a woman in the cellar."

"How?" I wonder aloud. "How could he fuckin' know that?"

"Something else for us to discover. Couldn't take it further last night. Not with the pastor there. Need to see the man on his own, and this time question him our way." Again Drummer strokes his beard. "Too many questions, too few answers. Something's fuckin' rotten in the church, and it goes way back. But it's not just the history that's interesting. Those guns we found must have come from somewhere, and in this trade, must be expected elsewhere."

"Was Hawk behind the gun running? Has he got his own pipeline, or was he using the Chaos Riders?"

"I'd say it's a fair bet the Riders were working for him. But who is he? The middle man? The man at the top?" Drum breaks off and tunnels his hands through his hair. "I've already got Mouse checking the pastor out, but if I'm right, it's the other man we should be more concerned about. It worries me they knew about the Chaos Riders and their recent demise. That means they were also probably complicit in Becca's treatment. Knew she'd been held in the cellar. And assumed she was dead because a charred, unidentified female body had been discovered there. But how the fuck they found that out, I've no fuckin' idea."

I feel a moment of compassion for Jill, but put it behind me. Thoughts of what went on in that building has my back tensing and stinging all over again. Jill's betrayal, her lies, and her last few moments are things I don't want to think on. "How did you leave it last night?"

"With deep suspicion on both sides." Drummer shrugs, then stands. "We better get going, Brother. With luck we'll find some answers today. Let's get this ball rollin'."

I follow him out front and sit on my bike, kicking up the stand as I wait for him to have a quick word with Wraith. Although I'm leaving Becca alone for a while, I'm itching to get going, though not looking forward to when we arrive. Having spent a year inside, even as a visitor I find the pen depressing. Even more so as we're meeting with Stub, the man who expects to spend the years he has left behind bars.

Still, it's a nice autumn day, and though the ride is relatively short, I enjoy it. The pain in my back has begun to recede as new skin starts to grow, so each time I ride it becomes easier. The feel of my real cut resting on my shoulders is still something I relish. Never want to be without it again.

Both Hawk and Stub are being held in the pen here in Tucson. As soon as we meet him, I find Stub seems relatively cheerful for a man who'll never be on a bike again, probably appreciating the break in the monotony visitors afford. He greets Drum and myself affably, then asks what we want. The Wretched Soulz are the dominant club in Arizona, and we're one of their support clubs.

After exchanging pleasantries, Drummer gets down to business. "We want information about a man with the handle, Hawk. Alexis Gardner is his real name. Be useful to know if you know of him, or if there's a way you can get close."

The corners of Stub's mouth turn up. "Know of him. He's in solitary at the moment. Man's got a temper alright. Got news that his wife was dead and smashed the place up. Guards shut him down fuckin' quickly."

"Thing is, Stub, we need to know more about him. His wife…"

"Ex," I say firmly. "Ex-wife." Hawk really must be a possessive motherfucker if news of what had been assumed was Becca's death sent him off the rails. Once again I wonder whether he knew exactly what sort of hospitality was being extended to his wife. On the other hand, his treatment of her didn't show he treasured the gem that he had.

Drum gives me a quick grin and corrects, "His soon to be ex-wife is not dead, but is under our protection." He goes on to explain the arrangements Hawk had made for her while he was in prison. He also, in hushed tones, lets Stub know what we found under Hawk's church.

Stub lets air out in a soft whistle. "That's some heavy shit." He thinks for a moment and taps his fingers on the desk before admitting, "I'm in with the Brand."

Drum and I both nod. It's hardly surprising. When you're in for a long stretch, particularly for life, it's not unusual to connect with one of the prison gangs for protection. The only issue is that they still expect that affiliation to continue when you're back on the outside. Of course, in Stub's case that isn't an issue, he'll never be out and free to have to pay back favours. The Brand is another name for the Aryan Brotherhood. Which makes what Stub says next come as a revelation, and possibly one of the pieces of the puzzle we're trying to build up.

"Hawk was sniffing around."

"To join the Brand?"

"Yeah. Him being a pastor an' all, thought he'd prefer to keep his nose clean. But you telling me about the guns…"

"It's only supposition that he knows about them," Prez says quickly. "But for the life of me, I can't fuckin' think it's anything else."

Stub runs his hand over his closely shorn head. When he talks he's thinking aloud. "I've got good standing. I've nothing to lose except privileges, so I take on the wet work for the Brand when it's needed." He gives a twisted grin. "Relieves the boredom at least. I'll get myself close to Hawk. No one gets into the Brand unless they're thoroughly vetted. He might not just want to get in for protection, but to set up contacts to move that shit, or for when he gets out. You know anything about him? He's white. Think he agrees with their agenda?"

"Hadn't thought about that." Drum's lips press together. "You could be onto something there."

"Leave it with me, Drummer. I'll see what I can find out."

Drum holds up his hand. "Just had a thought, Stub. Can you be the one to tell Hawk his wife's still breathin'? Get him a message? That she's with us and we'll offer him the same deal as the Chaos Riders."

"What deal is that?"

"Damned if I know, Brother. They were holdin' her for him until he got out. Be useful to know more about it."

Another grin. "You're suggesting I lead him on? Let him think you know more than you do?"

"Exactly, Stub. He might let something slip. Like what made the Chaos Riders do him a favour, what hold he had, or what incentive."

I can't say I disagree with Prez's plan, but there's something I don't like about it. If we play it his way Hawk can't be served with divorce papers anytime soon. While I don't give a fuck she's still married on paper, I know it nags at Becca.

When the business part of the visit comes to a natural end, a look of longing comes over Stub's face. "Before you fellas go, tell me about your rides."

The remaining time we have with him, both Drum and I tell him of our bikes. Drum goes further and describes his collection, and the Vincent Black Shadow his old lady, Sam, restored. We then talk about riding, the wind in our hair, sun blazing down. Stub vicariously lives through every word that we tell him.

By the time we get out I'm in desperate need of fresh air.

More puzzles. More questions. That's all we seem to have got today.

Back at the compound, I'm pleased to find Becca in the kitchen with the other old ladies. Ma's recipe book lies open on the table, and my mouth waters at the thought of them trying something else out from her collection. Might not have known the old woman long, but she sure could cook.

Before she spots me, I can hear Becca contributing. "I never thought of using oregano with that."

"Ma knew what she was doing."

"That she did, babe." Hyde leans over to plant a kiss on the top of Sarah's head. Sarah being the great-granddaughter of the woman we buried a few months back.

His action spurs me on to greet my own woman. I step up beside her, putting my arm around her, making her jump. Her face lights up when she sees me. "You doing okay, darlin'?"

"Yeah, I'm doing good. How was your meeting?"

"Good." I'm not telling her where I've been, and certainly not why. With Stub's help I'm hoping Hawk never gets to leave the penitentiary—at least not unless he's in a wooden box. But first we've got to unravel the mystery.

Dinner's delicious, as I'd expected, and after taking a moment to thoroughly ravish Becca's mouth and hand her a box I'd picked up down in Tucson, it's with a full heart and stomach that I walk into church.

"From the PDA out there, I take it you and Becca have made up?" Shooter's grinning and giving me a thumbs up.

"Christ. Another one bites the dust," Marvel complains.

"Beef won't know what to do with himself when he gets back."

I flip my finger at Joker. Beef won't give a fuck when he hears. He'll just be pleased Becca and I are together.

"How was Beef today?" Prez sends a warning look down the table and everyone at last leaves my love life alone.

"In good form," Blade tells us. "A little tired when I left, but he'd been talking all morning. He's been told he should be home in a couple of days."

The table's thumped, and 'thank fucks' go around as my brothers share my pleasure. It will be fucking good to have my old friend back. It's just not the same on the compound without him.

Drummer bangs the gavel. "Let's get the normal business dealt with, then we'll talk about what happened last night and today." The brothers who'd gone to the church nod, some who've not yet caught up look mystified. "Okay, Dollar. What's the money looking like?"

Dollar pushes his glasses up his nose and consults his tablet. "Good, now we've got back the money Rock stole."

"Didn't fuckin' steal it," I murmur as the others laugh.

"Shut the fuck up." Drum glares around. "Dollar, continue."

"Blade's found a place for a tattoo parlour. Good location. Not far from the Angels." I smirk. Get 'em drunk at our strip club and then over to be tatted.

Blade raises his hand. "Red knows an ink slinger that's got fed up with Vegas. He's coming to meet us sometime in the next couple of weeks."

"Any good?"

"Did Red's tats, and he ain't complainin'."

"That skull?" I ask, quickly perking up. It was an impressive job, hard to miss, placed on Red's bicep. As Blade nods I feel pleased. Be good to have someone to depend on once the skin that the Riders removed has grown back. "I'd like to sit in on the interview, Blade. Wouldn't mind letting him see what he'll be dealing with. See if he knows what he's talking about."

"Be good to have you, Rock. Maybe Beef too. Both of you are no strangers to needles."

He's right. Beef and I have dozens of tats. I reckon we can tell a good tattoo artist from a bad one.

Drummer's thinking. "Get him to bring his kit. If he seems likely, Rock, you up for getting another tat?"

There's a round of laughter and questions of 'where?', but I tap my thigh. "Got a spot reserved for him."

"You could always have Becca's name tatted over your heart."

There's an empty pack of cigarettes on the table that I throw, quite accurately, at Joker.

Shooter thumps Joker on his arm. "You could volunteer to have Lady's there instead. Oh, fuck me, yes. Lady could get a tramp stamp!" He bends over the table belly-laughing at his own joke. My lips twitch. It actually was quite amusing, especially watching Lady's face.

"If no one else has anything sensible to say, I'm bringing everyone up to speed on what's happened in the last twenty-four hours."

I lean forward, resting my elbows on the table, giving all my attention to the prez, who holds the brothers who weren't there rapt as he surmises what we found.

Peg whistles when he hears. "Under a fuckin' church?"

Wraith nods. "Purpose built, I'd say. Whatever's been going on has gone on a fuck of a long time."

"Becca's Hawk right in the middle of it?" Blade poses as a question.

"That's what Stub's trying to find out," I contribute.

"But Hawk's got Aryan associations? Or trying?" Bullet's shaking his head.

That's my cue. "Prez, I asked Becca about the membership of the church. Everyone is white."

Drum sucks in his cheeks, but then refutes, "Not many blacks in Tucson, few more in Phoenix."

"Hispanics though," Wraith suggests. "You'd have expected there to be at least one person of colour in the congregation. None? Now that's interesting."

Our bylaws used to say we were a white only club, but that got changed when Dart, previously a Tucson chapter member, now the VP in San Diego, married his black wife. We changed the outdated rule, and now allow anyone into the club. Anyone male, that is. No one objected, we'd more likely judge a man by how well he can ride rather than the colour of his skin or, I cast a look toward Joker and Lady, his sexual orientation.

Prez breathes in. "Let's sum everything up. The Herreras haven't come back to me since we took the Chaos Riders out. But I don't count that much more than a reprieve, now we're the only club they'll be fingering us to shift their guns for them."

"And we don't want to do that." Peg's comment sounds a challenge.

"Nah, Peg. We don't."

"Hawk's got guns…"

"And no one to shift them if he was using the Chaos Riders as his mules."

"If, Blade." Prez points to him. "I'd say it's likely, but I wouldn't want to say that's definite until we hear more."

A thought amuses me. "If Hawk was in with the Chaos Riders, what would the Herreras think of working with a club who had ties to fuckin' white supremacists?" If we'd had those suspicions before, we might not have had to take the Chaos Riders out. The Herreras might have done it for us. And I'd still have the skin on my back, and Beef wouldn't be lying in hospital. *Becca might be dead.* Or at least, I'd never have met her. Nah, all things considered, I wouldn't have wanted to draw a different hand.

CHAPTER 25

Becca

When Rock surprises me with a gift before disappearing into his meeting, I'm so stunned by the first present I've ever received in my life that I stay in the clubroom, turning the box over and over in my hands.

"What you got, Becca?" Darcy comes across. "Oooh. Nice." My blank face must register with her, as she resumes. "It's a phone."

I give her a duh face. Even I can see that. But my hesitation needs an explanation. "I've never had one before in my life. I haven't got a clue what to do with it."

Her jaw drops. "Never?"

"My parents wouldn't have allowed me to call anyone on it. We had a home phone which had no privacy." I realise long ago why they'd kept me away from a social life. *They'd been saving me for Hawk.* Keeping me pure until I went to the man who'd bought my virginity. "Hawk, well, to say he was controlling is an understatement."

"Open it then. It's the new model. Has it got any charge?"

She's talking a foreign language. How the hell would I know? I open the box as instructed, then pass the sleek device over to Darcy.

"Rose gold. Good choice. I like that." I've no idea what she's doing when she magically opens an almost invisible flap on the side and inserts a tiny card. The device soon lights up with an apple. She waits patiently, then hands it back. "Just go through the screens and we'll get it set up."

After half an hour I realise I can just about use it. Sam and Sophie have appeared, and now I've got all their numbers in my phones and they're gradually sharing the brothers and other women's numbers with me. My first text is to Rock, even though he won't have his phone in the meeting room.

Becca: Thank you

I beam with pride when I hear the message sent and do a little leap in the air. Sam puts her arms around me and laughs. Then really cracks up when my phone pings, making me jump and exclaim.

Soph: Welcome to the 21st Century

Tears prick at the corner of my eyes. I can't believe Rock bought me a phone. No one's ever done something so thoughtful for me before.

It's then I realise time's passed, and I'm feeling relaxed and enjoying the company. The heady thought hits me that if Rock and I are together I might be one of these women, this could be my home too. *Don't get ahead of yourself, Becca. Far too soon to be thinking about that.*

"So, you and Rock?" Sam sits down and tugs on my hand to get me to sit beside her. "He asked you to be his old lady?"

"I'm still married, Sam." Her question has made me feel guilty again over what happened last night.

She looks at me sharply, taking a moment to examine my face. "You're separated, aren't you? You owe nothing to that man."

"Nevertheless, I said my vows in church and before God." Primly I repeat what I'd told Rock. My face flushes as I remember in the end it was me who initiated things last night. *What did my vows mean to me then?* But then, Hawk had vowed to love and cherish me. He had a very strange way of doing that.

Leaning forward, Sam takes both of my hands in hers. "Were you ever in love with him, Becca?"

Sophie has come to join us. I look from one to the other and decide to tell them what happened. "No. I didn't even know I was going to be married." The story must sound unbelievable to anyone else. "I woke up on the day of my eighteenth birthday to be told it was my wedding day." My voice cracks as I recall it. *My hands shaking as I tried to hold the piece of paper with my vows written on it steady enough to read. My eyes blurring with tears, my voice weak as I made promises I knew even then I didn't want to keep.*

"Bloody hell!" Sophie exclaims. "Why did you go through with it?"

How can I make them understand? "My upbringing was really secluded. I only found out later that my parents and Hawk had it planned for the previous five years. That day, itself, was a whirlwind, I was dressed in white and whisked to church, handed vows I was supposed to say, and told not to embarrass my parents, or Hawk, in front of the congregation."

"For fuck's sake!" Sam exclaims loudly.

Eli, playing with a toy motorcycle, looks up and repeats in his high-pitched childish voice, "Fuck's sake."

"Oh…dear." She reaches down and pulls the miniature replica of Drummer onto her lap. "That's a bad word, Eli. Mommy shouldn't have said it." She glances at me and Sophie with a wry smile. "Ask him to say please and he ignores me."

Sophie rolls her eyes. "Tell me about it." Then turns back to me. "If you didn't write the vows, you were only saying what someone else wanted you to. Not anything you felt from the heart."

I grimace. "But I did say them. And in a house of God." A house of God with an arsenal of guns underneath.

"With Hawk as a pastor, it's probable God wasn't even listening," Sam snaps. "No one could call your marriage a real one. I bet one of your vows was to obey."

It certainly had been. I reply with a nod.

"And Hawk took that to extremes. Honey, you couldn't even dress yourself when you first came here. He'd got you so brainwashed you could barely survive without him." Her face brightens with a beautiful smile. "You deserve happiness. Even God must see that. It's obvious Rock really cares about you. I've never seen him act with anyone else the way he does around you. Once these men love they're all in. Don't give up on your chance of that. Divorce Hawk so you're legally free, but until you can, accept that morally, you were never tied to him."

Sophie has an odd expression on her face which I can't quite read. "Stand up," she suddenly instructs. I'm getting to my feet before I think about it. "Turn around and say, 'I divorce Hawk', three times."

I stare at her incredulously. And then burst out laughing. And do what she's said. Now both women are chuckling along with me.

We're still laughing when Rock and his brothers come out of church, and the man which Sophie and Sam think I can let myself think of as mine, makes a beeline for me. He curls his hand around the back of my neck and pulls me into him, nuzzling my hair, then bending and speaking softly, the words only intended for my ears.

"Want you, babe."

I'm unsure whether it was the stupid words Sophie made me say or Sam's conviction that my marriage wasn't a real one, but suddenly it's easier to shake off the shackles tying me to my exhusband. Shyly I look up to the man who holds me so tightly I can feel how hard and ready he is, and know my lady parts are reciprocating. Agreement comes naturally. "I want you too, Rock."

He keeps his arm around me as he leads me across the club-room. Someone looks like they want to talk to him, but he ignores them. As if my shorter legs can't go fast enough, he sweeps me up into his arms and carries me the last few steps to his suite.

Inside the room, he pushes me back against the door, then puts his arms under my ass and lifts me until I'm the same height as him. I hug my arms around his neck and my legs go around his waist.

For a moment his eyes simply stare into mine. I notice the hazel colour has flecks which are almost green, so bright they seem to sparkle. Leaning forward, he places his lips to the tip of my nose, then to my forehead. As his beard lightly scratches my cheeks I close my eyes and he places a gentle kiss to each of my eyelids. Now his mouth's at my ear, a gentle warm breath huffed out, his tongue tracing the auricle, then his teeth, closing, but not biting the lobe, making me squirm in his arms. In this posi-tion his hardness is pushing against the place where I'm so eager to feel him again, but tonight, it appears, he's not going to rush.

At last his mouth moves to mine, but first he contents himself just moving his head back and forth, kissing each side of my lips. While his touches are almost innocent, it causes my pelvis to buck against him.

"Patience." He chuckles. "I'm going to love you properly tonight."

I both hear and feel the admonishment as at last his tongue traces the line of my lips. When I open for him his tongue gently pushes inside and completes a slow exploration of my mouth. When he retreats I counter with a study of his. *We're learning each other.* If I hadn't already decided Hawk no longer has any hold on me, Rock would now be sweeping away all thought of him from my mind.

He's taking his time, but eventually pulls back, sucking my bottom lip briefly between his, then giving a tender peck to my upper lip before bending his head and kissing my chin before proceeding to plant more kisses in a line down my neck. My head rolls to the side as he continues his path until he reaches a spot more responsive than the rest, pulling at the skin and gently closing his teeth. Another rush of sensation makes me sigh.

"Rock..."

"Patience," he says again. "Put your legs down."

When my feet touch the floor I expect him to take me to the bed, but he doesn't. Again his eyes lock with mine, our gaze briefly interrupted as he pulls the pretty tunic I'm wearing over my head. He plants another gentle kiss on my lips as he unfastens my bra and slides the straps down my arms. His hands take a moment to circle my breasts, holding them in his large palms before he trails his fingers down my stomach.

Then he folds to his knees. As I lose contact with his eyes I look down to see him staring at his finger as it circles my aureole. As my nipple grows hard he covers it with his palm, allowing me to feel the warmth of his skin. He does the same to my other breast, slowly tightening his hold until he's gently squeezing my soft flesh. A glance at my face as he watches my reaction when he softly pinches the tip, then harder. A moan, unbidden, comes from my lips.

As if he can't hold himself back anymore, his mouth closes around my erect nipple, sucking it into his mouth. When he traps it between his tongue and the roof of his mouth my body comes alive and I throw my head back in pleasure.

"Rock."

He does the same to the other nipple, but his fingers return so he's not neglecting the first. I shudder as my stomach clenches.

Now he's moving down. His hands caressing as he goes, slowly drawing them down my ribs, making me twitch, but sensing I'm ticklish he doesn't linger. He presses his face to my abdomen, zooming in on my navel. I never knew that was an erogenous zone, but as his tongue circles in my clit throbs almost painfully. As if he knows, he stays there, drawing out my delicious torture. I'm scarcely aware that he's unbuttoned my jeans, and almost oblivious as he pushes them down my legs until he taps my calf, a silent request for me to lift my foot so he can slide off my sandal and free my leg from the denim. When he goes to the other I don't need prompting.

"I like this," he murmurs as he combs his fingers through my pubes. "Bare is good, but seeing you natural like this? Even better."

Touch me. Touch me there.

Instead he lifts my foot, making me put my palms flat to the wood of the door for balance, and sucks each of my toes one by one into his mouth. With a hand to steady me, he begins to kiss up the inside of my leg. Oh yes, he's getting there… When he reaches my inner thigh he stops, puts that leg down, then picks up my other foot and torturously slowly gives that appendage and limb the same attention.

Surely he must touch me there now?

"I adore everything about you," he tells me as he reaches the top of my leg. "You're perfect. Everything about you is perfection."

I'm still too skinny, still need to put on weight. But I don't bother to tell him. Instead I plead, "Rock, please…"

"What?" he asks innocently, but I can hear humour in his voice. "What do you want me to do, babe?"

"You know." This time it's my embarrassment that makes me squirm. "Touch me."

"Think I have been touching you." He chuckles.

I think he's been torturing me. But I can't put into words what I need. Such new sensations, I hardly know how to describe it.

I look down. He's kneeling at my feet, but it's no submissive pose. He's looking up at my face, wearing a mischievous grin.

Taking pity on me, he taps my inner thighs. "Spread." Another instruction, and once followed, he places his fingers just where I need them. As I gasp he slides them down to my slit and takes his hand away.

"Watch," he instructs. Obeying, I see him put his fingers laden with my essence to his nose and breathes in deeply, then one by one puts them into his mouth, his expression changing, his eyes closing as he sucks them clean while giving a mumble of appreciation as though tasting a delicacy.

My stomach muscles clench almost violently. I feel myself flush, my palms uselessly trying to find purchase on the door behind me.

Rock finishes cleaning his digits, then leans forward and plants a soft kiss to my mound, then another, and another, slowly moving to that area where I want, *need* his touch. His nostrils flare as he breathes in more of my personal perfume. Lifting his head, he lets the heel of his hand take the place of his mouth, pressing down on my pubis as his fingers gently rub the sides of my clit. I gulp back a scream, but still a strangled yelp comes out. I'm so sensitive there already.

Adjusting his assault, he moves his hand further down, covering my slit, then pressing in with one finger while simultaneously placing his tongue to my throbbing clit. The difference in sensation between fingers and tongue is staggering. Overly turned on, my clit pulses, the wet warm slide of his tongue against it causing all my muscles to tense at once. The rapid acceleration to my peak takes me by surprise as uncontrollable spasms wrack my body as a tumultuous tsunami of pleasure overwhelms me, so strong I'm not sure I can bear it. Shrill cries and wails come from my mouth as aftershocks continue to assail me.

Rock places one hand to my stomach, I think to hold me up, while with his other he gently massages my labia, keeping my arousal level high while intuitively understanding direct pressure on my clit would be painful.

As my twitching dies down he works to bring me to the peak once again. Before I met Rock I didn't know I could fly once, let alone twice. My legs shake, I feel totally drained and weak, and this time, when I come down Rock stands and puts his arms around me.

"You've killed me," I tell him when I'm able to speak.

"Not yet," he replies. Either as a promise or warning.

I make no protest when he carries me over to the bed and gently lays me down. Then he stands back and I can focus nowhere but him as he pulls his t-shirt over his head and then pauses with his hand on his belt.

There's a smirk on his face as I watch him pause his striptease. Damn, this man is covered in so many tattoos I guess it would be impossible to count them. *But I'll try.* If I lose count I can start back at the beginning, and, of course, I'll need to kiss each one.

The sound of his belt swishing through the loops catches my attention. Last night, after the first worrying glimpse, I'd kept my eyes closed, had been too embarrassed to watch him. My satisfied state now leaves me with no such concerns as greedily my eyes soak in what he's gradually revealing. He's commando. As his—untattooed—cock is freed from its confines, it bobs up looking very erect, the head so engorged with blood it's red and shining.

My gaze moves from it to his face. He's watching my reaction, and when I lick my lips he groans.

Suddenly finding strength, I pull myself up. Reaching out my hand, I touch the drop of pre-cum on the tip, and audaciously bring it to my mouth to taste it.

This time his groan is louder. "Fuck it, babe. Can't wait to be inside you." There's more urgency in his movements as he pushes down his jeans, a moment of self-deprecating mirth when he realises he's left his boots on. When he sits on the bed to take them off, chuckling, I put my arms around him, wishing I could feel my breasts pushing against his bare back, but the dressings still cover him from shoulder to the crack of his ass.

He must guess where my thoughts have gone. "Can't fucking wait for you to be on top, babe," he says, his hands covering mine. "Have to wait a while for that. But there's plenty other things for us to try in the meantime."

Completely undressed, he swivels on the bed. As I go to lie back he pulls me over onto my side facing him, then pulls one of my legs high up so it rests on his hips, leaving me wide open. A little press to my leg, telling me to keep it there, he touches me.

"Fuck, you're wet, babe. Fucking love it."

He waits no longer before pushing his cock into me. I feel the stretch, but welcome it. This is Rock. This is my man. As he takes hold of my leg again, holding it as high as it will go, he starts to power into me. It's a different angle, he's touching that spot inside while rubbing my clit. It doesn't take long before I'm tensing again.

"That's it, Becca. Come. Come all over my cock."

His words are so dirty it's all the encouragement I need, and the continual pumping extends my orgasm. Rock doesn't stop, doesn't give me time to recover, just keeps thrusting. He's going deeper than before, and I love the sensation.

Finding my mouth with his, he doesn't ask politely, his tongue lunges straight in, mimicking the action of his cock. My breasts are tight against his chest, his actions causing my nipples to continually graze against his skin. There doesn't seem a part of me that's not aware of him. I can't believe it when my muscles go into spasm again, tightening around him.

"Christ, Becca." This time Rock stops moving. He's breathing heavily, his breath warming my skin. He waits until I begin to relax, then pulls out.

I didn't think he... Oh. Now he moves away, then rolls me onto my stomach. Before I know it he's behind me, his strong arms pulling me to my knees as he gently pushes my head down.

"Oh!"

He thrusts in again, this time so deep I feel him bump against my cervix. A new experience, and one I already know I'm going to love. I'm so weak I can't move, but it doesn't seem he needs me too. He feels so good, filling me completely. As he hammers home I can feel his balls bounce against me.

Admiring his stamina, I realise he's exciting me all over again. *I can't, can I?* But his relentless lunges deep into my core drive me higher and higher until, "Roooocccck!" I scream as he propels me into space once again. This time I'm sure I see planets, the moon, and the sun as well as stars, and am only just aware of him roaring out his release behind me.

Now both our chests heave in unison. The air smells heavy with musk, neither of us seem capable of moving. As I try to get sufficient oxygen to speak, Rock leans forward and places a kiss between my shoulder blades, his tongue coming out to lick me.

"Fucking love the taste of your salty, just fucked skin, Becca." His voice rumbles, the vibrations causing goosebumps.

"Sweaty skin," I tell him. "You've definitely killed me."

He chuckles, and I feel his cock slip out of me, his cum dripping down my legs. He must feel it too, as he sits back on his haunches. Turning my head to the side, I see him watching, his hand tracing the path of the moisture trickling down.

I want to squirm with embarrassment as he says, "Best fucking sight in the world, Becca. Before you, I've never seen that. Never taken a woman bare." He looks at me. "Forgot the fuckin' condom, Becca. Sorry."

"I've got the implant."

My announcement causes him to grin widely. "Bare it's gonna be then."

I go to move, though my legs don't seem able to support me. "I need to wash," I tell him.

Rock's still stroking between my legs and watching as if it's the most satisfying sight he's ever seen. "Hmm?" he prompts, only half listening.

"Wash," I say conservatively, still trying to breathe properly again.

Rock slaps my ass, lightly, not enough to hurt, then leans over me again. "How do you feel about shower sex?"

Oh my God!

CHAPTER 26
Rock

Walking down to the clubhouse, Becca's hand clasped in mine, I'm unable to keep the grin off my face. Last night, *last fucking night*, was, well. I don't know how to describe it. I worshipped Becca, treated her as she deserved to be treated. Every touch, every kiss only serving to inflate my arousal so when I came it was the hardest I'd come in my whole fucking life. I can't ever remember treating a woman so reverently before, but once I started I couldn't seem to stop. After I made love to her, I fucked her. I'd woken her in the night and fucked her again. I'm so fucking addicted I can't stop.

Am I an asshole that I laughed when she declined my invitation to shower with me this morning? Or when she moved stiffly when she got out of bed. She'll be feeling me for the rest of the day, every twinge a reminder of me. I adjust myself in my jeans, I won't need a physical reminder. Just the picture of her in my head is enough to keep me hard.

"What you thinking about there, Rock?"

Realising I'm still wearing a shit-eating grin, I try to wipe it off as I look down at her. "Last night."

Her small fist bumps my arm. "Proud of yourself, are you?"

Picking her up, I swing her around. "Fuckin' right I am." I lift her to me and kiss her. "Fuckin' proud of you too. You've come a hell of a long way, Becca."

She glows at my compliment. "All thanks to you. If it wasn't for you I'd still be chained in that cellar."

Or she might be dead. The thought sobers me. Putting her down, she puts her arm through mine and we carry on walking. And fuck me if I don't just enjoy being close to her.

Just as we come up to the clubroom door it swings open, almost knocking into me. "Hey..." I'm just about to admonish whoever's coming out when Prez pushes past, along with Peg, Blade, and Wraith. Fuck me, Slick and Marvel are coming out too.

"Rock. Got visitors. Need you with," Wraith barks as he passes.

I react immediately. "Becca, go find the women and stay with them, okay?"

I'm pleased when she doesn't question me, just goes into the clubroom, her puzzled expression when she looks back over her shoulder the only sign she's concerned. Fuck yeah. That right there. That shows she'd make a great old lady. But I park that thought as I hurry down the track, catching up with my brothers.

Coming to the gate I don't even need to ask who's come calling, there's immediate recognition. But I can't remember getting a home visit from them before. It's members from the local chapter of the dom, the Wretched Soulz. Headed up by none other than their prez, Chaz.

Matt gets the nod to slide the gate open. Getting off his bike, the prez comes inside, his members stay where they are.

"Prez." Drummer greets him politely.

"Prez," comes the response. Respect given where due.

"Your boys want to come inside?"

The Soulz VP, Bull, still astride his bike, gives a stilted laugh. His prez sends him a dirty look, then turns back to Drummer. "Nah, this won't take long. Stub got word to us this morning as we were riding back. Stopped off to tell you. Thought you needed to know as soon as possible."

Drummer makes a go on gesture with his hand.

"Fact is we came to see if you were still breathing."

Now my prez stiffens, and around him all of us start taking this seriously.

"Yeah. Seems he got close to the man you wanted him to. Gave him the message you wanted passed on. About his wife? Well, that put him in a bit of a quandary. Stub didn't hang around to get details. He's gonna go back later. But seems your man already had you targeted as the primary suspects for taking out the Chaos Riders. You've got explosives on your compound…"

"Where?" Drum snaps sharply.

"No fucking idea. But they must have been planted recently. Your man was beside himself. Seems something's going to happen soon, maybe even today. He left exactly how it was going to be done to the man he hired. He thought his woman was dead, laid that at your door. Now he's crapping himself in case she gets hurt." His eyes sharpen. "Know you're going to be pretty busy. We'll meet when you've sorted it, Drummer." He gives a sharp nod.

With that, Chaz turns and goes back to his bike. There's the thunder of engines starting, and soon only a cloud of dust is left at the gates.

"Prospect. Get the women and children out of the club-house. Get them out in the open. Around the pool," Drummer orders even before the sound of the bikes begins to fade.

"Got it, Prez." Matt sets off at a run.

"Prez." Blade pushes past me to get Drummer's attention. "This place is sewn up tight. We need to get Mouse looking at the security tapes, but for starters, I reckon there's only one way anything can be brought onto the compound without us knowing."

"Unless we've got a fuckin' traitor somewhere…"

"Ain't got no traitors, Viper. Blade, whatcha thinking?" Drummer dismisses the notion one of us is responsible, as I would too.

The enforcer points to the shop behind us. "We had two customers who left their cars over the weekend. Not unusual by itself, but given the circumstances…"

Before he finishes speaking Slick's on his way over and rolling the doors up. There are two cars inside, up on ramps, in the middle of being worked on. Yelling at everyone else to keep out, he walks around underneath, then, clearly not having found anything, lowers them both to ground level.

I'm standing outside watching him, feeling useless. I'd offer to help but I don't know what I'm looking for. Doubt it's going to be something as handy as a spherical object with 'bomb' written on it.

Prez stares into the shop, then looks around at the men standing with him. "Agree with Blade this is the most likely, but I don't want something takin' us by fuckin' surprise. What else should we be lookin' at, Peg?"

In sergeant-at-arms mode, Peg's eyes narrow. "Along the boundaries. We're vulnerable if someone throws something over the fence. Mouse should check all tapes, and while he's doing that we'll have to do a perimeter check." He tugs at his beard. "And check out the clubhouse. There were hangarounds up last night."

"Good point, Peg. Get it organised, will you?"

He didn't need to tell him. Peg's already moving. Men come flooding down from the clubhouse, apparently the prospect had told them we got ourselves a situation. Heart, Paladin, Joker, and Lady almost skid to a stop. They're running so fast the others following almost crash into them like some kind of comedy sketch.

"What can we do?" Heart exclaims.

"Get those fuckin' boundaries checked." Peg starts assigning men. Nodding when he hears Mouse has already begun viewing the footage from the last couple of days. "Dollar, Blade, Shooter, Marvel, if you were with a hangaround last night, check out anywhere they had access to. Jekyll and Road, you too."

"Wasn't with a fuckin' hangaround," Road grumbles.

"Those that weren't," Peg glares at Road, "check along the fenceline. Look for anything that might have been thrown over. Tyre tracks outside, stuff like that."

"Found something, Prez." Slick emerges from the auto shop. "Like Blade suggested, it's in the fuckin' car. The white Ford."

"Can you disarm it?"

"Tricky. But I'll try." Slick's face is about as serious as I've ever seen it. He stands motionless for a moment, his palms cradling his bald head. "Need to get everyone well back."

"Timer or remote?" Peg asks quickly.

"Timer. Can't see when it's set for."

"Okay then." Peg starts to follow Slick. "The other car clear?" When Slick nods, he waves me across. "Get the second moved out, okay? Give Slick room to work. But push it, don't start it. And move fuckin' carefully."

I hope Slick's right to have cleared the Mustang. I walk across, note the keys are in it, and with my heart in my fucking mouth take off the handbrake. Heart and Viper come alongside. Walking by the open door with one hand on the steering wheel, I guide it as slowly and carefully as possible as we back it out, fearing any wrong movement we might make could set the bomb off. I exhale in relief as we manoeuvre it well away from the shop. When we're clear, my palms are sweating.

Prez turns to Blade. "Looks like we've got a minute at least. Got any gas stored in there?"

The man who manages the shop answers, "Yeah, not a lot. A couple of five-gallon barrels."

Prez's eyes narrow. "Think you can get them out without disturbing Slick or the car?"

Rolling his eyes as though annoyed with himself, Blade nods. "Sure can. There's also the Argon for the welding equipment."

I step up. It's the last thing I want to do, get close to the bomb once again, but I offer, unwilling to watch my brothers take all the risk. "I'll come help." Joker, Lady, and Marvel aren't far behind me.

We almost go into the shop on tiptoe. The hairs on the back of my neck stand up as I ease alongside the wall furthest away from the car Slick's crouched down beside. Getting a trolley, we slide it under the first barrel and start to wheel it out, taking it well away from the estimated blast area. Blade carries the Argon gas out on his own.

Then we return for the second barrel. *Fuck this!* I'm more than relieved when we make it safely back out into the fresh air. Joining my brothers, we watch Slick walking around the car, gingerly opening the doors. *Fuck, my brother's got some balls.*

"Fuckin' hell," Blade starts. "Sam was working on that just yesterday afternoon. Wanted to get a head start on it before the weekend. She can't have seen a damn thing." He shakes his head.

"Slick's looking under the seat," Viper points out. "Sam was looking at the engine." He looks distraught at the thought his daughter had been so close to the explosive.

I'm not surprised Blade has paled. I'd have done so myself. Drummer sucks in air loudly through his teeth.

The man we're all avidly watching steps out of the shop. "Right," he starts as if talking to himself. No one finds it strange he sounds tense and his muscles are bunched as though he's preparing for a fight. His hands though, they seem quite steady. Unlike my own.

"What you thinking, Slick?" Drum's loud voice makes more than one of us jump.

"I'm considering the best way to disarm it," Slick replies. "I don't want to rush this, cut the wrong wire…"

As his voice tails off we don't need more. He doesn't have to draw us a picture.

He returns to the car, then a few minutes later, Slick comes out the front again. "Okay…" he smooths his hand over his bald head. "Think I know what I'm doing now. I'm going to disarm it in a couple of minutes. First I've got to get the cover off." He looks at us and grins. "Wish me good luck."

It's so quiet it's as though no one dares breathing. Now it's not just my hands, my whole body begins to sweat, even though clouds cover the autumn sky. I loosen the neck of my tee with my finger. *Christ, I hope Slick knows what he's doing.* He can build a bomb, we all know that, but disarming one must be another matter.

No one's moving. No one's talking. Each of us keeping our fears to ourselves.

Slick should have bombproof clothing. But we don't keep that on hand in the club. *Maybe we should in the future.*

My nose itches, I'm almost afraid to scratch it.

Time ticks by. Slick doesn't update us further, which none of us comment on, knowing he'll be concentrating. The only thing we need to hear next is that he's rendered it harmless.

"Who brought that car in, Blade?" Drummer asks quietly.

"Never seen him before, Prez. Just a citizen. Nothing unusual. Sam might remember more about him. He was black, that's all I know. Twenties or early thirties perhaps? His name will be on the computer."

I note Drummer's face tightening as Blade mentions Sam and how close his old lady had unknowingly been to a bomb. Now I have Becca I can understand it. He shakes off his concern and turns back to Blade. "Mouse will only be able to check the name he's given us. Did you see the documents for the car?"

"Nah. Didn't bother. He reckoned the car was a gas guzzler. Sam was going to check the timin' and all that." Turning around I see Blade looking worried. I'd be too, in his position, but I doubt there was anything he could have done to prevent it or that he'd missed anything suspicious. "His friend followed him and gave him a ride back. Said he'd come back on Tuesday. I was just relieved it wasn't a rush job."

Their conversation over, not much more they can say, we all turn back to watch Slick again.

Now it's my ear that feels like a bug's crawling over it. Gingerly I swat the imaginary insect away.

Slick swears loudly, then shouts a warning. "Get back! Get back now!"

A split second then we're turning, not stopping to ask Slick anything more. He's done his best, but he's failed. Even before the blast I swear I feel heat at my back.

I'm moving, but it seems like I'm running in slow motion. Wraith's just ahead, but not by much. Peg's in the lead, Drummer comes up alongside.

Are we far enough now?

A flash like a lightning strike, a deep hollow boom closely following, the rush of air sends me off my feet. Smaller fizzes, pops, and more explosions.

My ears are ringing. I'm winded as I try to pull myself to my knees, shaking my head trying to clear it. Blind from the dust and sand sent up by the blast.

"Slick!" Peg must have shouted at full volume, as I can hear him above the roar of the flames. As the dust starts to settle I see him racing back toward the burning shop.

Slick.

Drum staggers past me, and again I just make him out, yelling, "Slick! Fuck!"

It's then I see Slick on the ground, unmoving. Being the last out, he took the brunt of the detonation.

CHAPTER 27

Rock

I manage to pull myself up, wishing my ears would stop ringing, and once on my feet run back as fast as I can hoping to fuck Slick's okay. As I near the shop a physical wall of heat hits me. Peg's gesticulating at Road, who's got some first aid training. Slick. The one thing that cheers me is Peg wouldn't be bothering to get him attention if he was already dead.

The sergeant-at-arms stands over Road as he examines him. "Can't we just move him? I can feel the fuckin' flames from here." He's still shouting, he must be deafened like the rest of us are.

"Give me a moment." Road's touching Slick gently, feeling for a pulse.

Slick, man. You better be okay. How the fuck could we tell Ella her old man's dead? Or Jayden, for that matter. Slick's been like a father to her.

Paladin's looking sick. His eyes meet mine and I know his thoughts are running along the same track as my own.

Joker runs up with a board he's got from somewhere. Carefully, Road and Peg roll Slick onto it. There's no shortage of volunteers helping to carry him away and out of reach of the burning matter, ashes and soot that are flying through the air. Something pops and lands just where Slick, only a second or two ago, had been lying.

Road walks alongside the makeshift stretcher. "Take him to the clubhouse, but be careful with him. If he wakes up try to keep him lying down."

Drummer's face is dark as he looks down at his stricken man, then at the fireball that used to be our shop. "We can't handle this. I've called out the fire department. Got a bus coming for Slick."

Looking down at the injured man, I'm concerned his face is completely white. The board is reddening, showing he's bleeding from somewhere. I feel helpless watching my brothers carrying him so gently. All I can do is hope he's not seriously hurt. I can do nothing for him. Staying at the shop is probably where I can best help.

I return to where Blade's standing, looking at the burning pyre which used to be his business. In his hands is a useless fire extinguisher. He might as well piss on it for all the effect that would have.

"Brother."

As I put my hand on his shoulder, Matt appears at a run from the clubhouse. He skids to a halt and looks around him, suddenly yelling, "Blade, need that over here." Coming over, he grabs the fire extinguisher out of the enforcer's hands. "It's set some undergrowth alight. At least we can stop it spreading." He's noticed something we've missed. Good on the prospect. Small fires have started smouldering, and he's right, we need to get on top of that shit.

Matt's tackling the larger areas, other brothers using their boots to stamp down or kick sand over smaller burns. Apart from Paladin and Road, who have stayed with Slick, everyone else has come back down here. The shop might be a total loss, but with the manpower we've got, hopefully the fire will be contained.

We're beating this. As we make progress I start to focus my thoughts on the fucker who has done this to us. *Hawk.* But how did Hawk come to the conclusion we were responsible for the body in the cellar? We'll be looking for answers to that later.

My slowly recovering ears pick out sirens, which become louder by the second. Two fire trucks and a police car soon appear. Known faces jump out of the first. Drummer updates Hammer, the paramedic, who races up to the clubhouse that he's more than familiar with—only a few months ago he was delivering Heart and Marcia's twins there during a wildfire. Darcy swings herself out, immediately searching for Peg, her face losing its tension when she sees he's okay and unharmed. The sergeant-at-arms, however, is the opposite. His face tightens when he sees her manhandling the hose. She's what, four, five months pregnant now? They have constant disagreements about her continuing to work. Which Peg obviously loses. After a quick explanation of what they're dealing with, Captain Slade puts his men to work. The police, once the fireman are organised, wait no longer to approach.

"Drummer." A state trooper comes over. "What the hell has happened here?"

Drummer turns around and shakes his head. "Accident. You know the type of stuff we work with in the shop. Gas, Arcon. Fucking assholes didn't notice a gas leak on that...car, there." The hesitation as the burned-out hulk barely resembles anything like a vehicle anymore. It's then I realise one of the doors flying off must have been what brought Slick down. It had been hard to see through the dust. Drum continues, "Gas leak. Sparks. Baboom."

The trooper eyes him sharply, but the prez's face is set. Disappointment, upset for the loss. Nothing suspicious to see there.

"We've got this handled, Officer," Prez tells him firmly.

"I'm sure you have." The trooper smirks. Then shakes his head, waves to his partner, has a quick word with the fire captain, then, thankfully, departs.

Drummer speaks softly. "They don't care. Someone wants to blow us up? They'd have been happier if they'd taken some of us out. Don't want them investigatin'. Whoever did this to us, *to Slick*. Well, they're going to pay. In blood."

"Hawk," I say quietly.

"Goes without saying. But he didn't plant the bomb. The man who did? Well, I want blood for that." Leaving me, Drummer steps forward. "You need me here, Captain?"

Slade shakes his head. "Your boys did a good job stopping it spreading. Might as well let us do what we do best."

"I'll leave the boys with you. I got business to go deal with."

As Drummer turns away the captain calls him back. He speaks quietly, but I'm close enough to hear. "Drummer. Look, I know you. You know us. You might have fooled the trooper, but auto shops don't just explode." As Prez goes to speak, he stops him. "You and I both know the cops aren't going to bother investigating. And there'll be no insurance claim put in, am I right?"

"You're right," Drum says through gritted teeth. Bikers don't do insurance.

"Which means whatever I find will be just between us, okay? I'll give it to you directly."

Prez stares at him for a moment before he nods his head. "Appreciate that, Captain. As I said, lazy douchebags didn't notice a leak, or think that the electrics would spark."

The captain eyes him for a moment before grinning. "Just what I'll put in my official report, though I might make it a bit more credible. Oh, and Drummer, before you go, any ammunition…?"

"Nothing," Drum says sharply. "We don't run guns or store ammunition in the shop. As you know, Slade, we run a clean club."

"I haven't seen anything different. But I need to be sure, that's my crew going in there."

While Slade's got a point, Drummer's right. All our ammo is stored under one of the old swimming pools where no one can find it. It's been missed by the Feds before now. As the captain goes back to what he was doing, Drummer waves Wraith, Blade, Dollar, Mouse, and Peg to follow him. Peg's reluctant to leave, but as Darcy takes a second to glare at him he throws up his hands in defeat and comes along with us. I've never understood it before, how much hold one woman can have over your life. Until Becca. Yeah, well, she's made everything come clear. If I was Peg, pregnant or not, I'd have slung her over my shoulder and carried her away, never mind what she wanted. But then, Darcy and Becca are two different women.

I stay for a while doing what I can to help, which means keeping out of the way of the experts. When I admit my puny efforts are futile, I finally return to the clubhouse just in time to see the paramedics, now using a proper stretcher, are already taking Slick out to the ambulance. He still appears to be unconscious, but for the moment, at least, alive. My hands fist at the sight of Ella and Jayden rushing behind him, Ella pale with worry, Jayden has red-rimmed eyes. Paladin is dangling his keys from one of his fingers, obviously preparing to follow them to the hospital. I move out of everyone's way, not wanting to impede them. Slick needs to get where he's going as fast as he can. But I do stop to question Road quietly before greeting Becca, who's making her way over.

"Slick?"

Road shrugs. "Least he's got is a concussion." He leans in conspiratorially and lowers his voice. "Until they do tests they don't know more than that. May have a brain bleed. He took a pretty hard blow to the head." He's right to speak quietly, the women don't need to hear the worst. It's best we all remain optimistic.

Then Becca's with me. She pauses a step away as if to reassure herself I'm all right. Seconds later she's in my arms and I allow myself a moment to treasure her. When she tells me she loves me, that's it. Pulling her to me I kiss her, pouring everything into it, reaffirming we're both alive.

"Was it Hawk?" Her voice breaks as she asks the question. "Rock, what if Slick…"

"Slick's going to be fine," I try to reassure her, but the look on my face must betray me. I can't promise her that. My heart bleeds for Ella and Jayden and the pain they must be going through right now. "As for Hawk," I continue, "we don't know at the moment, Ella. He's locked up. But he appears to have arranged this." I turn her to face me. "Sweetheart, in case it is down to him, we need to know Hawk's contacts. Do you know anything that might help? Does he know the sort who could arrange an explosion?"

Her eyes open wide as she shakes her head. "Rock, he is… was…a pastor. The only people I'm aware of are the elders at the church and the congregation. None of whom would know the first thing about something like this. I'm sorry, but I can't help. If he was involved in anything else, I didn't know of it."

Now my hands cradle either side of her head. "Think hard, Becca. Did anything ever strike you as strange? Any private conversations you overheard that you weren't supposed to? Anyone in particular come to your place and have meetings with Hawk?"

She bites her lip as she tries to remember. I know she'd do everything she can to help. But it seems she comes up blank. "I never even knew about the Chaos Riders, Rock. They never came to the house. He kept me isolated, remember? I really wish I could do something to help." Her eyes start to water, presumably as she knows she's being no help. "Parishioners used to pop in, of course, but I wasn't party to any private discussions. I think I remember the man we saw at the church visiting, but I may have been mistaken."

My fingers stroke her cheeks gently. "Don't worry yourself, babe. I didn't think you'd be able to help. I'm just covering all bases. Don't get yourself wound up." It's easy for me to say. I've probably said too much already, worrying her with my all but confirmation the explosion was in some way down to Hawk, organised by him at least. She'll think that means it's down to her, that she brought trouble on the club, and now Slick's in the hospital because of it. "It's probably nothing to do with him," I tell her. Too little, too late.

The mood around us is sombre. The women well aware not only have we lost one of our major businesses, but Slick has been hurt. Only one thing can be heard over the subdued conversations, Marcia and Heart's twins. She's trying to rock them and calm them, but they're both playing up and screaming. For a moment I wish I was still deaf.

Heart notices everyone heading toward church and asks, rather optimistically I think, "Prez, you need me?"

Drummer gives his kids a pointed look. "Nah, looks like you've got your hands full out here. Come on in when things have calmed down a bit."

Heart looks at the crying babies and grimaces. Grunt, the fucking wolfhound, has laid down near them, his head on his paws, his brown eyes focused on the babies. Even the dog looks concerned. But then a worried look seems to be his normal expression.

Still holding Becca, I watch as Sam gathers together the old ladies. Apart from Marcia, who is staying behind to watch over the children, everyone else is going to go to the hospital to support Ella and Jayden. Predictably Becca wants to go too. I don't want her out of my sight. Who knows what Hawk might be arranging now he knows where she is. If he's got other 'friends' like the Chaos Riders, he could get them to snatch her.

"Nah, babe. I want you here. Don't want you leaving unless I'm with you. Matt?" I call the prospect over.

"This is my fault, isn't it? Rock, I couldn't stand it if…"

"Nothing to do with you, sweetheart." Prez overhears and shuts her down fast. Even if it is, it's club business, and it's best if she's kept in the dark.

"Gotta get to a meeting, Becca. I'll see you soon, okay?" She goes on tiptoe to give me a kiss, then goes over to speak to Sophie. I watch her for a moment, wondering how well she's going to cope with what's happened.

As I start to move toward our meeting room Marvel comes in and catches up with the men moving in that direction. Drummer and Peg look at him with raised eyebrows. He was one of the brothers who'd been doing the final check of the boundaries. We'd found one bomb, but wanted to make sure there were no others.

"All clear that we can tell," Marvel tells us.

Peg nods to Drummer. "We searched the clubroom before I let the old ladies come in. Mind you, didn't have a cat's chance in hell to keep them out once Slick was brought up."

Marvel, like me, has his attention caught by the crying kids and then by the shaggy wolfhound cross carefully watching his charges. "Heart, ever considered training him as a sniffer dog? Fuckin' animal does fuck all around here." It's said good naturedly, and Marvel chuckles when Heart shoots him the finger. But actually, Marvel might have a point.

"Is it possible to train a wolfhound, Heart?"

"Whether it fuckin' is or not, we've got more pressin' things to discuss, Rock." Prez leads his way into church.

CHAPTER 28

Becca

After the amazing night with Rock, the events of this morning had come as a shock. The day had started so well. I'd had a new lightness of step when I walked down to the clubhouse alongside Rock. When he was abruptly called away I didn't mind entering the clubroom alone, while being curious and a little concerned as to why the men were rushing out.

But my worries were soon pushed out of my head. When Sam saw me, something about the look on my face—hopefully not the stiffness of my gait—must have given me away.

Coming straight over, she bumps me on the arm. "Looks like Rock gave you the full biker treatment last night. You went back for seconds then?" She grins knowingly.

"Oooh. Becca got shagged!" Sophie shouts out. "Well, did Rock rock your world? Come on babes. Let a sister know." As though it's bruise-Becca-day, she also knocks her bicep against mine.

"Was the Rock rock hard?" Ella calls out.

"Sis!" Jayden tries to look shocked.

Marcia's laughing. "You better give them something, else they won't stop. But keep it PG because of the kids. I think they're asking if he rocked your world."

I try to look prim but fail. "It was great." It's about all I can say. How do you describe sex of the type you never even dreamed existed? It's not just shyness, this is something I've never had before. Women to talk to, to laugh and joke with. Tears prick at the corner of my eyes as I feel emotional. I've barely dared think of the future, but could Rock and I be together? Could I make my home here with the rest of the old ladies? I'm fast coming to the conclusion there's nothing I'd like better.

Taking pity on me, Sam links her arm through mine and leads me across to the couch, absentmindedly passing Eli a toy bike he'd dropped as she passes. "What are you plans for the day, Becca?"

I'm afraid I have to admit I pout. "Rock and I were off to see Beef, but he got waylaid as I was coming in."

"Yeah, there's someone at the gate. Drum went running off too. Hopefully it won't take them too long to sort out."

The words are barely out of her mouth before the prospect, Matt, comes running into the room. "All old ladies and children to go out to the swimming pool." He's so out of breath the words are hard to make out.

Getting to her feet, Sam asks sharply, "What's going on, Matt." She holds up her hand. "And don't you dare say club business. If it's to do with our safety, then we need to have more information. It's not particularly warm, and we've got children to think about…"

"Bomb."

"What?" "Where?" The questions come from everyone, along with gasps of horror.

"Anywhere. Somewhere on the compound. Prez thinks around the swimming pool is the safest place."

"Right everyone. Let's get the kids and get out there now." Sam starts directing people. "Becca, could you give Marcia a hand with the twins please? Sandy, if you can take Eli I'll bring Grunt." I'm impressed by the way she immediately takes charge, and that there's no way she'll be leaving the dog behind.

Sam's so successful in organising us that the clubhouse is evacuated in orderly fashion, without any panic. It's only when we're all outside that we turn back and I realise I'm tensing up, waiting for what's become my comfortable place to turn into a fireball. I'm not the only one to be staring back, hardly daring to breathe.

"Mommy. Can I swim?"

"Not now, Eli. It's not warm enough." Sam's attention is caught by her son's question. It breaks the tension.

"Mummy!" Olivia's complaining to Sophie. "I want to swim too." Sam and Sophie exchange glances and both shake their heads together.

"Might as well make ourselves comfortable." Ella indicates the loungers.

Jayden comes over and gestures for me to give her the baby, who's luckily continued sleeping. I hand her over, grateful to do so before she wakes up. Even the teenager knows far more about looking after a baby than me. Then, no longer having a distraction, I look back again, wondering exactly who is searching the clubhouse for a bomb. *Rock?* I grow cold. While I wouldn't want to see any man hurt, I can't lose him. Not now I've just found him. My heart rate speeds up.

"Becca. Come sit here."

I realise I'm trembling as I go to join Marcia. "Is it for real?" I ask as I take the empty seat beside her. "Is it really going to blow up?"

Marcia purses her lips. "You know I was a cop?" When I nod, she continues. "Hopefully they've just received an empty threat. But you know these men, they're overprotective. They're going to take any warning seriously whether it's credible or not." She goes quiet, obviously thinking. "We've had no strangers at the clubhouse, no delivery comes there direct, the prospects bring stuff up from the gate. It's hard to see how any explosives could be planted."

"There were hangarounds up from Tucson last night," Sandy reminds Marcia.

Sam overhears and gives a very unladylike snort. "You see what they were wearing? Hard to believe they could smuggle anything in in those skimpy clothes."

"What about purses?"

Drummer's old lady shrugs. "I expect that's the kind of thing the men will be looking for. They'll have it handled." As she looks back toward the clubhouse the beating of my pulse speeds up again. The thought of any of the men poking around looking for something that shouldn't be there is frightening.

Sophie's cleaning dirt off Olivia's face with a tissue she's dampened with spit. She looks up when she's satisfied. "Loads of bomb scares back in London," she informs us. "Even my workplace was evacuated for a suspect package more than once. Never came to anything."

"Hopefully this won't, either." Sandy relaxes back on the recliner. "Carmen's at work, she's lucky she's missing all this."

As she names the hairdresser my hand automatically goes up to my hair. It's starting to grow out and could do with a trim to keep it tidy. I can't wait for it to grow long again. Spikes sitting up at all angles don't suit me. Carmen won't just let me leave it, but she knows what she's doing, we'd been discussing styles to let it grow while keeping it tidy. The thought of the talks I've had with her about my hair help keep my mind on mundane things, and as minutes tick past without anything happening my mind starts to ease. *It is probably just an empty threat.* When the sun comes out from behind a cloud giving a gentle warmth, I raise my face up. I start to think of Rock eventually being able to hold onto my hair when he's thrusting inside of me, which makes parts of me tingle.

"What you thinking about?" Sam nudges me with a laugh. *Busted.* I feel my face flame as I watch her pick up Eli and check he doesn't need changing. "Amy! Come back here. Stay with your mom. She needs help with the babies."

"But I want my bike."

"I'll get it for you later, sweetheart, but now I need some help." Marcia backs Sam up, her calm voice showing none of the concern I'm certain she's feeling.

Heart's daughter pouts for a second before skipping back, followed closely by Grunt, immediately going to Marcia and her young siblings.

We might be congregated around the pool rather than being inside, but a certain peace settles on us, particularly as time continues to go by and nothing happens. Once again I relax back, this time making sure I don't think of Rock and the intimate things we could be doing. The babble of voices, the squeals of children goes on around me.

The calm is shattered by a loud explosion, but not from the clubhouse.

"It's the shop!" Setting Eli down, Sam jumps to her feet and looks at the smoke billowing into the sky. "Soph, can you watch Eli for me? I'm going to see what's happened."

Not waiting for an answer, she plonks Eli down next to Olivia, and the two children, who'd jumped at the loud sound, but being too young to understand the significance, quickly settle back down, becoming occupied with showing each other their toys as Sam walks quickly away. The rest of us stay put in a stunned silence, not knowing whether to follow the prez's old lady or not. Looks exchanged between us indicate we're all on the same page. Having convinced ourselves there was no danger, the fact that there was a bomb on the compound is alarming.

"Was that the only one?" Sophie asks at last, concern in her face. "I hope everyone's okay."

"Best stay here, love. Wait until Sam comes back..." Sandy pats her arm.

Sam *is* back. Escorted by Matt. "Okay, okay," she's saying. "I get it. I'll wait here." While the prospect folds his arms and stands guard, she looks at us and shrugs.

"Is anyone hurt? Tell us that at least." I'm frantic with worry about Rock. I haven't just found the man of my dreams only to lose him.

But Matt looks on stoically.

"Oh my god. Someone's hurt, aren't they?" Sophie gets to her feet. "Wraith, no..." Her hand goes over her mouth, her face pales.

"Rock?" I ask anxiously, but get no answer.

"Heart?" Marcia questions frantically.

"Is Slick alright?" Ella and Jayden both stand at once. There's a twitch on Matt's face, which had remained impassive when other names were mentioned. "Nooooo!" Ella wails, then both her and her sister push past Matt, not giving him a chance to stop them.

As though it's started a tidal wave, all the old ladies are moving and racing in the direction of the clubhouse.

"Stop!" Matt calls out, trying to get in front. "We don't know..."

"Clubhouse is clear!" Peg appears at the rear entrance. I notice he's covered in dust, and there's blood on his forehead, but it looks like it's just from a small scratch. *Who else is hurt? And how badly?*

"Slick!" We're inside the clubhouse, my eyes rapidly scanning everyone standing, as Ella exclaims seeing Slick brought in on a stretcher. "Slick!" Getting no response, her hands flail as she goes to her old man. Jayden rushes to her side and captures one of her sister's hands in her own.

Drummer comes over and puts his arm around Ella, holding her back. "Slick got knocked out in the blast. Got the medics coming, Ella, sweetheart." She staggers, and he tightens his hold around her. I anxiously glance behind him, but the rest of the men haven't come in.

Where's Rock? What's happened to him? The medics appear, check out the injured man carefully, then waste no time transferring Slick onto a proper stretcher, and it's only when he's wheeled out that at last I see him. *My man.* Walking in, rubbing at his arm but otherwise looking alright. I push my way past the other men to get to him. He acknowledges me with a chin lift but finishes his conversation with Road. When I reach him, I pause a step away, just letting my eyes soak in the man who, for one awful moment, I feared I had lost.

"Rock." My voice comes out as a whisper.

He returns my gaze, then steps forward, then I'm in his arms, breathing in the perfume of my man, letting his scent, now tinged with smoke, consume me. I'd been so scared, worried I'd found him only to lose him. It's then I realise how much he means to me. He's my saviour, my rock. My. Rock.

"I love you." The words escape without me consciously intending to say them, drawn forth by the emotional turmoil of the morning.

His lips are on mine. It's not a gentle kiss. His hand curves behind my head, his fingers trying to find purchase on my short hair as he angles my face and ravishes my mouth. A celebration we're both alive and safe. He breaks off too soon.

He asks me questions about Hawk, enough for me to know that my husband is behind it. If it was possible to hate him more, this would have made me. I feel so guilty. If I hadn't come to the club this trouble wouldn't have come to them, and

Slick…Slick wouldn't be on his way to the hospital, quite possibly fighting for his life.

Drummer overhears the end of our conversation. But even his assurance that the bomb had nothing to do with me doesn't help. *What should I do?*

Sam is gathering all the women together. It seems the old ladies are preparing to go to the hospital to support Ella. Offering my shoulder to lean on is the least I can do.

"Can I go along, Rock?" If Ella suspects I'm the reason her husband got injured, she might not want me with her. But it wouldn't be a wasted journey. While I'm there I can also go and see Beef. We'd planned to visit him later, and he'll be wondering why we've not arrived. Beef will talk good sense and ground me.

But Rock's got other ideas. "Nah, babe. I want you here. Don't want you leaving unless I'm with you. Matt?" he finishes, waving the prospect over.

I want to question him. *What else does he know?* Is he just being cautious, or does he think Hawk is planning on getting me away and, heaven forbid, have more of his *friends* look out for me? Does Rock think I'm in danger? But I've no chance to ask. When the prospect comes up to us, Rock tells him enough for me to gather Matt will be my babysitter while he's in a meeting with his brothers. Then Drummer's voice sounds, and Rock disappears into church.

CHAPTER 29

Rock

S een too much fuckin' fire around here lately," Peg growls as
he walks to his seat. "What the fuck was that, Prez? What
shit is this Hawk involved in that he can order a hit like this on
the club?"

"That's what we're here to try to figure out." Drum tunnels
his hands through his hair. "Dollar. Will need you to look into
the financial implications of setting the shop back up."

"That's the tattoo shop down the tube," Blade complains.
"No auto shop, no new business. Fuck."

I look down at my hands, feeling guilt laying heavy on me. I
brought Becca back to the compound. I got us on Hawk's radar.
"I'm sorry," I mumble. "Shouldn't have got you involved with
Becca."

"What the fuck difference does that make?" Drummer snarls.
"You think we'd have turned that little girl away when we saw
what had been done to her? You have your brothers behind you.
Same as we were there for Marcia, Sophie, and not forgettin'
Sam. You expect us to turn our backs on anyone's woman?" His
stare focuses on me. "Well? Had it been any one of your
brothers, Rock, you say you wouldn't have done the fuckin'
same?"

I give him the evil eye. "Course I'm not fuckin' sayin' that."

"Then shut the fuck up." He glares at me again before saying,
"Mouse?"

Having got Prez's attention, Mouse clears his throat. "Not sure who we're looking at for this one."

"Let's start with Hawk." Wraith points at him. "Hawk got word his woman was dead, and somehow that we were responsible. We're just fuckin' lucky Prez and Rock went to see Stub, who was able to get a message to him correcting his information. If we hadn't been warned things could have been fuckin' different. Sam, Blade… Any one of us could have been in the shop when it exploded." He's right. It's not unusual for brothers to be working on their own rides over the weekend. Or the prez's woman, or their son, Eli, who loves nothing more than helping his mom.

Drummer pales for a second, then shakes his head and brings himself back to what we're dealing with. "Let's go through what we know. Hawk's a fuckin' pastor with a violent streak that put him in the pen. Not the type you'd immediately expect to know people who'd build and plant a bomb. Except he's also sitting on a church with one of the biggest arsenals I've ever seen underneath. He's got to be holding that for someone. We've just got to figure out who he's working with."

"Let's start with the man who brought the bomb onto the compound," Blade suggests.

"Nah," Prez contradicts. "We'll get to him. But I suspect he's just the delivery boy. I want to know who's behind it."

"Find him, find them," Blade suggests.

"Maybe, but let's think about this. Again, who's Hawk teamed up with?"

"The Herreras," Peg puts forward. "They would have fingered us for the hit on the Riders. They set us up to go head to head."

"I'm not so sure," Drummer considers. "If it was the Herreras they'd have moved those guns by now."

"They might have restocked. They might be using the church…"

"There was dust on those boxes," Wraith puts in. "That doesn't happen overnight. Those guns had been there a while."

Drummer raises his chin toward the VP. "I agree. There was nothing to suggest there'd been recent activity there. Which means Hawk's the key to all this. And Hawk was either friendly, very friendly with, or had something over the Chaos Riders. They were looking after his woman for him. So, what's the connection? In your time with them, Rock, you ever see them running guns?"

"It wasn't discussed in church, but remember I wasn't sitting around that table for long. Something of that type could have been going on. A few their members were on the road a lot. Of course, it could have been their boys they left in Phoenix who were more involved on that side."

"That would make sense. That's where Hawk's church is."

"Which could explain why the Herreras were prepared to give them a chance. They might have known they had experience of the trade. Could have been useful to them."

Drummer stares at the VP, then shakes his head. "If the Herreras were already using them, they wouldn't have offered the trade to us. The fact they did suggests we could be looking in the wrong direction linking Hawk to them. I don't think they were behind the bombing. And the Herreras would more likely be pulling the strings than jumping to Hawk's tune."

I raise my hand and frown. "Now the Riders are no longer in the running, we're the only ones in the game. Could be a message to play ball, or…"

"Or they'll take us out," Peg finishes for me.

Drum's hand slaps on the table. "Not their fuckin' style. Oh, they might fuckin' attack us, but they'd warn us first. Javier would have contacted me. Don't forget, we know Hawk ordered the hit." Shaking his head, Prez continues, "I just can't see a connection between Hawk and the Herreras."

"Why hasn't Javier been in touch?" asks Blade, his brow furrowed. "Think about it. They must know the Riders are out of the picture by now, so why haven't they come to us?"

Kicking his chair out a few inches, Drummer leans back, resting a foot against the table. One hand strokes his beard. "Things don't add up. You're right, Blade. I was expecting the Herreras to come knocking long before now. And then there's Hawk and the mystery of the guns under the church. None of this makes any sense. All we know is that someone planted a bomb in the club, and that Hawk was behind it. We know no more than that."

"Could Stub take Hawk out? He's gotta pay for what he's done some way."

That sounds like a fucking good idea to me.

Drum moves his hand from his beard and uses it to slam it on the table. "Fuckin' think for a moment, Blade. Don't give a damn about Hawk. He'll get what's owed to him. What I do care about is who he's dealin' with, and whether they're workin' for him or he's their mule. And who the fuck he arranged to have plant a bomb in the compound. We might have more than Hawk to worry about. At least we know where he is and how we can get to him when the time comes."

There's more fidgeting than usual around the table. Most of us are impatient to get to the hospital to see what's going on with Slick. There's an air of frustration that we're still sitting here talking. Drummer's got his phone close by, but there's still been no word about our injured brother. I know everyone will share my concerns that he hasn't yet come round after the explosion. It can't be a good sign to be unconscious for so long.

Matt knocks at the door, Peg disappears for a few minutes, Prez gives us a moment to talk among ourselves. When the sergeant-at-arms returns he's got Heart with him who brings the news that the fire's been put out and Slade and his team have left the compound.

Heart and Peg, both ex-service men, lean over the table and start examining some of the remains that the captain, good to his word, has passed over. The parts of a timer he'd found are now in front of us.

"Slick's the explosive's expert." Prez eyes the device. "But Heart, anything you can tell?"

"Basic timer as far as I can see."

Peg's nodding his head, "I had a quiet word with Slade. He was the one who found it, but its existence will be left out of his report. He agrees it was something simple to make, there are instructions on the internet."

"So who are we looking at?" Wraith asks.

"In my opinion?" Peg waits for Prez's nod. "Not a munitions expert. Just someone who has the ability to get explosives and do a Google search."

"Well that narrows the field," Marvel observes snidely, and receives a scowl from Prez.

"It's someone with a link to Hawk," I put in.

"Which would be useful if we knew who he was in bed with," Drummer says. "And we only know as much as we do because Stub told him his woman, *your woman*, was here yesterday. He arranged to have the explosives planted but couldn't get back in touch to stop it when he found out he might be putting Becca at risk."

"Stub managed to see him while he was in solitary," Peg puts in. "Presumably he couldn't get a message out."

"Didn't Stub get any more info?" I ask.

Prez replies, "Apparently not. He was too intent on getting us a warnin'. Hopefully he'll be able to go back and get more."

"Any Chaos Riders left? Out of Phoenix, perhaps?"

"Worth checkin' out, Blade." Drummer nods. "But the man who brought it in was black…"

"From what I saw, Prez, Chaos Riders was a whites only club," I inform him.

"What I don't understand is how Hawk knew to blame us for the attack on their compound. Didn't leave a callin' card, Prez." Wraith's looking perplexed.

"The Herreras might have their suspicions," Drummer throws at his VP. "Herreras knew they'd pitted us against each other. From that point on, Devils and Riders became enemies." Suddenly Drummer's eyes are on me. "Were there any Chaos Riders missin'? Are you certain we took them all out, Rock?"

I lower my head into my hands, then after a few seconds look up. "Prez, I wasn't in a good state that day. From what I can remember everyone was killed. But there may have been someone missing, I can't swear to it. I'm sorry." And I am. But I'd been brought up from the basement, hurting and bleeding. I hadn't been counting the men around me, just wanted to get out and re-join my true brothers.

Prez looks weary. "Okay, we're getting nowhere with the bigger picture. Let's turn to what we do know. Right, Mouse. What have you got on the fucker who brought in the car?"

"Prez?"

Again, Drummer's fist hits the table. "The motherfucker who tried to blow us up. Whatcha found out?"

Mouse, unusually for him, seems distracted. "Oh, yeah. Fucker gave us a fake name. Got a shot of him on the security camera, but that doesn't really help. Unless anyone knows him?" Mouse clicks a few keys on his laptop, then turns it around. We all lean in for a closer look, but by all the shakes of heads, no one recognises him.

Drum's eyes narrow when it's his turn to look. "First order of business. Find *him*."

There's a moment of silence while we take in Prez's snarled command. A silence broken by Prez's phone ringing. He draws it out of his pocket and looks at the display. Then puts it on speaker.

"Paladin. What's going on?"

"Slick coded in the ambulance. They got him back."

No one speaks as we listen to the young member's update.

"He's had a brain scan. His eardrum's ruptured and there's a big bleed on his brain. The cut to his head is insignificant, the scalp always bleeds like a bitch. It's the rest they're worried about. He's been rushed into surgery."

"How's Ella doing?" Drummer asks.

"She's in pieces, Prez." Paladin breaks off, clearing his throat before resuming. "She wanted to tell him something, was gonna tell him this morning before it all kicked off. She's just found out she's pregnant."

Oh fuck. We all know they'd been trying for a baby since the wedding, had all kinds of tests and shit, but it wasn't happening. Initially the brothers had been giving Slick some shit about the state of his swimmers, though we'd all backed off as time passed. Fuck of a thing if a couple want a kid and it's not happening. Which makes Ella's announcement tremendous and, given the timing, devastating.

"Sam's comforting her, Prez, but she's hysterical. Thinks Slick is gonna die and won't ever find out."

Slick should have been the first to know. Now he's going to be the last. *If* he survives to find he's going to be a daddy. Fuck. That man's wanted a kid with Ella for so long. No wonder she's distraught. This should have been such a happy day for them, and now Slick's fighting for his life instead of celebrating.

Prez ends the call, allows a brief pause before snarling. "I want the bastard that did this. I'm prepared to start with the fucker who delivered the bomb. Yeah, Mouse?" Prez looks up.

Mouse has been tapping away on his laptop furiously while Paladin's been speaking. Something about his expression suggests he's got something to say. "What have you got for us?"

"Hoped it would be easy, but it wasn't, Prez. False plates, fake name as I said before."

"Not unexpected," observes Peg.

Prez sighs. "Does that mean it's a dead end?" He's carefully watching the whiz with computers. "All we got is a fuckin' photograph?"

CHAPTER 30
Rock

Mouse looks smug. "When have I ever let you down? Darcy found the VIN on the engine. She let Marcia have it, and she's just messaged me what she's found out. She's traced it and got a name and address for the registered owner of the car. It's not been reported as being stolen." It's useful to have an ex-cop as Heart's old lady.

Drummer's eyes open wide. "Fucker wouldn't have used his own car, would he?"

Mouse shrugs. "Hadn't owned it long. Old banger. Perhaps he's stupid enough to think we wouldn't be able to trace it with the wrong plates."

Prez holds out his hand. Mouse places a piece of paper in it. "Bo Brayden," he reads aloud. "What the fuck kind of name is Bo?"

"Maybe his parents were Bo Diddley fans," Peg suggests, earning himself a glare from the prez.

"Well if this Bo is the fucker that lit up our shop, he ain't gonna have any worries about his handle anymore," Blade cuts in, his knife coming to a stop and pointing at me.

I watch it, wondering how this asshole's connected to Hawk. "Where is he, Prez?"

"Casa Grande." Prez reads more from the note. That's useful, it's about halfway between Tucson and Phoenix. An hour's ride or so.

"What are we waiting for?" I ask, half standing up. "I've got some fuckin' questions to ask him." Including whether anyone's out to take my woman.

"Sit the fuck down, Rock," Prez growls. "Have you forgotten about Slick?"

"What d'you want us to do, Prez?"

Drummer thinks for a second before answering the VP. "Blade, you okay to go check it out? No point us going mob-handed to find the fucker's not even there. If he's sensible he'll have gone underground, and it might take a while to find him." As Prez pauses, waiting for Blade's eager nod, I notice the strain showing on his face. "Next, I want some volunteers to stay here and see what can be salvaged at the shop. So that means Viper and Bullet are needed here to assess how quickly the rebuilding can be done. Don't want to remind you, but we lose good fuckin' money the longer the shop stays closed."

Hyde puts up his hand. "I don't mind stayin' to help."

"Whoever else wants to can go to the hospital. See what's going on with Slick."

While my palms are itching to get hold of the man responsible for putting Slick there, I want to be near my brother, and there when he comes out of surgery. I brought Becca here, so I feel responsible.

Drum must see me nodding, as he quickly stops me. "Not you, Rock. Want you with me. You too, Wraith." At my raised eyebrow, he continues, "Got a meet with the dom. I want to know exactly what intel they've got about this. Didn't have much time for more than the headlines earlier. Need to know the right questions to ask this Bo when we're face to face with him."

I frown. "Becca?"

"Can go to the hospital. If I know anything about women, that's where she'll want to be." He studies me for a moment. "She'll have the rest of the brothers with her. She'll be safe."

Peg leans forward, looking down the table at me. "I'll take her in the truck. I'll watch her like I'd watch my own woman."

I won't have too many worries if she's with the sergeant-at-arms. It had been easy to see how guilty she's feeling about Slick. Keeping her here on the compound, who knows what thoughts she'll build up in her head. Letting her be with the other old ladies will be good for her. Fuck knows, most of them have put the club through some shit in their time, they won't let her take misplaced responsibility. And knowing her, she'll probably like to catch up with Beef once she knows what's going on with Slick. I nod my thanks to Peg.

Drummer bangs the gavel. "What you fuckers hanging around here for, then?"

Outside in the clubroom Becca's sitting at the bar while Matt's tidying up from the party the night before. As I expected, she's looking worried. As soon as she sees me she slides off the stool. "Matt's just told me Slick's in surgery."

"Yeah, know that darlin'." I pause to allow myself to take a look at her, realising how far she's come from the woman I first met in the cellar, but what a long way she still has to go. I still have to be careful not to put too much on her. "Hey, I've got to go do something with Prez. Peg's gonna drive you to the hospital. You can check up on Slick for yourself and go visit Beef while you're there."

Her hand comes out to touch my arm. As she does, I notice she's trembling. "You going to be okay, Rock? You're not doing something dangerous, are you?"

The events of the morning have shaken her. Have reminded her what being in an outlaw MC is all about. Quickly I reassure her. "Nah, just going to have a chat with some friends. I'll be fine, and it shouldn't take long. I'll come to the hospital after-ward and bring you home."

"Ready to go, Becca?"

As she starts to move toward Peg, I take her arm and pull her back. "Not before you kiss me," I tell her, wanting, *needing* to feel her lips against mine once again.

"Hurry it up, will you?" Peg's tossing his keys and catching them impatiently. I flip him off and continue what I was doing. Then watch as my woman follows him out, throwing just one more concerned glance at me over her shoulder.

Fuck. I was the one longing for more excitement in my life. Needing it to feel I really was in a one-percenter club. Aggrieved that the brothers with old ladies and kids wanted to keep life calm and steady, something I had translated as boring. Now things have livened up I should be happy, but I'm not. All I want is for everything to get back to the status quo with both Beef and Slick home. To show my woman that she can feel safe here and not worry every time I go out on the road. How my outlook has done a one-eighty. I'd laugh at myself if things weren't so fucked up.

"Rock? You with us?"

Similar to Peg, Drummer doesn't waste time hanging around. Wraith's already waiting at the door, holding it open. Giving myself a mental shake, I follow them out to the bikes, Matt tagging along behind.

It's not far to the meet, which is halfway between our two clubhouses, a typical biker bar, quite busy on an autumn Saturday afternoon. While weekend warriors are wandering around outside admiring each other's rides, we park ours up where the Wretched Soulz's prospect is already guarding three bikes. Leaving Matt with him, we make our way inside. We find the people we're meeting in the dark depths at the back, their prez, Chaz, with his back to the wall.

A hand in the air brings drinks to the table, first ones for us, and refreshers for the men we've come to see. Drum pays the tab.

"Prez." Drummer salutes him raising his bottle.

He raises his chin in acknowledgement, then starts without preamble. "Spoke to Stub. Got another update for you." We lean forward, better to hear what he has to say as his voice drops. The table is set apart from the rest, but we're still wary of listening ears.

"Go on," Drum prompts.

"So, Hawk got intel that you killed his woman. Then you met Stub and he passed on the info she's alive."

"Know that. But how he got his initial info is what I want to know." Drummer's brow creases.

Chaz continues as if Drummer hadn't spoken, summing up what we already knew. "Week or so back he got word that you took out the Chaos Riders. That message included the face that a body of a woman was found in the cellar. Everything pointed to the dead bitch being his wife. He ordered a hit on your club-house in retaliation. When he heard his old lady was alive, he wanted to stop the attack in case she got hurt. Got a real hard-on for her apparently. Stub didn't fill in the background, as by the time he managed to speak to Hawk the attack was imminent, as you now know. Hawk said he couldn't get the word out to stop it in time." He pauses to have a swig of his beer. "D'you find anything?"

"Lost our shop."

"Fuck, sorry man." There seems to be genuine regret there. "I got to you as fast as I could."

"Appreciate the warning. Could have been worse. Got a man in the hospital as it is." As the prez of the Wretched Souls raises his eyebrow, Drum adds, "Slick."

He shakes his head. "Good man. Hope he pulls through. Think you've got more problems on the way. Might need to pull in some of your support."

Drummer's eyes narrow. "What makes you say that?"

"Hawk. Stub doesn't like him. Felt something was off. Got the feeling Hawk's in with a crew he can't quite control. And who can be quite ruthless. Violence for violence sake, you know? That's why he sent the warning. Didn't sound like he could stop the bomb being planted even if he got in touch with his contact. Sounds like it's an ugly crowd. And, the problem at the moment is we don't know who."

Hawk's in with some ugly types alright. The treatment he allowed to happen to Becca shows that.

"What do you know about the Chaos Riders, Chaz?"

The Wretched Soulz's prez shrugs. "Not much. They asked permission to set up in Tucson. Couldn't argue with their charter or rules and regs. They did it all right. We don't have trouble with your lot, Drummer. Thought we'd leave it to you to sort them out if there was a problem."

"Which there fuckin' was. A heads up would have been nice, Chaz."

"Noted and agreed. But you handled it. You know our position. We don't get involved unless we have to lay down the law. Knew you could take them if there was a need."

Drummer takes another drink, then picks at the label on the bottle. He's giving himself time to think. Chaz also downs more of his beer, his eyes never leaving my prez.

"What's going on, Drummer? Why were the Chaos Riders such a problem?"

"The Herreras tried to involve us in gun runnin'," Drum says at last, his eyes shooting up to meet Chaz's straight on.

The Wretched Soulz look at each other. "They're upping the trade? Or lost their own mules?"

"Fuck knows. But they were going to give it to us or the Chaos Riders."

"You couldn't just leave the Riders to get on with it?"

"Not a fuckin' chance. They made a play for our compound," Drummer growls.

"Can't blame them," the VP, Bull, says. "Got a nice set-up there."

"We like it," Prez tells him firmly, leaving him in no doubt we wouldn't give it up lightly. To anyone.

"So, the Herreras." Chaz beckons that he wants more.

Drummer seems to change the subject. "We might have come across something interestin'." He glances at Wraith, who nods his head. Reaching into his cut, Drummer pulls out a piece of paper, sliding it across the table.

Chaz picks it up, reads it, and I watch his eyes open. "This?"

"Yup."

"Who's?" He passes it to Iron, his sergeant-at-arms.

"The fingers all point Hawk's way."

Chaz's eyes squint at Drummer. "How's Hawk moving it now he's put away? His crew dealing with it?"

Drummer shifts. "Way I see it is the Chaos Riders were doing his carryin' for him."

"And they moved to Tucson to expand their business, maybe join with or take over from the Herreras. Over-confident cock-suckers." Chaz fits the pieces together.

"Exactly. Javier may have invited a snake into his camp."

Chaz suddenly sits back and laughs. "Hawk's locked up and his mules are all dead. Satan's Devils have got right up his ass. Got his woman, and," he points at the paper he's still holding, "presumably you've got the stash too. Christ, haven't heard a joke like it for years." He exchanges amused looks with Iron and Bull.

326

"He's still got somebody workin' for him. Else Slick wouldn't be on the operatin' table right now," Drum says grimly.

Chaz sobers. "Yeah. You're right. But if you're correct and no one's touched his stock, he's fucked up his pipeline." He pulls the paper toward him again, his eyes gleam.

"You want that lot?" Drummer asks, seeming to sense it's the right time.

Chaz seems confused. "You don't?"

"Fuck no. Not getting back into that shit." Drummer puts down his empty bottle. "I don't want that lot gettin' into the wrong hands. I suspect they're headin' south of the border, and want to see them on their way. Don't want shit like that in this town."

"Need a smoke." Chaz rises, his sergeant-at-arms and VP stand too. I slide my chair back to give them room to get out.

"Chaz doesn't smoke," Drum says conversationally when they're out of earshot.

I get in another round, with three extra of course. By the time I return Chaz and his men are back. The Wretched Soulz' prez wastes no time getting straight back into business. "How much do you want for them?"

"Your help. No money passes hands."

Chaz studies the prez, his surprise marked by his narrowed eyes. "Gotta know what I'm committing to here, Drummer. Man could make a lot of bank moving that product. Need to make sure I'm not paying over the top for it."

"First I need info from Hawk."

"That we can do without payment. Our brother Stub's got nothing to lose and gets bored out of his skull without doing the odd favour." Chaz has a silent conversation with his VP, then a few muttered words I can't hear with Iron. "I'll be asking Stub to talk to Hawk myself. Like to know more. Such as where the guns came from and who's expecting them. You can take it to the bank that someone is."

"My feelin's exactly." Drummer nods.

"You want this Hawk taken out?" Chaz's mouth twists. "As I said, Stub gets bored."

"Yes," I rush in, interrupting him with my one heartfelt word that's been my only contribution to the conversation.

Drummer looks at me sharply. "We need to have words about that."

Chaz leans back lazily on his chair. "What's he done to you, Rock?"

My face grows dark. "That woman he calls his? Well she's mine now. She would have died before he got released. He deserves death for what he did to her." Drummer goes to stop me, but I'm on a roll. "She married him legal, was forced to. She needs to get free of him. From what you say, the fucker won't agree to a divorce, and I don't want him hangin' over our heads for the next couple of years."

"You're right." Chaz nods. "Stub said Hawk went apeshit when he thought she was dead. Was keeping his nose clean, looking for early parole. Got the word and fucking lost it. Needed six guards to control him. There's no fucking way he'd agree to a divorce." He's only voicing what I thought. His eyes rest on me a second longer, then move to the man on my right. "Okay, Drummer, Hawk taken out, guns removed, and you keep your hands clean. That's the price you want us to pay?"

Drummer takes a good long swig from his bottle, then puts it back down. "Not exactly."

CHAPTER 31

Becca

Peg's got this gruff manner about him. I certainly wouldn't want to get on his wrong side. Although having seen how he is with his old lady I suspect underneath he's one of the good ones and has a heart of gold. It means a lot that he's driving me to Tucson, though I'm worried why Rock can't take me. The Satan's Devils are not men to let the person who planted a bomb on the compound off lightly, and it makes sense they'll be doing everything they can to find the culprit. They might be doing that right now. Is that where Rock's gone? Is he in danger? But if that's so, why haven't they taken their sergeant-at-arms with them, the man who the old ladies have told me is responsible for the safety of the club? There's no point asking Peg. Well, I've tried, but only got a dismissive grunt in response.

It's strange to think I've never worried about losing anyone before. Maybe that makes me shallow, but I've never loved anyone in my life. My parents I was dutiful to, gave them the respect they thought they deserved. I would have said I'd felt the right emotion for them, but anything was killed stone dead when, showing no remorse, they'd handed me over to an abusive man. Hawk, well, as my pastor I liked him enough, but from the moment we were married I'd come to hate him. Detested him for forcing me into a life I didn't want. Where nothing I ever did was good enough.

Every man and woman on the compound already means more to me than anyone else I've ever met. Rock? Rock's at the very top. I don't know how I'd survive were I to lose him now. I'd told him I loved him. While I might not have experienced that emotion before, I know it's the truth.

Peg leaves me alone with my thoughts as we drive into Tucson. Once at the hospital he walks at my side, his eyes ever flicking back and forth as though seeking out any possible danger. Unscathed, we walk up to the emergency entrance and find Viper outside, having a smoke.

"Brother?" Peg nods pointedly at the cigarette held between Viper's fingers.

"Still no news, Peg. It's got to me, alright?" It's only then I realise I've never seen Viper smoking.

Peg claps his hand on his shoulder as Viper gives us instructions where to find everyone.

As I enter the full waiting room behind Peg, I see Sam sitting on one side of Ella, Jayden on the other. Ella's openly crying, but silently. A crushed tissue in her hand is dapping at her red, swollen eyes. Sam's murmuring to her quietly, but she looks up and locks her eyes on mine as I enter. As a pastor's wife, I know how hard it is to give support under these circumstances, but suspect Sam inherently knows the right things to say. I suppose giving comfort has been ingrained in me, as, though I know Ella the least, I find it impossible to keep my distance.

Going over, I crouch down in front of her. "Slick's strong and fit. He's not going to let something like this bring him down."

Ella gives me a small nod, then hiccups and says, "That's what Sam's been saying, Becca. But the timing... I'm..." She can't seem to get out the words, so I cover her hand with mine.

"I know, sweetie, I know." One piece of information Peg had imparted on the journey. Her pregnancy.

It guts me to be here waiting to hear news of her husband. While I've not personally had much to do with him, I've seen him with Ella, and anyone could tell he was a good man. He treats Jayden as part of his family too. Noticing the teenager is also in tears, I take her hand and squeeze it. Paladin's sitting beside her, his arm over her shoulders. When he throws me a look of gratitude I have to look away. *This is my fault.* I know the bomb on the compound had something to do with Hawk. It's too much of a coincidence otherwise. I just can't figure out the reason. Feeling tears pricking at my own eyes, *of guilt as much as anguish*, I stand, unable to stay close to the stricken women anymore.

Peg's standing alone, so I go across. "What's the latest?" I ask quietly. "I didn't want to distress Ella further by asking."

"Still in surgery." He supplies the update he's heard. "Been a few hours now."

"Probably still trying to find his brain," inputs Joker, and he receives a cuff around his head from Lady.

Peg half grins at Joker's attempt to lighten the mood, but he looks tired.

"Should never have fuckin' happened," Dollar starts, but is interrupted by his phone vibrating. Taking it out he notes who's calling, then moves out into the hall.

No, it shouldn't have. It wouldn't have if I hadn't been here. I start feeling awkward. No one's blaming me or looking at me oddly, but if it wasn't for me, then Slick wouldn't be fighting for his life. *What if he dies?* How could I stand it? *Ella's pregnant.* What if Slick never finds out?

It's a subdued group waiting for news of Ella's old man. The longer we hear nothing, the worse the worrying gets. I eye up the brothers. Apart from Joker's failed attempt at levity, all are wearing sombre expressions, and there's barely any conversation. With one of their own possibly dead or dying, I suppose there's no plans to make or business important enough to discuss. All any of us can do is wait in a silence, punctuated by Ella and Jayden's sobbing.

There's a clock on the wall, the second hand jumping forward with each moment passing. It's almost hypnotic to watch. I'm in a kind of trance when I feel a soft hand in mine, and glancing up I see Sam, who's given up her seat to Sandy.

"I can tell what you're thinking, Becca. And you can stop it right now. We don't know why a bomb was planted on the compound. It might have nothing to do with you."

"Sam," I try to protest and tell her of course it does, but she doesn't let me continue.

"Even if it turns out it had something to do with Hawk, do you think anyone would blame you? Or regret that we gave you a home? Of course they wouldn't." She holds my hand tighter, as though sensing how close I am to pulling away. "You didn't ask for anything Hawk did to you. You didn't chain yourself up in the cellar. You didn't ask for your parents or Hawk to brainwash you. You've pulled yourself out of that hell, Becca. Don't go sliding back now."

"I should leave." It seems the only solution. Try to hide somewhere Hawk won't find me. Remove the heat from the club.

"That's the last thing we want you to do. Anyway, I doubt Rock will let you go."

But Rock couldn't stop me if I put my mind to it. *I wish I was mentally stronger and knew what to do.* But it still feels alien to think for myself. Even if I did want to go, what about the practicalities? I've nothing to my name. Even my clothes have been borrowed or bought with someone else's money. *Why do I have to be such a mess?*

"You're not a mess, Becca." I must have spoken my last thought aloud. Sam looks fierce, and again tightens her grip. "You're a survivor. Don't you ever forget that."

But looking around at the anguish in the room, my survival had too high a cost.

"We don't know," Sam refutes again, "that Hawk was behind it. Or if he was, the reason why." She leans in closer so only I can hear. "It might be in retaliation for taking out the Riders, and that would have happened whether you were there or not. You don't know for certain this is down to you." From her words, I suspect Drummer shares more with her than other brothers and their old ladies.

"It must have been Hawk. He arranged it," I insist, thinking how Rock had questioned me about people Hawk might have known. "I'm sure it's down to me." Through my eyelashes I sneak a glimpse at Ella. "It's my fault if Slick…" I can't even say it.

Seeing my distress, Sam speaks again. "Hawk made you feel responsible for everything you didn't do right. You've grown used to thinking everything is your fault. You need to look at things differently. Sometimes things go wrong however hard we try to do right. Own the guilt where necessary, but other times reject it."

I glance at her sharply.

"If Hawk did it, that's on him. Not you. You had nothing to do with placing a bomb on the compound, did you?"

Quickly I shake my head.

"You leave that guilt well alone, you hear me? Unless you knew or condoned it, which I know you didn't, nothing comes back on you."

"You'd make an excellent counsellor," I tell her, my lips curving slightly.

She grins. "I'm the prez's old lady. It comes with the title."

She's given me something to think about, but it's still hard to stay in the room with everyone grieving. "I'm thinking about popping up to see Beef," I tell her. It's a legitimate escape, and something I'd planned to do.

"Good idea, Becca. Anything changes down here I'll come up myself and tell you."

If I'd hoped for a reprieve I don't get it. For a start I should have realised that Beef, who's got Marvel with him, would only have one thing on his mind. When I've updated them there's been no change, Marvel leaves us to be with his brothers. I take in Beef's changed circumstances too. His face is paler than it's been for the past few days, and there's a drip once again running into his arm.

"What's all this, Beef?"

"Doctor's being overcautious, Becs. Don't let it worry you. The infection's come back. Probably stopped the darn treatment too early to save fuckin' money or something."

I perch on the side of the bed and take his hand. "This mean you're not coming home?"

Beef's eyes sharpen. "Now that's a lovely word for you to be using. The compound's home?"

I smile that he's picked up on it. "Not sure they'll want me there if anything happens to Slick, but yeah. I've got comfortable."

"Christ, girl. What happened to Slick wasn't your fault."

I lean forward and place my finger on his lips. "I've already had that lecture from Sam."

"Good. Now…" Beef tries to pull himself up but fails and uses the buttons to raise the head of his bed. I press my lips together, worried he seems weaker than he was. "Give me the dirt on you and Rock. I want to live vicariously through you."

As I feel my face flush, he continues, "Ah, like that, is it? Yeah, gonna want all the deets, babe."

"I'm certainly not telling you about my sex life," I say primly.

Then blush again when he grins and fist pumps the air. "At fuckin' last! You're admittin' you have one, that's a start." He allows me a moment to suffer embarrassment before going on. "Rock done the right thing and claimed you?"

I frown. "I'm not sure. It all went to hell when the compound exploded."

"Hey, I was told it was the shop," Beef corrects. "Don't exaggerate, darlin'. And if my boy's got his head screwed on straight, you'll be getting a property patch." This time it's him who stops me speaking by raising his hand. "Don't make that face. You know what we think of as property isn't the same as Hawk. Think we've had this conversation before, darlin'. But I'll remind you. You wearin' Rock's patch? Show's how much you mean to him, and show's other men you're taken. They so much as look at you wrong and Rock will stand up for you. And," he rubs his cheek ruefully, "I can tell you he's got a mean punch."

"He hit you?"

Beef chuckles. "Yeah, a time or two. You must have seen the sparrin' ring in the gym?" When I nod, he explains,. "We have matches once a month. Hardly anyone wants to take Rock on. That man can take a punch to the gut that would lay out any other fella. And yeah, he might have got in a couple of lucky shots while I was still nursin' the broken bones in my hand."

"All I could think of this morning, Beef, was that Rock wouldn't be hurt. I felt relieved when I knew it was someone else. Does that make me a bad person?" My voice has dropped to a whisper as I make my confession.

"Darlin', that makes you fuckin' human, that's what it does. If the positions were reversed, Ella would be thinkin' the same thing, and feelin' just as fuckin' guilty for it."

I bite my lip as I try to process his words.

"Like that, Becs." As I tilt my head in confusion he clarifies. "You're thinkin', workin' it out for yourself. When I first met you, you didn't question anything."

"I was never allowed to with Hawk."

"Or your parents. Never been allowed to think for yourself in your life."

I look down at my hands.

"Hey, Becs?"

"I can't be with Rock, can I, Beef?"

"Why the fuck not?" he asks, incredulously.

I shrug. "You said it yourself. I don't think for myself. I sometimes still panic when choosing what to wear. Rock's, well, he's, he's…"

"He's what?"

I respond to Beef's raised quizzical eyebrow, only able to say lamely, "He's a biker."

Now Beef smirks. "You do what he tells you in bed?"

Again my cheeks burn, which gives him the answer.

"All a biker wants, darlin. That's all a biker wants."

"*Beef!*" I punch his leg lightly.

"Oh, and it helps if you can cook. Look after the kids."

"Beef!" I say again.

"Look pretty, and you do that all right."

"Beef. Stop."

His face grows serious again. "I've known Rock a long fuckin' time, and he's my best friend. Love all my brothers, but him the most. You know what, Becs? Soon as I fuckin' saw you I knew what attracted him to you. Why he wanted to help and protect you. Take it from me, you're exactly what Rock needs and wants."

Once more my teeth worry my lips. "What if I change? What if I decide I like thinking for myself? What if I argue with him and challenge him?"

"Rock will be the proudest man in the world, darlin, when, not *if* you do that. Of course, you get too mouthy he might shut you up by puttin' his cock between those delicious lips of yours. He probably won't be able to resist anyway, not the way you keep drawing attention to them like that."

My mouth snaps shut.

CHAPTER 32
Rock

Then what, exactly?" Chaz lifts his beer again, sees the bottle's empty, and this time it's his sergeant-at-arms who gets fresh drinks. Including for us.

Drummer takes the new bottle and raises it to his lips before answering. "We don't deal in hardware anymore. Especially not the type we've discovered."

Chaz nods slowly. "Your loss is someone else's gain."

"Not always," Drummer replies enigmatically. He puts down his beer and sits forward, his hands clasped between his knees. "The Herreras want us to shift their...merchandise. We don't want to touch it."

"And you don't think Hawk was working for the Herreras?"

Drummer shakes his head. "I have no proof, just a gut feelin'. It just doesn't sit right with me. If he was the middle man for someone, perhaps, but no, I don't believe it was them. Don't know enough about the fucker, but he could be runnin' his own business. Herreras are a red herrin' in my view. Makes sense the Riders would introduce themselves when they stepped onto their home turf, and I don't doubt the Chaos told the Herreras they had experience in shifting stock. But Hawk's another matter, and we need Stub to find out where he fits in."

Chaz sits back and folds his arms. "So you think the Herreras have separate ideas about moving more plant. If so, they could step on the toes of the cartel."

"Exactly," Drummer agrees. "If I could get the cartel to pull the Herreras back into line, they won't be looking for more mules."

Chaz looks up to the ceiling for a moment, then he too, leans forward. "Cartel's starting to have enough of the Herreras. They pissed them off with that child grooming ring, then the slave auction. Their toes, as it were, are already feeling bruised." He looks at his sergeant-at-arms, who gives him a nod. "Tell you what, I'll set up a meet with the cartel and see what they feel about an increase in hardware from their Tucson relations. See if Javier got official sanction."

"Thing is," their VP starts, "I don't understand why he's gunning for you. Pardon the pun. What have the Herreras got against the Devils?"

Drummer raises his head and stares the Wretched Soulz prez straight in the eye. "Leave it that there's something. A favour we did for Leonardo."

"Who's dead."

"Figured that." Drummer nods. "When I couldn't make contact with him."

"This favour not looked on kindly by Javier?" Bull probes for more.

It's Wraith who answers his counterpart. "If he's in the know, possibly not."

Chaz taps his finger against his teeth. "You need us to get the Herreras off your backs. By dropping them in it with the cartel. You think that's gonna make Javier feel any more kindly toward you?"

"Not in the least." Drummer grins. "But he may think we're too slippery to deal with and look elsewhere. Or, not have a trade to run at all."

"And for this, we get the stash?" Iron asks, his eyes glowing in anticipation.

"Every last bit of it. All that's written on that paper."

Chaz pats the pocket he'd slid it into. "You think Hawk was the only one who knew where it was?"

"Doesn't look like it's been touched since he went inside. Riders were still breathing for three months but made no move to shift it. Don't know his pipeline, in or out, but I'd stake money the suppliers don't know where it's held, nor the delivery boys where to pick it up."

"Or," Chaz gets out the list and consults it again, "he could be equipping a private army. And you could be wrong about it being moved along. It might be exactly where it should be." His next smile shows all his teeth. "Fancy going to church, Drum?"

Drum's expression shows he hasn't thought through implications like that. "I'd place money that the new pastor doesn't know anything. But there was another fella with him. Didn't take to him much."

Neither did I. Not from the way he manhandled Becca.

"Someone must have helped Hawk put the weapons there." He nods at his sergeant-at-arms. "Something else to get Stub onto. And you get your Mouse working, Drum. We'll use our data guy too. Something about this Hawk is making me nervous. Oh, I don't mind taking his stock, but I'd like to know what's in the background. And who there could be on the outside, waiting to continue his business."

"Church." The corners of Drummer's mouth turn up. "I like the sound of that. Rock, ask Becca for the details of the services."

"I'm up for that, Drum." I'd like sight of her parents. But I might have to hold myself in check so I don't kill them.

Chaz is staring at me. "You can clean yourself up, hide your tattoos?"

I nod.

"As long as you're not struck down by entering you can come along. You got a woman you can bring along? Might help it look like we're good church-going folks."

I'm not taking Becca.

"I have," says Drummer. "And she'll pass. Got a sweet butt can accompany Rock if he doesn't want to bring his girl."

Chaz again looks thoughtful. "Bring Hawk's woman." His eyes flick to my mouth, which starts opening, and raises his hand to stall me while at the same time nodding to Iron.

The sergeant-at-arms makes a suggestion. "You've met the pastor, and this other chap might be there. If not, your girl might just spot something or someone who looks out of place, or who is taking a particular interest in her. It wouldn't be a stretch to say she's there because she's missing the comfort of her church. If Stub gets more out of Hawk, that could beef up our back story as well."

Chaz laughs as he slaps Iron's back. "I'm game. I got a woman I can drag along in her Sunday best. She can suck my cock on the way home, dual purpose." His grin gets even wider. "Never thought I'd step foot in a citizen's church, but there you go. And whatcha know? I'm already fucking looking forward to it."

We stand, do the manly handshakes and slaps on the back thing, then Chaz and his crew leave. Drum indicates we should hang around a moment, but before he can speak his phone rings.

Wraith and I turn away to give him some privacy. "You need to talk to Becca," Wraith tells me. "Find out who you should be watching out for tomorrow. Any players who don't seem to fit with the rest."

"I'd thought of that myself, VP." I frown.

He sees me tense. "You sure you're going to be able to keep your hands off her parents if you see them there?"

"I'll try, VP. I'll fuckin' try. But when I think they gave her to that brute, groomed her for him, and how they don't seem to give a damn where she is or how she's being looked after." I shake my head, baring my teeth in anticipation of what I'd like to do to them.

"You'll do more than fuckin' try," Wraith snarls. "You gonna have a problem, then you stay the fuck away. I'll go with Drummer."

He's not going to be doing that. I started this. I'm damn well going to finish it.

Wraith's glare softens, but only a bit. "People like that are taken in by the likes of Hawk. They may have thought they were securin' a future for their daughter. A pastor as a husband, for religious types you can't get better than that. Hawk told them he'd look after her. They probably think she's living the life of Riley somewhere."

Shaking my head, I let him in on something. "They knew he raped her. They thought that was okay." I take a deep breath. "You do that to little Olivia? Give her to a man and knowingly let him abuse her?"

His hands are around my throat before I finish speaking. "What you fuckin' talkin' about? Words like abuse and my kid never come out of your mouth at the same time together, you got it, Rock? You fuckin' got it?"

Croaking out a yes as well as I'm able, I show him I have indeed got it. Satisfied that the gleam from his eyes shows he's caught up too. Why I'd put Becca's parents in the ground with no second thoughts. No kid deserves to be treated like that.

"That was Joker," Drummer returns and says quietly. His eyes go to me then the VP, but if he notices the tension between us he chooses to ignore it. "He took over from Blade watching this Bo fucker's place. Dude just came home. Young black guy, about five-foot-six. Sounds about right. He's pretty certain he recognised him from that picture Mouse showed us. Come on, let's get out of here."

I'm shaking my head as we walk through the bar, noticing the glances thrown toward us. Wraith's and my altercation hadn't gone unnoticed, but mostly I read disappointment it hadn't descended into a full-on brawl. This is a biker bar, after all.

Once outside, Drummer pinches the bridge of his nose then looks at Matt, who's still guarding the bikes.

"Prez." I catch his attention. "Thought we'd only land the guy who had their car stolen. Can't believe we've caught the fucker himself first try."

Drum rubs the side of his nose. "Even Devils have to catch a break sometime. Let's bring him in. See who've we've caught in our net." He turns to Matt. "I'll call Blade. Get him back to the compound to meet up with you. Then you two can grab the truck, go to the address I'll text you and join Joker. Bring the package back. Blade should know immediately if it's the right fucker or not. He saw him bring the car in."

Matt stiffens as he catches up. "The package being responsible for putting Slick in the hospital?" Prospect is certainly not slow on the uptake.

When Drum replies with a quick nod Matt's features tighten, then without another word he goes to his bike. Guess his quick retreat shows what he thinks of a man who plants bombs.

I go sit astride my ride and lean forward over the tank. "Get what you want in there, Prez?"

Going to his own Harley, Drummer gives me one of his stares. "Getting fuckin' sick of this. More fuckin' questions than answers yet again. But we've caught Chaz's interest."

"They want those guns," the VP says. "Just want to be careful who'll they'll upset if they take them."

"Wretcheds don't give a fuckin' damn who they'll upset. They just want to know which direction they need to be facing."

So no one stabs them in the back. I know exactly what Drummer is saying.

Back at the hospital, we arrive moments after the doctor has updated Ella. Jayden's arm's around her, Paladin's holding them both. Murmured conversations discuss the news we've not heard yet.

Drummer's making a move toward Ella, Sam comes over and heads him off.

"Slick's out of surgery."

"He's still with us." Prez sighs with relief.

"With us, yeah. Out of the woods? Not quite yet." Sam looks drained. She's been holding it together for everyone. Recognising it, Drummer pulls her into his chest. She allows herself a moment of comfort, then tells us the rest. "They've stopped the bleed on the brain, but he's got a hairline fracture of the skull. A linear fracture they called it, so it should heal up fine. But they're keeping him in an induced coma to keep the swelling down."

My eyes flick to Heart. Docs did something similar with him. Trouble was, he took a long time waking after they withdrew the medication keeping him under. Then I look at Ella. Christ, I hope to fuck the same thing doesn't happen again. Ella's pregnant, she needs her man awake and to be here for her.

As though she feels my eyes on her, Ella pulls away from Jayden and comes across.

"Ella, darlin'." Sam steps aside as Drummer pulls Slick's woman in for a hug. "He's gonna be fine, sweetheart. If anyone's got a hard head, it's Slick."

She seems to take strength from the prez. There is something that's worrying her though. After a few seconds, she asks, "What if he can't ride again, Drummer?"

"What the fuck?"

Sam takes over from her old man. "Ella, sweetie. The docs said nothing about that, or any brain damage. Just said he might suffer headaches for a while."

"If he can't ride," Ella sobs, ignoring Sam's words, "then he won't be able to be in the club. That would destroy him, Drummer."

Drummer pushes her away and holds her at arm's-length so he can use the full force of those steely eyes on her. "Now you listen here, Ella. Slick's going to stay a brother whatever happens. He got hurt for the club. You really think I'd turn him away after that? And don't you be worryin'. Time's what he needs." He lowers his gaze for a moment, then looks back up. "Seems you've got an important job to do for your man. You're growin' his baby, and that's what you need to be concentratin' on. Try not to worry, darlin'. Your man's going to be fine, and you've got all of us behind you."

With a final sob, Ella seems to pull herself together. Her hands rest lightly on her stomach. As if being reminded of her duty to the child growing within her gives her backbone, she nods, thinks for a moment, then states, "Slick's going to be okay, isn't he Drummer?"

"Sure as fuck he is," Prez retorts.

I just hope that he's right. But Ella needs to think positively, and I reckon he's going the right way getting her started.

Knowing there's no point in all of us staying, Slick won't be coming round anytime soon, Ella, Jayden, and Paladin say they'll be waiting here, the rest of us going home.

"You takin' Becca, or want me to?"

"Thanks, Peg, but I'll bring her back on my bike." I grin at the sergeant-at-arms. "Just got to drag her away from Beef." I'm looking forward to seeing him myself. Fuck, it seems a long time ago that I set out this morning thinking I was coming here to see my old friend. Instead, we had to deal with an explosion.

I hear laughter as I approach Beef's room, but entering, the smile slides off my face. Beef's normally ruddy complexion is paler than it was last time I saw him, and he's hooked up to the machines and drip once again. But he's chuckling at something Becca must have told him.

He reaches out his hand. Going over, I clasp it. "Been keeping the shiny side up, Brother?" he asks.

I grin as I confirm, "And the dirty side down."

A nod of acknowledgement, then, "How's Slick?"

I update them, making the news as good as I can.

"Hey, Becca. Be a doll and do me a favour. I could do with a coffee. Anything for you, Beef?"

As Beef shakes his head, Becca takes my money and heads off to the cafeteria. As soon as the door closes behind her, Beef narrows his eyes. "Spill."

"Think we've got the person who planted the fuckin' bomb," I say succinctly. "Joker and Blade should be bringing him back to the club now."

He rolls his head back, then his eyes find mine again. "Wish I could fuckin' be there. Make him fuckin' hurt."

"You don't need to worry about that, Brother. He ain't gonna die easy, you can be fuckin' assured of that."

He nods, but even that seems an effort.

"You okay, Brother?" My eyes narrow in concern.

"Just another damn infection. Pumping me full of antibiotics again. Just can't wait to get out of this fuckin' place, Rock. I wanna go home." It's a heartfelt plea.

Resting my hand on his shoulder, I give it a light squeeze. "Can't wait to have you back at the compound, Beef. Place doesn't seem the same without you."

Suddenly his eyes seem to brighten. "That little girl you've got. One in a million, you know? Come through what she fuckin' has?"

Drawing up the chair to be closer, I sit down. "You don't need to tell me that, Brother. Fuckin' know it. She's doing great. Settling in well at the compound."

"She don't need nothing to set her back."

Acknowledging the sharpness in his tone, I reassure him. "I ain't gonna do nothing to hurt her, Beef. You know me better than that."

"You claimed her?"

"Going to," I admit.

"Get your patch on her, Rock. Sooner rather than later. She needs that."

"I'm not sure, Beef. I don't want to be another Hawk to her…"

He tries to sit up, but collapses back. "Fuck, feel so damn weak." He sounds annoyed with himself. "Look, Rock. She knows you're not Hawk. But I know she'll always need a strong man behind her, it's the way she is, not just the way she's been brought up. Give her choices, but help her to make them. You get me?"

I get him. "I'll ask her to be my ol' lady. I've already told her she's mine." I grin.

"Make sure she understands what that means. You watch out for her, you hear me?"

It's an easy promise to make. "I hear you, Brother."

Beef mumbles something. I lean closer and ask him to repeat it.

"Said I'm fuckin' going to miss sharin' a woman with you, Brother."

The thought of sharing Becca, even with him, turns my stomach. But her aside, I can understand where he's coming from. "Just got to get you out of here, Brother, and we'll find you a woman for yourself."

Weak he may be, but Beef's face fills with horror. "I'm no one woman man, Rock. You know me better than that. Keep to one pussy? Nah, that's not for me."

I grin again. Yeah, I thought that way too. *Until I met Becca.*

CHAPTER 33

Rock

It wasn't me! What are you doing? It wasn't fuckin' me." The words alternate between anger, pleading, and then even punctuated by a sob. "It's wasn't me. Get it?"

Last night, when they'd brought him back, Blade had confirmed we had the right motherfucker, definitely the man who drove the car onto the compound. But still he denies it. I've got here early, Bo's been hanging around all night. Well, strung up to the rafters. If it was anyone else I'd have sympathy knowing how that felt. But him? I hoped he suffered.

My brothers are trailing in around, only Lady approaches Bo, watching him shaking his chains, almost seeming disinterested as though he's nothing more than a specimen at the zoo.

As he walks in to join us I go over and stand next to Peg. "He must know why he's here."

"Yeah," the sergeant-at-arms answers. "But we haven't said anything. Which makes what he's saying so fuckin' interesting. Leave him strung up there long enough, he might give it all away by himself."

I stretch my hands, audibly clicking my fingers. "Where's the fun in that, Peg? I want my hands on him even if no one else does." I might have said fun, but I meant retribution. Unless we've got it very wrong, and from Blade's identification that would only be if he had a twin brother, he's the man responsible for putting Slick in a coma, and his old lady Ella in pieces at a time when she needs to concentrate on her health.

"Jekyll! Thank you." Prez's voice comes over the rest.

It catches my attention, and I turn to see Hyde and Jekyll appearing, Jekyll bouncing a hammer off his hands before holding it out to Prez.

We seem to all be here now, and brothers are in various states of preparation. Blade's sharpening one of his favourite knives, Viper's got something that looks like a vice, Bullet's got a bat. Me? I'm happy to just use my fists, they're my go to weapon of choice. Each blow I strike will be for my injured brother.

"It wasn't me! I didn't do nothing! Look, whatever you think I done, it wasn't me!"

Drum notices my arrival and nods. Then glances around, checking who else is here. Every member is, except, of course, Slick, Beef, and Paladin. Our youngest member being best placed to watch over Ella and Jayden.

As the prez steps forward, conversations die down. He approaches the man hanging, stopping without speaking when he's directly in front. Like everyone else, I watch, waiting. Drummer's a master at this.

Bo stops protesting. Visible tremors betray his fear, as does the shiny sheen of sweat running down his black skin.

Now it's Drummer's turn to bounce the hammer in his hand. He studies it for a moment before examining the man he's about to make hurt. Bo's so much shorter that even strung up, his face is the same level as that of the prez.

"So, Bo. We got ourselves a problem." Bo doesn't protest his name as Drum continues. "See, someone matching your description brought a car belonging to you onto our compound yesterday." He steps closer, his reasonable tone turning into a roar. "Car was full of fucking explosives!"

Bo yanks at the chains. "I don't know anything. I didn't know it was there. Why would I be driving around with a fucking bomb in the car? You think I'm stupid?" Christ, he's all but admitting it. Dumb fuck.

Drum regards him impassively. "Don't much care whether you knew about it or not. Fact is, the car exploded, and we got a brother in the hospital with a cracked skull."

"I didn't know. I didn't *fucking* know!" Bo's screaming, his eyes roaming the room looking for sympathy. "You can't hurt a brother for not knowing there was a bomb in his car. For fuck's sake, if I'd known I wouldn't have driven it." I notice he's stopped denying it was him.

"Your car. Your responsibility. And I ain't your fuckin' *brother*. You're going to pay for bringing it to us." Drum bounces the hammer again. "This here? This is gonna break your skull open, just like the bomb broke my *brother* Slick's."

"Fuck, he's pissed himself already."

"Usually takes them longer than that." Blade agrees with Heart.

"But I'm not going to use the hammer," Drummer informs him casually. As Bo looks like he's starting to relax, the brothers around me begin bouncing on their heels. We all know the prez too well. "No, I'm just showing this to you so you can start praying. Praying for this hammer to kill you and stop the rest of your pain."

Bo's eyes widen. Perhaps it's only now he realises just how much trouble he's in. Prez gives a signal to Viper, who's standing behind the hanging man. He doesn't see it coming, has no time to prepare, as in the same way the blast knocked into Slick. Viper swings a bat at his kidneys.

The pain takes a split second to register, then there's a shocked howl and Bo's head drops forward.

Prez wraps his fingers in the dark hair and pulls his face up. A face contorted by agony. "You talk to us, and this will go easier."

Bo's having difficulty breathing. Fuck, he only took one blow to his back and the man's darn near incapacitated. I've had harder hits than that in the ring. My look of disgust is mirrored on my brothers' faces.

"Who paid you? I want all the details. Every fuckin' thing you've got to say."

Bo's still gasping, but he's recovered enough to shake his head. "He'll kill me."

Drummer yanks back on his hair again. "And what d'you think we'll be doing if you don't? Takin' you on a fuckin' picnic?"

It takes a moment for him to process that. Fuck me, the man's crying. *Motherfucker.* Does he think tears will cut it with us?

"If I tell you, I want, I want…protection." Bo stammers the words out.

Fuck me! Is he really telling us he came onto the compound with the intention of killing some of us including, quite possibly, Prez's old lady if we hadn't have had a warning, and now he thinks we'll protect him?

I exchange an incredulous look with Heart, standing beside me, who asks, "What the fuck kind of dude we got here, Rock?"

"Pretty damn stupid one, Brother."

Without answering his question, Prez asks one of his own. "You ever seen a dismembered body, Bo? Ever seen what a bomb blast can do? Ever been in the fuckin' services and watched men blown up?"

Of course he hasn't. He's a fucking coward.

When Bo shakes his head no, no one's surprised.

"Well, then, this here's going to be an education." Prez waves Shooter forward, who's come armed with an axe. "Hyde, Marvel, hold his arm, will you?"

"I'll do this." Road steps forward. "Got a bit of practice in in the summer chopping down trees."

Before Bo can process what's happening, Hyde and Marvel have untied one of his arms, are holding him steady, and his arm's pinned on a bench which Shooter has brought up. Road takes a swing…

"Stop!" he screams. "Stop! I'll tell you everything I know."

Road manages to divert the swing at the last moment. Disappointing. Blade extinguishes the blow torch he'd lit to cauterise the wound. Didn't want him to bleed out before we had a chance to talk to him or have him make too much of a mess on the floor.

Bo's acting as though his hand really was cut off, pulling his arm against his body. He might not be the most intelligent tool in the box, but his imagination must work well enough.

Prez waits until he brings himself under control. "Just wanted to get your attention."

The man's blubbering, then when he looks at his wrist, vomit spews out of his mouth. Drummer neatly steps back to avoid it.

"Seems you weren't taking me seriously," Drum says conversationally. "I suggest you start talking now. If you stop, or tell me something I don't believe, I promise you, you won't have either hand left to jerk off with."

Just the threat of having part of his limb removed has stunned the man. Drum gives him a moment, and even moves away as though to let him take in the number of men watching him, none of whom show the slightest unease at what he'd been threatened with simply for not talking. If he could pale, he would be doing so now.

It's Blade who finally loses patience. Having swapped the blow torch for one of his blades, he waves it in front, menacingly.

"Got a call. Got money. Got asked to do it. Seemed a simple job. I was to place a bomb in your compound. Cased the joint first, didn't seem any way of getting in. Thought I'd buy an old banger and drop it off in your shop." The words tumble out one after the other. It takes a moment to process what he's said.

"You know explosives?" Peg snaps out.

"No. I never had anything to do with it. Man dropped it off. Said he'd set a timer. I made sure it wasn't going to go off with me anywhere near it."

"But you didn't care how many of us you took out." Drummer's tone changes again. "My ol' lady fuckin' works in that shop. She's pregnant. You could have killed her along with any of the brothers who'd be in there that day." He speaks so sharply his voice alone could cut a limb off. "Who was the man who brought you the bomb? And why you?"

"I head a small crew. We do jobs like put the heat on, you know? Man came to me with a message from Hawk."

Again Drummer steps forward. "How do you know Hawk?"

"I don't know him. I know *of* him. Seemed odd he'd come to us."

"Why odd?"

Fuck, Drummer's got some patience. This is like pulling teeth. *Perhaps I should suggest he does that for real. Might hurry things along.*

"Hawk's one of the white supremacists. Goes round with Nazi types. Only time he'd mix with my crew is to spit on us."

"So why did you take the fuckin' job?"

Bo shrugs. "It was good money. And we got a free pass for when we needed it."

Prez wipes his hand over his beard. As he turns to me I see him rolling his eyes. *Can Bo really be this dense?* Hawk wanted us to blame Black for it.

Peg's had enough and steps up himself. Bo's eyes widen at the sight of the annoyed sergeant-at-arms, who looks like he isn't going to pull his punches. He tries to scrabble backward. But Peg's not using his fists. Not just yet. Even so, the threat in his eyes has Bo shaking.

"You fuckin' stupid?" his voice thunders. "Even the fuckin' car was registered to you. You had to know we'd catch up with you."

"I didn't," Bo wails. "Tried to find a hot one, but couldn't get hold of one in time. Saw this old banger going for a song so I bought it. Cash. How was I to fucking know the dude would change the registration to my name? I used fake licence plates..."

"For fuck's sake!" I can't prevent the roar coming out of my mouth. "Don't matter if he's stupid or just fuckin' careless. End result is the same. Our brother's in the hospital fightin' for his life, and we're just lucky there's no one else in there alongside him."

"Name or description of the man who gave you the bomb?"

Bo cries out. "For fucks sake, I didn't ask him. He was white, that's all I know. You all fucking look alike, how can I describe him? Taller than me, heavy set."

"Sick of this, Prez," Dollar groans. "He's got nothing useful to give us."

Prez nods slowly. "Yeah, I agree. Time's up, Bo."

Bo's face looks terrified.

At that moment the door to the storage room opens, and in walks Truck, looking tired as he's just come off a twenty-four hour shift. Prez half turns, recognises him, then turns his attention back to the man strung up. "Don't think you want to be here for this, Truck." Truck's a firefighter as well as our prospect. He's got a reputation to uphold. We keep him out of anything that's not strictly legal. And delivering our form of retribution on a man who hurt one of our own certainly comes under that.

"Prez, I want to be here." Truck speaks in a chilling tone I haven't heard from him before. It even sends shivers up my spine. Without waiting for an invitation, he steps up alongside Drummer, his eyes shining with disdain he regards the man before him. Truck's a huge man, and at this second, as terrifying as Peg. "I attend fires started on purpose. Men, women, kids die. For once I'd like to see the person responsible getting what they deserve. Oh," he turns to Drummer, "I'll keep my hands clean. But I've heard the screams from people we can't get to in time. I've seen relatives devastated by their loss." He turns back to Bo. "Do you know how painful it is to burn? To have flames covering your body? And as for a fucking bomb, know your limb has been blown off? Have you any fuckin' idea what that feels like?"

We're all staring at Truck, seeing his hands clenching and opening at his sides. The big man's almost shaking he's so wound up. Blade nods, goes off to the side, and when he returns, takes a lighter out of his pocket and applies the flame to the blow torch he's brought back.

"I reckon we show Bo exactly what you're talking about, Truck."

Truck doesn't speak, nor protest as Peg steps forward and cuts Bo's shirt off. Then he undoes his jeans and pushes them down his legs, sliding his boots off with them. Bo tries to kick out to prevent him, but Joker and Lady step up and hold him steady. Soon we have a very naked black-skinned body in front of us. Idly I notice it isn't true what they say about Blacks. Well, no, it's not in Bo's case. Or maybe it's the circumstances.

"You fuckin' racist pigs!" Bo screams. "It's because I'm black…"

"It's because you hurt one of our own," Drummer says calmly and coldly. "Don't matter what colour your skin is. Go ahead, Blade."

Bo writhes as the heat of the blow torch approaches, and when it touches his skin he screams like the pig that he called us. The flames burn the skin from his back. As he goes rigid with pain, Blade continues without mercy down his legs. The air becomes tainted with the odour of burning flesh. It's vaguely reminiscent of barbeques we've had.

Truck crosses his arms, stoically watching the man's skin blacken, a darker shade than his natural skin.

"Burn off his fuckin' cock. Do it for Slick," Shooter yells out, causing a rumble of laughter. Yeah, Slick would certainly approve of that form of punishment.

Bo's almost unconscious, but comes back to life at the cry. "No, don't. Don't, I beg you!" For the first time it seems he's starting to accept he won't be getting out of this. "Don't do that! Kill me now!"

Prez gives Blade the nod as we all stare on, intrigued with the damage that a blow torch can do to a man's balls. First the hair singes and an acrid aroma reaches us. His cock has shrivelled so much it's almost invisible. But Blade homes in on his target.

I didn't think Bo could scream any louder, but he does, until the sounds cut off as he passes out from the pain.

Viper steps up with a bucket of water. One dousing doesn't do it, but the second causes moaning to start. Bo seems incapable of forming words.

Drummer views him impassively, then barks out, "You hear me, Bo? You understand me?"

A different moan seems to indicate he does.

"Slick was caught in the back by flyin' debris. From the bomb you planted. He might survive, he might not. Now we're going to show you what that must have felt like. To be hit by an object propelled at the speed of the explosion." He pauses and gazes around. "Each man takes his turn. Leave his head to me."

One by one we step up. When it's my turn I swing my fists at his chest, hearing a satisfying crack from one of the few ribs which hasn't already been broken. By the time we've finished it's hard to tell the man in front of us was ever a human being. Teeth smashed out, eyes blackened and closed, his arms broken but one still chained to the ceiling. I don't know whether he's still alive or not.

When it's Drummer's turn he walks around the back of Bo and swings the hammer with all his might, meeting his skull with an audible crack.

There's a moment of silence, then Prez speaks. "Take him down and bury him."

CHAPTER 34

Becca

When Rock returns from whatever he's been up to for the past few hours, his face is unreadable, tension radiating off him. So much so I don't dare ask what he's been doing. I think it's probably best I don't know. All the brothers had been missing, something the other old ladies didn't even feel the need to comment on. Taking my lead from them, I've been keeping myself busy helping in the kitchen. If Sam knew what was going on, she didn't enlighten us.

The women are easy company, and I soon settle in working alongside them, laughing at Sophie exaggerating her use of the English language and showing mock horror we were serving mashed potatoes and gravy with fried chicken. Even after two years of being here the VP's old lady still wants fries, *or chips as she calls them*, with hers. Our looks of disgust equal her expression of horror, and we've been called bloody heathens more than once this morning. I suspect it's her way of easing the tension, and that I'm not the only one wondering what's going on.

Finally the men appear, accompanied by an aroma that's hard to explain. A bit like they've been barbequing, but no grills are alight out back. As Wraith, Drummer, and Heart head for their women, Rock makes a beeline for me. He pulls me by the hand and, without speaking, almost drags me up to the suite. He's focused, not even stopping to talk to his brothers.

When we reach our destination he pushes me through the door. Immediately slamming it shut with his foot, he leans back against the wood, then waits, his eyes half closed, his brow furrowed. As the words come out, his voice sounds hoarse. "I need you, Becca."

His admission steadies me, lets me know whatever has got him so tense is not down to me. Whatever he's been dealing with wound him up tight.

He needs me. Just as I needed him. When I did, he'd been there for me. It's my turn now to take care of him. For a moment I stand undecided, knowing he's watching me through his eyelashes, letting me make the first move. My hands flutter by my sides, more used to taking direction than deciding what to do for myself.

That Rock's stance is unthreatening makes me braver. Without asking permission, I move toward him, going up on tiptoe and placing my lips against his. His mouth softens as I trace my tongue over the seam, and when he opens I take advantage and push inside. He doesn't take control, doesn't place his hands on my head, simply lets his tongue follow mine as I enjoy the warmth and softness of his mouth. *I love this man. So much.* Overcome with emotion, my only desire is to make him feel as good as he makes me. As I extend the kiss I bravely put a hand to his denim-covered cock, slowly tracing its form, squeezing gently, feeling pride as it lengthens under my touch. He moans gently into my mouth, a sign that what I'm doing is right. I fondle him again, and in amazement feel it steadily hardening.

Taking a deep breath to fortify myself, I drop down to my knees, and with shaking fingers, undo the button on his jeans. The hiss which comes from his lips tells me I'm still on the right track.

Fighting with myself so I don't look up to check I'm doing it right, I boldly push his jeans down over his hips. Having gone commando, his bulging, already hard cock bobs up to greet me. Ignoring the hard, tiled floor bruising my knees, I place my hand on the velvety smooth skin which covers the steel underneath. Then, with my other hand, balance his balls, gently massaging them, full of wonder and pride as his cock stiffens more.

His soft moan providing encouragement, I lean forward and suck one of his balls into my mouth, his pubic hair tickling my chin as I breathe in his heady, musky essence. My tongue continues to work, first one testicle then the other until I feel brave enough to slide it up the side of his cock and lick the drop of salty pre-cum off the tip. He hums as my tongue probes his slit, hoping to find more moisture leaking. I'm not disappointed. Again emboldened, I place my lips around the head, gently sucking it into my mouth.

A loud gasp. Reaching out his hand, his fingers toy with my hair. But he doesn't force me, doesn't push into my face, just holds me. A gesture of reassurance, leaving me in control. My tongue plays, licking up then down, a gentle suck to the head.

"Becca," he breathes out. His hands move away, then back, as though he's struggling with himself.

I smile into his cock, then open my mouth further, letting him slide inside, involuntarily gagging as he hits the back of my throat. I don't want to lose him, want time to get used to his size, so my hands go around his ass, holding him to me. He lets me experiment, trying to take all of him in. But he's large, too long and thick for me to take all the way. I manage as much as I can and swallow around him, one of my hands holding tight the length I'm unable to accommodate.

"Fuck, Becca. Don't know what fuckin' spell you're weaving. Never felt so fuckin' good."

It's not the first time I've given head, but the first I've done it of my own volition. Now I've free rein I want to take the time to enjoy this. The feeling of being in charge, of controlling him, exhilarating and welcoming. I suck him back in, hollow my cheeks, and swallow again.

"Becca, I'm close," he warns.

I want him. Want to feel his cum in my mouth, want to taste it and swallow it. While I've enjoyed teasing him, he's stretching my mouth and I won't be comfortable continuing much longer, so I massage his balls and fasten my pace as I bob up and down his shaft.

I take him as far back as possible. I feel his balls tense.

"Becca," he cries out. "Becca, fuck, Becca."

Warm liquid floods my mouth, and I swallow as fast as I can, not wanting to miss a drop. Some escapes onto my lips. I lick him clean, then my tongue comes out to get the bits that I've missed. Finally, I wipe the back of my hand across my mouth. Seeing his eyes now open and focused upon me, I lick my hand clean.

For a second, I worry. *Have I done it right?* Men like having their cock in a woman's mouth, but this time I wanted to give him pleasure, something he could get from no one else. A blowjob delivered out of love, not duty or force or an act to illustrate subservience.

"Becca." He bends slightly, curling his hands around my biceps, pulling me to my feet. His eyes stare into mine for a second, then his mouth is on mine. This time he's in control. His lips and tongue move frantically as though he can't get enough of me, seeming not to care he can taste himself on me.

I meet him thrust for thrust, our tongues swirling in and out of each other's mouths, almost duelling in our intensity.

When he finally pulls away he looks down in amazement, his pupils dilated and softened. "Fuckin' love you, Becca."

I grin. I can't help it. I wanted to ask him if I'd done it right, but his expression needs no word of explanation. It's clear that I have.

Then he's taking over. His hands still on my arms, he starts pushing me back to the bed before realising, once again, his jeans are around his ankles. We both look down. Just as I'd done the time before, I giggle.

"Minx." My chuckles erupt, and I don't care that he gives me an instruction. "Take off my boots."

I obey, dropping back to my knees, in my hurry fumbling with the laces. He lifts one foot then the other so I can take his boots off, and I help him slide his jeans over his feet.

Now he's stalking me. Crab-like, I scramble back toward the bed. Before I can get there he's impatiently lifting me in his strong arms and throwing me on it. He straightens, his breath coming heavily, his expression intense. But it doesn't scare me. I've raised the angry beast, and I don't mind a bit.

He tugs me to the edge of the bed, and this time it's his knees which hit the floor, and in the same motion pulling my shorts down my legs, taking my panties with them. I wait, poised, ready for him to begin, already knowing I'm wet and ready for him. But when he leans over me, his hands caressing my sides and smoothing across my stomach, it's unexpected. My skin ripples with anticipation just at his touch.

With a serious look on his face, his eyes fixed on mine, he lowers his mouth to my nipple, sucking it gently into his mouth. The zing to my clit makes me jerk. Then he applies his attention to the other, alternating between them until the nubs are hard and stand out.

Now it's me moaning. My body starts jerking again, without conscious thought trying to get him where I want him most. A huff of warm breath, then his tongue touches me, tracing my labia on each side. My clit's screaming for attention, but he avoids it. Suddenly his tongue sweeps inside my slit. The feeling is intense, wonderful, but it's still not where I need it.

Lowering my hand, I place it on his head.

"I'm getting there," he mumbles against me.

He pushes my legs further apart with his hands. For a second, he does nothing. I open my eyes, which I'd somehow closed, to see him looking at me, examining me. In embarrassment I try to close my legs, but he holds them open.

"You're fuckin' beautiful, Becca. Such a pretty cunt."

His words do something to me. I stop struggling only to be rewarded by a finger pressing inside me, then another, and then, *at last*, his mouth closes over my clit. A gentle suck while he massages my internal walls with his fingers, then he starts licking, seeming to automatically know what pressure I need and where.

Then I'm incapable of even thinking as a warm rush of feeling seems to reach from my extremities and land just where his tongue is. I'm breathing fast to get oxygen into my lungs, my nerve endings singing. I feel light headed as all my muscles tense and my stomach feels like a million butterflies are fluttering inside it.

I gasp, I stop breathing, the tension escalating until, until… Waves of intense pleasure flood my body, going on and on, extended by his now gentle teasing until, somehow understanding I'm becoming sensitive, he moves away.

He stands, pulls my body even closer to the edge of the bed, and plunges his hard again cock straight inside me. His hands grasp my ankles and pull them up over my head, lifting my hips from the bed as he thrusts in, deeper than he's been before. His eyes checking for signs of discomfort, but I'm feeling nothing but ecstasy knowing he's as far inside me as he can go. Such an intimate connection.

Then he starts hammering in, touching that place inside me, making my muscles contract all over again.

"Come with me, Becca."

I can't disobey him, his words, his beautiful punishment of my body. It would be easier to stop a volcanic eruption than my impending orgasm. As my sheath clutches at him he groans when I go over the top and my muscles convulse against him. He roars and starts pumping erratically.

"Fuckin' love this, Becca. Fuckin' love takin' you bare. Christ, you feel good." Each statement is punctuated by little jerks as he empties everything he's got inside me.

He lets my legs down, gently massaging them, then again, catches my eyes. "You okay, Becca?"

"Hmm." It's all the response I'm capable of as his fingers slide against my skin. It's the little touches, his outward concern that makes him so different than Hawk.

Once my feet are back on the floor he falls onto the bed, pulling me up against him and tucking me under his arm. "I meant it, darlin'. Feels so good skin on skin. I've been meaning to ask. How long have you got left on your shot?"

Silently I work it out under my breath, then sit forward with a jerk. "Rock! Rock. Christ. What's the date?"

"The twenty-fifth. Why?"

I'd lost track of time, no longer marking the days off. My hand covers my mouth. "It was my birthday on the eleventh. I'm so sorry. I'm a couple of weeks over already." I place my head in my hands, feeling like a fool. I'd got so settled here I hadn't given a thought to counting off the days. And I'd just got used to the idea I couldn't get pregnant.

"Hey. Hey, Becca. Look at me, sweetheart."

But I can't. I don't want him to hate me, to think that I've tricked him. "Look, I'll talk to Sam about…"

Realising I'm not going to face him, he pulls me back down to his side. Then he gives me no choice, taking my hands in his and holding them over my head. "Look, let's handle this in order of importance. You should have told me it was your fuckin' birthday. Would have wanted to do something for that. We'll have a late celebration, okay?"

I couldn't care less about my birthday. It's always passed without fanfare before.

While I'm still shaking my head he continues staring at me intently. "Could you be pregnant?" he demands.

Feeling tears prick at my eyes, again I move my head from side to side, but it's not in a negative gesture. "I don't know," I tell him, honestly. "My parents arranged it a week before the wedding. I was so stupid, I didn't know what was going on at the time. It's only later Hawk told me, and that it would be effective for three years. I don't know if the effectiveness wears off that quickly. But I'll sort it. Sam can help me find somewhere to go…"

"Damn it, Becca. Let me speak. Look at me." His voice, slightly harsh, pulls me up and stops my rambling. My bottom lip trembles. I know I've disappointed him, but I hadn't misled him intentionally. He waits until I'm able to meet his eyes before he gently rubs his hand across my stomach. "Let me have my say, yeah?" After I manage a small nod he continues. "You got my baby growing in there? I'd be the happiest fucker alive. You don't, and you want to keep trying? That's fine with me. You want to wait and get another shot? Again, I'm content. But I give you fair warnin' babe. One day, you'll be carryin' my children."

My mouth opens and shuts in confusion. *He wouldn't mind?* It takes more than a moment to process the idea. Hawk was adamant he didn't want kids.

"Gotta give me something here, Becca. I'd like to know where you stand." His brow is furrowed.

"I, I, er... I love you, Rock."

"But?"

"There's no but, Rock." I swallow to get moisture into my mouth so I can grab my slice of nirvana. "I'd love to have your baby. Babies, Rock. I just never thought..."

He guesses the rest, leans his delicious body over me, taking his weight on his elbows which he rests either side of my head. "I didn't want kids. Not until I met you. Now I know why not. I was waiting to find someone I wanted to spend my whole life with. Someone I could commit to. Someone I knew I loved and who I wanted riding up behind me. And that person I was waiting for is you, Becca. You complete me." He leans down and gives me a soft kiss. "Never understood Wraith or Drum, Slick or Heart come to that. But now I do. When you find the right woman, you know it." He gives a slight shake of his head as if bemused. "Even fuckin' resented the kids on the compound. Now I want to add to them. That's down to you, Becca. You've opened my eyes."

I know my shortcomings. "I hope I can be the woman you need. But I'm not sure. I'm damaged. I know that..."

"You're a fuckin' long way from damaged, Becca." He grins, "Dented perhaps. But nothing that can't be made right." He continues the earlier topic. "No condoms, no shots. Just my property patch. Hell, I might go the whole way and put a ring on your finger."

It hits me like a strike from a fist. "But I'm still married."

"Not in my eyes you're not. And soon, not in the eyes of the law either. Doesn't stop me giving you a patch. Just that the wedding will have to wait a bit longer."

Rock's making me picture a future when Hawk's no longer in my life. I'm smiling just thinking about it.

He rolls onto his side, taking me with him. As his fingers gently run through my short hair, he asks, "Your church, tell me about it." His abrupt change of subject takes me aback, and I need a moment to catch up with him.

"Why do you want to know?" I crinkle my nose, still reeling from the previous conversation, my thoughts swinging from elation to fear about how I could bring a child up. *Focus, Becca. He asked about the church.* "What information are you after?"

"What type of people attend it?"

"Upstanding citizens," I scoff. "People who like hearing about hell, fire, and brimstone. How all the sinners will be punished. Then they go off and do what they want Monday to Saturday. I know for a fact there was at least one man who was quite happy committing adultery, and then turning up on the Sunday all smiles with his wife."

"Hawk know?"

"Yeah. He used to laugh about turning a blind eye."

"And you've said there's no people of colour in your church?"

"God no," I retort. "Whites only."

"That down to Hawk?"

"He wasn't very tolerant," I admit, thinking back to some of the hateful things he would say. "I used to block out his rants. But all the country's woes were down to Blacks, Hispanics, and any others who weren't pure Ayrian descendants."

Rock isn't surprised, as though my answer was what he expected. "I know I've asked you this before, and you said no suspicious characters met with Hawk, or that you knew of. But a slightly different question. Hawk got any particular friends close to him? Anyone that was a member of the congregation he used to see more than others?"

My brow creases as I think back, examining Hawk's behaviour through new eyes. "White. Him for certain." Thinking of White joins the dots. "Rock? That man who was there the other night? Remember me saying I think he may have been to the house? Remembering White reminds me. That man was tight with him. I don't know if they ever came to the house together. Whenever Hawk had visitors, while they were there, I was sent to my room." I sigh. "All the congregation loved Hawk. He could do no wrong in their eyes. They'd all have been proud to be his friend. But he kept people at a distance. It was only White that I can recall acting friendly. Why the questions, Rock?" Another sign of my progress that I dare to ask.

His answer surprises me. "Because we're going tomorrow. Want to see what we're up against. What support Hawk has still got…"

"Going to church?" My eyes go wide. "They won't trust you."

"We need to go, darlin'. Don't know a church that doesn't open its doors wide to strangers."

"You don't know my church," I murmur. I think for a moment. "To be accepted you have to be one of their type. Scaler moved away. Not been heard of for a while. Might even be dead now. But he was the curate. Give them his name as a recommendation. Say that you worshipped at the All Saints Church, and you'll be welcomed. They all hate the congregation there, bunch of do-gooders they say. If you tell them you want a religion with teeth, they'll let you in."

"Know anything about the pastor who took over from Hawk?"

"I don't, sorry. He seemed okay when I met him. The other man with him the other night? I didn't take to at all."

"I don't fuckin' take to any man who has their hands on my woman," Rock growls. "You've said enough, darlin'. Given us some hints to get accepted."

I can only hope I've done enough.

Needing to change the subject, not liking being forced to think about the church and the people who went there, I let my hand wander across Rock's chest, examining the tattoos that he's had inked into his skin. My fingers linger on one. "Why the cards, Rock?"

"I like playing poker."

I frown slightly. "You gamble?"

My question, for some reason, makes him laugh. His arm tightens around me. "I know my limits, darlin'. Never lose more than what I can afford. You don't need to worry about that." His eyes glaze over, my question has touched a nerve. "My hobby, if you want to call it that, was why Drummer asked me to go into the Chaos Riders. Time was short, he had to think of something fast. Everyone knows I love a good game of poker, would go into Tucson to play. It didn't take much for them to believe I'd been on a losing streak." He taps his chest. "If it wasn't for the cards, babe, we might never have met."

And I'd still be languishing in that cellar. Or dead.

One look at him and I see he's thinking along the same lines. I try to lighten things up. "So, you could say our getting together was in the cards, then?"

"Could do." He chuckles.

"Will you teach me to play sometime?" Cards, or any games for that matter, had been forbidden when I was growing up.

He pulls himself up on one elbow, his eyes now alight. "That's an idea. Strip poker."

"You ever think about anything but sex?"

He answers my primly put question with another rich chuckle which comes from deep in his chest. "With you around? Never."

To prove his point, he kisses, first my mouth, then moves down to my breasts.

CHAPTER 35

Rock

"Yo." I'm half asleep as I answer my phone. "Yeah, Prez?"

I listen to the reason he woke me much earlier than I expected. Then agree to get dressed and go straight to his office. Eight am. After the night I'd spent alternatively fucking and making love to Becca, I'd hoped to have a leisurely lie in. Knowing there might be a chance it could bear fruit, something had driven me to do what I could to put my baby inside her. As a result, I'm drained and exhausted. We'd planned to go to the evening service, which meant I'd expected to have hours before we had to leave.

I wet myself in the shower, just enough to get rid of the smell of sex, which personally I'd prefer to carry with me all day, dress, and am entering church within fifteen minutes. When I go through the door I find I'm not the only one to have received an early summons.

Drummer is sitting at the head of the table as normal, Wraith and Peg are in their usual positions, as is Blade. At the opposite end are Chaz and Bull.

I jerk my chin toward my brothers, a more respectful nod at the prez and VP of the Wretched Soulz, then sit beside Peg as invited.

"Now Rock's here, let's get started," Drummer suggests.

Bull pulls out a pack of cigarettes and waves them toward us. Blade nods and catches the pack that's slid down the table. No one else takes up the offer, so it's only he and Bull who light up. Drum slides an ashtray down to them. Chaz grins up at a sign on the wall which suggests when the floor is full to use the receptacle provided, then a cloak of seriousness comes over him. He nods to Bull.

"I spoke to Stub this morning. You may be wondering about this early meeting. But there's a few things we need to go through," Bull starts, then pauses to take another drag. Smoke drifts up into the air. "Stub got to your man. Found a few things that are interesting." Another drag, and I shift impatiently, wishing he'd finish the darn cigarette so there'd be no more interruptions. "Okay, this is how it stands. Hawk has his own organisation and is a tight-lipped motherfucker. Doesn't trust anyone and runs it on a need to know basis. He took it over from the old pastor, who's dead by the way. It was agreed he'd keep getting a cut when Hawk took his place, but Hawk doesn't like to share. The old pastor had a convenient accident."

"The gun running out of the church goes back a long way." Drummer's steely gaze fixes on the Soulz's VP.

"Ever since it was built. As you said, few people knew about the basement. Very few."

"But someone else knows?"

"Yeah, Drum." Chaz takes over. "Two other people. Both very much breathing."

"Then why haven't they moved the fuckin' guns?" Drum's hand comes down over his beard.

Chaz shrugs. "They were waiting for their buyer to get ready. Then, now, of course, they're lost without their pack mules. The two fuckers working for Hawk are waiting for his instructions as to who's now going to move them."

"So they leave millions of dollars worth of equipment just sitting there?"

"Hawk likes to be in control," I butt in, thinking of Becca. "And I doubt he likes to be crossed. He'll want to sort out someone he can trust. Anyone else he brings in will find out their set up, they'll have to, to get that shit moved."

"Exactly." Chaz nods, a fleeting smile crossing his face. "As he got himself put in solitary when he heard about the Chaos Riders, he's not had a chance to set anything up as yet."

Bull leans forward. "Until now."

This time, Chaz's grin stays. "Stub managed to get some quality time with Hawk. Now there are two things that allowed him to get chummy."

Bull takes over again. "You know what it's like inside, especially if you're looking at a long stretch." He pauses, presses his lips together, and I imagine he's remembering he'll never see his brother on the outside again. "Wretched Soulz have a reputation, mostly untrue nowadays, but folks like Hawk believe we side with white supremacists. In the pen you need to have people behind you. Stub knew that, knew he was going inside, so had a swastika tatted on his neck before he went in. Didn't bother him much, as he knew it would gain him some protection."

"That's how he was able to become Hawk's best buddy?" Drummer looks interested.

"Yeah. That, and that he rides with us. Easy to persuade Hawk we were all on his side."

"Just don't tell Fagan." Bull laughs.

Drum's brow creases. "He's Hispanic, isn't he?"

"Yeah, and we've got a couple of black members. All good fuckin' men." Chaz grins again. "So," he takes up Bull's narrative, "Hawk's used to working with an MC. Offered Stub a decent enough arrangement to move the guns over the border. Gave up his contacts and everything. The profit from the sale goes to fund white supremacist activities. Oh, and some of the guns go to a Nazi group too."

"Fuck." Drummer looks disgusted.

"The one thing he kept back was where the guns are hidden. But of course, thanks to the Devils, we already know that." Chaz sits back looking satisfied, rapping his fingers on the table. "I'll take your deal, Drummer. We get the guns, sell them to Hawk's buyer. We'll divert the extra and keep them well away from the Nazi crowd. We'll keep all the money ourselves. At least it won't be used as intended. Then we'll help you get the Herreras off your back."

One side of Drummer's mouth turns up. "Can't say fairer than that. But we do need to know who Hawk's partners are. Can't afford any blowback."

"That's what we're after tonight. Avid churchgoers apparently. Men by the name of White and Butcher."

"White!" Peg snorts. "Fuckin' fittin'."

"Becca mentioned White and another man as being particularly close to Hawk," I butt in. "She think's one of them was the man who was there with the pastor the other night."

Bull glares at me, then continues as though he hadn't been interrupted. "Stub got a password, well, passphrase, that we can use so they know we've got Hawk on our side."

"Stub did fuckin' well," Peg observes.

"He did that," Chaz acknowledges. "More than that." He nods toward me. "You gonna take that girl as your ol' lady?"

"I am." I don't hesitate to reply and have to suppress a smile at the thought she might already be incubating my baby. Fuck me, never thought I'd be happy at getting a girl knocked up.

"Well, you ain't got anything standing in your way now. Hawk won't be a problem anymore. He sort of met with an accident last night. Shanked himself, would you believe?"

I wouldn't, and know it's just one more thing we can thank Stub for. My only regret is that I was unable to get up close and personal with him and put him in the ground myself. He tortured my woman for years. But he is dead, and any of his claims on her died with him. Becca's free. Now I do grin, then my face falls. "Stub get away with it?"

"Stub wasn't anywhere near him. Got thirty white suprem-acists to vouch for that."

Drum stares at Chaz. "Thought Hawk would be under the same protection?"

Bull shakes his head. "His beliefs might be the same, but no one fucking liked the arrogant dick. Stub, on the other hand, knows he's in for life and tries not to make waves."

Wise man.

"I just wish it had been me and that I'd made him hurt," I grumble.

Bull grins widely. "Oh, he hurt. Would you believe he tried cutting his wrists first, then had a couple of attempts at slicing his throat? He fell over a few times too, cracked his ribs and broke his nose Stupid man couldn't even kill himself properly."

Giving Bull a nod of satisfaction, I grin at last, hoping Stub's hands aren't too sore today. "Pass my thanks on."

A raised chin back.

"With Hawk dead, it will work well having your woman with us tonight, Rock."

Chaz's suggestion makes me sit up straight. I'd thought we could discuss that again and I'd get him to change his mind. I'd rather she was well away from danger. *Especially now.* "No fuckin' way." Chaz sits back, and I wonder whether having a hard, steely stare is a pre-requisite for being president of a club. "Look, I know I initially agreed to it, but she hates that fuckin' place. Girl's just recovering, I don't want to set her back."

Drummer is staring at me, his own steely eyes narrowed. "Not so fuckin' hasty, Rock. Let's talk about this." He points to Chaz. "Presumably you're thinking she can identify this fella, White?"

"Hate to ask her, but if he's a member of the church I'd put money on it she would."

"Prez," I start pleading. "Yeah, she can identify White. But if Butcher's the man we saw the other night, we don't need her with us. For a start she'll see her fuckin' parents…" I'd been thinking it over. It's why I hadn't mentioned it to her last night. It's my job to protect her from any unpleasantness.

Wraith's also giving me a hard stare. "She'll have us at her back," he assures me. "And you by her side."

Chaz is nodding. "The grieving widow wanting solace from her church. What better excuse for her to be there? Dress her in fucking black. She can discuss the funeral arrangements or whatever with the new pastor."

My head goes from side to side. "That's a whole fuckin' lot to put on her, Prez." I don't like the idea at all.

Chaz doesn't give an inch. "She gets upset, all the better. It will persuade them she's missing her husband." He breaks off and grins. "The kind of money Hawk was dealing with? Wouldn't be surprised if he was fucking loaded. Unless he's made a will that says different, all that comes to her now. Best she comes out of hiding if she wants to get her hands on the dough."

I'm still shaking my head. Becca wouldn't be swayed by money. Hell, she's never had any to spend herself.

"She's entitled." Drum seems to read my mind. "Whether she wants it or not, it's rightfully hers. Payback for all she had to put up with. Rock, I like that little girl. I think she's braver than you give her credit for. She volunteered to go back to the Riders to make sure you were safe. She'll do anything for you and, I suspect, for the club."

My lips purse as I think he's probably right. But at what cost to herself?

"I'll bring Sam along," Drummer offers. "Those two get along well. Sam will help keep her grounded."

There's a time for discussion and a time to shut up. As I look around the table I see no support for my assertion Becca should stay behind. Raising my hands in a gesture of defeat, I then sit back and fold my arms. Everyone knows I don't like it, but I won't argue further. If it's for the good of the club, my feelings need putting to one side.

There's not much else we have to talk about except for agreeing on a time and place to meet up later. Chaz and Bull go off on their way, I go back to my woman.

As I walk up the path I kick stones out of the way. Fuck knows how she's going to take it. I don't know which is best to tell her first. That she's now a grieving widow, or that tonight she'll most likely be confronted by her parents. *How's she going to react?* She didn't like Hawk, but gentle soul that she is, she might be shocked.

I open the door to my suite, hold out my hands, and she comes straight over. For a second I allow myself to enjoy the feeling of how well she seems to fit. With her in my arms I feel complete. *And now there's nothing stopping me making her mine.* Not that a piece of legal paper would have held me back, but she'd never have given me all of herself if, in her mind, she was sinning.

"Gotta tell you something, Becca." As her eyes stare trustingly into mine, I tell her, what for me at least, is the best fucking news I could have got. "Hawk committed suicide last night." She doesn't need any more details.

"Hawk's *dead?*" Her beautiful eyes widen. "Oh my God." She covers her mouth with her hands and I wait for her reaction, fucking hoping she doesn't waste one tear on him. Fucker doesn't deserve an ounce of compassion for what he put her through. Her face shows a myriad of expressions, pale with shock, eyes wide as she tries to digest the news, then her cheeks flush as her teeth worry her lip. When she finally speaks I'm surprised to hear her say, "Am I wrong to feel like a weight's been lifted off me?"

Hugging her close, I give her absolution. "Not at all, darlin'. Not at fuckin' all. He was an all-around bastard. Doubt there'll be many upset that he's dead."

"Suicide?"

Yeah, well that's the official version. "That's what they're saying. He probably couldn't stand being locked up."

She's still biting her lip. "It goes against the teaching of the church. I can't understand it. I never thought Hawk would do that. Even when I was chained up in the basement, I never would have taken my own life. It's a sin."

Resting my chin on her head, I reassure her. "Clearly Hawk wasn't as fuckin' brave as you, sweetheart. Man was a bully. Not unusual they turn out to be the weakest."

"I just never suspected…"

"Don't waste your time on him, Becca. He's gone. He's not coming back." Placing my fingers under her jaw, I turn her to face me. "Just concentrate on our future instead. You're mine now, no one can challenge that."

Smiling up at me, she agrees. "I'm yours."

I want to make sure she knows what I'm saying. "This is me claimin' you, Becca. You're my woman now."

I don't know how she's going to take it. She's just heard she's out of one relationship, and I'm asking her to commit to another. I can't read her face, it's gone blank. Her eyes are flicking backward and forward, her mouth opens and shuts. Then, when I'm wishing I waited longer to ask her, she suddenly squeals.

"I can be yours, now, Rock, can't I? I never have to worry about him anymore."

She was mine from the moment I saw her, chained up in the cellar. But I hold that back. "Sure can, sweetheart."

"I love you, Rock." Her eyes stare into mine, creasing as a smile transforms her face. "I can't tell you how much I love you."

"Love you, too, Becca."

With the affirmations of our feelings, I can't resist stealing a kiss. But don't let myself be distracted, and pull away after a few seconds. While I'd prefer to avoid it, she needs to be forewarned of the other topic for today. Attendance at this evening's church service. It doesn't come as any surprise when the blood drains from her face for the second time, and I immediately regret my part in it. Then once again her verbal reaction surprises me, and I see a little of the backbone Drummer's convinced she has, when she draws her shoulders back.

"Yes, I know White and we all saw the other man the other day. Of course I'll come with you. It would be better than just giving you a description." She's saying one thing, her expression showing she's thinking something else as she draws her eyes away from mine, looking down at the floor.

"Sweetheart?" I prompt.

"Rock, I admit that I'm scared. My parents are likely to be there too. What if they try to take me away from you? The congregation will have their back if they make a fuss."

Try to take her back? Over my dead body. "Whoa, sweetheart, hang on a second. Do you think for one moment I'm going to let you move from my side? Fuck, if they say one word to upset you I'll get you out of there fast. You trust me, don't you? Sam will be there, she'll take no shit either. As well as Drummer and Wraith."

Her lips thin briefly. "I hear what you say, but they will put pressure on me. I'm their only child, remember. And now I'm a widow who's in need of a man to look after her. A man they'll want to choose."

I curl my hand around her neck and pull her toward me. "Not gonna happen, darlin'. You've already got a man. Me. Ain't no room for anyone else."

She smiles briefly, then her brow creases. "Sam? She's going?"

"Yeah. She is."

Now she winces. "Rock, you don't know what that church is like. It's brainwashing, pure and simple. Twisting their view of religion to suit their own ends. Sam's going to hate it." She goes to sit on the bed, her head in her hands. "I've worked so hard to wipe my head of all the seeds they planted, but going back? I'm afraid they'll suck me in all over again."

"They're not going to do that," I tell her firmly. "I won't allow it. We'll all be there to keep your head in the right place. If you don't even want to talk to your parents, you don't have to." I take a deep breath. "Hawk's dead. You're free. As his widow you should get everything he left, unless he made other provisions. You need to come out of hiding in order to claim it."

"I'm not interested in money," she throws back at me without hesitation.

"I know you're not. But what he had should now rightfully be yours. We'll get the club lawyer onto it. You can do what you like with anything you get, hell, give it to charity if that's what you want."

She goes quiet for a moment, and again her facial expressions change swiftly as she thinks everything through. I give her time. Processing that she's now an independent woman, not a possession of Hawk's, clearly has many implications. "I owe you and the club, don't I, Rock? I've not paid for a thing since I've been here. Oh no. I do, don't I?"

Stunned that's the first thing she vocalises, I put her straight. "You owe us fuck all, Becca. You came here with nothing. I certainly didn't mind spendin' for both of us, and I know my brothers and their old ladies didn't either. As for the future? Well, you're going to be my old lady. I'll look after you for the rest of your life. It will be my fuckin' pleasure."

"I'll give any money to you. I wouldn't know what to do with it."

"No, you won't," I say, equally firmly. "You've still lots to learn, babe. I'll be happy to teach you. You take your time to decide what you want." I put my arm around her. "As long as you don't decide you want a fresh start away from me. Don't think I could live with that. Fuckin' love you, babe. I'm yours for life."

Her eyes widen. "Rock, I'm going nowhere. I've got the man that I love. How could I even think of leaving you?"

I kiss her, a brief meeting of our lips. "We'll figure everything out. Together, darlin'. Always together."

My phone rings. A glance shows she's again deep in thought, so I turn away to answer it. Immediately wishing I hadn't. What Drummer has to say isn't something I want to hear. "Fuck, Drum." My fist smashes into the wall. "Fuck, yeah. Okay." I end the call, but it's impossible to hide my distress.

Becca's quick on the uptake, sensing something is wrong. "Rock?"

How do I tell her? But she can already read me. As her hands reach out to rest on my chest, I'm sure she can feel my increased heartbeat. *Christ, I can hardly get my head around it.* After everything I've laid on her today, how is she going to react? Placing my fingers around hers, I ease her hands away from my shirt, but still the pain throbs through me.

She's watching me carefully, her eyebrow raised as she waits for me to explain. Her face has paled for the third time today, *and she hasn't even heard what I have to tell her yet.* With my arm around her, I lead her to the bed and gently encourage her to sit. Then, without letting go of her, park my ass beside her. I try to find the words, but for a few moments my mouth works, but I can't speak. Almost refusing to say it aloud. *If I don't voice it, it might not be true.* But it is. Delaying the news won't make the hearing of it any easier.

"Becca. Darlin'." I pause only to wipe my own watering eye.

Her brow is furrowed, her eyes lidded. "Rock, you're scaring me. Rock?"

I open my mouth, still nothing comes out. I swallow a couple of times.

"Rock? Is it Slick?"

My voice hitches when I finally get it working. "Not Slick, no. It's Beef. He's, he's taken a turn for the worse. Becca, he's slipped into a coma."

"Beef? No!" She gasps while studying my face as if trying to read some optimism there, before asking hesitantly, "Will he be alright?" But I can't give her that hope, she's sees that. A tear leaking down her cheek reveals she's intuited what's behind my words.

I explain the rest, trying to find my own comfort. "They're still treating him aggressively, but he's gone into septic shock. It's bad, Becca. He fought the bacterial infection off, but his weakened immune system means he's succumbed to the viral type."

She stands, her hands curling and uncurling at her sides. "He's strong, Rock. He'll fight this. He'll be fine. I want to go see him." She sounds so determined it's as though she's going to fight this typically fatal condition by herself.

Me too. Brother, if I could be fighting alongside you, as I have so often before, I would. But I can't fucking help. This is one battle you've got to take on by yourself. Fuck it, Beef, I was just talking to you yesterday. You've got this if you try. And you better fucking try, else I'll beat your ass.

"I want to go to him," she repeats firmly, seeming to think I'd missed hearing her the first time.

"That's what Drum said, Becca. Most of the club is getting ready to leave to go visit him. You ready to go now?" *To say our goodbyes.* But that, I sensibly keep to myself.

She stands, putting her hand trustingly in mine, both of us stunned and shocked. Becca trying to deny that the man who became her friend might be losing his life to infection. Drum's words, something else I don't tell her, echo in my head like a death knell, *there are signs his organs are shutting down.*

Beef. No. It's impossible, I can't lose him. We can't lose him.

CHAPTER 36

Becca

Matt and Truck are the only ones left on the compound. Even the sweet butts are coming along, Allie's driving them in her car. The old ladies are up behind their men.

When we arrive we take over the parking lot, the thunderous roar as bikes back into a line probably waking half the patients. Kickstands down, old ladies off, the men leave their rides unattended while we pile inside, going directly to the ICU. As the others peel off to the waiting room Rock and I follow Drummer, who, as appointed next of kin for all the brothers, persuades the medical staff to let the three of us into Beef's room together. Gowned up and masked, we go in to visit him.

It's hard to see the big man still and unmoving. His face is so pale it's almost translucent, even more tubes than were there yesterday are running into his arms. Behind me Drummer's speaking quietly with the doctor, but I pay them no mind as, without a thought to Rock's feelings, I climb up on the bed and gently cuddle up to Beef's side. The doctor starts shaking his head as if he's going to protest, then shrugs as if it's now too late to give anything to Beef except comfort. It's only then I see Rock's nod of approval, and he walks opposite me and takes hold of his other hand.

"Beef, Brother. What you doing? You've been sleepin' too fuckin' long. Gotta wake up, Brother. Time to go for a ride." Rock tries to rouse him, but there's no sign Beef's heard.

I force myself to be upbeat. Talk as I would normally, as though he can hear every word. "Beef, I got some news this morning. Hawk's dead. Killed himself apparently. I'm free and I'm going to be Rock's old lady. He's even said he'll marry me. Hey, I'll take bets he's going to ask you to be his best man. Sooner you can get out of here, the sooner I can get a ring on my finger. You gonna wake up so you can stand up beside him? Hear us take our vows?"

Rock glances over. "Yeah, right. The vows. I know what you'd be telling me, Brother. I won't be asking her to obey."

"You were right, Beef." I take over again. "I didn't dare hope, but you were right. Rock and I do belong together. Just as you said."

"You told me the same, Brother. Now I'm fed up seeing you sleeping like the dead. Wake the fuck up. Can you squeeze my hand, Beef? No need to crush my bones just yet, just a simple handshake to congratulate me. She's right, you'll be my best man, Brother. Can't think of anyone I'd like better. You reckon she'll want us in tuxes? Can you fuckin' imagine that?"

I give a weak smile. "I'd give a lot to see you both all dressed up. But doubt I'll get you out of your cuts for long enough."

"See? She fuckin' knows us already, Beef."

But Beef lies still and unmoving, only the shallow rise and fall of his chest shows he's even alive.

Drummer doesn't crack a smile at our banter as he comes across. "Beef, you've got work to do, Brother. Time to wake up." But even his best prez voice doesn't work.

"What did the doctor say?" Rock quietly asks.

Drum shakes his head. "They're not giving up on him. Pouring as much antibiotic into him as they can. But the prognosis isn't good. The initial infection weakened him, and this may be too much for him to fight off."

A nurse comes in, interrupting us. We move aside as she checks the equipment and replenishes the drip. She gives me a smile, and I remember her from before when I'd come to visit with Beef. As she leaves her hand squeezes my shoulder, the sadness in her eyes reveals far too much.

We stay for an hour, talking about anything we can think of to say. Eventually our words dry up, and we sit silent, watching him breathe, listening to the monitors beep.

"Rock, Becca. The others will want to say…will want to speak to him. Say your…goodbyes for the moment." Drum stands by Rock's side.

Rock drops his head, then his shoulders straighten as he leans forward, his hand taking Beef's once again. "Beef, Brother. You're the best fuckin' friend and brother a man could have. We've got rides to go on, things to do. We do everything together and will do again. Well, now I've got Becca, perhaps not everything. There's a limit to exactly what I'll share. But you fight, you fuckin' here me? You got this, you can do it. Tell you what, I'll even clean your fuckin' bike and get it serviced and ready for you. You got this, Brother. I fuckin' love you man, and don't you forget it." Then he does something I don't expect. He leans over and kisses Beef's forehead. "You'll be home soon, Brother. You'll be back." His voice chokes as he says again, "You got this. Shiny side up, remember?"

He pauses for a moment as though expecting a response. When there's none, he stands up, wipes moisture from his eye, then looks at me expectantly.

I can't say goodbye. I just can't. My voice cracks. "Beef, I love you too. You've been my first friend, you've helped me so much. Your job's not done yet. Still need you to steady me and put me right. I'll…" I swallow back a sob, unable to believe this might be the last time I see him, but he's already just a shell of the man he was. "I'll be waiting for you, Beef." I kiss him too, then find Rock's there to help me up.

"Send the next pair in," Drummer tells us. "I'd just like a minute with him."

Taking one last look at Beef, saying goodbye under my breath, refusing to believe it might be for the final time, I hold tight to Rock's hand as he leads me out. In a crowded family room, we find everyone else waiting. Rock shakes his head sadly as he gives them the update on Beef's condition, his voice breaking.

Wraith pushes away from the wall, Sophie beside him. Sam takes Olivia's hand as her parents walk away. Peg and Darcy follow. At this point, unless they get in the way, I doubt the nursing staff will mind how many are in his room. They're not exactly going to be raucous.

Rock takes my arm and persuades me back out into the corridor.

"Rock, I'd rather stay."

He looks grim. "Nothing we can do here, darlin'. We'll only get in the way. Beef's an old timer. Everyone will want to spend time with him."

"He might be able to hear us." If there's even a small chance, I want to keep talking to him.

"He won't be left alone. I promise you that. The brothers will be chattering so much he'll want them to shut up. They'll be there with him until...until he wakes up."

It's then I realise it's presumptuous of me. I've not known Beef as long as any of his brothers, or even the old ladies. It's right to make space so everyone who's breathed, eaten, and ridden beside him for so many years can tell him goodbye.

"While we're here, let's catch up with Slick and Ella. Fuck, I could do with some good news today."

Without waiting for my agreement—well, I'm hardly going to protest—I again walk with Rock to another floor where his other unconscious brother is being treated. The last we'd heard there had been no change in his condition, and with the devastating news about Beef, I'm worried Rock's not going to get any better here.

It's easy to spot Slick's room. Ella, Jayden, and Paladin are standing outside. Paladin's leaning against the wall, one foot flat to it, looking down at his phone. Ella and Jayden are on the opposite side, both holding hands.

Rock quickens his step. "Hey. Has something happened?"

Ella swings around. "Yes, the doctors are with him now."

"What? How is he?" Rock's voice breaks, and it's not surprising. Coming from seeing Beef, it sounds like he's fearing the worst.

Ella's face breaks into the smile I haven't seen her wear for days. "He's awake. They're running some tests, but the initial signs and his responses are good. They cautiously think he's going to be fine."

Rock lets go of my hand and sinks to his haunches, his head held between his massive palms. He rocks backward and forward for a moment, then looks up, his fingers tracing down either side of his face. "For real?" When Ella nods, he breathes out loudly. "Thank fuck."

"You okay, Brother?" Paladin asks, sounding concerned, as Rock, at last, stands, letting out a long audible breath as he does so.

"Just seen Beef," Rock answer succinctly.

Paladin meets his eyes, his expression letting us know he's heard the news. He jerks his head in a barely noticeable movement toward the woman and girl and shakes his head. He's right. Let them enjoy their good news for now.

The door opens, and the doctor comes out. He grins at Ella. "Mrs Andrews. You can go back in."

"Is it okay for him to have more visitors?" she asks.

The doctor glances at us. "Just two, maximum three at a time. He needs to keep quiet."

Ella turns to us. "You two pop in and see him first. I've already seen him awake."

Rock gives her a grateful smile. "Thanks, Ella. We'll just be a moment. I sure would like to visit with him."

He opens the door and ushers us inside.

Slick looks pale, his head bristly, in need of a shave, but otherwise his eyes are bright, his expression quick to smile as he recognises us. He holds out his hand and Rock clasps it, holding on a moment longer than necessary.

"Good to fuckin' see you awake, Brother."

The words make me think of the man we just left, the man who's unlikely to wake up. My eyes start to water. While I try to surreptitiously dry them, Slick notices and frowns, looking from me to Rock. "What's up? What's happened?"

Rock takes a deep breath, examines Slick for a moment, then lets out a sigh. "It's Beef. Doesn't seem like he's gonna make it. He's gone into septic shock." He breaks off, swallows, then chokes the next words out. "They… They think his organs are failing. He's in a coma, man. All the brothers are here to see him."

Slick closes his eyes. "Doc's told me I have to stay quiet, and fuck me, Ella's gonna do all she can to make sure I stay put. But I'll try to get Paladin to take me to see him later. Fuck, Rock, I'm sorry, Brother. I know how close you two are."

Rock says nothing, there's not a lot he can say. But when he holds out his arm in invitation I go to him and let him hug me close. We both need the comfort right now.

"Well, we'll be off now, Slick. Got places to be."

Slick narrows his eyes. "Thought you'd be stayin' with Beef?"

"No man, can't. We're going to church."

"Drum called a meetin'? Bit bad timin' if Beef's as bad as you say."

Rock gives a short laugh. "No. Well, he's comin' with. We're going to *church*. A real one. House of God and all that."

Slick's eyes sharpen, then open wide. "Fuck me. Church? For fuckin' real? Hey, you can't leave without givin' me more. Spill, Rock. Satan's Devils going to church? You'll all be struck down by lightning."

Now Rock grins. It's weak, but it's there. "Gets worse than that. Wretched Soulz coming along too."

Slick's eyes open wider. He glances at me, back to Rock, then waves with his hand. "I can't even…"

Rock looks down at me. "Becca, can you give us a moment?"

I nod. Sure I can. Whatever they're going to talk about is probably club business.

Ella looks up as I go out alone, so I explain, "Rock and Slick are talking for a moment. He won't be long. Slick looks good, doesn't he?"

"Yes, thank God," she replies, looking relieved. "I wasn't sure he was going to make it for a moment there. But I've just had a word with the doctor. He just wants to keep him in a little longer, do another scan, but he should be able to come home in a day or two. Will need to take it easy until his fracture's healed, but we can cope with that."

Something Beef won't do. I turn away, not wanting her to see the tears in my eyes. The direction I'm now facing puts me right in Paladin's line of sight. He nods slightly, and he's right. Let Ella enjoy her moment of happiness before she's brought back down again.

Rock's not too long, and soon we're back on his bike and returning to the compound. Drummer and Sam are already there. The mood is decidedly sombre as Sam drags me off to their house where she lends me some smart black pants and a black blouse.

When I've changed I come out to show her. "You look sufficiently like a grieving widow," she announces with a satisfied smile.

It's still hard to get my head around the fact I've no longer got a husband, nor that the only emotion that leaves me with is relief, along with a new sense of freedom. I certainly won't be able to convince people I miss him, but, "I can't cry for Hawk," I reply. "But I can turn on the tears if I think about Beef."

She pulls me in for a hug, but not before I see moisture in her own eyes. "Beef's a great guy. I'll miss him too. We all will, so much. I know he took good care of you for Rock. He was so happy to learn you were together."

"Rock's going to miss him terribly if he goes." Beef went downhill so quickly, it's difficult to take in. Sure, he was looking pale when I last saw him, but nowhere near death's door. He'd deteriorated so quickly.

"Honey, he needs a miracle now. Don't get your hopes up. Cases like this? There's only one way he can go."

For me, I speak fiercely. "I'm not giving up on him, Sam. I can't."

Her arms tighten briefly, then she lets me go and steps back. "It's good news about Slick, though, isn't it? Has Ella told Slick she's pregnant yet?"

"Not that I know. He's got to avoid getting overexcited, so she might be holding back for the moment."

She nods, then turns around and examines herself in the mirror. "Will I do? I don't own a dress."

"You'll do." I smile. "You look beautiful, Sam." I haven't seen her wearing makeup before.

Linking her arm through mine, she grins. "Off to church then?"

"Off to church." I try to keep the smile on my face, but it's not easy when half of me is drowning in unshed tears for Beef while the other half churns with fear.

CHAPTER 37
Rock

I'm wearing my dressiest jeans and a white button-up shirt. Drummer is similarly attired. The girls look great, clean, tidy, and presentable. While Becca's not made up like Sam—her red-rimmed eyes adding a touch of authenticity—the clothes she's been lent suit her. I make a note to take her shopping soon and buy her some decent clothes of her own. New underwear too. Fuck yeah. I'll have fun helping her choose that.

Forcing my mind away from what Becca could soon be wearing before my cock starts to take notice, I follow the others out to where the club's trucks are parked. Taking one, we settle inside, and after a quiet drive meet Chaz and Bull just outside of Phoenix. Chaz, flashy as always, is driving a restored 1960's Ford Mustang convertible. As a slight drizzle is falling, I take some satisfaction in that they're driving with the top up. The girl he's brought with him, I'm pleased to see, is modestly dressed. But the way she hangs off him gives away she's one of their whores.

Greetings exchanged, in convoy we drive to our destination, the church of God which hides a secret with violent promise underneath. I can feel Becca tensing the closer we get, and as I take her hand she holds it so tightly her knuckles grow white.

I don't tell her it will be okay. I know she's not afraid of the building, but the influence of the people inside. Instead of false platitudes I make her a silent vow, not to give her a chance to fall under their spell. It's my job to protect her, mentally as well as physically.

It's perfect timing. We arrive just moments before the service is due to start and take our seats in the back two rows. A few people turn around, their eyes opening. Although we're all dressed smartly, even without our cuts, you can't take the biker out of the man. While we wait for the pastor to appear I scan the congregation, noting two men in particular who interest me. An interest they're reciprocating if it's possible to tell by their calculating looks. One I recognise from the other night. If we're right, then that's Butcher in the third row back on the right.

"White. Is he here?" I murmur into Becca's ear.

"Left-hand front pew, in the middle."

It's as I thought. They're quick on the uptake that we might have something to do with Hawk. Maybe they even think we're Chaos Riders. Huh, that would be a laugh. As both men continue to watch us, I raise my chin. It seems it's the signal they want, and they turn their attention back to the front, but not before I've seen satisfied nods exchanged between them.

"Both men are here," I whisper to Drum.

"Picked up on that," Prez replies, his voice lower than I've ever heard it.

Then Pastor Alton appears and steps up to the pulpit. What he's saying I've no clue, being distracted by a gasp which comes from my side. Becca's looking at an older pair up in front of us. "Your parents?" I ask, softly.

I feel her shaking as she replies, "Yes."

I rush to reassure her. "Don't worry, Becca. Just stick with the story. You're under our protection now."

We stand and mime to a hymn, then sit back down and pray. Becca is the only one of us who kneels, her hands clasped together and pressed against her forehead. I doubt it would be too far a stretch to think she was praying for Beef, and while I don't speak to a God I don't believe exists, my mind goes to my stricken brother. As if on cue, my phone vibrates.

While the congregation have their heads bowed, I take it out and read it, feeling a bolt of pain go through me. It's Shooter letting me know they're about to put Beef on a ventilator.

Somewhere inside me I must have continued to have hope as the text hits me with a force I didn't expect. All I can wish for now is that he goes peacefully. *Brother. I'll fuckin' miss you.* The thought I won't ever see his cheery face coming out from the suite next to mine again guts me. I'm in a house of God, but still I don't waste time on a prayer. Why would anyone listen to me? Hopefully Becca's saying enough words for us both.

The quiet time ends, now we're up and singing again. Then we sit, and the pastor starts his sermon. The only reason I'm listening is to understand the sort of rubbish that brainwashed my woman.

"We have two weddings coming up in the next couple of weeks," the pastor starts, the congregation nodding and smiling. "Now's a good time to reflect on what the Bible teaches us about the relationship between a man and a woman. As Timothy reminds us, *1 Timothy 2:11.15*, 'A woman should learn in quietness and full submission. I do not permit a woman to teach or to assume authority over a man; she must be quiet.' Ephesians gives us more. *Ephesians 5:22.23*, 'Wives, submit to your own husbands as to the Lord. For the husband is the head of the wife even as Christ is the head of the church.' And in Genesis we hear a message directly for the wives. *Genesis 3:16* 'Your desire shall be for your husband and he shall rule over you.'"

The pastor looks around, his eyes lingering for a second on who I suspect are the poor, unwitting brides. If they believe this crap they'll turn out like Becca, frightened and scared of doing anything wrong. While I'd rather be anywhere else but here, I start to understand more about the woman at my side. If she's listened to this every day of her life, no wonder she's had difficulty adjusting.

"This is fucked up shit." Drummer speaks into my ear at the same time as Chaz turns around, shaking his head as if he can't believe what he's hearing.

"As you go forth into the holy state of matrimony," the pastor is continuing, "or if you are already married women, you must bend to the will of your husband. Your man is always right, you should broke no disagreement. For as Proverbs tell us, **Proverbs 21:19**, 'It is better to live in a desert land than with a quarrelsome and fretful woman.'

"I know you, Sara, and you, Wendy, have been brought up in the church. From children in Sunday School to the time you became adults, you have learned the teaching in Titus, **Titus 2:4.5**, 'So to train young women to love their husbands and children, to be self-controlled, pure, working at home, kind and submissive to their husbands'. I know you will have taken those lessons to heart and will go to your husbands and properly submit to them. You are never to challenge their decisions. The man of the house always knows best. He will provide for you, and whatever he gives you, you should be grateful and show your gratitude as a wife should."

I lean down and whisper to Becca. "You know this is wrong, don't you? It's just words from an ancient book written by ignorant men and twisted to suit some men's purposes."

I tune out the pastor as I watch for her reaction.

Her hands twist in her lap.

"Fuck, Becca. I'd laugh out loud if it wouldn't draw attention. Real men don't want a subservient wife, they want someone beside them, not walking behind them."

Suddenly she whispers back. "Then maybe I'm not right for you. I've been trained, just as Pastor Alton says. Taught to be a slave to my husband."

"Not anymore," I reassure her. "Just remember how much thinking you now do for yourself. Don't put yourself back in that mindset just because the fuckin' pastor's reminded you. The church did the damage, Hawk just compounded it. You're not the woman they brainwashed."

"I don't want to be that woman anymore."

"You're not." I risk a look at her face. She's worrying her lip again, and I'm sorry that we had to bring her.

Sam, sitting beside her, takes her hand. Though she speaks quietly, I can just about hear her. "For every Bible passage the pastor's quoted there are others that contradict him. Hell, I could probably find a quote that would persuade Drummer to buy me a new bike."

Drummer's hearing's good too. He raises a disbelieving eyebrow at her.

The sermon's over at last. Now the pastor's talking about upcoming events, including garnering support for a protest at an abortion clinic as if he's arranging a picnic outing. I've almost had enough and would be ready to walk out there and then, except I have to remember we're here for a reason.

I sit and stand when required until, *finally*, the pastor seems fed up with hearing his own voice, and the service draws to a very welcome close. As people start to file out from the front I see White and Butcher pushing their way through toward us. *Mission accomplished.*

"Let's talk outside," White suggests, ushering us out of the pew.

"Becca!" A shrill female voice cries out.

I'm cruel, but I do it for a good reason. "Remember Beef," I tell Becca harshly.

Immediately her eyes fill with tears, but she nods, understanding, as she turns to the woman who's approaching fast, a man coming along at her side. "Mom. Dad."

"What are you doing here, Becca?" The woman takes a step back, allowing her husband to stand right in front of his daughter.

Although intimidated, Becca stands her ground, making me as proud as fuck of her. "Have you heard about Alexis, Dad? He died last night in prison. He, he committed suicide."

Her mother obviously hasn't, as her hand covers her mouth and her eyes open wide. Her father stands stunned, then nods, giving her mother permission to speak. "Becca…" She seems at a loss for words.

With tears falling, Becca continues, "I wanted to come to pray. To get comfort."

Her father gives a smile which I notice doesn't reach his eyes. "Of course you did, Child. I'm pleased you came. You'll be expecting to come home with us now you've no man to watch out for you. Come, no need to waste time. You can have your own bedroom back tonight. We'll pray with you for forgiveness, and any of your failings as a wife."

Her failings?

"I… I didn't do a…a…anything w…wrong." Her initial bravery starts to fail her.

Her mother looks to her father as though again for permission, and then seems to speak for them both. "I can't take in that Alexis is gone, nor that he took his own life. But he wouldn't have done that if he'd had a good wife waiting."

It's time for me to step up. "I don't know why Pastor Gardner," I refer to Hawk politely, "decided to off himself. But I can assure you it was nothing to do with your daughter. What I can tell you is that he put her under our protection. We've been taking good care of her and will continue to do so."

"Your hair!" her mother explains, seemingly out of the blue. "Why did you cut it off. Alexis wouldn't like that…"

I grit my teeth in an effort not to blurt out that Hawk was the reason she lost it in the first place.

Not telling her he was now hardly in a position to explain, Becca tries to justify herself. "I wanted a new style."

"And gave no thought to your husband."

"Her husband is dead," I remind her bluntly. "Becca can make her own choices."

It was the wrong thing to say. Her father tries to take her arm. "Then you're coming home with us. Didn't you listen to the sermon? Seems you need reminding of your place…"

This time he's interrupted by White. "Mr and Mrs Salter, I'm sure you'll want to visit with your daughter. Especially on such a sad day." *So he already knows about Hawk.* "I need to talk to these gentlemen. Perhaps, Becca, you can catch up with your parents while we discuss business outside."

"A moment of prayer with the pastor will be in order," her father suggests, seeming pleased with the idea.

Becca's gone dead still. Sam puts her arm around her waist, glaring at her parents. "Becca's a married woman, well, a widow now. She makes her own decisions on who she wants to talk to. You're unsettling her. All the peace and comfort she found by coming here today is being ruined. Mr and Mrs Salter, I'm sorry, but she doesn't want to return to your home."

"My daughter's got no way of supporting herself. She'll have to come with us now she's without a husband."

"We don't know what provisions Hawk made for her yet. Even if she's left penniless she'll have a home with us, I assure you."

"Becca…"

"No, Mrs Salter." Sam's intent on getting her message across.

"Who do you think you are?" Becca's father challenges.

"Her friend," Sam states, earning her a weak smile from my woman. "Come on, Becca. We'll go sit in the truck and wait for the men to finish their business. Nice to meet you, Mr and Mrs Salter."

With the parting shot that's clearly a lie, and with her arm firmly fixed around Becca, Sam leads her away. Becca's parents are left with their mouths hanging open. I suppress a grin as I walk out, noticing Drummer is watching Sam carefully, making sure the girls get to the truck unmolested.

"You know what to say?" White advocates as soon as our group has removed itself out of earshot of the other parishioners.

Bull nods. "Absent in body but present in spirit. *1 Corinthians v. 3*." I hide my smirk. Particularly apt in the circumstances. I bet Stub had a chuckle at that.

White and Butcher visibly relax, though Butcher grimaces and looks up at the sky. *Uh uh*, I think to myself. *He'd do better to look downward.*

"So let's talk business." Chaz takes the lead. "Hawk gave us the job to move your stash."

"Thank Christ for that." Butcher speaks for the first time, and rather irreverently in my view. "We're running out of funds. We've got a big rally coming up."

"Did I hear you discuss the rally?"

Butcher swings around, the expression on his face changing swiftly, now one befitting a church-going man. "Ah, Pastor. Didn't realise you were there. Yes, these gentleman are helping with the finance."

Pastor Alton beams. "You're good men. And very welcome to my church. I trust you enjoyed the sermon?"

We murmur something that could be interpreted as affirmative.

Butcher obviously wants rid of the man. "Well, we need to get down to the details. I'm sure you've other parishioners to talk to."

"Yes, yes. Of course. Well, it was good meeting you. I hope to see you here again." Then he turns around and walks off.

Bull takes out his cigarettes, extracts one, and points it still unlit toward the pastor. "He know anything?"

"Fuck no." The church-goer persona has disappeared again as Butcher stares at the retreating pastor. "I've been keeping an eye on him, making sure he doesn't snoop." He nods at Drummer. "That's why I was here the other night. Pastor Alton wants the rally to go ahead, but won't dirty his hands making arrangements."

Chaz leans lazily back against the wall as Bull lights up. "Don't think there's a lot more to be said. We'll get the stuff shifted and collect payment. You just need to tell us where the pick-up point is." This, of course, we already know. It's extremely close to where we're standing.

"Hawk described the split to you?" White's turn now.

"Of course," he lies. He's no intention of giving these men anything.

"What club are you?" Butcher asks.

Bull rolls up his sleeve displaying the tat on his arm. "Wretched Soulz."

The two men exchange glances and chin lifts. Then White speaks again. "If your boys want some fun, you could join us at the rally. Bust a few black heads, send those fuckin' immigrants back where they belong."

Bull almost imperceptibly flinches, but his voice belies his physical reaction as he inhales then blows out smoke. He doesn't care when it wafts over their faces. "Sounds good to me. You'll have to give us the details. But for now, we want to get on with moving the…product."

"Course you do. And you've clearly got the manpower. At night's best."

I only half listen to them finalising arrangements. Satan's Devils' involvement ends here, and thank fuck for that. But it's interesting that Butcher and White do know where the weapons are kept, and I suspect that knowledge has signed their death warrant. But having heard what they plan to do with the funds they expect, they deserve it.

At last the discussion's finished. After handshakes all around the two men wander off.

Drummer turns to Chaz. "We can leave it with you now?"

The Wretched Soulz's prez is still staring after the men walking away. "Unless you want to be part of putting them in the ground. Did you catch they were the only two aware of Hawk's hiding place?"

"Much as I'd like to see them put down, I'll forego that pleasure and leave it in your capable hands."

"Perhaps I'll make them pray first," Chaz says casually, then his eyes narrow and he looks at me. "Understand your woman's problems better now, Rock. She really brought up with all that shit?"

"She was." I look at the truck for the hundredth time. My eyes have been on it while we've been talking, hoping her parents would keep their distance, which they seem to have done. Prez's old lady must have scared them off.

"Well, we're coming back tonight. Get this shit moved, loose ends eradicated, and take it from there, Drummer. I'll fulfil my part of the bargain and get the Herreras off your back. Warn you, they won't like it."

"Herreras will always be a thorn in our side," Drummer agrees, his expression showing it's not going to make him lose sleep. Then he takes Chaz's offered hand, pulls him in close, and they slap each other's backs.

I say my goodbyes in similar fashion to both Chaz and Bull, then we return to the truck and to Chaz's muscle car. The sweet butt is leaning against the hood, her blouse unbuttoned now, titties all but hanging out as she shakes them at her prez.

A final chin lift goodbye in response to Chaz's wink, then I've just put my hand on the door handle when my phone vibrates again. Taking it out, I read the text.

Shooter: Best you and Becca get to the hospital as soon as you can.

My eyes close for a second, then open. I pass my phone to Drummer.

"We'll all go," he says gruffly, while his hand rests on the back of my cut. "This will be hard for all of us, but particularly on you and your girl. We'll be there for you, Brother."

CHAPTER 38
Becca

Rock pulls me to him as he sits beside me in the truck. He holds me tightly, his head resting against my neck. I feel his chest heaving. *Something's wrong.* Although I've a good idea what it is, I allow him a moment, just letting the comfort I want to give him seep from my body to his. *It must be Beef.*

I'd prayed harder than I'd ever prayed before, begging even more than the times I sat in that church and my prayers involved giving me the strength to survive my marriage to Hawk. On my knees, I'd poured my heart and soul into my pleas for Beef's recovery. If I'm reading Rock right, my words were useless and had no effect at all. Beef's fate's decided before my request could be heard.

Drummer's driving, and he's not wasting time, his foot to the throttle, exceeding the speed limit. He's not speaking, his face is set in concentration.

It's a good few minutes before Rock pulls himself together sufficiently to explain. "We're going straight to the hospital."

"Beef?" But I already know the answer.

"Yeah. I'm sorry. It's not good, Becca." Each word seems like it's being dragged out of him. The tentative hope I'd been hanging onto starts to fade.

"Will we get there in time?" Beef might not be conscious, but I'd like the chance to see him one last time. *To say goodbye.* The word I couldn't bring myself to say this afternoon.

"Gonna give it a damn good try," Drummer says over his shoulder.

Nothing of consequence is said on that two-hour drive back to Tucson. Each of us lost in our own fears and recollections of Beef. Beef who'd been so good to me, taking me out of the clutches of Petty and Roller, comforting me while Rock didn't want to see me. Responsible for getting us together again. Beef, my first proper male friend. That a big man so strong could be struck down by an infection seems inconceivable.

As we draw nearer to the hospital Rock's arms are tight around me. I'm all but holding my breath, scared of what we're going to find. *Are we too late? Has he already gone?* Rock shudders beside me as if his thoughts are along the same lines. *Beef is Rock's best friend. Rock will need me. I've got to be strong for him.* I hate myself for not being able to find adequate words of support. I can't suggest Beef's no longer with us, nor can I pretend he's going to be fine. Anything I say would only be meaningless. My man's lost, or is about to lose, the brother he's been best friends with so long. The brother he'd ride with, laugh with, and, though this particular thought I don't much like but can't deny, fucked with. Could any two men ever be closer?

Drummer finds a parking spot. As we get out of the car Rock pulls his shoulders back, pauses for a second, then, standing taller, takes my hand as we follow the prez and his old lady.

Going to the ICU, Sam splits off to go to the waiting room, while Drummer, myself, and Rock go straight to Beef's. A nurse comes out just as we're entering. As she stands aside, I notice she's smiling, which registers as a strange expression in these depressing circumstances. But perhaps she's trained to give comfort in situations such as these.

"You can go in now. The doctor's just finishing with him."

Finishing with him. It sounds so final and such a brutal way of putting it. *Is he dead?* Has he been preparing a body?

"What the fuck?" Rock sounds, well, unlike Rock. His voice squeaking.

I'd been scared to look. I'd purposefully averted my eyes at the Chaos Riders' clubhouse, looking quickly away at the bodies lying around. I've not been face to face with a dead friend before. But as I raise my eyes I realise today's not the day I'll get that chance. Beef's pillow's been slightly raised, there's still oxygen tubes in his nose, IVs everywhere, drips still full of liquid. Beef himself? Well, his eyes are open and he looks alert.

I gasp, my emotions haywire. I grab on to Drummer to steady myself as Rock's supportive arm falls away and he almost leaps forward and takes hold of Beef's hand.

"Brother…" he stammers out. "Fuck it, I love you man."

"Love you too, Rock." Beef's voice sounds dry and croaky. But as I never expected to hear it again, I'll take that.

The doctor's still hovering, looking from his patient to us. Gradually a smile spreads over his face.

"What the fuck's going on?" Drummer asks.

The doctor looks at Beef, who gives a weak nod, permission to tell us everything. "That man there. Strong as an ox." Once started, he doesn't hold back. "Thought we'd lost him. One moment he was struggling to breathe, and we were going to ventilate. His blood pressure was rock bottom, his urine output nil, and his temperature sky high. Next moment he opened his eyes." He breaks off and shakes his head. "Never would have believed it if I hadn't seen it for myself."

"How is he now?" Drum asks sharply.

I watch the doctor, waiting to be told this is only a temporary reprieve. That we're still likely to lose him.

The doctor looks at a container under the bed. "Urine output's good." Then his eyes check the monitors. "Pulse rate a little low, but that's not unexpected. Blood pressure's creeping up and is already out of the danger zone." As if he doesn't believe it himself, he puts a thermometer to Beef's ear. "Temperature has come back down to normal." He raises his chin to Beef. "You must have an iron-clad constitution, that's all I can say. Somehow, you've fought off the infection."

"Prognosis?"

Now he shakes his head. "Speed of his improvement? I'd say the signs are good. He'll probably shock us again and make a full recovery in no time. But we'll have to run some tests. His immune system was pretty badly compromised after all. We'll leave it tonight, but tomorrow we'll do a full function test of all his organs."

"See," Beef croaks, actually grinning. "I'm a fuckin' medical miracle."

Rock still hasn't let go of Beef's hand, but his eyes find the doctor. "What time was this? What time did he start showing signs of improvement?"

The doctor consults the tablet he's carrying. If he's surprised at the question, he doesn't show it. "I can tell you almost exactly. As I said, I was called in as he was struggling to breathe. A couple of minutes after that? Say six thirty-eight pm."

Rock gets out his phone and consults it, then his eyes widen as he looks at me, then turns back to Beef. "Fuckin' miracle you called it. I reckon you got Becca to thank for that."

"Whatcha mean, Rock?" Drum looks confused.

"Six thirty-five was the time Shooter texted me and told me he was about to be put on a ventilator. Becca was on her knees praying at the time. You were praying for Beef, weren't you, darlin'?"

I was, but… I shake my head. "I admit my prayers were answered, but it has to be coincidence, surely." The big man above had never looked out for me before. *But perhaps he has been all along. He brought me to Rock, the man who saved me in more ways than one.*

Beef sucks on an ice chip and then manages a strangled laugh. "Divine intervention? And me a sinner?"

Drummer's looking thoughtful. "I'd have said there wasn't a God in that heathen place we went to. But you never know, present or not, He might have been listening."

Beef chuckles. "Or Satan's lookin' out for his own."

"Well I'm hard put to find a medical way to explain it." The doctor smiles. "Though I'd like to put it down to our expertise in our treatment. But if I were you, I'd be inclined to send up a prayer of thanks tonight."

Oh, I'm certainly going to do that.

Though all three of us are reluctant to leave, the doctor shoos us out with his assurance they'll be watching Beef carefully, and will let Drummer, as his listed next of kin, know if there's any change. We leave with much lighter hearts than when we had entered, confident that the medical staff won't want to lose their miracle patient.

Outside in the corridor, Drummer walks off as Rock stops and brings me into his chest. "I wouldn't have said I was a believer, Becca. But one things for certain, if there is a God, it wasn't one they were worshipping in that fuckin' church. *My* God would be the one who's with me when I'm riding, when I'm appreciating nature with the wind in my hair and the warmth of the sun on my back. *My* God wouldn't want women to be subservient, to be robbed of their choices and subjugated by a man. *My* God would be the one who brought us together."

Just like that, the shadows that had hung over me since hearing the sermon emphasising my screwed-up lessons of my past flee from me. Rock's right. And I prefer his God to mine, suspecting if anyone did, it was Him who answered my prayers and brought Beef back to us.

The waiting room is buzzing, everyone delighted with the prospect that their brother will be coming home. No one can quite believe it. I feel almost faint with all the emotional upheaval I've been through today. I know Rock wants to stay, but when Hyde offers to keep Beef company I'm glad, after a look at me, that he thanks Hyde and accepts. I've a strange confidence inside me that the man who's made such a miraculous recovery will continue to improve. While nothing will stop me coming back tomorrow, tonight I'll be able to rest knowing all will be well.

I'm a free woman. I'm Rock's woman. And Rock's complete knowing his friend will hopefully soon be back riding at his side.

"Only one problem," Rock says conspiratorially into my ear as we walk outside. "Bet the fucker could hear us when I promised to clean and service his fuckin' bike."

It's not that funny, but I laugh. And laugh. As Rock chuckles with me I realise for the first time today, my tears are not as a result of sadness.

EPILOGUE
Rock

Two months later

"That was a good fuckin' ride, Brother." Beef rubs his hands. "Might look into getting those heated grips, though. Getting a bit nippy out there."

"Heated fuckin' grips? You some kind of pansy now, Brother? Your compromised immune system making you fuckin' frail?"

Beef's retort with his fist to Blade's stomach shows there's nothing particularly weak about him. Blade staggers, recovers, and wheezes a laugh.

I flex my own cold hands. It's true, the early December day had turned chilly, but I'll leave the wraparound handwarmers to Beef. My eyes turn away from the brother I'd given up all hope of ever riding with again, and instead find Becca. We've got visiting members from San Diego up here today, so she's wearing her property patch. I watch as she confidently pushes past them, making her way over to me.

I hold out my arms, and she steps straight into them, raising her head for a kiss. She's become a rich woman, my old lady, or will be soon, when the lawyers sort out what Hawk had left. He'd died intestate, and with no other living relatives, everything he had will come to her. Becca's still adamant she doesn't want it. We don't need it, I make enough for us both, but I'll encourage her to do what she wants with her new-found

410

wealth. Personally, I think she should keep it, she earned it for the time she was abused by her ex-husband. But if she wants to give it away, I'll be alright with that too. As far as I'm concerned, everything and anything she wants, she can have. She deserves it.

Her hands are still touching my cheeks as she pulls her lips away. I notice her face is glowing as she starts curling her hand around my neck and I allow her to pull my head down so she can speak into my ear. "Rock, er..." she starts quietly.

"What is it, Becca?"

"I did a pregnancy test."

My breathing stops as I look down at her. "Well?" I prompt, anxious to know the answer.

"It looks like we've made a baby."

I can't help it. I pick her up in my arms, swing her around me and shout out my pleasure at the same time. "We're gonna have a kid!" I yell to the packed room.

While others are congratulating me, Beef sounds grumpy. "Fallin' like fuckin' flies."

Swinging around sharply I stare at him, seeing his face soften as his eyes fall on Becca. Then he pushes me away and takes my *pregnant* woman in his arms, cradling her head in his big paws. "Couldn't be more fuckin' pleased for you," he tells her gently. Then turns to me and slaps me on the back. "Hey, Rock's gonna be a daddy," he tells everyone, as if they hadn't already heard.

It's Slick who comes over next. He's beaming. "Won't be more than a couple of months between our rug rats."

"Becca! Congratulations!" Ella's already by her side, and fuck me, the other women are coming over, and I've now lost my woman. But I'm not worried. She'll be back. She and I, well, we belong together.

"Church! Now!"

At Drum's roar we start making our way into the meeting room. My back is sore by the time I arrive from the number of times it's been slapped. Thankfully the skin's healed over completely now.

Inside, we jostle for places around the table. Dart, who used to be one of us, and who's now the VP for the San Diego chapter, takes a spot next to Peg, so we all have to move down one. Extra chairs have been brought in, and Niran, also from San D, squeezes in beside Joker, and his brothers, Pennywise and Salem find spaces for themselves too. I flex my elbows, trying to give myself more room.

"Mouse not comin'?" Wraith asks.

As Prez gives a brief shake of his head, I realise Mouse has been missing more times than he's been present lately. When he is around he keeps to himself even more than usual. There's something going on with the man, but as far as I know, none of us have got to the bottom of it. Drummer seems easy about it. As long as he's available on the end of a phone and can work remotely, he's giving him a pass. I frown, my good mood slipping as I wonder what the computer guru has got going on in his life. I seem to have reached that disgusting point in my life when I want everyone to be as happy as I am.

Prez bangs the gavel. "Okay, assholes. Let's kick this off. Fuckin' good to see Dart here. As you know, his ol' lady's helping Rock's woman get her inheritance sorted."

There's banging of the table. Dart looks around. "Fuckin' good to be back sitting around this table, Prez. Good run, eh, brothers?" Niran, Pennywise, and Salem all nod.

"Yeah, thought we'd come see how the mother chapter rolls," Pennywise answers for them all.

"Right, back to business. Dollar?"

"Shop's up and working again now. Better than ever. But we had to use Ma's legacy, and that means the tattoo shop's on hold for now. Sorry, Rock."

I shrug. It will still be some months before I can get the scars on my back tatted over. While I'd have preferred to go to someone who works for us and whose livelihood depends on doing a good job, instead I'll just have to find someone the brothers recommend.

Having run through the normal business, Drummer takes the floor. "Beef and I met with Doc. Seems we'll have to find ourselves a new medic."

"What the fuck? He's been patching us up for years," Blade observes.

"Yeah, like when you cut yourself with one of your knives," quips Viper.

Blade spins his knife until it points at the man who's spoken. "One time. That was one fuckin' time. It slipped…"

"Yeah, yeah," a few people call out.

"Lucky you didn't lose your dick!" Joker puts in.

"Shut up!" Drummer glares around the table.

"Missed this," Dart murmurs, earning him a death stare of his own.

"If you'll fuckin' listen." Prez resorts to banging the gavel, and gradually we quiet down. "Doc blames himself for Beef's wound getting infected."

"Man couldn't have done more." Beef is shaking his head. "Gave me antibiotics after he removed the bullet. The hospital wouldn't have done anything different. *And* he got me taken in at the first sign there was something wrong."

"Doc's a good guy," Peg puts in. "He knows his stuff. And Beef's right. He made the calls as he saw them and called them right."

Drum sits back, smiling with satisfaction. "That's what Beef and I told him. But he thinks he's lost our confidence, so I said we'd put it to a vote."

We vote. It's all ayes to keep Doc on retainer. Heart records the decision in his book.

"Just one more thing before we go. Chaz has been dealing with the Herreras on our behalf. Heard something which is worrying. It might come as no surprise that we're not their favourite people."

"Leonardo Herrera sanctioned those killin's," Peg reminds him.

"But Leonardo's dead. Javier's at the head now, and it was his cousins we took out."

"Fuckin' ace," Peg snarls. "We take out their dirty laundry, and now get the fuckin' blame for it?"

"Seems like," Drum replies. He doesn't seem happy. "You're all aware Butcher's on Chaz's payroll now." Yes we are, and that was one more mystery solved. Butcher turned out to be a dirty cop. He was the one who'd got into the police records and read a female's body had been found in the Chaos Riders' clubhouse. Using his police credentials, he was also able to get messages to Hawk. In addition he was being paid by the Herreras, and when they'd pointed their finger at us for taking the Riders out, he passed that info onto Hawk. We needn't worry about him. Wretched Soulz have got him sewn up tight. White? Well, White had met with an unfortunate accident.

The prez's eyes fall on Paladin at the end of the table. "There's one way they can hurt us. Butcher's heard Herreras' whisper of retaliation. Cartel's hit them hard, they've lost the gun and the skin trade. They're looking at the girl who got away and inadvertently brought them down."

Paladin stills. "Jayden," he breathes out.

"How old is she now, Brother?" Drum's question surprises me.

"Sixteen and a half."

"You still gonna want her as your old lady?"

Paladin's yes is so firm and committed no one mocks him. Even Slick stays quiet. "I've done what you said, Prez. Stayed clear."

Drummer nods. "Age of consent is seventeen in Colorado. I've had a word with Hellfire. If we think there's a risk to Jayden, he's offered to let you transfer there. Temporarily or permanently."

Now Slick sits up. "Not sure I'm happy with that, Prez. As for my ol' lady..."

"You want her alive and well, don't you, Slick? Paladin's done as instructed. He's watched over her but not stepped over that fuckin' line. They've both waited. It would have happened in eighteen months anyway, I'm just suggestin' we pull the timetable forward. You really gonna object to keeping her out of harm's way, Slick?"

Slick's brow furrows, then he glances at Paladin. "Can I speak to Ella before you make a decision?"

Paladin raises his chin. "Got a lot of time for you both, Slick. And anyways, I need Jayden's view on it. Yeah, this should be a family decision."

Slick nods back. "Appreciate that."

"It's on the table," Drummer sums up. "Let me know what you decide. And right now, it's time to party and show these San D fuckers exactly how the mother chapter rocks." He bangs the gavel, which is the signal for talking, stamping, and table thumping before a mass exodus to the clubroom.

The sweet butts are ready and waiting. Cars pulling up outside with the hopeful hangarounds from Tucson. Showing things are very much back to usual, Beef catches my eye, grins, gives a shake of his head, then walks off smartly to get first choice.

Becca's deep in conversation with Ella, probably discussing early pregnancy or some such shit. *Fuck me, she's pregnant!* I grin, then go over. As soon as she sees me, she stands.

"You want to stay here, or go up to the suite?" I try to give her choices as often as I can.

"Nah, we've just finished, haven't we, Ella? And thanks, I'll give that a try if I start feeling nauseous in the mornings."

Slick chooses that moment to approach. He's certainly not giving Ella much choice as he takes her hand, pulls her up, then carries her out bridal style with just giving me a wink in passing.

Which gives me an idea. Within seconds Becca's in my arms, her hands shooting around my neck for balance, and I'm making my way through the room. Becca's laughing, releasing one hand to wave at Alex, who's been giving her legal advice, and Alex and Dart's young son, Tyler, who's looking the picture of health. I see Dart coming over to quickly usher the pair out, presumably having seen Beef getting settled on the couch with a hangaround beside him.

Once in our suite I put Becca down, then go to the drawer of my bedside table. I stand, my back toward her as I start to speak. "Becca, you comin' into my life. You've given me something I didn't even know that I needed." I turn around. "I was restless, bored. Didn't even know what I was lookin' for until I found it. Thought my restlessness was down to missin' excitement. Couldn't have been more fuckin' wrong."

"I think we've had enough excitement to keep us going for a while," she offers, giving me one of her glorious smiles.

Not answering, I approach her. She's standing, head tilted to one side as if wondering where I'm going with this. "I love you, Becca. You've given me so much already, and soon we'll have a family of our own." I drop to one knee and hold out the ring I'd kept hidden. "Will you marry me, Becca?"

Her eyes widen, and I swear I can see moisture glisten there. Then she looks down with an impish grin. "Is this one of the choices you always give me?"

I chuckle. "I'll always give you a choice, Becca. Every fuckin' time. If you turn me down now, I'll just keep asking until I wear you down."

She makes me wait for it. Then, "Yes. Yes. Yesyesyesyesyes! I'll marry you, Rock!"

I jump up, slide the ring on her finger. "Marry me soon," I implore. I want to tie her to me in every way that I can. This brave, special woman of mine. I know with her upbringing she'll feel more comfortable having our union made legal. "Soon?" I repeat.

"Tomorrow?"

"Works for me, sweetheart. Fuckin' works for me." Placing my hands under her sweet ass, I lift her up, knowing she can feel my hardness. My cock's as stiff as iron whenever she's around. Our mouths meet, move together in that now familiar dance.

"Fuck me, Rock," she pleads as she pulls away breathless.

"My fuckin' pleasure," I respond, placing her *gently* down on the bed.

The door of the suite opposite slams shut, but not before we can hear loud giggling. Beef's brought a woman up to his suite. Becca catches my eye, and soon we're both chuckling without voicing a reason.

But I understand. Beef, my best friend and who's become hers, is here, very much alive. He's beaten the fuckin' odds, septic shock is fatal in six out of ten cases. I'm not going to complain at any noise he's making. He deserves all the pleasure he can get.

Now I'm going to have my own family, and his or her Uncle Beef will be right there beside me. Brothers for life.

I feel the luckiest motherfucker on top of the fuckin' world. No longer at rock bottom, a place I never want to visit again.

Becca giggles once more, my eyes snapping back to her. Thoughts of Beef disappear right out of my head as I stalk toward her with just one idea in my mind. I'm going to fuck my soon-to-be wife.

THE END

JOKER'S
FOOL
SATAN'S DEVILS #7.5

Joker

A gay man in a straight MC needs to stay under the radar. I hate who I am, and whatever is said, it isn't a choice. I can't help my nature, but I can suppress it. If I could change, I would in an instant.

I hate Lady's Man from the first moment I see him. He's obviously straight, even his handle shows how the women all flock to him. I detest him for arousing impulses in me that I should be better able to keep hidden.

He's upsetting my well-ordered life. I thought I had everything under control, but no, not when I'm around him.

I jump at the opportunity to transfer from Vegas to the Tucson club. I wouldn't have been so quick to switch clubs had I known Lady was going to come with me. There's no escape, and no running away however hard I try.

Vegas was a relatively quiet club. In Tucson we're thrust in the middle of slave trafficking rings, even coming up against the cartel. In the midst of the fighting Lady forces me to face up to those yearnings I've always tried to keep buried. But admitting who, and what, I am could have dire ramifications.

SATAN'S DEVILS #7.5: JOKER'S Fool

OTHER WORKS BY MANDA MELLETT

All books can be read as a standalone.

Blood Brothers

A series about sexy dominant sheikhs and their bodyguards

SATAN'S DEVILS MC

- *Slick Running* (#3 – Slick & Ella)

- *Targeting Dart* (#4 – Dart & Alex)

- *Heart Broken* (#5 – Heart & Marc)

- *Peg's Stand* (#6 – Peg & Darcy)

- *Rock Bottom* (#7 – Rock & Becca)

Coming soon:
- *Joker's Fool* (#7.5 – Joker & Lady)

Sign up for my newsletter to hear about new releases in the Blood Brothers and Satan's Devils series:
http://eepurl.com/b1PXO5

ACKNOWLEDGEMENTS

When I wrote *Turning Wheels* eighteen months ago now, it was to be a one-off spin-off from my other series. But the bikers got into my heart and soul and kept stepping up to tell me their stories.

Rock hadn't told me much about himself before I started writing this book. All I knew was how he'd got his name. But then it all started unfolding in front of me, and I hope, through the story, you came to love Rock as much as I do. He's certainly easy on the eyes to look at.

As always, I have to give heartfelt thanks to my amazing team of beta readers. Ladies, you rock! Mary, Danena, Colleen, Sheri, Terra, Zoe and Nicole, you gave me tremendous feedback which help me get *Rock Bottom* to where it is now. Thanks must also go to Steve, my husband, who's also a beta reader. I can't express how much I value his encouragement and support.

My editor, once again, is Brian Tedesco, and while thanking him I also have to apologise for the parts which made him squirm. Sorry for making some of this hard reading, Brian.

I've been dealing with a few issues while writing this book and have had to pull out of Kindle Unlimited. My apologies to those readers who used to read my books on KU. It all happened in a rush, meaning I quickly needed versions of all my books in alternative formats so I could publish to the major online retailers, Apple, Nook, Barnes and Noble, Kobo, Google Play etc.

Lia Rees really deserves top billing in the acknowledgements as not only has she formatted *Rock Bottom* and produced the amazing cover, but she also scrambled to re-format the other twelve books so I could publish wide in the quickest possible time. I can't thank her enough for the way she responded and helped me out. Lia's worked with me since the first book I published and I'm so grateful to the author who pointed me in her direction.

Once again thanks go to Deb Carroll my PA. Love working with you, Deb. I know you enjoyed my special chapter, and hope it brings you what you were looking for.

Last, but not least, the greatest thanks of all go to each and everyone of you who've bought my books. Especially those who've contacted me or left a review. I love getting feedback and knowing what you think. One message saying you love my characters and their stories inspires me to write more. So please carry on reviewing or messaging me. I make notes of all the characters you want to know more about, and promise I'll get around to them all in time. I, unfortunately, only have one pair of hands.

Now I've got to get back to writing, so I'll say goodbye. But only for now, because there'll be another Devil coming soon.

STAY IN TOUCH

Email: manda@mandamellett.com
Website: www.mandamellett.com

Connect with me on Facebook:
https://www.facebook.com/mandamellett

Sign up for my newsletter to hear about new releases in the
Blood Brothers and Satan's Devils series:

http://eepurl.com/b1PXO5

ABOUT THE AUTHOR

After commuting for too many years to London working in various senior management roles, Manda Mellett left the rat race and now fulfils her dream and writes full time. She draws on her background in psychology, the experience of working in different disciplines and personal life experiences in her books.

Manda lives in the beautiful countryside of North Essex with her husband and two slightly nutty Irish Setters. Walking her dogs gives her the thinking time to come up with plots for her novels, and she often dictates ideas onto her phone on the move, while looking over her shoulder hoping no one is around to listen to her. Manda's other main hobby is reading, and she devours as many books as she can.

Her biggest fan is her gay son (every mother should have one!). Her favourite pastime when he is home is the late night chatting sessions they enjoy, where no topic is taboo, and usually accompanied by a bottle of wine or two.

Photo by Carmel Jane Photography

Printed in Great Britain
by Amazon

26859149R00245